"Great reworking of the Excalibur myth with a female hero."
- *Patricia McGrew, Sensual Romance*

"Once again Ms. Burke has delivered an awesome tale sure to give the readers many hours of entertainment. I hope she will soon take us on another adventure to the Light Isles."
- *Nicole La Folle, Timeless Tales*

Discover for yourself why readers can't get enough of the multiple-award-winning publisher Ellora's Cave. Whether you prefer e-books or paperbacks, be sure to visit EC on the web at www.ellorascave.com for an erotic reading experience that will leave you breathless.

www.ellorascave.com

Ellora's Cave Publishing, Inc.
PO Box 787
Hudson, OH 44236-0787

ISBN # 1-84360-621-6

Merlin's Kiss, 2003.
ALL RIGHTS RESERVED
Ellora's Cave Publishing, Inc.
© Merlin's Kiss, Stephanie Burke 2003.

This book may not be reproduced in whole or in part without author and publisher permission.

Edited by Martha Punches.
Cover art by Bryan Keller

Warning: The following material contains strong sexual content meant for mature readers. MERLIN'S KISS has been rated Hard R, erotic, by a minimum of three independent reviewers. We strongly suggest storing this book in a place where young readers not meant to view it are unlikely to happen upon it. That said, enjoy…

MERLIN'S KISS

Written by

STEPHANIE BURKE

Merlin's Kiss

Chapter One

"Run Arthur, run!" Brieana screamed as they raced through the crowded encampment that had sprung up around the famous sword.

"If you hadn't called Lord DeLacy an ass-eared lout," the voice behind her whined, "we would not be running!"

"Arthur! If you had stood up for me," she panted between words as she ducked behind another fall of rocks, "I never would have had to defend myself!"

"We need to hide!" the pale young man gasped. "I wish I had never thought to take you for a walk in the moonlight."

"You are right about hiding," she groused as they ran past still another stone formation, ignoring his less than complimentary comment. "Behind there!" she cried as she grabbed his hand and darted behind a particularly large boulder. "We need a weapon."

"Well, we would not need one if you had not kicked him in the privates!" he whined again.

Absently spying the hilt of an abandoned sword embedded in the rocks of a rise, Brieana ran to it and with deft fingers, began to probe the sword base.

"I would not have kicked him if he had not grabbed my person."

Golden-haired Arthur scurried up the hill behind her. "Whatever you are doing, do it faster!" he urged. "I can hear them coming. He must have the whole garrison with him."

Giving him one last disgusted look, Brieana gave one mighty yank and the abandoned sword pulled abruptly from its rocky sheath.

7

Stephanie Burke

"And what do you think to do with that?" Arthur sneered at her while pushing an unruly lock of hair behind his ear and looking down his nose at her.

"Well, you are supposed to be the mighty warrior," she growled losing patience with him at last. "You use it!"

With that, she shoved the sword into his hands and began to count the seconds before he would turn to her for help.

Not everyone knew it, but Arthur was the weakest swordsman in the area. And for the hundredth time, Brieana wondered why she dressed in the armor of the Black Knight to save his sorry hide in battle.

Then she took another good look at him as the moonlight illuminated his near perfect features, and she remembered. She was a fool for good looks and a great body. Certainly she did not risk her very life time and time again for his mental acuity.

Even as he began to turn to thrust the sword into her smaller, albeit more capable hand, DeLacy and his men appeared at the base of the hill and froze in their places.

"Excalibur!" he shouted in shock, and soon the murmurs and cries of him and his men drew the rest of the encamped warriors to view the new king of the Britons. "Arthur has drawn Excalibur from the sacred stone! All hail Arthur, King of the Britons!

As one, the assembled warriors dropped to their knees to pay homage to the one who would be king. Arthur looked puzzled for only a moment. He was a little dense, not stupid. He thrust the sword high into the night sky.

"Excalibur!" he roared as he shoved Brieana behind him, nearly knocking her down in his eagerness.

"But I..." As Brieana began to protest, strong hands grasped her shoulders and spun her around.

"My Lord Merlin!" she gasped as she turned to view the powerful mage. "I was just going to..."

"All hail Arthur!" he boomed in a loud authoritative voice.

8

Merlin's Kiss

Brieana had always respected the older man as her friend and Arthur's mentor. She had often thought him quite handsome and charming, with a deep sense of justice. He would help her.

"My Lord," she said louder as he drew her away from the prostrating men. "I drew Excalibur from the stone." As she thought about that fact, she came to a startling but wonderful realization. "I am King, uh, Queen of the Britons! I am the true ruler!" Then turning excitedly to Arthur, she cried, "I am Queen! Tell them, Arthur!"

Then Arthur was faced with a difficult decision. A decision many great men have been forced to make. He looked at Brieana's luscious lips and then to the men kneeling before him. Love or power? He stared at her long curling hair, as dark as raven's wings, and her almond-shaped, green cat's eyes, then to the teeming mass of masculinity that knelt at his feet ready to do any and all of his bidding. He looked back and saw love and a little fear reflected in her beautiful eyes, eyes that begged him to do the right thing. Love, or power? He knew what he had to do.

Facing the crowd, he declared in a ringing voice, "By right of strength and virtue...I, Arthur, have drawn Excalibur from the stone. I am king!"

"*Nooo!*"

The fierce roar of approval emanating from the new king's army drowned out Brieana's scream of denial.

"My Lord Merlin!" she cried desperately as she ran to the sage, tripping over gravel and kicking up dust, and pulled on the sleeve of his long tunic. "You know the truth! I do not lie! Please tell them!" she begged as she looked into his bottomless black eyes.

Slowly, he turned away from her.

"Let us leave our 'new king' for now. We have much to discuss." Then to the crowd, "Leave us!"

Shocked, she stared at the back of the man, her closest friend, her confidant, in horror. Betrayed! Those who she had held closest to her, those that she had trusted, had betrayed her.

Angry? She was pissed! How dare they keep her rightful kingdom from her?

Manipulated! It all now made perfect sense. She had been manipulated by the master.

"You knew, My Lord Merlin." Wide eyed, Brieana faced a most painful truth. "That is why you planted the idea of a moonlight walk in Arthur's head with your talk of how beautifully the moon shines down upon the mountains. You planned this!" Her voice broke as she made her accusations, her pain becoming audible and dreadful to bear.

With a tired sigh, Merlin nodded his head. Resigned, he motioned to his adopted son. "Come here, Arthur."

"Why did you not tell them?" she railed at her former beau. "I drew the sword from the stone!" Shock had leached all of the color from her face, but anger had returned it with a vengeance.

"A mere girl like you?" he all but smirked.

"Hush!" Merlin's voice thundered across the now empty land. Turning to Brieana, he calmly replied, "Arthur could not have drawn Excalibur from the stone. That would have taken true strength of character."

Proudly, Arthur nodded and looked down his nose at Brieana as the insult flew over his beautiful, but nearly empty head.

Disgusted, Merlin shook his head before turning to Brieana.

"What is done shall remain done. There is now no way to alter this course."

"And that is that!" Arthur added with a self-righteous smirk.

"Insolent pup!" Merlin roared. "Guard your tongue, boy! She has saved your ungrateful backside in battle as the Black Knight and has made you a hero in the process."

Merlin's Kiss

Arthur looked blank for a moment, then his eyes snapped back to Brieana as a dull red highlighted his cheeks.

"I was wrong about DeLacy," Brieana stated with the last of her anger. "Arthur, you truly are the ass-eared lout."

Then she turned to Merlin in confusion.

"But why, My Lord Merlin? You, who always counseled us to follow the truth and right way of things. But then you...you..."

This final betrayal of trust did what no insult or warrior could do. Tears welled up in her green eyes and rolled down her face.

"I had so many dreams. You even encouraged me to put them to paper and not miss the slightest detail. My Lord, why?"

The strength leaving her limbs, Brieana sank to the rocky ground and cried silent tears.

Merlin sighed with true regret. He hated using people and cursed the necessity of it this time. Because of him, the strongest person on this whole accursed island cried, defeated and broken, at his feet. His heart ached as he looked at her bent form. No more! No more manipulations.

"My Lord Merlin..."

"Brieana," he began to explain as he bent to cradle her cold still form to his shoulder. "They never would have accepted a woman. Not in this day and in this age. They would only follow a man. And since there was no one else available, I chose Arthur."

"But what about my dreams, My Lord? To finally have something of my own?" she rasped in a gravely voice. "I have nothing now, no home, no family, for Arthur surely would not want me now!" She remembered the look on his face as he found out who was protecting him in battle. She gestured to the 'new king' who was preening and fighting off an imaginary beast with the most powerful weapon of their time. "I have nothing!"

11

Stephanie Burke

Merlin knew that she was right. He had neglected to plan for this eventuality while he sought to secure the future of the land.

"I have lost what was destined to be mine by birth and by legend. Then you tell me it is because I was born a woman? What about my round table, my society of honest and noble warriors? I am a woman, yet you admired my ideas as I wrote them down and presented them to you! You, who taught me warfare, admired my knights and their laws modeled after the truths that you yourself taught me after my family perished at the hands of unsavory warriors. You, who taught me justice; is this justice? Justice is denied me!" Dismay filled her as she mentally whirled in a volley of conflicting emotions. "Where is your justice now?"

"I have wronged you," Merlin admitted. "Now I will try to right that wrong and deliver to you some measure of justice."

He rose to his feet and moved away from her. In a loud voice he cried, "Rock of Ages!"

After a moment, a rough gravely voice boomed from everywhere, and yet nowhere, "Ah, Merlin, my good friend! It is good to see you. It seems just yesterday when you requested that I hold onto the Lady of the Lake's gift to you, until an honest and true leader and warrior appeared. I can see that she stands beside you. Yes, she is a true leader of men."

At the sound of the booming voice, Arthur immediately ran to stand behind Merlin and fearfully looked over his mentor's shoulder at the mountain.

"I thank you, my friend, but I find that I must ask another boon of you."

"Anything, my friend!"

"The world is not ready for a female leader, not ready to take orders from a woman."

"This is true, my friend. In all of the time that I have existed, no man has yet to heed advice from a woman. Many a great battle could have easily been won or avoided by listening

Merlin's Kiss

to the counsel of a woman. The centuries meld together in my mind, my friend, but what you say is true. I may cease to exist before a woman is allowed to rule."

"A sad fact, my friend," Merlin commiserated. "But in seeing to the future of the Britons, I have wronged this one. I may never live to see a time when a woman is respected enough to hold so strong a power, but with your help Brieana, the true sovereign of Briton, will. Please take and hold her in safety until a time when she will be given the recognition and honor that she deserves. Hold her safely until that day."

"It will be done, my friend."

As Brieana's gasp of fright filled the air, Merlin added another request. "Also, let only a man of equal strength, honesty, power, loyalty," and looking over his shoulder at the cowering Arthur, he added quite loudly, "and courage release her!"

"It is done, my friend," spoke the mountain.

Shocked speechless by what was unfolding before her, Brieana was easily pulled to her feet and maneuvered to the edge of a silently appearing precipice. After mumbling a low incantation, Merlin pulled a golden torc, seemingly from thin air, and held it up so that she could see the rubies and emeralds that studded its surface. Reverently, he pulled her long dark hair aside and placed the torc around her neck. As it touched her bare skin, Brieana felt a shock that shot from the top of her head down to her toes, but she had no time to dwell upon that curious phenomenon, for Merlin began speaking.

"I apologize, My Lady, and now seek to right the wrong that I have foisted upon you this day. I have tried to give you more than I have taken away from you. In truth, I pray that you can forgive me, my heart. Now Brieana, I seek to make your dreams come true."

With that, he muttered something under his breath and pulled her into his arms for a passionate kiss involving searching tongues and firm masculine lips. Arthur coughed nervously behind them as Merlin ravaged his former intended's

Stephanie Burke

mouth. He broke the kiss as Brieana began to respond, and tenderly brushed a lock of curling hair from her face.

"Be happy," he whispered, before pitching her over the edge.

"*Merrlinnn!*" she screamed as she fell, only to be caught in an amazingly soft, yet strong stone hand that had reached out of the heart of the mountain itself. Immediately, Brieana fell into a deep sleep, compliments of Merlin's extraordinary kiss, as the hand gently fisted around her and rejoined with the cold hard stone of the mountain.

"It is done, my friend," the voice boomed. "She will sleep until the proper time. Fare thee well, my friend." The voice faded as absolute silence filled the land.

Merlin walked over to Arthur and closed his hanging jaw with a snap of his fingers. As he steered his pupil away from the mountain, he reached within his robes and pulled out a small bound book.

"What is that, Merlin?" Arthur asked, still a little frightful and looking over his shoulder at the mountain range growing smaller and smaller with every step.

"A final gift from Brieana," he answered.

"I thought that you liked her. The way that you kissed her…"

"More than I like you, at the moment," came his reply.

Finally, Arthur let out in a rush, "If you liked her, why did you imprison her in stone?"

"Insolent cub! Yes, I liked her, and you saw what was done to her. Imagine what I could do to you! I merely attempted to correct a wrong that I had foisted onto her for the good of the island. You would do well to learn from her example. Now read that journal!"

After a quick perusal of the text, Arthur snorted and turned to his teacher.

Merlin's Kiss

"Cam-e-lot? Who would name a kingdom Camelot? It sounds like a disease only cows or sheep could get! Better yet, the name of a really good harlot! Camelot! Who ever heard of a kingdom named Camelot?"

* * * * *

In the distant future...

Kerian growled his frustration as he followed the trail of the winged monster that sought to evade the seasoned warrior. He had been tracking the beast and still the drack managed to elude him. Now he was irritable and tired as the sun began to set and cold night to emerge.

"You had to hide in these accursed mountains!" the warrior murmured as he stopped to lean against a bolder.

This particular drack had slaughtered a few of his chums — a small grazing animal that was a cross between an ancient cow and a sheep — before making good its escape to the mountainous regions that surrounded his castle. If the drack reached its home nest, it would tell others in its coven where chums could easily be had, and soon he would be overrun by a horde of the hungry beasts.

Kerian did not want that to happen; he also did not want to spare the men needed to hunt down the winged lizard, so he alone was chasing down the fleeing beast himself.

No one had ever been this high in the mysterious Dark Mountains before, and he did not relish being the first. Uncorking a water bottle from his waist, he tilted his head back and let the cool water flood his parched throat. Damp tendrils of snow-white hair dried on his forehead as the cooling night winds blew down the gravel path.

He should make his soldiers climb the mountain for exercise, he thought as he capped the bottle and reattached it to his rawhide warrior's belt that encircled his slim hips. Again standing at his full height, he lazily stretched his broad back, enjoying the pull of firm solid muscles as they moved beneath his dark bronze skin. His amber eyes flashed with excitement as he again took up the trail left by the lizard. He might have despised the circumstances that forced him to the hunt once again, but the great Warlord loved the chase.

He walked a few more paces before he spotted the purple hide of the drack he sought.

His lips stretched into a full grin as the lizard turned and caught sight of him in the waning sunlight. With a shriek of fear, it took off up the mountainside.

With a roar, Kerian pulled his sword from the sheath on his back and took off after the drack. Adrenaline gave his booted feet new lift as he leaped over small boulders and large rocks. His muscles burned as he pistoned his leather-clad legs faster and faster.

His eyes caught sight of the six-foot-long creature's tail as it dashed into a small cave. With a shout of triumph, he exploded into the cave and straight down as the ground sharply gave way.

"Schlat!" His voice echoed around the small tunnel as he tumbled head over heels, only to land in a heap of brown leather and white hair.

Remembered training had him tossing away his sword as he fell, but still the five-foot razor-sharp blade landed inches away from his head.

He groaned and looked up to see the drack circling above him, hissing in laughter as it glided on pastel colored wings.

Slowly climbing to his feet, he took a moment to dust off his sleeveless leather war vest and leggings before retrieving his still quivering weapon.

With quiet dignity, he examined the many cuts and abrasions that now covered his arms and chest. Finding no serious wounds, he looked up at the drack and smiled.

"The first battle to you, my brother. Now be warned that I shall sew my new leggings from your purple hide."

Merlin's Kiss

The drack seemed to falter for a moment while it took in the measure of the man it faced. This was no green fighter seeking glory by bringing home a drack skin. This was a warrior who meant every word he said and looked to have the skill to carry out his threat. Landing at the top of the shallow gorge, the purple lizard leaned in for a closer look at the man.

What matter a few chum? it thought as it stared into the unusual amber eyes of the man.

"What is mine, I protect," the man answered.

With a gasp, the lizard stumbled back a few paces before gaining control of itself.

You hear me? it cautiously questioned as it skittered back to the ledge to peer at the man.

"Did I not answer you, youthling?"

Kerian now examined his sword's special blade. Serrated for a foot near the hilt, it was double-edged and heavy. The sword was more frightening than the man who deftly returned it to its special sheath.

Kerian knew that the curious drack would soon mature into a full-blown drackoon, capable of breathing ice and eating a whole herd of chum. He also knew that all of the drackoons in the area knew him—the one human who was capable of picking up and understanding the almost silent language of the drackoons.

You are Kerian! it gasped, fear making its eyes widen. Everyone knew of this mighty warrior and...

"I am, youthling. You voided my agreement with Gren when you violated the treaty. This act will not go unpunished." Turning his back to the suddenly mute drack, he ran both hands along the rock wall to feel for crevices and handholds. At his action, the whole of the mountain began to tremble and shake.

I meant no offense! the drack cried out as it skittered back in fright.

17

Stephanie Burke

Kerian too jumped back from the wall as it made an unusual rumbling sound and began to drop pieces of stone upon him. He frantically searched for the cause.

With a flash of blinding light, the wall seemed to splinter into pieces as a booming voice cried out, "At last!"

The stone in front of him exploded into a thousand more pieces, spewing out dust and gravel, and a body tumbled from the cold embrace of the wall. Automatically, Kerian reached out and caught the body before it tumbled to the hard, rock-strewn ground.

Amazed, he stared into the still face of a woman, and not just any woman. This woman was beautiful beyond compare and completely naked! Her dark hair was the only thing that protected her modesty and hid certain parts of her body from his sight. Around her long, delicate looking neck lay a curious band of gold and jewels. He noted that the jewels sparkled as if recently polished. Amazingly, her body was warm and clean smelling after being imprisoned inside her stone coffin, but this woman wasn't dead. The gentle rise and fall of her barely covered breasts gave mute testimony that she was still alive, if not conscious.

Being the logical creature that it was, the drack decided it would be in its best interest to leave the scene before something else happened. But before it could take to the air, a commanding voice stopped him.

"And where do you think you are going, youthling?" Kerian demanded. He did not know what to make of strange women popping out of stone, but he decided the best thing for him was to get her to some type of safety and fast, then he would have his answers. The quickest way was, unfortunately, on the back of that purple pile of untanned leather that had tricked him into falling into this pit in the first place.

I was…uh…returning to my coven to…uh…warn them that the new herd of chum in the valley…belongs to you?

Kerian adjusted his hold on the naked female and slowly shook his head.

Merlin's Kiss

I'm not? the drack silently questioned.

"You're not," he confirmed.

Then I guess I am...uh...getting you out of the...uh...mantrap?

"You are."

How do I get myself into these fixes? With a resigned sigh, the drack spread its pastel colored wings and slowly descended into the pit where the two humans were...temporarily delayed.

"By what name are you called, youthling?" Kerian asked.

Zorn, replied the drack as it carefully settled beside the famed warrior. *Why do you ask?*

"I like to get the names of all my next meals," Kerian growled as he glared at the rather tall beast.

The drack seemed to pale under its leathery purple hide.

Kerian shook his head at the young beast then again turned his attention to the woman. It was getting cold as the evening winds began to blow, and in her unclothed state, the woman would suffer from exposure to the elements. There was no hope for it. He placed her carefully on the ground and began to strip off his war vest. It would not offer much protection, but it was better than nothing.

As he pulled the vest from his back, the drack let out a gasp when his bare skin was exposed. Kerian stiffened at the sound, but then shook off the feelings of shame that accompanied the scars. He peered over his shoulder at Zorn and raised one platinum eyebrow.

"Something disturbs you, youthling?"

No, nothing, the drack quickly assured. *Your back by surprise took me.* Then it stopped as it thought about what it had said. *Oh dear.*

Kerian said nothing, but turned back to the woman and began to dress her in the meager vest.

Glad, I will be, my services to offer up to you, Great Kerian, Warlord of Mirage.

"Will you be silent?" His low tone evoked instant quiet as he guided the woman's limp hands into the armholes of the vest and tried not to notice how very soft her skin was. His main priority was to get her back to the castle and find out who she was and where she had come from, not to pay attention to those rosebud lips, the same delicate shade as her pink nipples. Or to ogle the soft thatch of hair that shielded her womanhood. So soft, he thought, like the softest of silks. His fingers itched with the urge to touch it, to run his fingers through it. To discover what womanly secrets she hid behind that soft bush.

To offend, I did not mean. Instantly contrite, the drack inched forward to get a better view of the woman.

She was like no other woman he had ever seen. The color of her hair alone, dark as the midnight sky, marked her as an outsider, foreign to these shores.

Who is she? it tentatively questioned.

"I know not," Kerian replied as he lifted her limp body into his arms. "But I know that we must get her to the shelter of Mirage before she becomes chilled."

Taking the subtle hint, Zorn positioned himself in front of the warrior so that he could place the body of the woman across its back, no easy task because the drack stood almost as tall as Kerian.

Once she was positioned to his liking, Kerian climbed onto the back of the drack, carefully avoiding any placement of his legs that would impede its wing movements, and motioned it to rise.

The flapping of its delicate looking wings caused the dust to rise and pebbles to fall in the small pit as they began to rise out of the hole that had trapped the man.

As soon as they cleared the gaping maw of the pit, the drack carefully flapped its wings until they cleared the small tunnel that led to the mantrap. Free of the confining womb of stone, the drack gracefully climbed higher in the sky, before

Merlin's Kiss

folding its wings close to its body and diving down the mountain path.

The feel of the wind whipping across his face brought back the freedom Kerian had experienced as a child, before the days of Shala. His hair flew wildly behind him as he raised his face to the cool kiss of the night winds. It had been years since he had experienced the exhilaration of a night flight. And despite the troublesome youthling that carried him, Kerian found that he was beginning to enjoy the ride.

The cool night wind was having an altogether different effect on the other passenger that rode draped over the back of the drack. Brieana's eyes began to flutter as she felt an unaccustomed coldness wrap around her body. Her small awakening groan was lost to the wind, so it came as a complete shock to Kerian when her eyes popped open and a yell of a never before heard magnitude pierced the night sky. Brieana had opened her eyes to find herself face down on some kind of beast and a mountain range passing, flying beneath her very eyes.

"Eiiikkkk!" she yelled as she tried to jerk to an upright position. She let out another scream as her upward movement was impeded by…hands? She almost missed the muffled curse as she tried to turn and fight against the restraining hands that held her on such an unnatural and unusual ride.

"Woman, be still!" a low voice commanded. The quiet intensity of the words caused her to still all movements as her brain struggled to assimilate what was happening to her. Eyes still drawn to the passing landscape, she let out a low whimper of fear, all the while hating herself for her cowardice. What had happened to her? Where was she? Her whole body shaking, she sucked in a deep breath as strong hands gently turned and lifted her so that she sat across a very hard set of masculine thighs. A battle-scarred finger lifted her trembling chin and she beheld the face of her captor.

Kerian had been surprised by the woman's reaction but quickly saw the danger of having her struggle on the back of the

Stephanie Burke

flying drack whose complaints now filled his head. He quickly understood the source of her panicked outcry. Few people ever have the privilege to take to wing with a drack. He brought her upright and across his lap so that the land passing at a dizzying pace would not frighten her. It was utter fascination that made him tilt her face upwards so that he might view a woman who seemed to be birthed right out of a mountain.

"Your eyes are amber!" was the first thing that rasped from her parched throat. Her voice was all but unrecognizable after her long sleep, and that bothered her. How long had she been under Merlin's spell? Bits and pieces of memory came to her.

"Yes. A common color for a common soldier."

Yet there was nothing common about the man who held her within his steely grasp. His forehead was high and wide, set off by a peak of soft silver/white hair. That same hair cascaded behind him, the wind whipping it into a frenzy of motion, and exposed his high cheekbones, strong jaw and a stubborn chin with a deep dimple in the center. This man was better looking than Arthur, that rat, but he was a stranger to her.

"I have never seen eyes of that color!" Kerian softly exclaimed as he took in the woman he held. Her eyes were the green of the Forbidden Forests that surrounded and protected Mirage from invaders. They were beautiful eyes, surrounded by long black lashes and slanted just so to give her the look of a claw beast, the feline creatures that inhabited those very forests. Her face was heart-shaped, with a pointed stubborn chin, yet there was an air of strength that seemed to surround her. But who exactly was she?

Faring how is the Lady? Zorn's voice intruded upon his thoughts. *Has she recovered from her fright?* There was a hint of amusement in its voice and it chuckled at the female's predictable reaction.

"She is fine, youthling. Best you concentrate on how you will escape my skinning knife instead of the reactions of a scared woman."

Merlin's Kiss

"I'm not scared!" her gravely voice replied. "Just a little startled. And who are you talking to?"

"The drack," he answered, long used to people giving him funny looks because of his strange abilities.

The drack in question tilted in a small acknowledgment causing Brieana to throw her arms around the man's neck while muffling a small shriek of fear.

"Do you mean to do me harm?" she asked, deciding that a direct approach would get her answers from this man. He did not seem the type to mince words. "And who are you?"

"I am Kerian, Lord of Castle Mirage and you are on my lands, therefore under my protection unless you prove to be injurious to mine."

Again he spoke without rancor and with brutal honesty. He readjusted her hold upon his neck and she became aware of her dress, or rather, lack of dress.

Just as calm as this Kerian, she asked, "So then, what happened to my clothing?" Getting hysterical at this point would only prove too wearing. She was already practically naked and flying in the night on some purple-winged beast—at least it looked purple in the waning light. What more could happen to her?

"This I know not. Maybe you can explain why you were expelled from the belly of a mountain after you tell me your name?"

"It is Brieana. Brieana of Belfore."

Whatever else she was going to say was lost in a deep gasp as she first caught view of the castle they were approaching.

All lit up from huge cauldrons of burning pitch, the place looked massive. Its outer wall seemed to stretch for miles around and it was back-dropped by dark mysterious- looking woods. It had to possess at least five large towers and was surrounded by a smoking moat. This place was nothing like she had ever seen before.

Stephanie Burke

"I don't think that I'm in the Britons any longer," she managed after taking in the fast-approaching castle.

"I have never heard of such a place. We are on my lands and that is my home, Mirage."

"Mirage? This is beginning to feel like a nightmare," she choked out before a great blackness surrounded her and she tumbled into oblivion.

Chapter Two

Brieana woke to the feel of the softest of silks caressing her back, and something hovering around her. She cracked one eye open only to jump straight up in the bed she was lying on and scramble to what passed as a headboard around this strange place.

A purple dragon was staring straight at her, quaking in what had to be anticipation of an easy meal. Before she could open her mouth to scream, a voice invaded the quiet of the dimly lit room.

"I can hear you, youthling. And hiding behind the skirts of this Brieana will not save you. Now come and let me start on my new leggings."

It was Kerian! And he was about to walk in on this vicious creature just waiting to attack!

Pure instinct took over. Just as the door opened, she grasped the end of the silken blanket that covered her and with a rolling dive, aimed her body right at the purple menace. The fleeting thought, *Why do I have to always protect the men around here?* flashed through her mind before she effectively knocked the purple monster off all four of its feet.

"Dragon!" she roared, as Kerian stood in the room in open-mouthed astonishment.

Never before had he seen a woman perform such a feat! Even as he watched, she tossed the coverlet over the confused drack's head and ran for the door, long hair flowing behind her.

"Quickly," she cried as she skidded to a halt before him. "Before it uses its breath of fire to char us both to cinders."

Such was her excitement that she never even noticed that she was slaying a savage beast and saving their lives wearing little more than her skin. But at his refusal to move, and his close examination of her softly swaying breasts, realization came crashing down upon her.

"Oh!" Suddenly the raging monster thrashing around on the floor, tangled in the blanket was forgotten as she hunched over and tried to use her hands and a few hanks of strategically placed hair to shield her nakedness.

"There is no need to run from the drack. Zorn is a young one and has not yet attained the age where he can spew forth elements from his mouth." Kerian tried to be polite and turn away from her nakedness but found himself transfixed by the sway and movement of her naked body.

"Besides, dracks spit ice, and this one will not attain the age necessary to perform such a task for some time. He has more important things to do, anyway. Like becoming my new leggings."

Oh, please, My Lord Kerian! Zorn wailed at hearing his words. It was bad enough that this...foreign woman had entangled him in such a simple trap, but for Kerian to finally make good on his threats was too much for the young drack to bear. *Is there not some way that, the loss of one chum, I may make up to you?*

"You will cease this begging, Zorn. It is unbecoming of one of Gren's kin. And it was more than one, youthling."

"To whom are you talking?" Brieana nearly screamed. Seeing that the warrior made no move to attack the beast, she could only assume that it presented no danger. But whom was the man speaking with?

She backed up to the bowl-shaped bed and reached one arm behind her to grope for the remaining sheet. It would serve as a cover until she could find some clothing of her own.

"Yon drack," he muttered as he watched her yank the sheet from the crumpled bedding and struggle to wrap it around her trembling body without exposing more of it to his view.

Her limbs were long and finely muscled and gave explanation for her ease of movement when she attacked the

26

Merlin's Kiss

drack. Even hunched over as she was now, he could see that she was not as tall as the women that occupied his keep, but was of a pleasing height. Odd, but she awakened protective feelings in him that he had never thought to feel again.

"But I hear nothing!" She turned to look at the hapless creature as it finally untangled itself from the blanket. It was roughly the size of a large horse, with its wings tucked closely to its body, but moved with an almost liquid grace. It mournfully stuck its head out of the blanket and an almost pleading expression crossed its face.

"Why, the poor thing is terrified! What is wrong with it?"

She lost a little of her fear at the beast in such a vulnerable position. He looked as though he needed her help. Again Kerian's low velvet voice flowed over her, causing her nipples to tighten in reaction and her to wrap both arms around herself to hide the telling reaction. She frowned at the strange occurrence because only once before had that happened—when Merlin had kissed her. That bit of memory was clear. She would contemplate it later, she thought. Better to pay attention to what the man was saying.

"He fears rightful retribution for crimes that he has committed."

The drack whimpered and again attempted to bury its face in the blanket, as if it would hide from the quiet wrath of the man. Kerian took a few steps into the room, smiling at the picture that the woman, Brieana, made swathed in the sheet and trying to appear unconcerned about her present predicament.

"What are you going to do to it?" Always champion of the underdog—look at Arthur—she was ready to defend this unknown creature. Besides, now that her initial fright was over with, she thought it looked kind of cute, in a fierce, livestock-eating kind of way.

"Since I cannot recover what was stolen," he glared at the drack until it whimpered softly, "I will use its hide to keep me

27

warm this cold season, in place of the eaten chum's wool that I would have used. It is a fair trade, is it not?"

Sensing an ally in the foreign woman, Zorn scuttled over to her, dropped low to the ground and rested his massive head against her thighs, forcing her to collapse onto the bed and almost lose her sheet to gravity. He looked up at her with pleading eyes that seemed to scream, *Help me! From this madman, save me.*

Before she could reply, the door opened again and in walked the most beautiful woman Brieana had ever seen. Her eyes were a light brown and so at odds with her nearly white curly hair flowing down her back, that her appearance proved to be most shocking. Her bronze skin glowed in the candlelit room and her steps were sure and confident as she approached the bed and the woman who lay sprawled across it.

"Shala," Kerian murmured and bowed low to the tall woman.

Gracefully, she pulled aside the long skirts of her bright green gown and perched on the edge of the bed. She turned those golden brown eyes upon Brieana, who still struggled to sit upright with a lap full of drack, and parted her ruby red lips into a smile.

Brieana felt as if a hungry wolf was staring at her, as she watched the woman's perfect white teeth glint at her. Unconsciously, she gripped the sheet covering her body closer as she attempted to move away from this exquisitely menacing creature.

"I am Shala, mistress of this keep, and I welcome you, mage."

In confusion, Kerian looked down at his stepmother. The woman had on her best dress and now she, who never welcomed anyone, was offering a greeting to his strange guest and calling her a holder of magic.

Merlin's Kiss

"This is Brieana, Shala," he introduced. "And I don't believe that she is a mage. Or are you?" he asked turning to the suddenly weary looking woman.

Before she had a chance to speak, the woman spoke sharply to her stepson.

"After all that you endured to learn to treat me with respect, Kerian, you seem to have forgotten those lessons quite easily."

Although his face remained impassive, Brieana saw his muscles tighten slightly at what had to be a dig, and she decided that she would watch what this woman did and said closely.

"My father is no more, Shala," he calmly retorted. "And his lessons will never be forgotten." His amber eyes bored into her golden ones.

"Excuse me, but I am no mage."

Brieana interrupted the fierce stare-down with her comment. Her wariness was turning into dislike as she saw Shala turn her nose up at Kerian, though she did not know why she felt the urge to defend the man. It must be her protective instincts rising up to assist the man after she saw the well-hidden spot of vulnerability that he displayed at the woman's hurtful words.

"Of course you are, my dear. Why, I feel your aura of power. I have felt it since you entered the walls of Mirage," Shala insisted.

"I have no powers, Shala. You are mistaken."

Shala stared hard at Brieana, causing her to nervously reach out and rub the jeweled collar encircling her neck.

She felt a warning flash travel through her body and then she clearly heard the drack say, *To the foreign woman, ill will your stepmother means.*

Brieana turned startled eyes to Zorn.

"What did you say?" she gasped.

Stephanie Burke

Shala's eyes widened as she jumped from the bed. "You speak to that horrid beast!"

Even Kerian seemed shocked.

"I thought that you could not understand the words of the youthling?" Although his face did not betray the emotions running through him, he wondered if it were true. Was there another one as cursed as he?

Hear me you can? Zorn managed, almost as shocked as the others.

"He asked me if I could hear him." She turned to Kerian for confirmation, receiving a nod in reply.

"This cannot be!" Shala cried as she looked from Zorn to Brieana. "Where did you get those powers, girl?"

Shala's eyes looked questioningly at Brieana.

"I have no powers!" Suddenly feeling trapped again, Brieana reached for the comforting touch of the jeweled torc and felt an almost instant lessening of her fears.

"It's the necklace! May I examine it?"

Confidently, she reached out a hand to finger the precious stones embedded there. She had felt the flash of magic, of true power, as the dark foreign girl touched the source of her energy, and Shala wanted to make sure of the source of power!

Brieana tried to scoot backwards, uncomfortable again with the woman's close proximity. Even the now silent drack scuttled back as the woman eased closer. But before she could move, Shala's fingers reached out and touched the torc.

Almost instantly, a bright flash of blue light exploded from the torc, throwing a startled Shala across the room. With a muffled thump, her body struck the stone wall and she bounced to the floor, all of the air forcibly leaving her lungs as she landed then rolled to her side.

The drack let out a startled shriek as he leapt back and Brieana stared wide-eyed at the fallen woman for a moment, before struggling to rise and aid her.

Merlin's Kiss

"I did not... I do not know how... What just happened?"

One trembling hand rose to her lips as she stared at the fallen Shala.

Kerian observed the woman on her knees in the bed before him. The drack now held a defensive position in front of her with semi spread wings as if he feared an attack to her person, and she still looked innocent and very vulnerable.

"What kind of magic do you possess, Brieana of Belfore?" he breathed out, his voice dropping deeper with his shock. He shook his head to break out of his stupor and swiftly walked over to his stepmother. He quickly knelt to check and see if she were still breathing. He rolled her over to her back and was gratified to see the slow rise and fall of her chest.

Groaning slightly amidst a tangle of shiny white hair, Shala tried to struggle to sit up, but Kerian held her to the carpeted floor until her brown eyes were open and her trembling stopped.

"Are you well?" Brieana asked cautiously as she crawled to the end of the bed to closer observe the woman, still struggling to keep the sheet covering her body.

With Kerian's help, Shala shakily rose to her feet.

Brieana did not feel comfortable around the woman, but her necklace's strange reaction frightened her. She did not want the woman hurt; she just wanted her to give her some space. What was this power that lay around her neck? For truly, all that she could recall of it was that a man, a powerful man, had placed it there.

Knowing that she had found the information that she was looking for, Shala decided that it was time to retreat and observe the strange girl and assess the necklace's power. Now she had no doubts that the strange piece of jewelry was the source of the energy that she had felt, not anything emanating from the child. The bolt of energy that had knocked her back contained magic in its truest form, and she wanted to know more about it.

31

Stephanie Burke

"I am fine, my dear. Please excuse my actions. I thought that the necklace looked familiar to me, and sought to see if it was indeed like my old family heirloom. We might be related, you and I. It would be wonderful to have a real family at this point in my life. I did not expect it to act as your protector."

Family? Ha! Zorn growled. *Never in all of my days, to gain someone's affection, have I seen such an obvious ploy!*

Kerian forced himself to turn away at that moment, almost overcome by the humor of that statement.

"And just how old are you, youthling?"

As drackoons recon it, forty cycles! the indignant drack replied, a small smile gathering on its face as it lowered its wings to settle at its side again, now certain that no one would harm its new protectress.

"Good. Now that you have experienced forty years of life, I will feel no guilt when I fashion my new leggings from your hide."

The humor left the drack's voice as he turned to Brieana and wailed, *Oh gracious Lady! Speak with the Warlord I do beg you to, and my life spare! Listen to you, he will! Protect this graceless lowly creature you can!*

Brieana felt a smile crease her lips and lighten the tension in the room. She knew that she should be frightened now that the beast's voice was inside her head, but he was just too amusing for her to remain frightened for long. Besides, his voice felt right in her mind, as if talking to him were natural.

"That beast is speaking ill of me, is he not?" Shala asked as she glared at each of them in turn, before a smile once again graced her red lips.

"Guard yourself well, Brieana. Strange things happen when dracks are around. Am I not right, Kerian?" Her voice held amusement as she observed her stepson.

This time, Kerian visibly winced as his stepmother gathered the remains of her dignity and slowly started for the door.

Merlin's Kiss

"Welcome again to our home, Brieana, and please do not let this incident worry you. Your power is there to protect you, and when you get to know us a little better, I'm sure you will feel safe." With one last considering look at the drack, Shala quit the room.

"So that was your stepmother." Brieana looked at the warrior as he again forced his emotions under tight control. She was still taken aback at the events that had taken place so quickly in this room, but strangely enough, she felt safe with Kerian.

"I really do not know what happened to cause the energy that tossed her so, Kerian. Yet, it was good of her to forgive so quickly. In her shoes, I would have been furious."

Perhaps she had misjudged the strange woman, especially after she so gracefully excused Brieana's necklace's reaction to her gentle touch.

"I too must apologize, little one. I did not know that Shala would try and touch you, making you feel as if you had to defend yourself. I would like you to feel safe in my home, yet I can understand your defense."

While unexpected, Kerian could see that Brieana was just as surprised at the flash of energy that had repelled his stepmother as they all were. Maybe she just possessed a piece of protective magic and did not fully understand its use. Maybe the women of her continent were protected with the strange necklaces that surrounded their throats. "Where are you from, little one?"

"I come from Belfore, in the Britons. That is where we are now, although I don't recall this castle being here. I must have been asleep for quite a few years."

"The Britons? Are they one of the smaller new continents?"

"Do not be silly, Kerian. We are on the land of the Britons! This island is so enormous, we need a good king to unite the clans."

She looked into Kerian's baffled face and felt the first stirrings of unease. The word "king" did not feel right either.

Stephanie Burke

Some lost memory was prickling at the back of her mind, demanding that she pay attention to it.

"We are on the Britons, are we not?" she asked her voice now a bit husky with her growing uncertainty.

"I know not of what you speak, Brieana. I have never heard of a clan called Belfore, nor of these Britons that you speak of."

He looked at her in growing concern. Could she be ill? Was she from the Dark Isles? That might explain her unusual coloring, but not how she emerged from the solid stone of a mountain.

"No Britons?" She was beginning to remember something. Again, her fingers rose to caress the torc, and then understanding exploded into her mind, and her memories returned fully.

"Merlin!" she gasped, eyes growing wide with horror. "Merlin did this! I was queen! He took it away from me and put me to sleep!"

Zorn's head shot up at the mention of the great mystic's name. Kerian noticed this, but continued to question a suddenly pale Brieana.

"You are a queen?"

"I unsheathed Excalibur from the stone and I am the true Queen of the Britons! Then Merlin put me to sleep! How long have I been asleep, Kerian? How long?"

Noticing her near hysteria, Kerian sat on the bed beside her and took both of her ice-cold hands within his, noticing how tiny she was in comparison to the rest of the women he knew.

"Listen to me, Brieana. I know nothing of these Britons that you claim to rule. We are on the Light Isles of this new earth. There are no kings or queens here. Only clan leaders."

"Merlin did this to me!" she exclaimed as her eyes widened in shock and understanding. "He said that I would sleep until I would be accepted as ruler and that only a man my equal in strength could free me."

Merlin's Kiss

As she turned her large expressive eyes to his confused amber ones, a startling revelation came to her. An epiphany so startling that her reserves of strength withered away and her nerves snapped! "If you managed to awaken me, then you are my perfect mate!"

He watched as her eyes again rolled to the back of her head and she collapsed into a dead faint.

"If she is my equal in strength," he said to no one in particular as he eased her limp body back into the pillow of the bed, "then I am a lot weaker that I thought. That is the second time that she has done that!"

Zorn said nothing, but there was a strange glint in the young drack's eyes. In fact, he looked as if he knew something that Kerian knew nothing about. He turned speculative eyes towards the warrior as Kerian beat a hasty retreat from the room.

Shala was almost right about one thing. Strange things did happen when a drack was near, but only if they gave you that certain look.

Stephanie Burke

Chapter Three

"Damn that woman!"

Kerian eyed the soldier standing in a fighting crouch before him. He had actually managed to penetrate his defenses and slice a thin, stinging line across his forearm. All because he could not keep his mind off of berry-colored nipples and her declaration that had them all but mated.

"Again, Sato," he declared in a loud voice.

His soldiers, men and women of the fighting ranks, eyed him curiously. Not often did a warrior land a blow against the Warlord of Mirage. They anxiously awaited the continuation of the match. Was the Warlord losing his edge or was Sato that good?

Neither! They watched as Kerian focused his complete attention on his opponent. Drawing in a deep breath, he bent his knees slightly and drew his practice sword before him, one hand holding the great weight of the four-foot blade, his other hand held out to his side for balance.

His sparring partner made a daring lunge forward, high on the blood of his previous small victory. With the grace of a dancer, Kerian knocked aside Sato's weapon with one deft blow. And while the soldier was reeling from the maneuver, Kerian's fist connected solidly with the underside of his chin, knocking him neatly to his backside.

"Never let an assumption of victory cause you to act rashly, my friend," he cautioned as he offered the felled man a hand up. "Your enemy might surprise you."

Once on his feet, Sato performed a quick bow of respect before stumbling off of the practice field.

"Let this be a lesson to all of you!" Kerian continued, raising his voice so that all of the assembled warriors could hear.

36

Merlin's Kiss

"Never let your guard down." He glanced at his bleeding arm so that they would know that he spoke of his mistake. "And never anticipate a victory. The battle is won only when the last man has fallen either to your sword, or to his knees in surrender."

With a curt nod, he dismissed his troops from practice and went to seek the comfort of his own solitary thoughts.

* * * * *

"I worry about him."

Shala's voice floated over to Brieana, causing a small shudder of unease to shiver down her spine. The woman had been nothing but kind to her, yet she felt a great sense of unease in her presence.

"Kerian?" she questioned as she looked out onto the practice field, now devoid of all movement, from the large doorway to the castle. "He seems perfectly fine to me."

After her last fainting spell, Brieana had not seen the warrior at all. Zorn, her constant companion, had kept her company in the days since she had arisen from her bed. She assumed that he stayed with her more for his own protection than any hidden dangers in Mirage, yet the skittish drack had stayed by her side. For that she was grateful.

She still had no idea where she was or how long she had been sleeping, but she was beginning to suspect that she had been spellbound for quite a time.

"He seems restless, edgy, more prone to mistakes of late." Shala's voice drew Brieana away from her musings. "I wonder what is troubling him?"

Again Brieana felt a strange quiver of unease. There was nothing telling in the other woman's words, yet she seemed to react...coldly to her stepson.

"Why do you not ask him? I have not spoken to him since the incident in my sleeping chamber."

Stephanie Burke

Maybe he senses that the witch will seek to do the great Warlord harm! Trust her, I do not! Zorn's agitated voice intruded in Brieana's head and she fought to stifle a giggle as she turned accusing eyes to the purple beast.

Shala's eyes narrowed as she viewed the drack, but said nothing. She knew that he was speaking unkindly of her, but that did not matter now. Soon, there would be no secrets from her.

"I, too, have not been able to catch him in an unoccupied moment, dear one." Shala continued ignoring the play-by-play between the drack and the young woman. "If I could, I would seek to ease his…burdens."

Again, Brieana felt a shiver of discomfort as she listened to Shala's words. The woman had been nothing but kind to her. She had given her a wardrobe of beautiful dresses and sturdy pants, including the brown leather pants and tunic she was now wearing, as well as necessary toiletries, but Brieana's instincts were screaming for her to get as far away from the woman as possible.

"I think I shall go and talk with him, Lady Shala. Perhaps I can be of assistance to him."

"Very good, child." Shala seemed pleased to hear of her plan. "And if you need any assistance at all, please come to me. I want you to think of me as a mother. After all, it is quite possible that we are indeed related. With the similarity of the necklace and all."

With a pat to her head, Shala walked away, as regal as a queen, and disappeared down the hallway that led to her personal chambers.

"Very good child, indeed!" Brieana huffed as the drack's silent laughter filled her head. "She speaks to me as if I were a babe! I was once the Queen of the Britons, and she pats my head as if I was a green girl in need of comfort!"

Better a pat to the head, gracious Lady, than a knife to the back! Zorn stated with some finality.

38

Merlin's Kiss

"You do not like her because of her opinion of dracks, my dear Zorn. I do not know why I react strangely to her, though. Maybe it is the torc."

She absently fingered the reassuring warmth of the golden band before turning her attentions again to the empty practice field.

"I could have bested him, Zorn. Or at least gotten under his defenses quicker than he would have expected."

I have, of that, no doubt, my Lady. Shall we go inside now?

Zorn knew that she was making up her mind to go and seek Kerian, and Zorn would have rather avoided the Warlord now. Although he had Brieana's erstwhile protection now, that could change at any moment. And he was just uncomfortable being away from his coven for this long period of time. *Oh, those cursed chum are going to be the death of me!* he silently wailed.

"No, your appetite is going to be the death of you, my friend," Brieana laughed, shaking off her dark musings as she decided to find Kerian. "Now let us go and seek Kerian, before he disappears again."

* * * * *

Closing the door to her inner chambers, Shala allowed distaste to show across her face. Her golden brown eyes narrowed in anger as she gritted her teeth and rested her forehead against the wooden door of her abode.

"What does this girl have to do with my plans? Why can I not get near the little bitch without feeling the warnings of that accursed necklace?"

In blinding anger, she lashed out at the door with one slippered foot and failed to note the dark presence seating on a chair before her fireplace.

"Mind your temper, my beauty, lest you prematurely age that wondrous face of yours."

Stephanie Burke

Shala sucked in a deep breath and fought to compose herself.

"And just when did you arrive?" she asked as she straightened her gown and smoothed her hair before turning to face the creature sitting in wait for her. "And how did you breach my defenses?"

As usual, the creature sat in the shadows, having extinguished all of the candles in the room, save for the few that graced the entrance of her room. He seemed to love the shadows and loved to incite fear by operating behind a menacing dim light that they provided.

If she peered closely, she could make out a large humanoid shape that seemed oddly distorted. Again she wondered if she should be thankful that the disgusting thing that was her ally did prefer the dark.

"Your little...safeguards were amusing child's play to one of my nature, Shala. You should know by now that I can easily overcome any spells that you attempt to use against me. Besides, is that any way to treat such an honored guest such as myself? You should not have gone through all of that trouble on my account."

"State your business, Dagon, and let us put aside this pretense."

"As you wish, gracious Lady."

He watched her with yellow glowing eyes as she gracefully walked deeper into the dim light of the room. He smiled as he noted her displeasure at his unexpected visit. But she had no reason to protest his visit. She needed him and what he could give her.

"My people are waiting for a word from me, Shala. All is in readiness and shall proceed according to plan."

"Good. I want that miserable bastard dead!"

"How sweet. Your maternal concerns touch a hidden chord within my bosom, Lady. Your tender affections threaten to

Merlin's Kiss

overwhelm me." His low laugh sent shivers of fear and anger down her spine.

"Your emotions are not a concern of mine, Dagon, but we seem to have a slight problem."

"Problem?" The coldness of that one word made the skin on her neck crawl, but she fought down her fears and responded.

"There is an added complication. There is true magic here, Dagon, magic even more powerful than anything that I have ever sensed emanating from you."

"And where is this new untapped source of energy, my Lady?" Although he seemed to have remained in his relaxed pose, she could tell that his whole attention was now fixed upon her.

"A useless vagabond wandered into Kerian's presence and the soft fool took her in. I was going to eliminate her and that disgusting drack that follows her, but she possesses a magic that I have never felt before. It repelled me, Dagon."

"What is the source, Shala? Do not mince words with me."

"It is around her neck, Dagon. She wears a strange jeweled necklace. That is the source of her powers."

"So, kill her and take it." Dagon waved his hand as if the matter was a small trifle, and not to be concerned about.

"Are you not listening to me? It repelled me, Dagon. I am the most powerful mystic on this isle and it repelled me!"

"You are not much of a mystic to begin with, my dear," he snorted as he relaxed again into his seat.

"You still do not understand, Dagon!" Agitated she began to pace the dimly lit room. "How can I possess this magic if I cannot get near enough to take it? Any mystic knows that any protective amulet cannot be removed unless the wearer is dead. How can I kill her if I cannot touch her? The spells that you...gifted me with, do not work! She will require a personal touch after I discover where she has come from."

41

Stephanie Burke

"Your magic is weak, Shala, and always has been. You are only as good as the twisted thoughts that emerge from your pretty head and the thing that rests between your thighs! I will rid you of the little girl, so you need not feel threatened any longer. But still, you owe me the agreed upon price. And if you try to use any magical tricks gained from the possession of this amulet, I will return, and your shrieks of agony will echo over this land that you love— your fate will be the fate of your people for generations to come. Do you understand me, my beauty?"

"I understand, Dagon! I understand pure uncorrupted magic. And when it is in my possession, you will regret your words!"

Then all that she heard was the thump of the chair as it hit the carpeted floor. In a blur of movement so fast it was almost undetectable by the naked eye, Dagon swooped across the room, his dark power extinguishing candles in his wake. Before she could draw another breath, cold taloned hands gripped the delicate flesh of her slender neck and lifted her clear off of the floor.

"Guard your tongue, witch. All that you have has been given to you by me, and I can easily take it away from you along with your life. Your fool plan did not work years ago and those drackoons you loathe so well protected the heir. Because of you and your scheming, I had to wait for this time to extend my grasp on this stinking wasteland of a planet. If you try to cross me, Shala, I will kill you, pure power or no. Do you understand me, my lovely?"

Shala fought for every breath as small gurgles of distress escaped from her restricted throat. Her hands uselessly clutched at the fingers that held her suspended above the floor. Eyes wide in true terror, she managed to express her acquiescence and Dagon slowly released her to drop into a quivering heap at his feet.

Bending low, he lifted her chin with one curved talon, gently brushing the hair from her face with the other hand.

Merlin's Kiss

"I do so hate to use force with my lessons, my sweet, but you must understand my position."

He drew her face to his and a cold wet tongue traced a path across the heated flesh of her face and withdrew before touching her lips.

Shala shuddered at the feel of his rough tongue caressing her skin, shuddered in both disgust and arousal.

She stared as his yellow eyes melted into a red so bright it was almost demonic.

His long dark hair fell around her face, shielding her from the outside, creating a dark tunnel from which his eerily angry eyes glittered.

She felt his taloned hand dig deeper into her skin and whimpered at the remembered feel of that claw digging into the flesh of her hips, raising and lowering her, demanding that she take more of him.

She stared up into his red eyes and shuddered at how close he came to possessing her soul.

"Do not try to deceive me or play me false, Shala. I offer you the chance to redeem yourself and rule these lands as you see fit. Do not make me regret my decision."

In a flurry of movement, he was gone.

Shala sat on the floor of the dark chamber, fighting to regain control of her gasping breath and pounding heart. With one shaking hand, she reached up and wiped the wet residue from his tongue off of her face, anger turning her brown eyes red.

"I understand you, Dagon. And when I possess pure magic, I shall take you and your devilish minions and send you all straight to the hell you escaped from! This I vow with my last breath!"

Chapter Four

"Kerian!"

Brieana's voice carried across the rocky ledge to the man seated on the boulder, staring across the land to the great expanse of the Dark Mountains. He turned and watched the small woman running towards him with her drack companion. He noted the long fall of her dark hair trailing behind her and the gentle sway of her unbound breasts against the brown leather of her tunic as she drew near.

He also noted the skittish approach of the drack, which kept the woman between the two of them, as if she could protect him.

With a curse, he turned his head back towards the mountains as the source of all his recent troubles approached him.

"Kerian." Her voice sounded a bit breathless as she stepped closer to his rock perch. "What are you doing here, all alone?"

"I am thinking, Brieana." He tried to keep his voice cold and distant, but her mere presence was melting his icy resolve not to interact with this female.

"Of what, may I ask?" She gingerly positioned herself on the stone beside him while Zorn immediately skittered to her side, peering at him over her shoulder.

Noticing the look that he was getting from the youthling, he replied, "Of my winter wardrobe, Brieana. Of what color chum's wool tunic I will have made to match purple leather."

Zorn gulped and ducked his head out of sight behind the boulder, poking one eye up to see if the great Warlord made any move towards him.

"Stop that!"

Merlin's Kiss

At her sharp tone of voice, Kerian turned to her and raised one silvery eyebrow.

"You are scaring him, Kerian. Zorn has been a great comfort to me over these past few days."

"A comfort, Brieana? This walking appetite has been a comfort to you? What has caused you unease?"

For a moment, Brieana seriously considered telling Kerian about the unsettling feelings that she got whenever his stepmother was present, but she decided again that they were just feelings of jealousy she felt. Shala was a beautiful woman; self assured and confident in her place, unlike herself who still did not know where she fit in, in this different, yet so similar new world.

"I do not know," she finally answered.

Gentle breezes lifted her curling hair and blew tendrils of it across her face. Kerian watched as she, in an unconsciously sensual movement, lifted her face into the light wind and closed her eyes, almost moaning in her enjoyment of the cool air.

Kerian felt a tingling sensation below his waist that signaled the beginnings of his erection, one that he would not be able to hide from either her or her pet drack.

Bending at the waist, he made an effort to cover up his burgeoning maleness, before he embarrassed himself.

Brieana watched as Kerian's straight white hair fell forward, obscuring his face and hiding him from her now attentive view.

"Are you in pain, Kerian? You were not hurt during your mock battle?"

"No," he nearly growled, which was odd for him.

Kerian was the most composed man that she had ever met. Even Merlin had been known to give into a fit of frustrated shouting when Arthur did something particularly inane, but not Kerian, her ordained mate.

Stephanie Burke

"Then what is troubling you? Even the Lady Shala commented on your unusually reticent nature."

Thinking up ways to torture me, he is, my Lady! Zorn cried. *Contemplating making leggings, he is, from my unworthy hide.*

"Kerian, you would not harm Zorn?" Brieana asked, looking between the cowering drack and the still man.

"Leave me, Brieana," he flatly stated.

What was wrong with him? Why was he in such a dark mood?

Concerned, Brieana reached out her hand to touch his shoulder, and recoiled at the heat that she felt.

"Kerian?"

"Take that accursed youthling and go! Go before something happens that both you and I will regret!"

"Go where?" Brieana's concern swiftly turned to anger. How dare this man speak to her in such a tone! She knew that she held no power here, but she demanded the respect that other women got in this strange new world! She would not be ordered around like a child!

"Where shall I go, Warlord? To the forests that everyone tells me that I cannot explore? To the mountains that everyone claims are too dangerous for me? Or shall I go back to where I came from? Find me a passage back to my home, and I will gladly leave you this day! Do you think that I enjoy being treated like a little girl, Kerian? I was a warrior in my time, a fierce fighter! I was a queen! Now look at me! Look at me!" she screamed as he continued to study the ground between his feet. "I am a woman full grown and I demand to be treated with respect!"

Kerian slowly raised his head, his unbound hair flowing backwards to rest against his bronze shoulders, as he took in the angry woman before him. In her anger, she had risen to her feet and stood in a battle stance, her hair so at odds with her temper, flowing gently in the breeze. Her chest heaved, again drawing attention to her breasts and her face reddened with her flash of

Merlin's Kiss

temper. Her green eyes glowed, and the exotic shade made her all the more beautifully exotic in her anger.

"What do you see, warrior?" she rasped in a dark tone. "What do you see when you look at me?"

"Trouble."

With that, he rose rather stiffly to his feet and left her standing there in front of his boulder, with the cowering drack. But the drack was not cowering. He was eyeing them both with something akin to speculation in his eyes.

Chapter Five

"What do you mean, we are going on a journey?"

Brieana was stunned at Kerian's announcement. After he had left her in the field of rocks, she had stayed there until her temper cooled and then made her way back to Mirage.

As she looked back on the confrontation, she decided that Kerian was a bit stubborn, but that was a trait that made for great leaders. She had been accused of being a bit stubborn herself, many times.

But when she began to recall his face, so calm and still, devoid of emotions, she was suddenly plagued with the idea of ripping off that facade of calm and exposing the real emotions that lay underneath. The more she thought on it, the more appealing the idea became.

Now she looked up at him as he loomed over her in the dining hall, and patiently waited for his answer.

"I am going to rid myself of at least one potential problem."

"Brieana is no problem, Kerian. Please remember your manners, do." Shala interjected from her seat beside Brieana.

When her stepson had entered the long dining hall, Shala knew that he had come to some conclusion about the woman. She would not allow her stepson to be rid of the girl until she possessed that necklace and the powers that came with it.

As he had approached the raised dais where the long wooden table sat, with determination in his stride, Shala realized that she might have to defend the little witch that she wanted to destroy.

"Me?" Brieana asked, drawing stares from the assorted people seated at the table. "I am a problem?"

Merlin's Kiss

"You are not my problem. I will not let you become one. That is the problem."

He pointed to a corner where the drack sat comfortably by an empty fireplace, warily eyeing the two in conversation.

"You are going to murder Zorn?" Brieana half rose from her seat as she stared open mouthed at the man in front of her.

Murder! the drack shrieked with a sound heard by all. In a flash, he shot across the room pell-mell, knocking over a cook's assistant bearing a large tray of hot fruit- filled sweet cakes, causing them to fly across the room like miniature cannonballs.

Amid shrieks of outrage from the assistant and the many people splattered with the hot syrupy fillings, Zorn raced back and forth, causing chaos wherever his wildly flapping wings managed to strike.

Kerian watched in stupefaction as a candle-stand went flying into the lap of one of his best warriors catching his pale beard on fire. As the reasonably frightened man jumped to his feet, he knocked over the table, dousing his eating companions with roasted chum, steamed vegetables, red wine, and of course, the fruit pastries.

There was another shriek as the man, stumbling to a nearby wash basin to douse the flames in his facial hair, knocked over another bunch of fruit-coated warriors, rendering one man unconscious as his head cracked against the stone floor, and causing his best runner to shriek in pain as several fighters fell onto her prized feet, breaking a toe.

But the mayhem did not stop there! In an effort to help his flaming and smoking comrade, another warrior picked up a basin of wash water, tossing it from across the room in an attempt to douse the flames, but missed and instead doused the people seated at the high table, Kerian included.

At the sound of Shala's disgusted shriek, the room quieted. Even Zorn found a spot, cowering behind one of the previously spotless tapestries that hung on the wall behind the high table.

Stephanie Burke

Brieana, still in her half-risen position, blinked the water from her eyes as she slowly pushed her mass of sopping hair out of her face. She looked wide-eyed at the destruction of the once pristine room, in amazement. The room had been completely destroyed in less that a minute. The human torch had managed to put out the flames, but now stood in a sodden puddle after dumping the whole wash basin of water over his head. His beard still smoldered as his eyes shot death to the drack behind the high table. A whimpering woman was seated on a table, sans her leather running slipper, clutching her foot and moaning that she would never run again. The unconscious man was placed on what remained of a broken table and carried from the room to the infirmary. She turned her eyes then to Kerian.

The greatest Warlord Mirage had ever spawned, stood in a puddle of dirty water, his long silvery-white hair a sodden tangled mess that constantly dripped dank water. His favored brown leather vest lay plastered to his broad chest and his pants adhered to his rock hard thighs like a second skin, exposing every muscle of his legs. Her mouth went surprisingly dry, considering her soaking wet state, at the sight of his body exposed body, but went even dryer when her eyes reached his face.

For a man who let no expression cross his face, he was doing a good imitation of anger. No, more like rampaging anger heralding the approach of some great disaster. His eyes, so slanted down into furious slits, beamed amber death at Zorn while his face, usually so serene, was screwed up into an attitude of complete and utter hostility. Brieana was surprised that the heat of his anger did not evaporate the rivulets of water streaming down his visage. His wrath, felt by all in the subdued room, was a palatable thing.

"I was not planning on murdering the beast," he gritted out through his tightly clenched teeth. "I was planning on taking him home."

50

Merlin's Kiss

"You were?" A joyous expression lit up Brieana's face, drawing the attention of all to her exotic beauty. "You are not going to turn him into winter leggings?"

The cold water not only soaked Brieana, it caused the nipples of her breasts, those breasts that Kerian could not stop thinking about, to harden into little peaks that pushed against the wet leather of her tunic. In her excitement, she gave a little jump, causing her full breasts to sway against the material.

"No," he replied, his anger tapering off as his blood rushed to his nether region.

His response to her did not go unnoticed by Shala, who filed that information away for future use. It seemed that her walking corpse of a stepson was enamored of the little witch. This might prove interesting, very interesting indeed.

Abruptly he turned, his boots making a squishing sound as he left the dais.

"Will one of you please order the cleaning of my hall? And get that drack out of my sight!" he nearly roared in anger, mixed with a healthy dose of frustration.

Brieana watched his exit with fascinated eyes. How...strong he looked. How masterful. Her insides started to tingle, like they did when Merlin kissed her, but all the pleasant feelings vaporized as a quivering voice intruded into her private thoughts.

Releasing me to go home, he is, to my coven? Zorn asked, peeking out at the destruction that he wrought from behind the tapestry. Then his whole countenance changed. Brieana swore that he was smiling.

"I do not know, Zorn. Not after the chaos you caused," Brieana pointed out as she again looked over the room that now resembled the aftermath of a battlefield. Even Shala did not escape. While the woman was directing two servants in the clean-up effort, her once perfect green gown was wet and stained.

51

What matter a few accidents, my Lady! Home, I am going! The Warlord's word, everyone knows, is his bond! With that, he happily trounced out of the room, nimbly avoiding those casualties of the war zone that he created.

"His word is his bond?" she mused out loud.

"Excuse me, my child?" Shala asked coming once again to loom over Brieana and making her back up a few steps. If Shala noticed her aversion to her company, she never said a thing about it.

"Nothing, My Lady." She quickly spoke as servants bustled around them, cleaning off the high table and mopping the water from the floor.

"Then it is time that we go and change. I would not have you catch your death, my dear. That would not do at all."

Silently, she followed the woman from the hall to her chamber, but all the while Zorn's words echoed in her head. His word was his bond.

* * * * *

"Stupid insufferable creature!" Shala growled as she closed the door to her inner chamber.

"I am beginning to suspect that you do not care for me, my love."

In the heat of her anger, Shala failed to notice that all of her previously lit candles were now extinguished. She shivered as she felt the cold presence in her room.

"What do you want, Dagon. I am not in the mood for games."

"Only to tell you that my plan has now been set into motion. Your stepson will disappear during his trek to the Dark Mountains."

"How do you know that he was traveling there? I only just found out myself." Shivering in her wet dress, Shala made no

Merlin's Kiss

effort to cross the room to her armoire. She did not want to get too close to the dark creature that stood in her path and she wanted to know how he obtained his information. If he had a spy planted within her household, she wanted to know about it. Because if he did, his power was even greater than she feared, and that would make his eventual elimination more of a problem.

"I have my ways, beautiful Shala," he murmured as he made himself more comfortable in the chair that he had claimed as his own.

"Are you spying on me, Dagon? Do you not trust in my loyalty?" She cautiously crossed the room to the covered window he used to easily enter and exit.

Dagon muttered something low underneath his breath and a flame appeared in the air in front of him, illuminating his face.

Shala sucked in a breath and turned her face away in disgust as the features of his face were clearly exposed.

Dagon was a painfully beautiful man. If not for his high forehead and strong determined jaw, his delicate features would appear feminine. His large almond-shaped red eyes glowed softly in the light of the mystic fire he conjured. His nose was a straight sharp blade that perfectly matched his perfect cupids-bow upper lip and the sensuously full bottom one. His smile exposed perfect white teeth and drew attention to the double set of fangs that dropped slightly lower than the rest of his teeth. His smile was telling.

"Do you not like the look of me, my beautiful Shala?" He laughed as she turned her face further away.

With a wave of his taloned hand, he caused the flame to extinguish, returning the room to its previously dim state.

"I make it a habit to keep tabs on you, my dear. I want to know everything about you. Like, for instance, your stepson will take your little witch to the mountains with him."

Shala sucked in a shocked breath. Take that little girl to the mountains with him? She would lose her opportunity to get the

53

Stephanie Burke

necklace from off of her dead body without Kerian or that cursed drack being aware of her death.

"He wants her, you know," Dagon added. "He wants the little witch to warm his bed, my beauty. Maybe even to love."

"Shut up!" she growled at him, causing him to break down into laughter once again.

"Jealous, my sweet? Have no fears, my dear, dear, Shala. I will kill them both on the trail and you never need worry about the Woman of Legend bothering you again."

"Woman of Legend?" That snapped her out of her angered stupor. If Brieana was the Woman of Legend, that means that she could control the...

"A myth from our past, Shala, a children's tale told to give the peasants hope," he sneered.

He did not know the importance of the Woman of Legend, what power she could possess? Brieana was this woman?

In the ancient book of spells that Dagon gifted her after the consummation of their arrangement, there were old stories involving a woman from the past who would make her way to the future, bringing incredibly powerful amulets with her. Was that why the strange necklace rejected her touch? Because of Dagon's dark magic?

"Do not kill her, Dagon, not yet anyway."

"Why not, my love, do you not want the little bitch dead?" he asked, clearly playing with her.

I will wipe that smile off your lips, Dagon, she silently vowed.

"I want to observe this Woman of Legend. I want to learn her secrets. And for that, I will need more power."

"But you find me repulsive, my beauty. Your disgust touched me even at a distance from you. Why would you wish more of my power within you?" He relaxed deeper into his chair, smirking at her with his softly glowing eyes.

"You are the only one who has what I need, Dagon. I will do anything to get what I want."

Merlin's Kiss

"Well, since you asked me so sweetly, I'll give you what you want, beautiful Shala. But in the end, it will cost you."

In another one of his swift moves, Dagon was across the room and had Shala in his arms in the space of an eye blink. Her dress quickly hit the floor as he bore her to the bed.

"Remember, my fine Lady, you asked for this," he growled as he took possession of her lips.

His hands stroked an unholy fire within her body, her lust and her eagerness for his tribute rising with sudden force. Her arms gripped his cold hard shoulders and he buried his face in her neck. Her whimpers of pleasure increased as his soft baby fine hair trailed over her breasts. His cold tongue contrasted with the heat of her skin.

"You taste alive, my love." He groaned as he dropped his face to her breasts to tease and torment her nipples with his tongue.

Shala whimpered at the sensation of cold against hot and grasped his hair to push his head lower.

"So eager, my love," he murmured as he acceded to her wishes and dropped his head between her legs.

Shala's whole body arched off of the bed as the power of his touch filled her very being. Her head whipped back and forth on her coverlet as the pleasure-pain filled her. Instinctively, her hands left his hair to pull at his back. That's when the shock of his cold leathery wings penetrated her lust-hazed mind. For a moment, she had forgotten who he was. That was a dangerous thing to do.

Noticing her cooling ardor, Dagon chuckled. "Remember, you asked for this, my love." Pulling his head away from her heat, he rose proudly above her, fully extending his wings and blocking out what dim light the few candles provided. "And now, you get what you asked for."

A strangled shriek exploded from her body as Dagon filled her with his immense length. Pleasure and pain vied for dominance of her body, with pleasure winning out. Her legs wrapped around his waist to bring him closer to her as her arms wrapped around his neck. Again he chuckled as he began his slow hard movements.

"You will do anything to get what you want?" he questioned, his passion rising with every thrust.

"Dagon!" she cried, raking her nails down his shoulders to grip at his thick wrists positioned above her head holding his body above her.

"Yes, I hear you, my beauty. You will get what you asked for."

His words breathed in her ear, caused her to clench around him, urging him to move faster.

He ran one taloned finger down the center of her body, lightly scraping her soft skin, before retracting it to stroke the very seat of her desire.

Uttering a scream, she rose against him, her inner muscles fluttering around him.

Laughing, he threw back his head; he spread his wings to the fullest above their gyrating bodies as he felt his release building up in him.

"Shala!" he cried out as her movements tipped him over the edge and his dark magic fought to explode from his body.

Muttering under his breath, he cast the spell as he felt his control slipping.

"Together!" he cried and groaned as her inner muscles began milking him, attempting to steal from him his breath, his essence, and a small portion of his great power.

"Dagon!" she cried as her release rocketed her among the stars, moaning as she felt him explode within her, drenching her in his power.

Dagon moaned and gently dropped his sweating body to cover her, letting his leathery wings relax and drape both of them. He felt worn out, as if a piece of his soul had been ripped out, unlike Shala, whose body had begun to hum at his release.

Merlin's Kiss

Shala floated, drifted on a plane that she had only felt once before, when she first consummated her union with Dagon all those many years ago. She relaxed beneath him, mentally calculating the changes in her body.

She could feel his magic coursing through her, his heightened sense of smell letting her know the candles were just about burned out. She could hear a servant passing by the door to her outer chamber and could feel the blood flowing through Dagon's veins.

Now, while he was so replete with ecstasy, it would be so easy to reach under her pillow and grab the dagger that she kept there. So easy to plunge it into his black heart and end his threat for once and for all.

"Do not even consider it, my beautiful Shala." His whispered words wafted across her skin.

"I...I was not—"

He cut her off as he tightly curled in his wings and lifted himself off her body. "You think like me, my precious one. And in your position, and given the circumstances, I would gladly plunge a knife into the sweet skin of your back. Besides, the feeling that you have will not last much longer."

"What do you mean, Dagon? The last infusion of magic that you gave me is still felt to this day! Why will this feeling not last?"

"Because I have decided that you need to be controlled a bit more, my spiteful beauty."

With a wave of his hand and few muttered words, a mystic fire exploded into being above the bed illuminating both of their naked bodies.

Shala again grimaced at the sight of his body. Although his face and form were human, Dagon's body was a patchwork of ugly raised scars and wounds. His retractable wings, leathery and large, were coiled behind him. His hands, with talons retracted, traced over his body, materializing a tunic and short pants that his kind preferred.

Stephanie Burke

"What do you mean, Dagon?" Again she asked as she reached to the floor to pull what remained of her gown around her body. As she moved, she noticed a sudden lethargy in her limbs and she felt the need for sleep.

"Only this, my beauty. I have decided to curtail your movements, just a bit. I have made you quite pregnant, my dear."

He stopped to laugh at her shocked expression.

"I cannot be pregnant! I have cast the spells…"

"I keep telling you, my flower, that your little spells may mean something to these pitiful humans that occupy Mirage, but to me they are meaningless and easily brushed aside."

Shala stared at him in shocked anger.

"And please do not think of doing away with the seed, my dear. It is my heir that you carry and I will be most unhappy with you and this land if anything were to happen to it. Thus, I have curtailed your plotting, but just a bit, and I have guaranteed my, shall we say, participation in the glorious future of the Light Isles!" His laughter boomed around the room.

"I shall leave you now, my dear, to recover from the process. I have given you a bit more of my magic powers, but not enough to do what you would so dearly love to do. Sleep well and remember."

In a lightning fast move, his hands were at her throat, talons extended to test their sharpness against the tender flesh of her throat.

"I will be watching you, my love, watching you very closely."

In another flash of movement, he was gone.

As sleep overtook her, Shala muttered, "You just made a big mistake, you winged fool. Now I have more reason to get rid of Kerian, the Woman of Legend, and of you, Dagon. My child will inherit this land and will rule in my passing as I see fit!"

Merlin's Kiss

Then she passed out, the strain of carrying Dagon's seed too much for her body. But she was unconscious with a smile on her face.

Chapter Six

"I want to go with you!"

"No!"

"I want to go with you!"

"No!"

Brieana was losing patience with her warrior. She didn't know when she started thinking of Kerian as hers, but she suspected it had begun when he promised Zorn could go home. Maybe he was her true mate after all! She had begun to have doubts, but his treatment of the drack after the "accident" had been more than equitable. He hadn't killed the silly lizard, and that made him rise a bit more in her esteem. But now he was just being plain unreasonable.

"You have to let me go! I want to take Zorn home. He is my friend, Kerian, and where I come from, you do not abandon friends."

"No!" he all but shouted.

Brieana had cornered Kerian at his practice field a few scant minutes before a mock battle was to take place. He had no time for the woman's foolishness. He would not be responsible for her on the long trek into the mountains. Kerian had visions of her petite body shivering with the fever that came with over-exposure and even worse, dashed to the rocks below like someone whom he had once loved. She was too small and delicate for such a journey!

"It is out of the question! You are not built for the rigors of life on the trail, Brieana. I do not want to see you hurt!"

The concern underlying his words went completely unnoticed by Brieana. All that she heard was that another man did not think that she was capable of handling herself.

Merlin's Kiss

"Not built for rigors of trail life?" she questioned with narrowed green eyes and a sneer on her lips.

Any of yon soldiers, best you can Lady! Zorn urged from behind. During their conversation, the young drack had walked up and claimed his favorite place, at Brieana's side, well behind her but still near her side.

"Stay out of this, youthling!" Kerian ordered as he watched the fury build in his beautiful castle guest. For some strange reason, Zorn wanted Brieana along on this journey. He had to pause and wonder why. Before he made any headway into the matter, Brieana rallied herself for attack.

"He does not have to stay out of it, Kerian. He, unlike another stubborn male of my acquaintance, listens to my stories of my true home. I was a warrior there, battle tested and dangerous. Pick any of your fighters, Kerian, and let us duel."

"Why would I do that?" he asked, platinum eyebrow arched over one amber eye.

"Because if I am bested, I will stay here without any complaint. But if I win, you have to take me with you."

Kerian took a step back and eyed the small spitfire before him. She barely reached his shoulder, yet she was offering him a challenge. He noted how her flash of anger brought a little color to her cheeks and made her eyes sparkle. She was enjoying this battle of wills. Moreover he was confounded to understand why her enjoyment had become paramount to him.

"All right, Brieana. You have your challenge, but let me warn you, my word is my bond and I expect you to honor your word as well."

"Agreed!" she instantly, cried. This was going to be fun. Eager to get the battle started, she gleefully ran her hands down her leather-covered thighs. She was again wearing an oversized tunic and tight leggings, provided no doubt by Shala. She looked beautiful and kissable, not like the fierce warrior that she claimed to be.

"Best Sato," he demanded, his face as usual devoid of any expression. "I want this done quickly so that you will not get hurt."

"A mere trifle!" Brieana bragged as she walked past him to select her weapon from the sword cart. "Just ready extra rations for our journey, Kerian. I work up a powerful hunger after being on the battle field."

Love her confidence, do you not? Zorn asked as he watched Brieana make a careful selection. *What matter a few extra rations, when she is made happy, warrior?*

Kerian looked suspiciously at the drack. After learning that he would not be made into a winter wardrobe, Zorn had gotten uncharacteristically brave.

"Why are you suddenly so content?" Kerian asked. He was beginning to feel like he was being manipulated.

What mean you by that, Warlord? Soon to be home, safe among my coven, I am. That is all. But he continued to watch Brieana.

She did look as if she knew what she was doing; Kerian had to grudgingly admit. She tested the balance and heft of each blade, before making her selection. Once satisfied, she swung the sword a few times, then approached Kerian.

"I am ready," she announced as she reached his side.

"Then by all means, let us proceed." He turned and cupped his mouth to shout, "Sato? A challenge!" Instantly the practice field, filled with the fighting men and women of Mirage, became deathly silent.

Bowing to his lord, Sato announced, "I am ready!"

"Not me, my friend," Kerian corrected.

Sato looked around for the warrior who had issued a challenge to him, but only saw the little foreign woman, Brieana.

"Who?" he finally asked, looking more than a little confused.

"The Lady Brieana," Kerian confirmed.

Merlin's Kiss

There was a moment of shocked silence, then the field exploded into laughter.

"Her?" Sato asked rudely, ashamed that his lord would give him such a piddling challenge.

"And why not me, you braying ass?" Brieana exclaimed, obviously angry at the reception her challenge had met.

"I did not mean...My Lady, I..." but Sato could not find the words.

"Do you accept?" Kerian's almost deadly quiet voice filled the field causing a sudden death to the revelry taking place there. When the Warlord of Mirage spoke in that tone, he got results.

"I will be pleased to accept the challenge, My Lord," Sato replied, firmly in control of his emotions once again.

"Then let us proceed!" he commanded.

Brieana nodded her thanks to her warrior, and strolled casually onto the field, Sato doing the same. They met in the center of the now empty practice field.

"Lady," he nodded to her, thinking that this would be quickly done with.

"Sato," she returned respectfully before bending slightly at the knees and holding the sworn in an unfamiliar stance.

She held the great weight of the dulled sword with two hands instead of one. Sato figured that it was because the sword was too heavy for her. It would be easy to knock the weapon from her hands.

In a surprise move, he quickly lunged forward, hoping to knock the sword from her hand and end this humiliating battle, but he was in for a surprise.

Brieana had expected such strong-arm tactics from the arrogant male, and had played upon his assumptions like a piper played a flute. At his lunge, instead of backing up, she pivoted to her right and knocked his blade downwards. When

63

Stephanie Burke

he paused, surprised at her maneuver, her right hand lashed out and made direct contact with his right cheek.

He quickly stepped back and swung out at her head. Again she deftly side-stepped his maneuver and brought her sword back up into a defensive position.

Angered to be dealt such a blow, Sato again lunged at her, at the last minute pivoting to deliver a powerful double strike to her sword, hoping to make her wrists go numb and cause her to drop her weapon.

No such luck.

Brieana went to her left knee, using her sword to deflect the blow, then hooked her right leg around his knees, knocking him off balance.

As he struggled to regain his footing, Brieana rose to her feet, striking his sword at the base, hoping to disarm him and end the fight right there. But Sato was better trained than that.

He took the fall onto his back and using his momentum, kept rolling backwards until he again landed on his feet. Then from a crouched position, he lunged at Brieana's legs, all thought of this being a farce of a battle leaving his mind.

Again, as graceful as a dancer, Brieana side-stepped the forceful lunge and took advantage of his extended position. She swung around behind him, hoping to deliver the winning touch, but his sword was there deflecting her blow. Using his own weapon to hold hers at bay, Sato quickly turned and once again faced his small opponent.

Brieana smiled into his face and waited for his next move. He had to understand that brute force would not work with her in warfare. Her trick was to deliver her blows without being caught. At this, her small stature was an asset. She had the speed that he lacked. That coupled with her experience in war made her a formidable opponent. Taking a step back, she deliberately left herself open, and Sato immediately took advantage of it. Swinging his sword at waist level, he went for the small break in her defense, just around her waist.

64

Merlin's Kiss

With Sato being unbalanced again in his attempt to quickly end the match, Brieana again stepped around his blade and delivered a punishing kick to his right wrist, the one holding the sword.

Instantly Sato's hand became numb and he felt his sword slipping through his limp grip. Just as quickly, Brieana stamped the sword out of his hand and laid the blade of her sword against the back of his neck.

There was stunned silence on the battlefield. No one could believe what they had just seen! The tiny foreign woman had bested Sato in a mock battle! She now stood victorious, her blade held to deliver the death strike and waited for Sato to confirm that the battle was truly lost.

"Do you yield?" she asked, panting with the exertions of the battle.

Having no other choice, Sato nodded. "I yield." His voice carried plainly across the silent field.

With a jaunty smile, Brieana removed the blade from his neck and offered him her hand.

Sato slowly rose to his feet and eyed Brieana with some admiration. "Where did you learn to fight like a demon possessed?" he asked in awe.

"Battle has a way of teaching its victims, Sato. I am battle tested several times over, and use any seeming disadvantage to my advantage."

He nodded as if he understood. "Experience is the best teacher," he considered.

"Kerian?" Brieana cried as she walked towards the silent Warlord.

Just like the others, he could scarce believe what he had just witnessed. Brieana had the skill of one of his most experienced fighters.

"What kind of world did she come from?" he asked to no one in particular as he watcher her victorious approach.

65

A harsh unfair one, Zorn replied as he too watched his mistress approach, now quite sure of her identity.

Kerian looked at the purple lizard for a moment before returning his attention to Brieana.

"I must learn to pay attention to her future stories," he replied, eyeing the drack from the corner of his eye.

Zorn got that look in his eyes again and Kerian quickly turned away.

"So how soon will we be leaving, Kerian?" Brieana questioned, still slightly out of breath. "And will I get to carry my own sword?"

"In two days time," Kerian replied. "We must be sure to have all of the provisions necessary for this journey and I want you measured for you own sword. It will take that long to forge it."

Brieana's eyes lit up for a moment, then shadows clouded their bright green.

"I have a sword," she replied, her happiness leaving at some unpleasant thought.

"Where is it?" Kerian asked. He knew how people got attached to their weapons, even naming them sometimes. Why, he even had his own special blade, used only in battle. He would find her sword for her. That would make her happy. "I do not remember seeing it in the cavern with you, but we can stop there on our journey back and search for it."

"My sword is not there," she replied, almost angrily. "My sword was the greatest weapon in all of the Britons. No other could match its might."

"Then where is it?" Kerian asked. If her sword held the same power of her necklace, then it was powerful indeed. He did not want that power falling into the wrong hands.

"It was stolen from me," she replied after a tense moment of silence. "It was taken from me by stupid men who feared the truth."

Merlin's Kiss

"What truth was that?" Kerian asked stunned. It would take a powerful force indeed to disarm this woman. He had seen proof of her prowess in the mock battle staged with Sato. It must have been a great warrior who stole such a weapon from her. That or a close friend betrayed her. The thought left an unfamiliar sour taste in his mouth.

"The truth is simple, Kerian. It was that a woman was just as great as they were could lead them into a new era of peace and prosperity. That was a truth that they refused to accept. And so, here I am, stuck in a place that I do not know, with no future before me and a cloudy past behind me."

"The one who enchanted you took your sword?" Kerian asked, angered at the Merlin who she cursed with startling regularity.

"Yes, he did," she replied. "And Excalibur is lost to me, forever."

She looked so lost and alone standing there struggling with her emotions, that Kerian felt great pity for her.

"I might not be able to bring you your mystic sword, Brieana, but I can design one that suits your personality now. It might not be much of a comfort, but I understand the pain of betrayal."

His bitter tone snapped her out of her own morose thoughts and she looked at her warrior. What betrayal had he known?

"What happened?" she asked as she took a step closer to him and rested her small palm upon his leather-covered chest. Kerian sucked in a deep breath at the contact. Separated as they were by the thin leather, he could still feel the unique heat that she generated within him at her mere touch.

"I do not wish to dwell on the past," he replied more sharply than he usually would have, the force of his desire for her roughening his voice. "I prefer to dwell upon the future. And that is the journey into the mountains to return your pet lizard home."

Stephanie Burke

Hurt by his sharp tone. Brieana withdrew her comforting hand, and Kerian almost begged her to return it, but gained control of himself.

"And my sword," she reminded him. "Your word is your bond, and you gave your word that you would design my sword."

Although Brieana was hurt, a well-made sword was better and more dependable than most men were any day.

"That I did," he returned, and turned to the men and canceled practice for the day.

With one hand barely touching the material of her tunic, he guided her towards the armory to be measured.

He would give her this sword, if that was the only thing that he could give her. He would take her on this journey, and then he would find out where she belonged and return her home. That was all that he could give her. He could not give her his heart, which was what a woman of her caliber deserved. He had no heart left to give.

Merlin's Kiss

Chapter Seven

"When will my sword be ready?" Brieana asked as she dutifully walked behind Kerian as they started out on their journey to the mountains. She paused for a moment to adjust something that he called a bedroll that strapped to her back. It contained blankets made from the soft yet durable chum's wool, some foodstuffs that he called freeze-dried, and an odd assortment of metal implements. Some were for cooking, some were for hunting and others made no sense to her whatsoever.

For instance, the little metal box filled with little wooden sticks called matches. How the tiny little things started a fire, she didn't know! Everybody knew in order to build a fire, you needed oil or candles, or at the very least a dry sturdy stick and a piece of dry wood. But she supposed that a few changes could have happened in the years while she was asleep, but she doubted that people had found a way to create fire out of thin air.

Keep up, please do, Zorn yawned as he loped along behind her. *Busy will be, the rabbits, later tonight.*

Brieana snorted at his comment, as if rabbits might do them some harm, but she adjusted her roll and rushed to keep up with Kerian's long strides. Besides, night was far off.

Kerian breathed in the fresh crisp air of the morning, inhaling it deeply into his lungs and relishing it with the expansion of his chest. He loved physical activity and hiking was one of his favorite pastimes from his youth. Now that he was Warlord and Master of Mirage, he found that he did not have the time to indulge in the activities of his younger days. Therefore, he planned to enjoy every moment of this trip. Sure, he had Brieana and his attraction to her to deal with, and Zorn, but he would put unpleasantness behind him and concentrate on enjoying his time out.

Stephanie Burke

"Well?" her husky voice demanded. "Kerian, when will my sword be ready?"

"By the time we return," he replied as he turned to face her to gauge her reaction.

"Really?" Her green eyes lit up and a smile lightened her whole face. The lightning dawn sky made everything around them seemed surreal. It was like a dream, back lighted by the hazy purple sky, her supple body swaying with each step. He wondered what her body would feel like underneath him, calling out his name in a fit of passion.

"Did I not say so?"

His gruff answer caused a frown to replace the burgeoning smile on her face, but she quickly hid her feelings. If he wanted to act the barbarian, that was his problem. She was going to enjoy this trip, even if he glowered the whole way.

"Good," she shot out, then pushed ahead of him, disdaining to look at his muscular body clothed in blue leather leggings and the matching vest he seemed to prefer. She also did not notice the way his war belt pulled those leggings dangerously low on his slim hips.

"Slow down, there has been a rabbit infestation reported in this area."

"Humph!" She turned her nose up at that and marched onward on the rocky path.

"They travel in packs and the vicious little monsters have been known to devour a man whole in a few moments." His face was stern as he gave his lecture, his silver eyes boring deeply into hers.

"Of course I believe that rubbish!" she snorted, turning her back to him. How dare he try scaring her, after treating her like an ignorant clod?

As she angrily stormed ahead, she began to notice the natural beauty of this place, how much it reminded her of home. The grassy plains that Castle Mirage sat on slowly gave way to more rugged and rocky terrain. The further she walked, she

Merlin's Kiss

found that among the dark green grass and wild flowers, small pebbles began to give way to large rocks, then to boulders. The dawn air was crisp and clean and burnt her lungs a bit, but it felt good on her exposed skin.

Kerian insisted that although the days were still hot, she should wear a long sleeved tunic and leather pants. Today's set was made entirely of black leather that made her feel a bit dangerous. Her own war belt, a scaled down model of Kerian's, contained her water skin, a knife and another long knife that he called a machete. It also contained more things that Kerian deemed necessities for survival. She did not mind the extra weight, her black armor at home weighed more, but she found it a bit uncomfortable as she stalked ahead. Slowly the beauty of the place dissipated her anger at Kerian's harsh words, and she began to notice the wild life scuttling around.

Several large birds that resembled falcons flew lazily overhead and often dove down for a quick meal. Small, brightly colored lizards scurried across the path, their rainbow-hued scales shining in the early morning. Then there were several little bunny rabbits swiftly traveling across the path, paying no heed to the humans that trod on, invading their territory.

Travel so quickly, must we, Zorn whined, pulling her attention away from the furry little creatures.

"So that we may get you home and the sooner that is, the better I will feel, youthling."

"You do want to return home, do you not, Zorn?" Brieana asked, waiting for her traveling companions to catch up with her. "You must be excited about going home to your coven again."

But missed the cook's baked meat pies, I will! Zorn whined. The giant purple lizard had grown quite accustomed to castle life and felt a bit reluctant to leave his pampered existence.

"But think of all that you have experienced! How many dracks can say that they spent time in a real castle among humans? Every one will look up to you! And think of the ladies Zorn."

What matter, they? he testily asked, causing Brieana to look at him with a grin on her face.

"Oh, you will find that it matters, come mating time."

At her words the drack cocked his head to the side, as if considering her words, then a grin split his purple face.

An advantage, it will be, will it not?

"You had better think of the advantages of hiding your purple hide from Gren's wrath when she finds out that you violated our treaty."

Zorn's head, once held high with his importance, quickly slumped down low and he looked as though he was contemplating the advantages of hiding from his leader's anger.

"Why must you spoil everyone's happiness, Kerian? If you have nothing positive to say, then please, shut up, do!"

Again in a huff, she stormed ahead, nearly stepping on one of the little bunnies.

"Oh!" she cried out in surprise at almost finding one beneath her boot. "I am sorry, little fluffy fellow." She bent down to get a closer look.

"Brieana," Kerian's low voice warned. "Step back slowly and make no sudden moves."

"Really, Kerian! It is just a harmless little bunny!" She ignored his tense muscles as he began to ease his sword out of his war belt.

She turned back to the little brown bunny rabbit. He had white ears and a puffy little tail. His pink nose was twitching in the cute way that all bunnies have.

Suddenly, she heard a low growl. She looked around to find the source, but there was nothing in front of her but the rabbit. She looked back at Kerian and Zorn to see if they too had heard the strange noise, but they both looked to be preparing for battle, bodies held ready to spring at a moment's notice.

Merlin's Kiss

"Back away from the rabbit, Brieana." Kerian spoke in a low calm tone, causing her to wonder what was wrong.

As she turned to shoo the little fur-ball away from the unseen danger, her little friend looked up at her and bared his teeth.

Instead of the tiny overbite that most rabbits have, this one had sharp white fangs dripping saliva. The growls became higher, building in volume until it was apparent that the threatening sound was emanating from one little brown rabbit. Before she had a chance to get over her shock, the little beast's eyes widened as it reared back on its hind legs and prepared to attack.

Brieana gave a sharp scream as the little rodent went airborne and headed right for her throat. Just as her short life was passing in front of her eyes, strong hands gripped her shoulders and tossed her aside. She felt the heat from the small rabbit body as it sailed past her head, inches away from her throat as she fell to the ground. As she watched, horrified, the little bunny took off down the path, kicking up little puffs of dust in its wake.

"Are you harmed?" Kerian demanded as Zorn took off like a cannonball after the brown menace. "Are you well?"

Kerian knelt at Brieana's side, blade held in readiness as his sharp eyes scanned the area for more of the little pests.

"That rabbit tried to kill me?" she said, her words sounding incredulous even to her own ears. She lay in a stunned pile of leather and legs as she watched Zorn disappear after the rabbit. She turned wide eyes to Kerian. "It leapt for my throat."

Kerian said nothing as he ran his hands along her legs and arms, checking to see if she damaged anything in her fall. He grunted at the feel of how tiny her limbs were, than he began to get angry.

"I warned you about the dangers of rabbits but you refused to heed my warnings, Brieana, and almost got yourself killed. We were very lucky today. I told you rabbits hunt in packs, and

Stephanie Burke

if that one had not been a lone straggler, we might be fighting off a pack of wild hungry rabbits! This land may appear tame, but there are a lot of hidden dangers here."

He rose to his feet to glare at her. Then he realized that he was shaking, and not out of anger. He was shaking out of fear.

Fear was an emotion that he had never thought to feel again, because fear made you vulnerable. He did not want to be made vulnerable because of this woman! He had to get Zorn home and repair the damage that Zorn had done to their treaty, and then he had to find out where this woman came from. Then send her home!

"Rabbits eat vegetables," she insisted. "They do not eat meat." She was still in shock.

"Not in my generation, nor in my father's, father's generation, nor his father's, father's generation, Brieana. And not after the Great War!"

"Great War?" Brieana questioned as she got to her feet, feeling a little unsteady, but fine. "Where has Zorn gotten off to?"

Kerian turned her to face him when it looked as if she might try to run after the purple beast.

"Dracks eat rabbits," Kerian replied. "And the Great War was a cataclysm of destruction. It almost ended man."

"What? Did Arthur misuse Excalibur?" she questioned, shocked that Merlin would let the fool do something so, well, foolhardy.

"There was no sword involved, Brieana. Our ancestors lived in great castles with large paved roads and used powerful machines to do their work for them. They are the ones who created now-clear-air weapons. They destroyed everything, leaving few survivors in its aftermath. They say that it took hundreds of years for the air to be clean again."

Brieana shook her head in denial. He had to be making up some fantasy to scare her! Nothing has so much power that it could wipe out all of mankind!

Merlin's Kiss

"It is true, Brieana. All know of the tale. It is true."

"But if what you say is true Kerian, then I must have been enchanted for hundreds of years! That is not possible! I have only been asleep for a short time."

She shook her head from side to side as if she meant to defy the truth. What he spoke of could not be real! If it was true, then there was no way for her to go home and reclaim Excalibur and her queenship! If he spoke true, then the world had changed without her, and there was no place for her in this new one.

Seeing how upset she was, Kerian decided to change the subject. What he was thinking was surely impossible. But if that were true, then she was from Earth's past and not from the Dark Isles. If it were true, then there would be no way to send her away from him and all of the unsettling emotions that she had awakened inside of him. The thing that scared him most—he was beginning to enjoy them.

"Leave it for now, Brieana," he soothed after she looked as if she would break into tears. "Let us continue on our way. We have a long journey ahead of us."

"Zorn!" She called out to remind him as he started to walk away. "We cannot leave him!"

"He will find us," he assured her as she paused to wait for the drack.

The sun was now rising over the mountains and filling the land with light. Exposed by the light of day were the dim shadows—outlines of the boulders that peppered the trail. The shadowy mountain that rose majestically before them still had to be conquered. Yet, Kerian took in the beauty of his land awakening to a new day and wondered, as he watched Brieana in the midst of this waking miracle, why her presence made the day more beautiful.

Brieana turned to face Kerian, the rising sun casting his face in shadows and giving him a golden aura that surrounded his whole body. He was her port in the face of the storm that had become her life. He was her mate, chosen by destiny, her equal

75

Stephanie Burke

in all things, as predicted by Merlin. Yet, he was so distant from her. And the feelings he created within her!

She decided to ponder these thoughts later. For now, they had some hard traveling to do and she did not want to make any more mistakes. She would listen to this man, until she found out her purpose for being here. Then she would move on to fulfill her destiny, with or without him.

Merlin's Kiss

Chapter Eight

I need to have sex! Kerian thought to himself as he eyed Brieana examining her feet for blisters. "If I find the sight of a female inspecting her toes arousing, it has been far too long."

He ignored the look the drack was giving him and tried to remember his last sexual encounter.

"I know it was before the chum sheering last year, or was it after?"

He simply could not remember the last time that he had indulged in the carnal act!

He shook his head in dismay, deciding he needed a break from camp and some time away from his little mystery woman.

On quiet feet, he walked out of their makeshift night camp and into the shadows of the mountain. When he reached a wide ledge, he decided to sit there and observe the moonrise. Nothing was as beautiful as watching the moon fill his land with its pale white light. The nightly illumination made his home look magical as it outlined the walls of his castle and made the surrounding land glisten like a field of diamonds. His breath caught at its beauty. He needed this land as much as it needed him.

As gentle night breezes whipped loose tendrils of his hair around his stoic face, he thought of the threat to his people. He had been receiving warnings of a Dark Isles invasion and the thought of war troubled him. No one had ever met a person from the Dark Isles before, and he worried about the abilities that they possessed.

Again his thoughts turned to Brieana. Was she of the Dark Isles, a spy sent in to reconnoiter and report their weaknesses? He didn't think so.

77

Stephanie Burke

As they hiked over rough terrain, he replayed Brieana's words in his mind. She claimed only a man equal to her strength and wisdom could have freed her from her stone prison, and he was the man to emancipate her. Was she his destined mate? He had always felt different from his people. Women either shied away from a leader with his strange powers, or they wanted to sleep with the living curiosity who spoke to dracks and proved that he would kill to protect them. However, Brieana was different.

She could understand the language of his special friends and she was a warrior like none that he had ever seen. She fought like a seasoned veteran of war, yet managed to look so delicate and fragile while doing it. She was a mystery and he was afraid that she could awaken emotions long since beaten out of him.

He looked over his land again, his amber eyes looking sad and a bit lonely. He was destined to be alone and to protect. That was what great leaders did. He would use his abilities to protect all of his people and not for his own selfish gain. That trait had cost him much before.

Brieana walked softly across the gravel and rocks of the plateau where they camped. She noticed Kerian rise and leave the comforts of their fire and wanted to know where he was going. She quietly followed him and now hung back in the shadows as she watched him look over a view of his land. He seemed so sad and lost that tears almost came to her eyes.

"I know you are there, Brieana."

His low voice startled her for a moment, then she boldly stepped forward to sit beside him.

"How did you know it was me?" she asked as she examined his still profile.

"Your smell, Brieana. You smell like wildflowers."

"I do?" She could hardly contain the pleasure in her voice, but she managed to keep it hidden.

Merlin's Kiss

"Yes. It is a dead give away of your location to your enemies. In the future, you should endeavor to refrain from using perfumes."

Her eyes widened in shock and then anger as she took in his words.

"I do not wear perfume, Oh Great Leader of Men. I wash with the same soap as you!"

"I meant no offense!" he quickly added, knowing that his harsh word would hurt her feelings. "It is just that I can track your scent easily. It is a different scent than what I am used to." Like the scent of female flesh, his treacherous mind reminded him. How long had it been since he smelled that particular scent?

"That is fine, Kerian." She acquiesced, noting his suddenly sullen expression. "I am glad that you can track me easily. If I get lost I know that you will find me."

He felt his heart melt a little at her confidence in his abilities, but he quickly tried to shore up the breach.

"What is it like?" Her words interrupted his thoughts.

"What?" he asked, forgetting that he was supposed to be remembering all the reasons why he needed to find a place for her and why he needed to harden his heart towards her.

"What is it like to rule all of this, to have your own kingdom?"

"This is not a kingdom, Lady. This is a clan. And I am ruler here by virtue of right and might. Mirage is the largest of several clans that make up the Light Isles. I am ruler only here and no place else."

"But what is it like to rule?" Her eyes watered a little at the thoughts of her lost kingdom and her unjust treatment. "What is it like, to have people follow your every command?"

"It is a lot of responsibility, Brieana. These people depend on me to be strong and just. They know that I will provide protection for them and their families, so they serve me well. I

Stephanie Burke

need them to tend to my chums and my farmland. Without them, this place, Mirage, would cease to exist."

He continued, "There is a balance here, Brieana, and I do my best to keep it maintained for the good of us all."

He seemed to feel the weight of his castle on his shoulders at that moment. He looked like he was in so much in pain that Brieana had to reach out and caress his face. Surprised at her touch, he turned to face her, and caught his breath at the picture she presented, all soft and feminine, and with concern for him shining in the depths of her green eyes.

"You sacrifice a lot for them, do you not?" She examined his still face and wondered what had hurt him so.

"I have sacrificed everything, Brieana. I have nothing left to give."

His amber eyes shone with longing for a moment, his steely control cracked and she caught a glimpse of his hungry soul. Her lips parted at the sight, her eyes filling with tears for him.

"Don't!" he cried out, seeing the moisture gathering and clouding her eyes. "Don't waste your tears, Brieana. I am not worthy of them."

He started to turn his head away from her, to jerk away from her painfully gentle grasp, to deny her tears, her trembling hands, and her feminine smell, but her small hands restrained him.

"You are worthy, Kerian. If you were not, I would not be here now."

Her heart broke for the pain that he must have endured during his life. But she could admire the results of his struggles. Kerian was a quiet, intelligent, compassionate man. Everything that she respected and strove to be.

"Brieana," he began in a warning tone. "I am losing myself and I don't know how to find the balance within. You make me dream of impossible things." Like a life filled with happiness and joy. Like children who would love and respect him and a

Merlin's Kiss

land filled with everlasting peace. "I am not good for you, no matter what your magician has said."

"I make decisions for myself, Kerian," Brieana began just as heatedly, her hands still holding his head in place. "I am a grown woman and I know what is best for me."

Kerian felt the rough calluses on her hands and the small delicate bone structure that lent them such amazing strength. Her very touch burned his face. Within her grasp, he felt something that he had never before experienced with a woman, and that was dangerous. She was making him start to believe in happily ever after and in a future that seemed impossible for him. He had to let her go, but before he did, he decided he must have something else to tide him over for the rest of his solitary life.

"I'm going to kiss you, Brieana. Now."

His low husky words sent a jolt of mingled fear and desire throughout her body. But she stood firm. She wanted to feel his lips on her, to carry the taste of him within her memory to replace the unmanly fumbling of Arthur and the demanding dominating touch of Merlin.

Gently, as if she were a delicate treasure, he cupped her face and drew her close. Her eyes closed, shielding her bright green orbs as he slowly lowered his lips to her slightly parted mouth. She gasped at the first brush of his lips, almost questioningly across hers, getting to know the feel of her.

He quickly breathed in the gasp she let escape, the very life breath of her, and savored its flavor. He again lowered his head, tilting a little to the side, as he firmly pressed his lips to her softer, more delicate ones.

Fire exploded along her nerves at the gentle brush of his lips. It started a quaking deep within her body. Soft tingles down her chest, causing her nipples to tighten and her to moan softly. In an attempt to deepen the kiss, she parted her lips and tugged on his face. Responding to her needy gestures, he pulled

Stephanie Burke

her closer and accepted the invitation by gently thrusting his tongue into her mouth.

Her eyes widened for a moment, before they closed on a groan and she lost herself in the magic of his kiss, of his tongue invading her, of his flavor exploding in her mouth. This was like nothing that she had ever felt before, something that she could quickly get addicted to.

Softly, she brushed her tongue against his and delighted in the return of the tingling. She tentatively thrust her tongue into his mouth and almost cried out at the heat that she felt.

Kerian felt his control slipping. His little Brieana was like fire in his arms. She caused his senses to heat up and his passion, once dormant, to rise to the surface. One taste was not enough. He had to have more of her, more of her special taste, more of her softness. Then, she tried to take over the kiss by invading his mouth!

Kerian lost his battle for control. In a flash, he tore his hands away from her face and gripped her small waist. Never breaking off the kiss, he lifted her, making her straddle his lap, so that he could deepen the kiss. His hands, large and rough, began a gentle exploration of the soft skin protected from the cool night air by her tunic.

Brieana sighed as she felt his fingers creep up over her stomach and caress her back. Never had she been touched quite like this and she wanted it to go on forever. She leaned forward to deepen the kiss, and trembled as her tightening nipples rubbed against the soft leather of her tunic. What would they feel like brushing against his rough hands, his stiff vest, his bare chest?

"Kerian?" she panted, breaking off the kiss and sighing as he began to pepper her face with little glancing touches of his open mouth.

"Yes, love?" he answered, still lost in a fog of need for this woman.

Merlin's Kiss

She buried her hands in his hair, marveling at the silky texture of it, lazily running her fingers through it, causing him to growl his pleasure.

"Kerian," she began again. "I..."

We eat, when? a loud voice complained in both of their minds, causing them to guiltily move apart and stare at each other in disbelief.

Hungry, I am! Zorn complained as he padded around the corner to stare at the couple still entwined and wearing twin looks of surprise and alarm. "Rations, we eat, yes?"

"Uh, Zorn, go away!" Brieana stuttered out as she attempted to find a graceful way to dismount Kerian. "You have no sense of timing!"

Not time for mating, this is! Time for dinner! the exuberant purple lizard again cried out as he sat down beside them, an attentive audience to their little passion play.

"You are really becoming a nuisance!" she declared as she finally got off of Kerian's lap and turned to face him, cheeks flaming red. But what she saw on his face caused her to lose all color.

"This can never happen again, Brieana," he said, his deep voice filled with some inner anguish.

"Kerian?" she questioned, feeling his deep emotional pain and not understanding it.

"I will only end up hurting you, Brieana, and I cannot live with that!"

He rose to his feet and stalked off, disappearing into the darkening shadows, as if she never existed.

"Thank you so much, Zorn!" Brieana cried, turning to the youthling with tears in her eyes. "He will never want me again!"

Worry too much, you do, Lady. Come to you, the Warlord will, when the time is right. Not the night, was tonight.

Brieana's tears instantly dried up. Did this drack know something that she did not?

83

Stephanie Burke

"What do you know, Zorn?" she asked stalking towards her purple protector. "What do you know about Kerian and I?"

Speak to Gren, you must! the drack said as he cautiously backed away from his Lady. *The answers you seek, Gren has!*

"Tell me, you rotten purple...menace! Tell me what you know!" She took another step forward and Zorn took off with a flash of purple skin.

A good night for hunting, tonight is! he declared as he took to wing. *Many rabbits tonight. For rations, no need!*

"Coward!" Brieana called after him, standing in the small clearing, arms akimbo and a scowl on her face.

"I guess I eat rations alone tonight!" she muttered to herself, walking back to camp.

Once there, she sat in a huff by the fire then smiled as she realized what her drack, her special, beautiful, wonderful little drack had said. "Kerian will come to me when the time is right!"

With a smile, she tore into the store of meat that Kerian insisted that she pack. Suddenly the cold fare tasted like ambrosia and the cool night was magical again!

Merlin's Kiss

Chapter Nine

Shala leaned over the side of her bed and proceeded to vomit up her meal, just as she had for the past three days. She whimpered as the spasms wracked her body and caused sweat to bead up on her forehead.

"Damn that Dagon!" she whimpered as her body continued to heave.

"Is that any kind of reception, my dear, for the father of your child?"

As his amused voice filled the chamber, the candles began to slowly extinguish themselves, leaving the room dim but for the soft morning sun flowing in through the opened drapes at the windows.

"Come to gloat?" she asked and again leaned over the side of the bed to spew out what was left in her stomach.

"Charming," he drolly muttered as he fully materialized in the room and walked over to his usual chair across the room. "And I wasn't aware that I needed an invitation to visit, my pretty. After all, you are the mother of my child."

With a negligent wave of his hand, he created a sphere of energy and sent it flying across the room to float above her bed.

"What is it you want, Dagon?" Shala asked as she pulled herself up into a sitting position and raised one trembling hand to the mass of matted hair covering her face. She forced herself up in the tangled covers and eyed the ball of blue/white energy floating weightlessly above her.

"Only to let you know that your beloved stepson and his mysterious woman will reach that glorious creature Gren in a matter of moments."

He chuckled at the pitiful sight of her before continuing. "If I followed my first inclination, my dear Kerian and his lovely

85

Stephanie Burke

traveling companion would be already dead and this little conspiracy of yours would now be at an end. But I have let your," he eyed her quaking body and let out a little laugh, "considerable charms sway my decisions."

He lazily lifted his foot and rested it on the chair that sat opposite to his and watched the sickly woman sitting in the bed glaring at him.

"And why should I care about that wretched beast?" She carefully raised her hands and cupped the sphere of light. It pulsed within her light clasp and she felt a nurturing warmth enfold her.

"Oh, you don't, my sweet. That is what makes you so, shall we say…attractive? But then again, *Gren* was never one to murder her offspring, now was she, my pretty? Hmm. You two ancients don't have a lot in common, do you? But that is not an issue, at this point. Your cooperation, my pretty, is."

He settled back comfortably in his chair before turning to meet her curious gaze. "Can you not picture it, my lovely? What will your precious Kerian think when he discovers you fat and bloated with my child? Will he turn away from you in disgust, yet again, my sweet? What will you do then, my little pleasure puss?"

"Damn you, Dagon!" she cried out, then quickly covered her mouth with her hands. Yelling at him was not good for her stomach. "What is your point?"

"Why, to let you know that this whole thing could have come to a…satisfactory conclusion years ago, my dear, had you managed to seduce your beloved stepson and rule through him. But no, he rejected you and then you came crying to me. Jealousy is not a pretty thing, my dear. It ages you prematurely. And your jealousy comes with too many complications." His sarcastic voice rang clear through his amused tones.

"Why are you here, Dagon?" she finally forced out, her face pale with the loss of color and her eyes rimmed in dark shadows. "Are you here to torment me? If so, you can go

Merlin's Kiss

straight to hell! You can do no more to me than you already have!" She motioned to her weakened state and ravaged face. "I don't need you, Dagon!" She clapped her hands to her stomach as her agitation made it heave and convulse.

"But who else will have you, my sweet, looking as you do?" he tutted, amused to see her vanity had been pricked as she raised hate-filled eyes to him. "I believe that your darling Kerian has found a new love interest, and that leaves you once again, crying and begging and beholden to me, my precious jewel." His laughter rang out across the room causing something inside of Shala to snap.

Without any thought and acting on reflex, she raised her hand and a pure beam of energy shot from her palm, aimed directly at Dagon.

Acting as if the death bolt headed in his direction didn't bother him in the least, Dagon raised one hand and Shala watched as her powerful bolt of energy was absorbed easily into his body. He turned eyes, red in his anger towards her.

"Big mistake, my beauty." His tone rang cold and strangely detached as he stared at the terrified woman on the bed.

"Dagon…I…I didn't…"

In a flash, he was across the room and on her bed, looming dangerously over her. "Not very smart, my precious, and here I thought that you were my best pupil." His large leathery hand reached out and gently caressed her perspiring face, a face now completely devoid of color.

"Any student of dark magic knows the basic rules, my pet. I guess you were not paying attention."

His hand suddenly snapped down around her throat and began to slowly tighten. "Any magic that I give you will not harm me, my pretty." His cold hard voice filled her with dread. "It will only make me stronger."

His fingers tightened around her throat and she tore at his punishing hand, attempting to loosen his grasp and free herself from the dark possibility of an instant death. Her eyes widened

Stephanie Burke

in terror and she began to pant with fear as he continued to apply pressure.

"The only reason I haven't snapped your pretty little neck like a twig is because I have a use for you. I will use your body to carry my heir and I will use the power you will inherit after I kill your uninterested lover to ease my conquering of this pitiful pile of rocks and the wretched souls who reside within. Other than that, my sweet, you mean nothing to me."

He shook her a bit to emphasize his point, his voice as cold as a drackoon's breath.

"And now, have I made myself clear, my precious? Do you finally understand me?" When he felt her attempts to nod in the affirmative, he quickly released her. He smiled as he let his hand wander down her chest and cup one breast, fuller now with her pregnancy. He chuckled in her angry face as he felt her nipple harden with excitement. Then he quickly pulled his hand away, as if the touch of her naked skin was too contemptible to bear.

"Take this, my precious." He called over his shoulder as he moved away from the bed. "It wouldn't do for the peasants in this castle to discover the reason that you are puking your guts out every morning is because you carry my child."

He raised his hand in the air and the energy sphere, which floated above the bed during their confrontation, drifted gently to rest against her chest.

"After all, we wouldn't want anyone to know of our plans too soon, now would we, my dear? Besides, my child will grow faster than a human child. It won't be that long until she leaves your womb."

As he spoke the lights began to rise in the room, and he slowly began to fade from view.

Shala sat there as the ball of energy began to disappear within her body with a curious warm tingling sensation.

"This will restore your energy, my pet." Shala sighed as she felt strength returning to her weakened body. "And it will

Merlin's Kiss

ensure that your pathetic excuse for a body will not reject my child."

Shala sat up with a start, concerned as that comforting warm feeling from the orb of energy began to turn into a burning stinging ache.

"Oh yes," he added as his body disappeared leaving his glowing eyes eerily watching her. "And it will only hurt for a little while," his laughing voice declared just before all traces of his presence vanished.

Shala's cries rang about her chamber for at least fifteen minutes.

* * * * *

"When will we get there?" Brieana asked as Kerian helped her down from a large boulder, one of many which seemed to litter the path they were following.

Pulling his hand back and quickly stepping away from her, he answered, "Not long now."

Kerian had returned to their makeshift campsite later in the evening and went directly to sleep. No comment was made of the wonderful kiss that they shared, nor did he mention what could have happened if Zorn hadn't shown up and interrupted the burning caress.

"Well, I for one will be happy to get there."

She walked along behind the swiftly striding Kerian who seemed to delight in each movement, as if pushing his muscles to the point of exhaustion was an enjoyable past time.

"Is it getting hot, or is it just me?"

Deceptive, the heat is, my Lady, Zorn added as he gracefully spread his wings and landed lightly next to Brieana. *Keeps the eggs healthy, the heat of the mountains does.*

"In that case…" Brieana began to unlace the front of the green tunic she wore, but a word from Kerian stopped her.

Stephanie Burke

"Don't, Brieana. The temperature could turn cold around the next corner at this altitude. The mountain itself holds the heat, but the winds blow cold and fierce."

She eyed Kerian questioningly, noticing that he still wore his war-vest instead of a tunic, and raised her eyes to him for an explanation.

"I am used to the changing weather here, Brieana, and you are not. Leave your tunic alone."

If she exposes one inch of her flesh, Kerian thought to himself as he hurried along the familiar path, *I will not be held responsible for my actions.* Ever since he had gotten a taste of her, all he could do was hunger for more. She was an addictive drug he would do well to be rid of. She made him dream of the impossible. Maybe Gren would have some answers.

"If you are sure, oh fierce leader," she muttered as she sped up to keep up with his long ground-eating strides.

Almost there, we are! Zorn cried out as they passed yet another boulder, which now seemed to be landmarks for Kerian and Zorn.

"I can't wait to meet Gren!" Brieana declared happily. "It will be nice to finally learn of my destiny."

"And if you have no destiny?" Kerian almost angrily asked. He stopped so suddenly on the path that Brieana crashed right into his back. Suddenly he found that he wished that Gren would tell her that she wasn't special, that her destiny was to stay and mate with him. But that was an impossible dream.

"That is a cruel thing to say, Kerian!" she hotly cried as she looked at her would-be mate. She sure hoped that Merlin knew what he was doing when he chose this man for her. "Of course I have a destiny, and Gren might be able to tell me what it is! And what do you care, anyway? You've never believed a word I said."

"I am beginning to believe," he finally allowed with a sigh. "You are too skilled at what you do. I have never seen a woman of your small stature able to defend herself so well."

Merlin's Kiss

It was true. During their time together, Kerian had begun to believe the wondrous tales that Brieana told. Raised with magic, it took little convincing to make him believe that a person could be bespelled and cast to drift asleep through time. What he was having problems believing was that this woman was meant for him.

Brieana broke out into a wide smile at his backward compliment, but she took it as a positive sign.

"So Gren might be able to tell me of my destiny, Kerian." She strode past him and rounded a curve in the trail. "And maybe she will tell me where my kingdom..."

Kerian stood there, waiting for her to continue, but was met only with silence.

"Brieana?" he called out. He turned and discovered that Zorn had disappeared too, and he began to panic.

"Brieana!" he called out more urgently as he unsheathed his large sword and raced around the corner.

"Brie...umph!" He ran straight into a large immovable object that bounced him back on his rear. Only his training saved him from a nasty injury as he rolled, using the momentum of the fall to turn into a neat flip that landed him on his feet. In a flash he was up and standing in his battle stance, sword held at the ready.

Kerian? a deep voice boomed in his head.

"Dalis?" he asked as he began to relax his battle stance and uncoiled muscles that stood flexed and ready for action. "Is that you, old friend?"

Kerian! My brother! boomed the deep voice and Kerian looked up and up and up to see the teal face of the large drackoon that he had run into. *After all of these years, to see you, is good, my brother.*

"And you, my friend!" he cried as he sheathed his sword and strode forward to the drackoon who was roughly the size of a small building.

91

Your mate, this woman? he asked as he motioned with his tail at the mute and paralyzed Brieana.

"Brieana?" Kerian called as he walked over to the still body of the dark-haired woman. "Brieana!" he called again as he snapped his fingers beside her ears.

"Did you freeze her?" he asked Dalis as the amused Drackoon looked on at the couple standing on the trail.

Of course not, my brother. But answer my question, you did not!

"She is not," Kerian grumbled as he tried to awaken Brieana from her stupor.

Regret this, do you not?

Kerian was saved from answering by Brieana's low voice whispering, "Big. He is so big and green."

Kerian sighed, relieved that her shock was leaving her, and began to chafe her hands. "More like a blue-green, Brieana." She nodded absently, her eyes now focused on the larger version of her beloved Zorn.

"I have come to return something to you, my brother," Kerian said, turning away from Brieana and looking at Dalis. "Have you by chance lost a purple stomach with wings and feet?"

Zorn! The teal drackoon sighed with long suffering patience. *What now, done, has the youthling?*

"Only break the treaty by eating a few of my best chum, crippled my best runner — she is lucky to have escaped with her life — and turned my household upside down!"

"Zorn is not that bad!" Brieana left her stupor to defend her friend. "He has taught me a lot about this place when I was lost and alone!"

Ignoring their conversation, Dalis cried out in a booming voice, *Zorn!*

Brieana immediately clapped both arms around her ears as if she could stop the echoing voice rattling around in her mind.

Zorn! he cried again.

Merlin's Kiss

"Stop it!" Brieana cried as she struggled to get used to this new drack voice inside her head.

Understand me, you can? Dalis's surprised voice spoke much softer inside her head.

"Yes!" Brieana answered as she peeked through her cradling arms. "And he wasn't that bad. You might have scared him to the next island."

The Woman of Legend! the drackoon voice sighed in her mind as he looked in awe at Brieana.

Here I am, father, Zorn appeared finally, looking dejected as he stared up at his father with great sad eyes.

Trouble, you cause, know you? his father asked, a smoldering look on his face. Kerian almost felt a shaft of pity for the youthling, but that was quickly dropped as he answered.

The Woman of Legend, found her, I have!

"The what?" Kerian demanded as he looked between Dalis and Zorn. That was the second time that he had heard that particular title and it was causing him considerable unease.

The Woman of Legend, my brother. Get her to Gren, we must. Foretold, it is, that when the Woman of Legend appears, darkness great will follow.

The word darkness caught Kerian's attention and Brieana saw a fission of shock cross his usually patrician face.

"What about the dark, Dalis?" he asked, an unusual note in his voice.

Explain later, I will. Get her to Gren, we must! Zorn, to wing!

"Gren?" Brieana asked, almost excitedly.

My mate, Lady. Hurry, we must.

Turning towards Kerian, Dalis lowered his body so that his friend could scramble onto his back. If Dalis was offering to fly them to the heart of the coven grounds, this situation had to be dire. The great drackoon co-leader never allowed anyone on his back.

Stephanie Burke

Hurry, my brother, he urged Kerian and called to his youthling, *We fly, Zorn. To wing!*

"Brieana, you ride with me!" he commanded as he settled himself carefully on Dalis's back, settling his feet so that they would not interfere with Dalis's massive wing span. That done, he turned and reached a large hand down to her.

"But...I..." Brieana struggled to hide her fear of her first conscious flight on the back of a drackoon. She knew that something important was happening because of everyone's reactions to her speaking drack, but she was still deathly afraid to fly. To her, it was unnatural.

"You fly with me Brieana," he said as his amber eyes bored into her very soul. "I will take care of you."

Kerian looked deeply into her eyes as he made that statement and Brieana got the feeling that he was speaking about more than just caring for her during this flight. She looked at his hand, so strong and able, and knew that if she took it, she was risking more than a ride on a drack.

Finally, she reached out and took that large hand with her smaller one and knew that they were making unspoken plans for the future. Kerian would protect her, fight with her, support her, no matter what. She was willing to take the chance.

"I trust you," she said and she was quickly settled in front of her reluctant mate.

They both knew then and there, right at that moment, that between the two of them, something special had begun.

Merlin's Kiss

Chapter Ten

"I am flying! I cannot believe I am flying!"

Despite the urgency of their trip, Brieana marveled at the speed at which they traveled. Feeling safe with Kerian's warm arms surrounding her, she settled back and watched the passing scenery, trying to contain her excitement.

Kerian understood exactly how she felt. As a small boy, when he was first granted a ride on Gren's back, he had cried tears of happiness. He had felt buoyant, a lightness that he had never before felt. Even now, with the wind whipping through his hair, his platinum locks waving behind them like a flag, he couldn't resist turning his face into the wind and delighting in its chilled kiss as they raced across the rocky land.

He fought the urge to raise both hands in the air and cry out his joy to the world, like some untrained youth, because he knew that his actions would frighten Brieana.

He sighed softly as she nestled closer to the heat that his body provided and inhaled her special scent. She still smelled of wildflowers and fresh morning dew.

"Oh Kerian, look!" she cried out as they approached what looked to be the smoking mouth of a volcano. "Is that where the coven is?" She leaned away from him and he felt a shaft of cold where her body had once snuggled close to him. In her fascination, she had forgotten her fear as she pointed to the mountain in question.

"It is," he answered, placing a restraining hand around her waist. If she continued to squirm, she just might fall off of Dalis's back.

My Lady, sanctuary for the drackoon, this is.

"Sanctuary?" she asked before Dalis started a dive that would take them right into the heart of the mountain.

95

Stephanie Burke

"Ohh!" she cried out, even as Kerian's arms surrounded her, holding her close. She felt her hair lift straight up into the air, almost as if it was going to be pulled right out of her head, and fought against the urge to cry out as she turned to face Kerian. But he couldn't suppress the laughter that exploded from him in great guffaws.

"It has been years, Dalis, since I have felt the fierce bite of the wind in a drackoon dive!" He threw his head back in pleasure as he relished the feel of the now warm air caressing his bare arms and face.

Too long, my brother! Dalis's voice held a hint of regret as well as amusement. He enjoyed giving this privilege to this stoic man who held so much pain within his heart. *Between visits, too long, much!*

Brieana was speechless as Dalis pulled his wings in close to his body and zipped through a small entrance near the mouth of the volcano. She felt the pressure slam into her ears as they entered the tiny opening.

"Oh my!" she gasped as the walls seemed to shimmer with a thousand incandescent points of light, as they sped past. The jet crystals imbedded within the walls reflected the light a thousand times over and made her feel as if she were flying through a giant black pearl.

"Duck," Kerian whispered in her ear as he pushed her forward, and just in time, too. Suddenly, Dalis ducked low, as an overhang suddenly appeared out of nowhere. Quickly, Dalis dived again and for a moment the walls closed in so tightly, that Brieana felt for sure that they would be scraped raw on the rough crystal surface.

Before she could contemplate such an injury, they popped out of the hole and into a whole new world.

The central room of the large chamber had to be at least seventy feet high. There in the walls were imbedded the rarest jewels and precious metals shaped to form a story. As Dalis lazily circled the chamber, Brieana could see the pictures clearer and was shocked to see several that resembled things from her

Merlin's Kiss

past, fire breathing dragons, magical griffins, and a few who looked exactly like Merlin himself.

She did not have long to contemplate this, however, for with Dalis's entrance came the clamor of a thousand insistent voices, all buzzing in her head.

Who is that? they asked. *Dalis brought back, who, with him? Is that Zorn? Happened to him, what? Warlord, is that?*

With so many questions buzzing in her head at once, Brieana began to panic. Her head began to ache and she became confused and disoriented.

As Dalis spread his wings, slowly pumping them backwards, and coming to a graceful stop, Brieana almost fell from his back. If it were not for Kerian's strong arms supporting her, she would have landed on her face.

"Take deep breaths," Kerian whispered softly to her in a low monotone to her. "Give your mind a chance to adjust."

Brieana whimpered in fear as she instinctively reached for the torc that hung around her neck.

The moment she touched it, she felt an inner calm begin to flow through her body. She relaxed against Kerian and felt her mind slowly began to adjust, to block out the background voices and to concentrate on those that were important to her.

Well, is she? Dalis asked with some concern as he turned his large head and observed Brieana's shaken state.

"She is fine, Dalis. Remember how long it took me to adjust to all of the drack suddenly being spoken in my head the first time I visited? Give her a moment to adjust."

So saying, he carefully slid off of his friend's back, Brieana still cradled within his arms, and landed softly on the ground.

Not ill, she is? a soft voice asked from behind.

Brieana roused herself enough to look over Kerian's shoulder at the smaller purple drack who eased up next to his father.

97

Stephanie Burke

"I am fine, Zorn." She replied and nodded to Kerian to indicate that she wanted to be set down. "I was just overwhelmed for a moment, but I am better now."

"Are you sure?" Kerian asked as he observed the color return to her cheeks and her curiosity return. "It took me quite a few visits to adjust to so many voices inside my head at once."

"You did not have Merlin's gift, Kerian," she said proudly as she caressed the torc. "I do."

The Old Father! a voice cried out in surprise. *The Old Father, she speaks of.*

While they were talking, a small group of drackoons had surrounded them, anxious for answers as to who Dalis had brought into their midst.

Surprised, Brieana looked around and gasped at the colorful sight that met her eyes. Drackoons in every color stood around them, watching her with just as much curiosity. There were large drackoons the size of Dalis with bright red, blue and yellow hides. Some were black and some were the purest of whites, while still others were silver and gold. And scattered among them were dracks, some the size of Zorn others small enough to sit on her shoulder without causing her discomfort, all in vibrant jewel tones.

"They are beautiful!" Brieana breathed in awe. "I have never seen such a collection of living jewels."

Fortunate, we are, a softer, more feminine voice rang softly through her mind. *From the Warlord standing beside you, a great deal of our fortune comes.*

"Gren!" Kerian cried out in true pleasure, his face lightening up and for once showing his happiness.

Brieana turned around and her mouth dropped open. Standing before her was a drackoon, the only drackoon present with platinum hide and glittering purple eyes. She was large and poised, yet definitely feminine from the gold tipped wings that rested softly upon her back, to the soft motherly expression she wore on her face as she watched Kerian.

98

Merlin's Kiss

"True-mother," he addressed this regal creature as he went down on one knee before her.

To your feet, Kerian! she cried out amused and exasperated at his actions. *No need, there is, for this tribute that you bestow on me. I should be the one bowing, in truth, to you!* she laughed as she gracefully glided forward and nuzzled the man gently.

Laughing, Kerian rose to his feet and Brieana caught her breath at the change happiness brought to his face. The years and the cares seemed to melt away from him, leaving him looking younger and more alive and carefree than she had ever seen him.

"I have brought you back a present, True-mother. A little purple nuisance that I am happy to return."

Zorn! Gren cried out as she looked anxiously around for her offspring.

Here, mother, I am, Zorn said softly, a pitiful expression on his face as he slinked forward.

Of all my children, you are, Zorn, the most troublesome.

Everyone exploded into laughter at hearing this.

Turning to Brieana, Kerian added, "She has had over two hundred children."

"Oh my!" Brieana cried out, looking towards Gren to see if she could tell how having that many children would affect a drackoon.

Understands, she does, Dalis spoke in a low ominous tone, and just as suddenly the room quieted again.

The Woman of Legend! Gren softly exclaimed and quickly her statement echoed around the room.

The Woman of Legend, was whispered by almost every drackoon in attendance.

Then, my mate, it is time, Gren solemnly said as she turned and motioned Kerian and Brieana to follow her.

Like a plow through freshly turned soil, the sea of drackoons parted for the humans in their midst and Gren

Stephanie Burke

solemnly led them to a smaller cave, surrounded by large torches.

"*Enter please,*" she said, nodding towards Brieana.

As Kerian made to wait for her outside the chamber, Gren motioned him inside too.

You too, my non-son. Concerns you, does this also.

They were even more surprised when she motioned Zorn to follow behind Kerian before she too entered and Dalis stood guard at the door.

"Can you tell me, please, of my destiny?" Brieana asked as she looked about the room.

In the center of the wide tall chamber, sat a stone pedestal. On that pedestal sat a ball of light, roughly the size of a man's head, so bright it almost burned her eyes to look directly upon it.

Look child. Gren motioned to the pedestal. *The cold that burns, look at. Tells the story, it does.*

"What story?" Brieana looked anxiously around for Kerian and sighed with relief as she saw him standing a few feet behind her.

Our history, child. Your destiny.

At Kerian's urging, Brieana stepped closer to the pedestal and held in a cry of fright as the ball of light began to pulse. Instinctively, she reached for Kerian and felt a measure of comfort when she felt his large rough fingers close around her hand.

With the other hand she reached for the comfort of the torc and felt the strange jeweled collar began to tingle.

They all looked on in awe as the pulsing light began to glow and fill the room with its cold light. Brieana's eyes grew wide as the light continued to pulse and glow until the whole room was engulfed in its cold fire. Just when she thought her heart could take no more, the light exploded and before her very eyes, pictures began to appear.

Merlin's Kiss

First was the earth, but it was an earth that she had never seen before. It was loud and congested and filled with strange wagons that moved without horses. And the people, the people were dressed so strangely. Women were dressed in strange short gowns and men wore strips of cloth tied around their necks like nooses. And everything was moving so fast. The people moved quickly into strange box shaped castles and forts where they seemed to argue with each other.

She saw that the land, the grass and the trees were being cut down and cleared out for more of these large box homes. And the animals were disappearing. Instead of roaming freely as they were meant to, they were locked inside cages, forced to live in a strange environment and give up their birthright, the skills that made them special, to become puppets and slaves for these oddly dressed humans. Just when she thought that she could take no more, the pictures changed and before her flashed scenes of war.

Instead of the honorable combat and chivalrous fighting that took place in her time, large armies flew in metal birds that dropped fiery death from above or sat in large metallic wagons that spit out exploding cannonballs. Death was instantaneous and indifferent. The innocent, the guilty, the soldiers' own armies killed indiscriminately, each wanting to conquer the other.

Then there was an explosion.

Red, orange, and blue fire spilled from a large gray mushroom-shaped cloud and she watched as wave after wave of heat scorched the land, killing everybody in its path. And she saw nation after nation of peoples dying from some painful wasting sickness that she was sure came from the death cloud. The great land masses disappeared and were replaced by two islands. Surely all was lost, but then she saw something moving in the barren lands.

She saw people, survivors of every race and nationality, merging to become one. They divided themselves into two groups, one moving towards a dark island that glistened in the

101

Stephanie Burke

sea like a golden brown sand jewel, and a lighter island that glittered like a sparkling emerald and showed sprouts of new life.

Together these people, black, white, red, and yellow, merged to become one people dedicated to creating a new life for themselves on this green island. The other island soon became lost in a dark haze and nothing was seen from the many peoples who had settled there.

The pictures changed again and she saw a group of people who resembled Kerian and his family, grow and divide into peaceful groups. Instead of going back to the old ways, these people began to fight with swords in honorable combat, although they seemed to strive for peace. She saw castles go up and people continue to work the land with strange new animals, similar yet different from the creature that she was familiar with. She saw the drackoons emerge from their hiding places and interact with the people. She saw hope. Then the pictures began to fade.

Blinking to clear her eyes, she looked around the room to see Kerian staring in awe at the pulsing light, that was once again the size of a man's head, and blinking as if to clear his eyes too.

"What was that, Gren?" she asked softly. After watching that presentation, her voice seemed odd and out of place. "Was that what happened to the earth?"

Yes, child. While asleep, you were, the world changed rapidly and for good, not always.

"But that should have taken hundreds of years to happen, Gren. Was I asleep that long?"

Already, this answer, you know, Gren stated as she watched the young dark-haired woman accept the confirmation of the facts, as she knew them to be.

"And what does this have to do with my destiny?"

You, child, are the Woman of Legend, away from a dark fate, to lead us, destined.

102

Merlin's Kiss

"Me?" Brieana cried out in shock. "But Merlin said that I would have my own kingdom to rule! There is no kingdom here!"

And your rightful kingdom, already completed, was it? Gren slyly asked.

That caused Brieana to shut her mouth and think.

"No, Gren. It would have taken hard work and dedication to turn the Britons into a fit kingdom, but I had Excalibur there."

Ahh, the Old Father, the riddles he creates! Gren chuckled.

"Old Father?" Brieana asked as she looked at Kerian's confused expression. He knew the history of his world, even though he had never seen it in such brilliant color, but had never heard of an Old Father. He shrugged his shoulders and looked towards Gren.

The Old Father's gift, you wear. She enlightened them with a chuckle.

"Merlin?" Brieana exclaimed, as her eyes grew wide in shock. "So, the old stories were true."

"Can you fill me in, please?" Kerian asked. "I thought Merlin was the one who cast the spell of sleep over you."

"He is, Kerian. But the old legends say that his mother was a great sorcerer and that his father was a…dragon."

"Dragon?" Kerian asked confused. He had never heard of a dragon before. Were they related to the drackoons?

Fire breathing ancestors, all! Gren chuckled when she saw the look of surprise cross Kerian's face.

"Fire breathing?" he asked. The only thing he knew about breath as a weapon came from the drackoon, and they breathed ice.

Belief is hard, is it not, my non-son? Gren asked with a chuckle. *From him, through my veins, magic flows.*

"But what has that to do with me?" Brieana asked. "I can accept that I am the Woman of Legend, but what am I supposed to do?"

The clans. Unite! Gren said as she turned and motioned for a wide-eyed Zorn to leave the room.

"Unite the clans?" both Kerian and Brieana echoed together.

"But…but…How?" Brieana stammered as she followed behind the silver/white drackoon and her youthling.

A quest, you must go on! Gren called over her shoulder as she passed her mate and motioned them to follow.

The center chamber was now cleared of all the drackoons and dracks as Gren and Dalis led them through a short maze of tunnels that descended deeper into the mountain.

"A quest for what?" Brieana wailed as she followed after the quickly walking dracks. "This destiny business is harder than I thought it would be!" she whispered to Kerian as he hurried along with her.

A queen, what made you? Gren asked as she entered another large open chamber, presumably her personal place. *Have you what, made you special, did?*

"Excalibur!" she cried instantly as she entered the large chamber and smiled in surprise. This room was filled with flowers and light. In one corner sat a plush pile of furs and in the opposite sat a large platform made of the jet-black crystals that lined the cave entrance.

Then find Excalibur, you must! she said before she settled down on her comfortable pile of furs. Dalis chuckled from a corner, yet still stood guard just inside the room. Zorn sat near his mother.

"What about this great darkness, Gren?" Kerian asked as no further questions came from Brieana, his Woman of Legend.

The Woman of Legend, your path follows, my non-son. To find what you seek, you must follow her.

"But this great darkness, Gren. Does it have anything to do with the information I have been getting? Are the Dark Isles getting ready to invade?"

Merlin's Kiss

This, you know, Kerian. This I tell you, your path follows the Woman of Legend, my non-son.

"If we don't succeed in finding Excalibur?" Brieana asked, joining in the conversation, wondering what would happen to his land and its strange inhabitants.

Doomed, we are all, then.

Her answer brought a stunned somberness to the room. After a moment of silence, Kerian said, "Then we must succeed. If Brieana is to be Queen of this land, I will do whatever is necessary to save it and my people."

This, I know, my non-son, Gren said sadly as she watched this man struggle with the foretold shift of power. As usual, Kerian accepted her word instantly, without argument. If Brieana would be queen, he would make it so.

Accompany them, you will, Zorn! Gren ordered as she watched surprise and displeasure fill her youthling's face.

Mother! he wailed as he thought of spending more time with the hostile Kerian, of another uncomfortable trip away from well prepared meals.

Treaty, you broke, treaty, you fix! That was that. Gren was leader of them all, especially when it came to her children.

Go you now, and prepare to leave.

Now! Dalis commanded, adding emphasis to his mate's command.

Head dropped between his shoulders, Zorn left the room, tail dragging and looking utterly dejected.

"I shall prepare to leave, also, my True-mother," Kerian added, with a thoughtful look on his face. "If my information is correct, we haven't a spare second to waste."

I shall accompany you, brother, Dalis said and together they exited the chamber, leaving Brieana standing in the center of the room with a confused look on her face.

Troubles, you have? Gren softly asked, knowing that Brieana would confide in her as Kerian did.

Stephanie Burke

"Merlin's spell, Gren. It confuses me."

Woman of Legend, you are. Foretold long ago, that she who appears different and the language of the Old Father's progeny speaks, the Woman of Legend is.

'That I understand and accept Gren, but what about the second half of his spell? Only a man equal to my strength and loyal only to me can release me. Kerian does not seem to want a mate, Gren. Am I to share my kingdom but not his heart?"

Your quest, complete, Woman of Legend. In time, revealed, it all will be.

"But…" Brieana protested, but Gren cut her off.

Your heart, trust, Brieana. In time, all will be made clear.

Sighing in defeat and knowing that Gren had to be Merlin's descendant and a wizard—they had always striven to be mysterious and never reveal facts until they wanted to—Brieana walked over to the platinum-colored drackoon and dropped to her knees before her.

"Thank you, Gren," she said before embracing the drackoon leader. "I don't know where I would be without you."

A favor, I ask? Gren questioned, sadness in her shining purple eyes.

"Of course, Gren!" Brieana said, startled and confused that this great creature would ask a boon of her.

Him, look after. Him, protect. Vulnerable, my non-son is.

"Without question!" Brieana declared. "But why do you call him your non-son?"

To tell, his tale, Gren sadly spoke before closing her eyes in grief. *When time is right, all will be revealed.*

Brieana sighed and placed a small kiss on the drackoon's face before rising to leave the chamber.

"One of these days, Gren, you will have to show me how you breathe ice!" she called back, amusement again in her voice.

A great display, one day, you will receive, Woman of Legend, Gren called out before she closed her eyes and slept. Humans

Merlin's Kiss

were tiresome, she thought, but worth the effort. They could be trained.

Chapter Eleven

"...now we need a clue as to where this sword could be hidden."

Brieana walked in on the tail end of Kerian's statement but instantly knew what he and Dalis were talking about.

"Excalibur?" she asked as she walked up to the small group of drackoons that had gathered in the central chamber. "Are you speaking of Excalibur?"

Yes, Lady, Dalis answered as he looked over her shoulder, presumably for his mate.

"She is resting," she added kindly as she saw his concern.

The magic, it does, take a lot from her. Dalis sighed sadly.

"Gren supplies the magic that keeps the coven hidden and powers the knowing crystal. Although I have never seen our history played out before in such vivid color."

The torc, it is, Dalis said as he made a gesture towards Brieana's neck. *"Years I spend as Gren's mate, much I too learn. The Old Father's magic aids Gren.*

"I have never seen the like," Brieana breathed, still filled with a touch of awe at her history lesson. "Such strange and violent people."

"And we very well might revert to their behavior if we cannot find this sword of yours, Lady," Kerian spoke and motioned her to step forward.

"I have an idea where it might be," Brieana said to the profound relief of the drackoons gathered around.

Tell us, Lady, several voices urged. *Where is Excalibur?*

"Well, we need to find the Lady of the Lake. If anything had happened to that knave Arthur, Merlin would be sure to return the Lady's gift to her."

Merlin's Kiss

Then she paused for a moment. "What did happen to Arthur?"

For a moment, silence reigned in the room.

Arthur, Lady? Dalis asked, wearing a very confused look upon his face.

"The one who was made King in my place! Merlin's special project. Whatever happened to him?"

Known to us, that is not, Dalis said thoughtfully. *But revealed in time, it will be.*

"How did I know that you were going to say that?" Brieana sighed as she again turned to Kerian.

"Anyway, all we need do is find the proper lake and call upon the Lady. She will aid us, I am sure."

"That is easy enough," Kerian said with a satisfied nod.

"Why, there are hundreds of lakes here!" Brieana objected. "And we haven't much time, Kerian. We need a map."

"There is no need, Lady." Kerian insisted. "Trust me."

"I trust you, Kerian," she conceded with a sigh. "So tell me, great Warlord, where is the lake I seek?"

"In the Forbidden Forests, Lady. That is where we shall find your sword."

"Really, Kerian?" Brieana asked, eagerness showing on her face. "Have you been there and seen my sword?"

"No, Lady. But the only lake in existence is in the Forbidden Forests."

"The only lake in existence?" she said with some dismay, her hand reaching out to rest on his forearm.

"The rest ceased to exist some time ago, Lady. Only this one remains and is rumored to be a beautiful magical place."

That settled, Brieana sighed with pleasure.

"Then we shall retrieve my sword, unite the clans and peace will reign."

"But we have to get there first," Kerian reminded her.

109

Stephanie Burke

Fly you there, we shall, Dalis offered with the resounding approval of several drackoons. *Honored to help, we are.*

"I wish it were that easy, Dalis, my brother," Kerian bemoaned with a sad shake of his head. "The trees in the Forbidden Forests grow too thickly for comfortable flight and there may be many hidden dangers that we know nothing about."

Help, we shall, still, Dalis declared. *Afraid, we are not.*

Several drackoons backed up his statement with cheers of agreement.

"But then, who will look after Mirage?" Kerian asked.

Suddenly there were mumbling among the coven.

Ask this of me, why, brother? Dalis said, mood suddenly deathly serious.

"The darkness, Dalis. I fear it has something to do with Mirage. I have been hearing things, Dalis. I am afraid to leave it for too long a period. While I am on this quest, you and your coven are the only ones I trust to protect Mirage, for the both of us."

Understand, this, brother, Dalis responded solemnly. *Fly you, we shall, to the border.*

"Thank you, Dalis," Kerian said, relieved that his home would be protected from the darkness a while longer.

"But then, how will we get there?" Brieana asked. She knew that in order for Kerian to make this request of Dalis, something serious had to be brewing around his castle. Otherwise, Kerian would have never asked another to shoulder his responsibilities.

"By...unicorn," he finally said with a fatalistic look on his face.

"Unicorn?" Brieana asked with some wonder, before Dalis and the drackoons burst out in laughter.

"We really get to ride on the backs of unicorns!"

"And a more ornery creature has not been created," he said with a sad sigh.

Merlin's Kiss

"But they are so beautiful!" Brieana insisted. "All fluffy and white."

"They are black, Lady," Kerian cut her off. "Black as their stubborn hearts and souls. They are intelligent creatures who will only move when they think they have reason to. I keep grazing land open for them for the sole purpose of keeping an eye on them."

"But, they only come to virgins and are known for their sweet temperament!" Brieana denied. This was one fantasy creature that she didn't want to lose her dreams about. "They can't be anything like those horrid little bunnies."

"The only virgins they like are the kind that feeds them, curries them, and stays out of their way. They are not nice creatures, Lady. Trust me."

"Oh dear," Brieana sighed as she took in the serious countenance on his face. Kerian never told jokes. "So I guess we ride on these mules with horns, then."

"Mules?" Kerian asked.

"Never mind, I'll explain on the way."

* * * * *

As they waved to Dalis and his two drackoon companions, Brieana turned to Kerian.

"They are wonderful, aren't they? I can see why you love them so."

"I have given my life to them," Kerian said and a sad expression crossed his face.

"Kerian?" Brieana reached out and laid a hand on his arm, but he quickly gathered himself and shook off her gesture.

"Shall we begin, Lady? We are not far from Mirage."

"You called me Brieana before, Kerian," Brieana said turning and starting after his retreating back.

Stephanie Burke

"That was before I knew you were my Queen," Kerian said over his shoulder as he nimbly navigated the rocky trail.

"But…" she began, only to be interrupted by Zorn.

Prepared dinner, think you, the cook? he asked with an eager expression and a growling tummy.

"Tell me again, why are we taking my walking wardrobe?" Kerian growled with an annoyed look in Zorn's direction.

"Because Gren told us to," Brieana muttered, giving an encouraging look to the suddenly less hungry-looking drack.

Need me, you must! Zorn put in. *Important too, I am!* he added as an afterthought.

Kerian snorted and shook his head in disbelief. "Unicorns and a drack. When will this madness end?"

* * * * *

"He's coming." The soft voice circled the room, drawing Shala away from sleep and effectively ending her afternoon nap. "Shall I end this game now, my precious one?"

"Won't you go away and leave me in peace?" Shala demanded as she struggled to an upright position on her bed.

"But then, who would look out for your interests, love?" he purred as the lights began to dim and she felt him settle his bulk at the foot of her bed. "Now then, shall I end this little game that you insist on playing, or do we see what develops?"

"You know I desire the information that they carry, Dagon. Otherwise I would have let you kill them while they were on the trail."

Suddenly, he was across the room and Shala swore that the air around him became amused and condescending.

"An interesting turn of phrase, you have, love. Let…as if you ever had any say so in what I do."

"You need me, Dagon, so let us stop playing these silly games," she cried hotly as she rose to her feet and stormed over

112

to her wardrobe. "If the clan leaders saw you, they would kill you where you stood."

"And what would they do to you, fair princess, consorting with these Dark Isles monsters and all?" he asked as he clicked his tongue in reprimand.

"They would never know, Dagon, because I would never tell them."

"But when your charming child popped out and looks...so much different than the rest of you, tell me, my dear. What would they do to you?"

"I'll say I was forced!" she cried out in anger, her face flushing and eyes glowing the same fiery red as Dagon's.

"Try again, my sweet. Everyone knows that you must be a willing participant to bear a Dark Isles child."

"They do not!" she chuckled, sure that she finally had the upper hand with this dark creature.

"But they will by sundown, my sweet," he said with a bored laugh. "Did you actually think that I would leave an opening for you to exploit? You did?" he asked before breaking out into sarcastic laughter.

"How, Dagon?" she asked, her voice a little choked with the knowledge that she was right back to being a pawn in his games.

"With the information that I have been seeding your peasants with, my dear. How do you think that your stepson has been getting the information about our movements? And by nightfall, everyone will know this little tidbit about those Dark Isle monsters!" He chuckled. "Inspired, don't you think?"

"Why would you do such a thing, Dagon?" Shala almost screamed in anger. "You jeopardize us all!"

"Nonsense, my pet," he said with the confidence of a man who knows exactly what he is doing. "What better way to make them all gather together in one place? Can you imagine it love, all of those poor unsuspecting fools, waiting here, ripe for the killing. It stirs the soul and does my poor heart good."

Stephanie Burke

Shala stopped for a moment to absorb what he was saying. His plan was, quite actually, brilliant.

"And with the clan leaders gone and their people defenseless, they will flock to Mirage for protection and declare Kerian their sole leader. And when we take care of him and that youngster he travels with, all the power will be mine!"

She smiled brightly and once again the beauty of her face shone clear. The heat in her eyes cooled and they changed into the color of molten gold. Her full lips parted in a wicked smile as she contemplated all of the glory that would be hers.

"Don't you mean ours, my pet?" A sinister dark voice intruded into her private fantasies.

"Yes, of course," she quickly added, not wanting to anger the troll more than she had already. Her only excuse was overactive hormones from carrying this blasted baby. "I meant to say ours."

"You lie very well, my pet, but please remember. I hold the true power here." In a flash he was across the room, large leathery wings spread, in a menacing way, blocking out the dim candlelight as he towered over her. "Which brings me back to my original point, love," he said as he slowly folded his wings.

Shala was unable to look away from the grace and beauty in which he moved. A rough finger softly outlined the skin of her face and neck before he again turned away and took his seat.

"What point is that?" she managed to force out of her suddenly tight throat as she damned herself for still desiring the slug.

"Shall I put an end to your games and kill the man outright, or do I wait and let him fill your head with all of this Woman of Legend trash? Such a tough choice, too."

He crossed one leg over the other and watched her as she began to lay out her clothes. She had such a nice body; a body made for strong wings and dark magic. Pity she was such a bitch.

114

Merlin's Kiss

"I want to know what that drackoon told them, Dagon. It might be important."

"Since you ask so sweetly," he began but then Shala crossed the room naked, and stood before him.

"Grant me, the mother of your child, this one request, Dagon."

Grasping one large scarred hand, she pressed it to the small curve of her stomach and tried to hold in a shiver of excitement she felt at his touch.

"Get dressed, Shala," he commanded, amusement turning up the corners of his mouth. "Your body holds no pleasure for me. I gave you my child to, uh, clip your wings a bit. Your stale feminine wiles will work on me as well as they worked on your stepson."

Shala's mouth dropped open in indignant anger before her eyes began to glow red again.

"Damn you, Dagon!"

"You know dear, that is usually the reaction of someone who has been out- maneuvered and backed into a tight spot in which they know they cannot escape," he chuckled.

Stomping her foot, Shala turned and began to don the red gown she had laid out to wear, her back stiff and her movements jerky.

"I will let you learn of their visit and of drackoon magic, my sweet. I suddenly find myself in a generous mood." And it would give him time to allow his soldiers to follow them at a leisurely pace and set up for their eventual ambush and death. Shala was becoming too dangerous and he felt that it was time to strip her of a little more of her power.

"What are you up to, Dagon?" Shala asked as she angrily tied the front laces of her gown. He had to be planning some devilment.

"I have reconsidered, my dear. I will give you, the mother of my child, this one little wish. After all, are you not taking good care of my heir?"

115

Stephanie Burke

"Thank you, I think," Shala muttered as she turned to exit the room. "Just don't be here when I return."

"I wouldn't think of overstaying my welcome, precious," he purred as the lights began to rise in the room and he again quickly disappeared from view. "After all, I want to keep the little mother happy."

"Humph!" Shala huffed as she slammed the door on his amused laughter.

"Let the braying fool have his laugh now!" she murmured to herself. "If that brat has brought back the information that I need, I will be the one laughing last."

Merlin's Kiss

Chapter Twelve

"Welcome home, Kerian. I was so worried about you." Shala walked forward, both hands extended in welcome, her red gown gracefully sweeping the floor behind her. "I see you have also returned to us, Brieana. I worried myself sick over the two of you."

"Shala," Kerian answered as he briefly held both hands before ushering Brieana through the castle doors.

"You have returned to us safe and... What is that doing back here?"

Shala halted her well-rehearsed welcoming speech when she caught sight of the purple drack who proudly stepped in behind Brieana, like a bodyguard.

"My journeys have not yet come to an end, Shala," Kerian answered. "And in my own home, I have no need to answer any questions that you put forth. Zorn is here at my behest and that is all that you have to know."

"Of course," Shala assured, but inwardly she was seething. *How dare he bring that beast back into my castle?* she thought angrily. *Soon, Kerian, soon all of this is mine and you will be but an unpleasant memory.* "I was just shocked by his appearance, Kerian."

He nodded gruffly, then turned to enter the main hall, an excited Brieana and a cautious Zorn following close behind.

"Have Sato brought forth to me," he commanded a nearby sentinel. "I will need him to gather two agreeable unicorns. Tonight, we journey."

"Tonight?" Shala cried in alarm as she rushed after the trio. "But surely you have time for a meal and a rest in a good bed?" If they departed so quickly, she would never be able to pick that child's mind for the information she needed. If she were to

117

posses the magical talisman she wore around her neck, she would need to know all of the secrets that came with its possession.

Meal? At her words, Zorn's head shot straight up and he rushed to the great table set against the far wall of the main hall.

Kerian shook his head as he watched the purple drack head for his favorite spot behind Brieana's seat and position himself to grab choice morsels she would throw his way.

"Speed is necessary, Shala. We will have to decline. I have to prepare for a long journey."

"But Kerian," Brieana nearly wailed. "Can we at least wash and eat?"

Kerian turned to Brieana, mouth open to remind her of the darkness approaching, but stopped as he took a good look at her. Her usually bright green eyes were a bit dull with fatigue and her skin had lost some of its luminescence. Too many shocks in such a short time, he supposed. Her clothes were travel-stained and she moved stiffly as if she were in some discomfort. She deserved one night of rest, he decided, before he took her off to the wilds of the Forbidden Forest.

"We will stay the night and continue on our quest tomorrow," Kerian said and tried to hide the flash of warmth in his chest as her eyes lit up with pleasure.

Gently, he caressed her cheek with his big, rough hand, and smiled as she nestled closer to him.

"Excellent. Then I shall give the orders to prepare an early supper so you all can rest. Brieana, child. If you follow me, I shall help you bathe."

Shala's voice contained a bit of sharpness that Kerian ignored, but Brieana quickly picked up on. Stepping away from her Warlord, she turned to face Shala.

"That is not necessary. I can bathe myself," she said as she tried to figure out if the strange note in Shala's voice was anger or...jealousy?

Merlin's Kiss

"Nonsense, child. Let me help you. After all, you must be exhausted after your journey." Then quickly motioning to one of the waiting servants, "A bath and drink in Lady Brieana's sleeping chambers, please."

The serving woman looked more shocked at the please added to the order than the reappearance of the drack. "Milady." She nodded before taking off towards the back stairs.

"Now, Kerian," she added. "You go off and make your plans for your, ah, quest, and I will take care of Brieana."

Nodding, Kerian looked towards Sato, who was approaching him from a side entrance, and moved to intercept his best soldier, his thoughts focused on the preparations for the journey ahead.

"Now come with me, Brieana," Shala said as she took her by the elbow. "Off to your rooms."

Come, I shall, too! Zorn's voice echoed in her head as they started up the stairs. *Trust her, I do not!*

With that pronouncement, the drack disappeared up the rear stairs. Shaking her head, Brieana turned to listen to what Shala was saying.

"And I have a special wine that will help you relax until mealtime," she said as she bustled Brieana down the hall. "Your bath should be ready soon."

As she flung open the door, Shala clucked her tongue in disapproval as she saw Zorn lying contentedly at the foot of Brieana's round bed.

"I thought that creature was enjoying a repast below," she stated as she glared at Zorn.

"He is a little over-protective of me, Lady," Brieana explained, ignoring the youthling's snort in her head.

"Well, as long as he stays out of the way. The castle is no place for pets."

Stephanie Burke

Pet her, I will! Zorn's annoyed voice rang in her head, although the drack never changed positions and looked to be lying sleepily on the floor.

"Come, Brieana. Time to prepare you for your bath."

Brieana fought to hold in a giggle as Shala ushered her across the room and into a padded bench.

"First, I will check and see if you picked up anything in you hair while you were...journeying about."

With her hair, I will start, also, Zorn stated as he lazily stretched and yawned, showing off his razor-sharp claws and long dangerous teeth. *Pluck it out, strand by white strand, I will!*

Brieana again stifled a laugh as Shala looked at her oddly. Then shrugging her shoulders, Shala produced a hairbrush and began to quickly pull it through Brieana's tangled curls.

"It must feel safe to be back with normal people again, and away from those large beasts. They can be so...frightening when seen up close."

As is, her face, Zorn drolly replied as he opened one eye to glare at Shala.

This time, Brieana burst out into giggles.

"What is that vile creature saying about me?" Shala finally demanded, throwing down the brush in a huff. "You might as well tell me, because I know that it is insulting me!"

Insults, you have not seen yet! Zorn replied and Brieana again burst out into helpless laughter.

"Brieana?" Shala demanded, tapping her foot in impatience, her face almost as red as her gown.

"He... Well, I... You see..."

But then the door burst open and servants bearing a large wooden tub and buckets of steaming water entered the chamber. Following behind them, a servant came bearing a small tray.

"The wine!" Shala said as she rushed forward to take the tray from the servant. "You will drink while your bath is being prepared."

Merlin's Kiss

Turning her back to the busy workers and Brieana, she began to prepare the wine.

Chuckling to herself, she wrapped both hands around the goblet and began to mutter the ancient words. There was a small popping, which she covered by calling out, "Here we are, Brieana. From my personal stock!"

Trust her, I don't! Zorn cried out as Shala approached with the silver goblet. *Drink it not!*

"Zorn," Brieana sighed, shaking her head at the drack. "Just because she doesn't like you," she whispered, "does not mean that she will try to harm me!"

Lady, no! Zorn called out as he leaped from his reclining position and crouched down between Shala and Brieana, with exposed teeth and a low growl.

"Zorn, No!" Brieana shouted as she stood and glared at the little purple youthling. "That is enough!"

"*Schlock!*" Shala cried out as she took a step back. That vile creature suspected too much. She began to shake with her rage, barely managing to control it. He would have to go if she was to put her plan in action.

"As I have said, Lady, Zorn is a little over-protective of me." She soothed the shaking Shala.

"I mean you no harm, Brieana, and if it will make the difference, I will sip from the cup myself."

So saying, she lifted the goblet to her lips and proceeded to quaff a goodly portion of the wine. "See, no ill effects, Zorn. I will not try to poison your mistress."

"Now, please go and find Kerian, Zorn." Brieana was now just a little exasperated with her bodyguard and wanted nothing more than a few hours of rest before they had to start another arduous trip. She may be a bit uncomfortable with Shala, but the woman was offering to help ease her tired body, and that was good enough for her.

But, Lady...? Zorn whined as he cocked his head to the side and glared at her.

Stephanie Burke

"Go, Zorn. I am tired and in need of a bath. Nothing will harm me here."

Shoulders slumped in defeat, Zorn quietly exited the room and went in search of Kerian.

"About that wine?" Shala asked as she approached Brieana. She was truly thankful that the one lesson Dagon had given her still held true. Dark magic could not harm the one who controlled it.

"Yes, thank you Lady Shala. I could use it about now."

Noting that the servants had all left the room to continue with their other duties, Shala smiled at her unknowing victim as she closed the door to the chamber. Walking over to Brieana with a smile, she handed her the goblet.

"To your health, child."

Smiling at the toast, Brieana lifted the cup to her lips and drained it in a few swallows.

"Now, to the tub with you," Shala motioned to her as she walked over to help her disrobe.

Once naked, Brieana headed straight for the high wooden tub and gracefully sank down into its warm depths. She sighed as the water, treated with essential oils and a wildflower fragrance, seemed to caress her whole body. Every inch of her skin was suddenly drenched in perfumed bliss and she laid her head against the back of the tub and sank down until its murky depths came up to her shoulders.

"Comfortable, dear?" Shala asked as she handed her a sponge.

"I have never felt so good in my life! Thank you, Lady Shala." She closed her eyes and relaxed as the steam wafting up from the water caressed her face and made her quite sleepy.

"Shall we have a bit of conversation, dear? Would that be agreeable?"

"Yes, Lady Shala." Her words came out almost as if she was in a trance.

Merlin's Kiss

Brieana was so tired that she barely registered answering any questions from Shala. Her thoughts seemed to jumble and all she could concentrate on was the warm feelings coursing through her body.

"Well, child, what did that creature, Gren, tell you?"

"I am the Woman of Legend." The words seem to slip out from her tongue, and it bothered her a bit, but the tub was so relaxing and wonderful…

"What makes you so special, child? There have been many great female leaders." Her question came out clipped with her rising anger. How dare they name this little brat the Woman of Legend when the title should belong to a more powerful individual? Someone like herself!

"Excalibur, Lady."

"What?" That startled Shala right out of her anger. "Ex…Calibur?"

"My ancient sword, Lady."

"And where exactly is this sword?" she asked, impatiently. This might be the key she needed to bring both Dagon and Kerian to heel!

"With the Lady of the Lake, Lady Shala. That is where Kerian and I travel in the morn. We will fetch the sword and bring it back here so that I…"

"Very good, child." Shala interrupted as she rose to her feet. "Don't fall asleep in the tub and drown yourself. Wouldn't want anything to happen to you, at least before you complete your quest."

Hurriedly, she quit the room, leaving a totally relaxed Brieana to drift in her tub, her conversation with Shala evaporating like the heat of the water in which she dozed.

* * * * *

Stephanie Burke

"She will bring it to me, and then I will rule!" Shala mumbled to herself as she raced to her chambers. "I will take that sword, Excalibur, and I will rule all of this isle!"

She slammed the door open and quickly made her way to a hidden alcove in the back of the room, her workshop. There she pulled out a sealed box, and caressed the ornate wooden lid. Inside were the old cast-off spells that Dagon had given her after their first joining years ago. Her foolish teacher had overlooked one thing, though. Contained in the old spells was a spell to awaken the legendary Man-Demon with the lost name. Once she possessed the sword, she could easily do away with Brieana and Kerian, but it would take a bit more to rid herself of Dagon. This spell would do it!

She returned the box to its hidden cache in the wall and giggled to herself. "What delicious irony, little one!" She recently had taken up the habit of talking to her unborn babe. She found it oddly comforting. "Your father has given me the means to destroy him, and he doesn't even know it! He thought that these old spells could do nothing to the great and powerful Dagon! But we will show him! We will show him and he will die screaming!"

Her laughter echoed the hallways outside her chambers and a servant passing by shuddered and made a sign to ward off evil.

Merlin's Kiss

Chapter Thirteen

"Are you sure you wouldn't rather walk?" Sato looked up at the Warlord with something akin to anguish on his face.

"No. And I will require two of them." Kerian looked down as his most feared soldier, besides himself of course, paled beneath his golden skin.

"You do not ask much, Kerian." Even Sato seemed a little surprised at the sarcasm that came from his mouth. Hoping that the Warlord was too worried about the coming journey to notice his little slip, he quickly continued.

"Why not let the drack fly you there?"

Me? The word echoed in Kerian's head, and being caught off guard, as he was, he flinched before he could recover his equilibrium.

Turning to face the drack in question, he sighed angrily at the purple lizard.

"Must you shout, Zorn?" His words were controlled and cold, as if to make up for his momentary lapse.

Realizing that he had approached Kerian without his usual human shield, Brieana, Zorn slunk forward, frightened but determined.

With you, I must speak, Lord.

Respect was the last thing he expected out of Zorn. The youthling had a way of raising his ire then hiding behind Brieana, but the way he approached told him that this was a serious matter they would be discussing.

"Two unicorns, by tomorrow, Sato!" Kerian demanded of his still reluctant soldier.

"Aye, my Lord!" Sato rapped out. When the Warlord used that tone, people jumped to obey. Why me, he thought as he gathered his strength for the battle that awaited him. He turned to leave just as Zorn stopped in front of Kerian.

"You wished a word, youthling?"

Yes, Lord. Worry, I do, about the Lady Brieana.

"Why would you worry, Zorn? She is safe in her chambers in Mirage. My own stepmother is tending her as we speak." He ran a tired hand through his sweat-dampened hair. Once out of the cool air of the mountains, it always took his body a few hours to adjust to the warmer climate on Mirage.

The reason, that is, for my worry! I trust her not!

"Youthling, has she given you any cause to believe that she would do Brieana harm? I know that she is not the most likable person on the Light Isles, but that is no reason for her to wish to harm Brieana!"

The torc, Lord, he answered as he raised his head and looked Kerian dead in the eyes. *Reacts it does, to evil.*

His words sent a shiver down Kerian's spine before he controlled the instinctive reaction. He looked deep into Zorn's purple eyes and saw only earnest concern there.

"What could she do here, under my roof?" Kerian asked, his mind striving for an explanation. Shala had always been different, but he never thought her cold enough to harm Brieana. She had no reason to! Unless she noticed his attraction for the dark-haired former queen. Was she still angry about his rejection all those years ago? Was jealousy a strong enough emotion to cause her to wish to do another harm?

Poison! Zorn said the one word with malice and Kerian immediately turned and headed for the back stairs. For Zorn to be so concerned there must be a reason.

* * * * *

"Lady? Are you within?"

Merlin's Kiss

Kerian slowly opened the door to Brieana's chamber and peeked inside. An agitated Zorn waited in the hall, his thick tail whipping furiously back and forth.

There was the high-backed wooden tub that Shala herself preferred to use, but where was Brieana?

Stepping into the room, he looked over to her bed and saw the covers still unrumpled, the bed perfectly made. There were no other alcoves in this chamber so that meant she could only be in one place. But why did she not answer when he called?

"Brieana?" he called again, louder this time, and waited to hear her low voice commanding him to leave the chamber. When she did not respond, he broke out in a cold sweat.

Slowly walking towards the tub and dreading the worst, he looked over the edge and saw her sitting there, staring off into space.

"Brieana?" he again asked as he looked down upon her relaxed body.

The oily water hid none of her body from his view. He stifled a groan and struggled to ignore the quick rush of blood to his cock, hardening it, making it throb against the tight leather of his leggings as he hungrily eyed her breasts, gently bobbing in the tub. The caress of her now cool bath water had hardened her nipples and made the rosy peaks stand out in stark relief. He looked down further and saw the curly thatch of her pubic hair and wondered what that secret alcove would look like, smell like, and taste like.

Shaking himself free of his carnal lusts, he reached down and placed a hand on her damp shoulder.

"Lady? Are you well?"

"I am fine, Kerian," came her dazed voice.

"What is wrong with you?" he asked, concerned about her lack of reaction to a man standing there watching her nude in her bath.

"I know not, Kerian."

Stephanie Burke

"Brieana? Are you uncomfortable sitting in that water?"

"Yes, Kerian. I am."

"What is going on here?" Kerian demanded as Zorn slipped into the room.

"You are asking me questions, Kerian. And I am answering them." Her voice came out in a monotone that cast a sharp edge of fear in Kerian.

Did this, your stepmother! Zorn growled angrily as he paced back and forth in front of her bed! *Drugged her, she did!*

"Brieana?" Kerian tried again as he ran his hands through his hair again. "Do you not wish to leave the bathtub?"

"Yes, Kerian," she answered, but remained frozen in place.

Biting off a harsh curse, Kerian reached into the cool water and slid his hands beneath her, flinching at how cold her skin was.

Brieana just sat there, looking straight ahead and making no move to assist him.

"Why would she do this?" he demanded of no one in particular as he swiftly carried her across the room to the bench at the foot of her bed.

"So that she could question me, Kerian."

"What!" Kerian's voice echoed around the room while Zorn's shout echoed around his head. Brieana didn't even flinch.

"So that she could question me," she repeated again.

Muttering under his breath, Kerian commanded himself not to notice how silky her skin was as he grabbed a rough drying cloth and wrapped her securely within, having to lift each arm to accomplish his task.

Taking another cloth, he began to chafe the warmth back into her skin.

"What was so important that she had to drug you to get her answers instead of just asking me?"

Merlin's Kiss

"Excalibur, Kerian," Brieana said in her deadpan voice. "She wanted to know about Excalibur."

Designs, she has, on power! Zorn all but shouted as he rustled his wings in his growing anger. His lips parted to show his razor-sharp teeth as he growled his frustration. In that moment, Kerian caught a glimpse of the strong, terrifying drackoon the youthling would become after he reached his cocoon state.

"I will question Shala on this matter!" Kerian lifted Brieana with one arm and flipped back the covers on her bed. Easing her between the clean silken sheets, Kerian again felt a burst of anger directed towards his stepmother. There had to be a reason behind her madness, and an antidote for what was causing Brieana to behave like an addled slave.

"You stay here and let no one enter, unless it is me. Understand, Zorn?"

Understand you, I do! the youthling declared as he took up a defensive position beside the bed. One would have to be crazy to try and get past an angry drack and his sharp teeth to harm Brieana.

"Close your eyes, dear one," he gently commanded Brieana, a painful note in his chest when she obeyed. He was so used to her snappy comebacks that her instant compliance caused a sharp pain in his heart. "I will fix this, I swear it on my life!" He placed a gentle kiss on her forehead and stormed from the room, his amber eyes almost glowing red with his anger.

Any servant unlucky enough to pass him quickly gave him wide berth as he made his way to Shala's quarters. Within moments, the whole castle knew of his hot anger and whom it was directed towards.

* * * * *

"Why?" Kerian demanded as he loomed dangerously over his stepmother. "Why would you do such a thing?"

129

Stephanie Burke

"Her loyalties, Kerian," she replied with a demure look on her face. "I felt leery of this strange creature and wished to know what she was hiding."

"You could have asked me, Shala!" His cold fury enveloped the room with a dangerous aura.

Shala fought down a delicious little tingle as Kerian lost a little control over his emotions. When he was like this, he reminded her of Dagon, and thoughts of him made her mind wander to the last coupling that they shared, the one that left her with child. Abruptly, her desire faded.

"And how did I know that she hadn't cast some spell over you, Kerian? That necklace she wears contains powerful magic. Besides, the drug will wear itself out in few hours and she will sleep like the dead. She needed rest anyway, the delicate little thing."

She rose from her chair and walked over to her large stone window and jerked back the drapes, flooding the room with the last rays of the setting sun. She smiled at the colors the spread out across the sky, the fuchsias, the pinks, the turquoises, and absently patted her abdomen.

"Have I not always kept the best interests of this land foremost in my mind and heart, Shala? Have I not given everything that I am to keep Mirage stable and productive?"

"Yes, Kerian," Shala said soothingly as she turned from the window, her most engaging smile on her face. "But as mistress here…"

"Lady, you have no power here, other than what I allow you!"

The smile abruptly left her face.

"Listen to me, and listen well, Shala. You have no right to interrogate or drug anyone that I bring into this castle! Have I made myself clear, Lady?"

"Yes, Kerian," she bit out, anger making her eyes simmer with red fire. She balled her fists at her side and fought the urge

Merlin's Kiss

to hurl a black bolt of energy at him. That would ruin her plans and she needed the big buffoon to fetch that sword!

"Mind my words, Shala. Or you could easily find yourself wandering the badlands looking for a clan to take you in!"

The slamming of the door punctuated his last remark, and in a fit of temper, Shala angrily threw out her fist and shot a powerful beam into the stone wall beside the door.

She was so angry that she never noticed the room darkening and the curtains easing together/closed/shut to envelop the room in darkness.

"Tsk, tsk, Shala. You seemed to have overplayed your hand with your darling stepson." His low sinister laughter filled the room before, in a blur of dark color, Dagon made his entrance.

"I was expecting you, Dagon. I knew that you wouldn't roam far." With her anger defused by her little tantrum, Shala turned and calmly faced the second troublesome man in her life.

"Were you, my pet?" he asked, sarcasm dripping from his every word. "You know that I can't leave my little...baby love for long!" His cynical laughter again filled the room.

Getting straight to the point and hoping to end this little conference quickly, Shala ignored his baiting and announced her desires.

"You can't kill them yet, Dagon."

Cold silence filled the room.

"I can do as I please, my pet!" he said in a low tight voice as he ran one finger down the side of her face.

Shala fought an instinctive reaction to jerk away from his cold touch, and instead stood her ground.

"I still need them, Dagon."

"Why do you need those incompetent, powerless creatures, Shala? Tell me this and I might grant your...request."

He made his way to his favorite chair and settled himself comfortably.

Stephanie Burke

Fighting the urge to kick him out of that seat, Shala crossed over and took the seat across from him.

"It is very simple, Dagon. I want them to complete their quest. They are after a symbol of power. Once I have that, no clan will try and contradict my power. They all will bow to me and follow my every command."

Intrigued despite himself, Dagon leaned forward and paid attention to her words. "What symbol is this, dear heart?"

"A sword." She sat back in her chair, pleased to see that her prey had taken the bait.

"What kind of sword, dearest?"

"A sword named Excalibur."

Dagon's amused laughter again filled the room.

"The famed Excalibur, Sword of Legend for the Woman of Legend?" he demanded as tears of mirth filled his eyes.

Shala's smile froze on her face. "What is so humorous, Dagon?"

"That puny sword is no match for my might, Shala. If you were thinking of having them fetch it for you so that you could turn it on me, you are mistaken!"

Shala took a deep, surprised breath. The sword was more than a symbol of power? It was reported to have power too? She was saving the man-demon to deal with Dagon, but if this sword had power, could the torc amplify it?

"I would never attempt to do such a thing, Dagon!" she quickly shouted, striving for outrage. "Not only are we partners, you are powerful enough to kill me if I tried."

"Ego stroking will not work with me, Shala." He chuckled. "It was a nice try, though."

"Dagon!" she again cried out. "The sword is but a symbol, nothing more. The clans will respect it and it will ease my takeover of the clan leaders. That is all."

Dagon studied the pale-skinned woman before him. This bitch was up to something, and even though it annoyed him, it

132

Merlin's Kiss

intrigued him as well. What was she plotting? It would be so entertaining to let her little game play out. He was curious to see where it led.

"Very well, Shala. Your stepson and the little child have received a reprieve. I will allow them to complete this quest before I give the order to eliminate them."

"Do you have to say it that way?" Shala growled, annoyed with him and with herself. "The way you put that makes my actions seem so cold and hard."

"Dead is dead, Shala," he said as he leaned close enough so his cold breath caressed her face. "You are a murderess, and I am your accomplice. Learn to accept yourself for what you are. I have no illusions as to what I have become, and that is the first step to total power!"

Shala stared at him, absorbing his words for a moment, before a trembling hand caressed her stomach.

"And now, I must take leave of you, my dear. My minions have arrived and I must see to their orders. Once I set them in motion, I refuse to alter their course."

"I understand," she muttered, still rubbing the slight bulge in her stomach.

"You'd better, my dear. You can easily be erased and replaced."

Before she could comment, there was a rush of cold wind and Dagon was gone.

"You just gave me leave to destroy you," Shala muttered as she sat there in the dim light the rising moon cast into her room. "I will rule this kingdom as I see fit and my child will rule beside me! Your own arrogance has destroyed you, Dagon," she chuckled to herself. "And you are too puffed up with your own imagined importance to even notice when I deliver the death blow. You will rue the day you did this to me, Dagon. On my life, I swear it!"

Chapter Fourteen

Brieana awoke feeling ravenous and refreshed. The sun had hardly made an appearance in the purple pre-dawn sky when suddenly she was just…awake. Tossing her hands over her head in a long catlike stretch, feeling rather energetic and frisky, she threw back the covers and leapt to the floor. And landed on something warm, leathery and moving.

"Zorn!" she cried as she tumbled back into bed. "What are you doing?"

Guarding you, Lady. He opened his mouth in a wide yawn, exposing razor-sharp teeth in his cavernous mouth.

"From what?" she asked, fighting to free herself from covers that seemed to want to twine about her and keep her in place.

Shala! the drack snarled, extreme venom in his voice.

"She did nothing to me, Zorn!" she spat out a mouth full of sheet and glared at him from a tangle of hair and blankets.

Drugged you, she did! he insisted, while rising to his feet and pacing the room as if suddenly pregnant with impatience. *Evil, she is!*

"Drugged…?"

Brieana tried in vain to remember the events of the previous evening. She remembered making Zorn leave the room and undressing, but not much more than that. Had she been drugged by Shala? She struggled to remember but her mind hit a brick wall.

"What happened, Zorn?"

Drugged you, she did! A truth speak spell, she used! Zorn stopped beside the bed to glare at her in return. *Forsake my duty, you made me.* As he said that, he appeared more sad that angry.

Merlin's Kiss

"I...I do not know what to say, Zorn." Brieana was truly amazed. She had thought that her unease around Shala was due to her not knowing her purpose in Mirage. Now she saw that the feeling of unease was a warning she should have paid heed to.

Killed, could have been, you! Lost we are, without you!

Brieana felt a wave of shame flood through her. Last night, all she could think about was a hot bath and a warm meal, so secure in her destiny was she that she behaved as if the outcome of her quest was a foregone conclusion. What would happen to the Light Isles if she had been killed? What would have happened to all of these people? Her selfishness could have spelled disaster for the very ones she was bound to protect! From now on, she would put her own selfish needs second. She would be a good leader first.

"I most humbly apologize, Zorn." Brieana managed to pull herself to her feet and stood before the faithful drack protector, using the sheet as a cover-up. "From now on, I will listen to your counsel. You know more about this world than I. Can you tell me where Kerian is?"

For our quest, preparing provisions he is.

"When I dress, will you take me to him, Zorn?"

Yes, Lady, Zorn cried in obvious relief that she was at least going to listen to him. He turned away while she dressed. He understood the reasons why she would wish to hide the body that Kerian found so delightful. Human women were so pale, bumpy and soft. Their skin did not pulse with their life force and they had no wings with which to reach for the sky. There was no accounting for taste, he thought as he listened to the rustle of her clothing as she pulled them from the chest of clothes Shala sent down and began to dress. Well, at least her clothing lent some attractive color to her, but why anybody wanted to ogle a naked human was beyond him.

* * * * *

...and her skin was as soft as the mist-refined spleetar *silk. Her rosy nipples were like little ripe fruits, just begging to be picked, uh, licked. The curly thicket of hair that rested between her legs was like a lush forest he longed to explore. Her muscled thighs were...*

"Kerian! Watch out!"

Kerian turned just in time to see the large black unicorn bearing down on him! With natural agility, he stepped aside and barely avoided being trampled to death by the female unicorn.

He could have sworn he heard laughter as the cursed beast thundered by in a cloud of dust. He hit the ground face first in a tangle of platinum hair and swear words.

You have to keep alert when dealing with unicorns, he reminded himself. They were treacherous creatures.

"That was a close call, Kerian!" Sato cried as he raced to assist his lord to his feet. "You have to keep alert when dealing with these treacherous beasts!"

Kerian sighed at the gentle admonishment he received from his second in command, and waved away his helping hand. As he rose to his feet, he glanced to where the marauding female had joined her mate, both highlighted by the dim early morning sky. Graceful dancers, they tossed their heads and pranced as if taunting the mere humans with their strength and beauty. Both had the usual shiny black coats of their breed, but the female had a gold blaze running down her face, blending perfectly with her mother-of-pearl horn. The male was a calmer version of his mate, but with no distinctive markings to differentiate him from any other unicorn. And like the others, his black coat was a startling contrast to the purity of his mother-of-pearl horn.

"Would you not rather walk?" Sato looked none too happy with the evil glint in both of the unicorns' red eyes.

"Would take far too long," Kerian answered as he eyed the unicorns that were, in turn, eyeing him.

"Yet it would be safer," Sato said with a grimace.

It had taken him nearly all night to track two of the most amiable unicorns on their land and bring them both back to the

Merlin's Kiss

castle. He looked as if he had been twelve days into battle and was on the losing side. He ached from every part of his body and was desirous of nothing more than a bath and bed. That is, until he learned of the confrontation between Kerian and Shala.

"About the Lady of the keep...?" Sato began.

"Watch her, Sato. I do not trust her. She wants something that Brieana has knowledge of, and I fear for all of our safety. I had almost forgotten the old rumors about her dabbling in dark magic, but the way she is reacting to Lady Brieana has me worried. A little knowledge is a dangerous thing, my friend. And if she has a little knowledge of magic, there is no telling what she could unleash upon us."

"As you wish, Warlord." Sato knew for Kerian to share this confidence with him there was indeed something not quite right about Shala.

"Thank you, my friend. I know that there is a lot of unease directed towards the drackoon upon the Dark Mountains, but if anything should happen, go to Dalis and accept his help, Sato. It is important that you obey me in this."

Sato hid a tremor of fear that accompanied each mention of the dreaded drackoons, but he remembered what Kerian had sacrificed to help the large lizards.

"But I have not the ability to communicate with them as you do, Warlord."

"Words are not necessary, Sato. If they see you, they will come. Heed their advice and follow their lead. They will make their words known to you. They have been on this Isle longer than any of us and they are very wise."

Sato nodded acceptance of the order and Kerian felt a small bit of the burden that he carried ease a little. Between the brave Sato and the wise Dalis, Mirage would be safe from all marauders.

"Now go and find your bed, my friend. You look as if you need the rest."

Stephanie Burke

"Good journey, Kerian!" Sato nodded to his leader and headed for his personal chambers. All he could now see was bath, food, and bed, and not necessarily in that order.

* * * * *

The sound of Kerian's disgusted voice rang clear in the gently lightening sky. Brieana, dressed in a tunic, another one as black as night, entered the clearing beyond the practice field to see Kerian wrestling a saddle onto a jet-black unicorn that constantly side-stepped and snorted at him. So awed was she by the sight that she froze, causing her grumbling protector to slam into her back.

"I have never beheld such beauty," she breathed as she watched the play of muscles on both equine and man. Kerian moved with a grace that spoke of his strength as he gently settled the saddle onto the unicorn's broad back. The unicorn tossed its glossy black mane as it accepted the weight upon its back.

Then out more, you need to get, Zorn grumbled.

Brieana refused to eat in the same hall as the woman who had drugged her, so Zorn was deprived of his large breakfast. Instead, Brieana had stopped by the kitchens and a cook gave her a loaf of bread fresh from the oven and a hunk of cheese. Zorn had to make do with a few scraps that the cook tossed his way. Even now Zorn longingly eyed Brieana's package as they stood in the fields.

Suddenly, the unicorn Kerian was handling lifted its muzzle into the air as if sensing something, then it zeroed in on Brieana standing there. In a flash, it broke away from Kerian and raced towards the woman and the drack.

"Brieana!" Kerian cry broke the spell that she was under, and she noticed the unicorn bearing down on her, head lowered in an attack position.

Merlin's Kiss

The torc around her neck began to grow warm as the danger approached, and instinctively she raised a hand to cover it, then she stood frozen and watched as black death bore down on her. Her first sight of a fabled unicorn held her in thrall.

In the background, she could see Kerian racing uselessly after the charging equine, a look of horror on his face as he realized that he would be too late to stop it.

Brieana felt more than saw Zorn leap in front of her, but still she didn't move, seemingly compelled to watch this beautiful destructive creature bear down upon her. Just as the creature was close enough for her to smell the heat of its huge body, she raised one hand and shouted.

"Stop!"

It was almost comical the way the massive equine pulled up. In fact, it braked so suddenly that its haunches almost scraped the ground as its front hooves scrambled for purchase. The dust cloud it created cloaked Brieana from Kerian's view, and he felt his heart, the heart that he refused to acknowledge, break as he pictured her bleeding, trampled body beneath the large hooves of the unicorn.

As he raced into the dust cloud, he stopped in amazement, his hands spread out in supplication, his mouth open to shout his denials to the heavens.

Brieana stood in front of the murderous beast, gently stroking his muzzle as he preened under her attentions. The ever-watchful Zorn stood by her side, a look of cautious acceptance on his face as he observed his Lady and the black beast that would be carrying them.

"Are they not glorious, Kerian?" she asked as she continued to stroke the unicorn's shiny coat. "They are a bit of fantasy come to life."

"I thought... I saw... Are you all right, Lady?" Kerian seemed unusually flustered as he approached her, his eyes examining every bit of her body for signs of injury.

Stephanie Burke

"I am a bit dusty now, but otherwise fine. For a moment, this large fellow had me frightened, but like all men, he just needed a firm hand and some ego stroking. Is that not right, gorgeous one?" she crooned to the now docile unicorn.

"I thought you were going to be killed!" His voice was low and dangerous, showing his anger more eloquently than with words.

"I am fine, Kerian. I think that it has something to do with Merlin's gift. But I am not too sure. But I know that this little angel would never hurt me."

As Kerian stepped closer, the 'little angel' bared its teeth and snorted at him. It was the unicorn equivalent of 'get bent' and Kerian knew it.

"Can you now understand the unicorns too, Lady?" he asked as he stared at the beast, a dangerous glint in his eyes. It was the Kerian equivalent of, 'if you hurt her, you will pay.'

"No, I cannot, but I know that he will never hurt me. What is his name?" Her green eyes sparkled up at him as she continued stroking the equine, making Kerian picture her eyes glinting as they stroked a certain part of his anatomy, slowly, from the base to the tip. Would her hands feel just a bit rough, but warm, adding delightful friction as she sped up? Would his natural lubrication ease her motions as her thumb made small circles around the head of his cock, moving in time to the deep throb that was sure to make his sac tighten with the need to release his hot seed? Shaking off his fantasy, he answered her question.

"He has no name, Lady. He is a unicorn and that is what I call him."

Brieana frowned a little at that, but smiled brightly after a moment.

"Then I will name him, Kerian. From now on, he is Magic, Black Magic."

Kerian sighed at the strangeness of this woman. She had to put a name to everything she came in contact with. Her sword

140

Merlin's Kiss

was Excalibur, her kingdom, the whole bloody thing, was called Camelot. Now she had named the unicorn Black Magic! Before long, she would be naming each chum that he owned!

"Very well, Lady. We will call this unsociable creature Black Magic."

The unicorn seemed to take offense and snapped at Kerian, but he ignored him. The smile lighting up Brieana's face made him forget his earlier annoyance and the rude beasts.

"How do you fare this morning?" he carefully asked, looking for any signs of the drug.

"I am fine, Kerian. But that is the reason that I sought you out this morning, instead of awaiting you in the hall. Why did your stepmother drug me?"

Kerian sighed and took her hand as she stepped closer. "She is a strange one, Brieana. She has never really been a mother to me, although she has defended me at a time when I was unable to defend myself. She is just cautious of new people and protective of Mirage. This is her only home and if something ever happened to it, she has no clan to turn to. She thought that we were keeping some knowledge of Mirage's welfare from her and sought answers."

Brieana made a face at his words, but he quickly continued with his explanation.

"I do not condone what she did, Lady Brieana, and I told her as much, but I can understand her fear. Rivals wiped out her clan before the treaty went into effect and gave us this uneasy peace that we now share. I think she is more afraid of losing her home than anything else. Still, what she did was dangerous and unnecessary. I have warned her about you, and I am sure that she'll keep her distance from now on."

"I refuse to be in the same hall with that woman now, Kerian. I can also understand her reasoning, but what she did was sly and underhanded. If she wished to kill me if she found out that I was a threat, she could have easily done so. What kind

Stephanie Burke

of potion did she use anyway? I cannot even remember what I told her and it had no effect on her!"

"No effect on her?" Kerian pounced on that statement like a hungry bloodhound.

"She tested her witch's brew before she served it to me, Kerian."

"She must have an antidote for it then," he decided as he stored that piece of information away. "But she will trouble you no longer."

"That is true, Kerian, because I refuse to go back in there with that madwoman!"

Nodding his understanding, Kerian released her hand, noticing how small and warm it felt nestled in his, and turned back to the area where he was readying the unicorns for travel.

"I mean it!" she called after him as she started to follow. "Do you understand, Kerian?"

It was an interesting procession that followed the Warlord as he walked back to the female unicorn. First there was a red-faced and sputtering Brieana, followed by a somewhat docile unicorn that snorted and stomped at everything that passed him, including insects and the wind, yet gently nuzzled his new mistress' shoulder. Bringing up the rear was a disgruntled and grumbling purple drack, with his wings held tight to his body and his tail nearly dragging the ground.

Finally when they reached his objective, the female with the golden stripe down her face, Brieana's mouth slammed shut.

"I suppose you wish to name her too?" he asked as he removed something from the pack on her back, neatly avoiding her snapping jaws and disgusted looks.

"Blaze. Her name is Blaze, Kerian, and she is a fierce protector."

Kerian rolled his eyes as Brieana rushed over to stroke this unicorn too into blissful docility. He bit back a feeling of jealousy as he brought his cloth-wrapped package forward.

Merlin's Kiss

"If you are done playing tamer of all animals great and small, I have a promised gift to offer to you."

Brieana turned around, a delighted smile still on her face as she assessed Kerian's words.

"What have you promised me, Kerian?"

"Have you forgotten so quickly, Lady?" he teased as he presented the package to her.

Abandoning her new living toys, Brieana eagerly reached up and took the gift from his hands. The weight of it almost seemed familiar to her as she quickly unwrapped it.

"My sword! Kerian, it's my sword!"

"As promised, Lady."

But Brieana was already lost in the wonder of the object that she held within her hands. This was a sword like no other. Its curved blade was serrated on the inside curve and spiked on the outer. The hilt was fashioned with an ornate silver hand guard and a single emerald embedded in its pommel. The black leather grip fit her small hand perfectly as she hefted the blade to test its balance. This was a warrior's sword. With it she could protect herself and any others they deemed worthy.

"This is beautiful, Kerian," she sighed as she gave it an experimental flick with her wrist. "You designed this for me?"

"Of course, Lady. I also remember saying that I could never restore your lost sword to you, but I may have a chance to do just that."

"Thank you, Kerian." She looked up at him with tears in her eyes. No one had ever given her a gift quite like this before. Merlin gave her the torc, but that was all part of his schemes, and Arthur never gave her anything at all. "I have never before received such a thoughtful gift, any gift for that matter."

Touched by her obvious regard for the weapon, Kerian again felt a swelling within his heart. No one ever touched him like this small dark-haired woman. Her every tear had the power to render him useless.

Stephanie Burke

"Then shall we go and claim your sword and birthright, Lady?" Kerian asked. Anything to stop this awful, awful, wonderful burning sensation in his chest. "Shall we go and save your kingdom?"

"Yes, Kerian! Yes!" Her passionate answer caused an uncomfortable tightening in his loins as he pictured her entreaty under different circumstances, mainly under him.

"You have eaten?" he asked, his voice a little tight with his growing desire.

"I have food with me," she replied, still looking at the sword with glazed eyes.

Bread and cheese, as if a meal, they make! Zorn grumbled still miffed about his lost meal.

"Then let us be off!" Kerian turned to Blaze and, deftly avoiding the bite that surely would have caused him lots of pain and the unicorn great satisfaction, he settled himself upon her saddled back.

Tucking her sword into a scabbard on Magic's saddle, Brieana quickly scrambled onto her seat atop the great stallion, and turned to face Kerian.

He looked a bit uncomfortable sitting on Blaze's back. The way he kept shifting signaled that he was in some discomfort. *Perhaps it is just the transition from drack riding to unicorn riding,* she decided as she watched him ready himself for their journey.

"Not what you want to be riding, Kerian?" she asked slyly, referring to the ease in which he rode drackback.

"Not at all, Lady," he gritted as her words sent another erotic picture running through his head. A picture where she was beneath him, thighs wrapping tightly around his waist as he rode her to a mutually delightful finish. "Not what I had in mind at all."

Blaze snorted as if she could read his mind and was amused by his private fantasies. Zorn gave him another odd look, which he ignored, and skillfully turned Blaze into the

144

Merlin's Kiss

direction of the Forbidden Forest. Putting the pleasures of the flesh, with great difficulty, out of his mind, he gestured in the direction that they were supposed to go.

"Your destiny awaits, Lady!" he called to her as he urged Blaze into a fast gallop.

"Our destiny, silly man!" she called to him as she kicked Magic into a full gallop and raced her future mate to their fortune. "You are just too silly and vain to realize it!"

Stephanie Burke

Chapter Fifteen

The smell of damp vegetation and moist earth filled Brieana's senses as the darkness of the forest closed in on her. They had been traveling for hours inside the dark wooded areas and only just now had the forest truly closed in on them.

With visibility at a low, Brieana followed the clip-clop of Blaze's hooves and tried to get as close to Kerian as possible. For once, Zorn was quiet, not even complaining when Kerian sent him off to hunt like a drack, instead of mooching people food. But it was the silence that unnerved her most of all.

When they entered the forest shortly after daybreak three days ago, the birds were chirping and the insects were droning; now there was total silence. The tall trunks of the strange trees seemed to absorb any sound and emphasize an atmosphere of doom.

When they crossed the bubbling cold river that Kerian had warned her about, she had not felt this sense of an unnatural presence, even after she wanted to test his theory and fall in. They had to stop for the night and build a fire, things he had not wanted to attempt that early, but because the cold had sapped all of her strength, Kerian felt it was for the best.

She had not felt this sense of unease when she wandered over to the beautiful flowers that Kerian and Zorn had warned her about and almost lost her nose as she bent for a close inspection of Man Snapper flower. She had only wanted to see the teeth that they had claimed the flower possessed. How was she to know that they moved about the earth on root-like feet to more easily obtain a meal?

Not even the fireflies that now spat fiery acid at their prey had unnerved her like this small clearing they had stumbled upon.

Merlin's Kiss

"Kerian?" she whispered as if afraid to draw some unknown monster's attention to her and her party. "Is this place natural?"

Suddenly there was a rustle and quick footsteps behind her. Twisting in her saddle, and automatically reaching for her blade, she looked back and saw…nothing.

Pulling Magic to a halt, she turned and closely examined the trail behind her. Still nothing.

"Kerian, did you hear that?" she called out, and was met with silence.

She faced front, only to find that Kerian was nowhere in sight.

"Kerian?"

Then there was another rustle to her right. Her nerves screaming and pressure building up in her chest, she whipped towards the sound and again saw…nothing.

"Beware… Beware her ire!" a low voice seemed to whisper in her ear.

Magic shied sideways as if he too heard the warning, and Brieana spent a few moments calming him down.

"Zorn?" she called out, but her trusty drack bodyguard was not with her.

"Zorn!" she called out louder, fear beginning to build up pressure in her chest. "Kerian? Answer me."

"Beware, beware her ire!"

Whipping to her left, the direction of the whispered warning, she again heard a rustle and then nothing. But she had no time for contemplation, for Magic, frightened by the low voice, reared up on his hind legs, as if fighting with some unseen enemy.

"Beware. Beware. Beware!"

The voices were coming in from all around her and Brieana could feel a cold sweat building as the unfamiliar metallic taste of terror filled her mouth.

"Beware!" to the left.

"Beware!" in front of her.

The hair on the nape of her neck rose and the voice taunted her from behind.

"Beware, beware her ire!"

Whipping out her sword and turning her unicorn around, Brieana again saw nothing, but could hear the rustle of…leaves? "Who are you?" she cried out, her heart pounding painfully in her chest. "Where are you? What do you want?"

"Beware!" came from the right.

Giving in to her building hysteria, Brieana swung the sword to the left as she jerked Magic around to see what was tormenting her. Nothing.

But before she could recover, the voice whispered from in front of her.

"Her ire, beware, beware!"

"Stop it!" she screamed, fear lending her voice volume. "Show yourself! Coward!"

An enemy that she could see, she could fight. This unseen menace preyed upon her fears and caused her to react like a green soldier, going into her first battle.

"Beware!" the voice taunted and Brieana gave in to her hysteria and began to swing her sword like a madwoman.

"Stop it, stop it, stop it!" she screamed, frustration drying up her fearful tears before they could trickle down her face. "Leave me alone!"

Then there was a clang, and a painful vibration flowed up her arm before her sword was knocked aside.

"Brieana?"

"Bastard!" she screamed as she dove at the thing that had disarmed her, taking them both to the soft packed earth.

Her flailing arms and legs landed many a good blow as she fought for her life.

Merlin's Kiss

"Brieana!" It spoke her name again in Kerian's voice. Kerian?

Brieana slowly opened her eyes to look up at the hideous beast that now held her in its death-giving grasp.

"Kerian?" she whispered as she saw who stood above her. "You bastard!" she screamed and let her fist fly.

"Brie...oomph!" her fist connected neatly with his right eye and he jumped to his feet, knocking her off his body.

"If you ever play such a mean-spirited jest on me again..."

"What are you talking about, woman?" Kerian moved a few feet away from her, more for his protection than anything as he covered his aching eye with one large hand.

"That whispering 'beware,' and all of that! Are you trying to frighten me?"

"I have no idea what you are talking about, woman!" he growled as his fingers gently prodded the rapidly swelling flesh of his eye.

"Then who was it, Kerian? Zorn?"

Yes, Lady? The purple drack sauntered into the area with something squawking and flapping in his mouth.

"Was it you, you little purple rat?" She spat the words at the youthling, causing him to open his mouth in astonishment and drop his meal. He had never before seen his Lady so angry, even though he had to admit the red tint to her skin made her more attractive.

Although neither Zorn nor Kerian had experienced all of the Forbidden Forest, and its secrets, they both knew the stories of strange happenings that occurred there. Perhaps Brieana's experience with the mysterious voice and their getting separated were things they could attribute to the strange area.

"Beware, beware her ire!" The thing Zorn dropped squawked as it ran in circles around the group standing there, all looking in astonishment at the bird thing.

Stephanie Burke

"It's a Sage Chicken," Kerian growled as he glared at Brieana. Walking over to the befuddled chicken, he knelt down on one knee and gathered it to his chest.

"Sage Chicken?" Brieana paused in her angry pacing to watch in amazement as Kerian cradled the bird in his arms, gentling it. The only chickens she knew of were good when cooked in sage, but she had a feeling that Kerian was not speaking of spices.

"They have lived in the Forbidden Forest forever and often warn travelers of danger. They also happen to be a favored snack of the drack."

And rare, too, they are, Zorn agreed with Kerian as he hungrily eyed the quaking bird in Kerian's hands.

"Rare?" she asked still thrown by the idea of a talking chicken.

"Drackoon don't venture into forests much, Lady." Kerian glared at her, his eye still watering and smarting from her sneaky punch. Brieana, realizing that she had hit an innocent man, backed guiltily away and went to retrieve her sword.

"Beware, beware her ire!" the chicken interjected, breaking Kerian's gaze from Brieana.

"Who's ire?" Kerian asked as he continued to soothe the chicken's ruffled feathers.

"The Lady Lake, her ire is great!"

"The Lady Lake?" Brieana rushed over to Kerian's side, the sword forgotten as she heard what the talking bird had to say.

"Her lover's scent. She smells it much! Stay away from her jealous touch!"

"Lover? Smells? What is this chicken speaking of?" she demanded as she looked from one puzzled face to another.

"Beware, beware of her ire! Beware, beware!" the chicken clucked as it struggled to be free.

Afraid of doing it injury, Kerian released the bird and quick as a flash, it took off for the darkness of the trees. Zorn, seeing

Merlin's Kiss

his would-be snack getting away, gave chase and soon both were lost in the darkness of the forest.

"What did that bird mean?" Brieana turned to Kerian, but the Warlord had already turned his back to her. "Kerian?"

"Not that you would believe my answers." He angrily searched the ground till he saw the gleaming edge of his large war sword. Its serrated blade gleamed in the dim light for a moment, before he walked over to where the unicorns were peacefully grazing and slammed the sword into its sheath.

"What are you speaking of?" she asked as she continued with her search and let out a triumphant crow when she spotted her sword.

"I told you that I played no jests on you, yet I was the first person whom you accused!"

"You were the first person that I saw, Kerian." Brieana tried to explain as she too made her way over to Magic and replaced her sword. The unicorns seem unusually docile around Kerian. She figured it was because you could almost feel the heated anger rolling off of him in waves.

"Yet after I told you that it wasn't me, you persisted in believing the worst."

"I am sorry, Kerian. I was frightened, not thinking. It will not happen again."

"Likely story!" Angrily he grasped Blaze's reins and pulled the unicorn through a tall thicket of trees.

What was wrong with him? She had apologized and yet he was still not looking at her, Brieana mused as she grasped Magic's reins and followed him.

"I also accused Zorn," she called out, trying to figure out what was wrong with her Warlord. Men were so complicated. She would never understand them, not if she lived for more than a thousand years, which was what she had done. Men were still the most confusing species on the face of the earth!

"Zorn once told you that I won't lie, and you believed him. Why the sudden mistrust, Brieana?"

151

Stephanie Burke

He almost sounded hurt. That was it. Brieana paused as the light suddenly dawned upon her. She had hurt his feelings.

"Kerian, wait!" She rushed forward to stop him, to explain her frustrated hysteria, and nearly slammed into his back as he suddenly paused on the trail. Looking over his shoulder to see what had stopped him, Brieana felt her mouth drop open as the most beautiful lake she had ever seen spread out before her.

"This has to be it!" she breathed in awe.

"Brieana?" Kerian motioned her to his side and gave a terse warning. "Arm yourself, Lady. We approach the unknown here and the Sage Chicken did warn us."

Wondering about his precautions, Brieana did as he asked. She had already hurt his feelings and didn't want to alienate him by pointing out that the Lady of the Lake was a helper to Merlin, so she placed the sword in her war belt. She noticed that Kerian did the same as he released the unicorns to graze.

"Behind me, Lady," he whispered as he cautiously picked his way down the soft packed earth of the forest floor, to the bright green grass growing around the lake.

When nothing happened, he motioned Brieana to his side and together they looked out over the beauty of the lake.

"She has to be here!" Brieana said, excitedly. "I can feel her magic here!"

"I feel nothing, Lady, but this is as good a place as any to rest. But let's keep on guard. There might be hidden dangers."

Nodding her approval of his plan, Brieana hurried back for the unicorns.

"What about Zorn?" she called over her shoulder. "Should we not go and search for him?"

"The youthling will return when he smells the cook fire, Lady. He is all stomach, but then, most dracks are before they become drackoon. Zorn has a few years of being a youthling before he becomes a full-grown drackoon, but I believe that he is storing up energy for the process."

Merlin's Kiss

Amusement tinged his voice now when he spoke of Zorn. Even though Brieana knew Kerian cared for all drackoons, she never thought to hear of his affection for the purple troublemaker.

"You have forgiven him, then?" she asked as she led the unicorns over to Kerian. Together they began to unload the sleeping blankets and what supplies they would need for the night.

"He was behaving as a drack. I expect no less from a drack. All creatures must stay true to their nature."

"And me? Have you forgiven me, Kerian?"

Kerian paused in unsaddling Blaze to observe Brieana.

She was a born queen, denied her birthright, and had no reason to trust a man. From comments she had made, all the men in her life had let her down, from Arthur, the little boy she fancied herself in love with, to Merlin, who cast her into a stone prison for many a year. Brieana had learned mistrust from an early age. He was a fool to think that he could earn her trust so easily.

"There is nothing to forgive, Lady." He tossed the saddle aside and moved on to Magic, ignoring the growls and snaps from the unicorns. "You must stay true to your nature."

"And just what is that supposed to mean?" Brieana tapped her foot in the lush green grass of the little valley surrounding the lake. Forgotten was its blue/green waters and pale tan sand. She wanted an explanation for his statement.

"I mean, Lady, that you must follow your heart. If your heart has learned distrust, then you will find it hard to trust others." He shrugged as he went about settling the unicorns and picking out an area to camp. "For now."

Brieana started to run over and demand an explanation for cryptic words when she caught his last words, "For now." What did that mean? Was Kerian trying to change her mind about trust? Did he want her to trust him, to start some type of relationship with him?

153

Stephanie Burke

"I will go and gather water for our evening stew, Lady," he called over to her, wondering about the bright sparkle in her eyes and the bemused look she now wore across her face.

"Be careful, Kerian!" she called over to him as she spread out their blankets and began to gather up small stones to build a fire ring. "I don't want anything to happen to you."

"I wonder what is in her mind now?" Kerian quietly asked himself as he went to fetch the water. "Women!" There would never be a man who could understand them.

Merlin's Kiss

Chapter Sixteen

As the sun began its downward path, bathing the calm waters of the lake in a kaleidoscope of warm colors, Kerian and Brieana finished their meal of traveler's soup and bread. Kerian had packed enough supplies for a long journey, but they had hardly made a dent in the provisions. Now, settling back after their final meal for the day, they both paused in their clean-up chores to admire the sun lowering in the west.

"Is it not like a dream, Kerian?" Brieana asked as she gathered up the bowls they used for eating.

"I have never seen the lake before, Lady, so this is a rare treat for me. I have seen the waters surrounding the Light Isles, but never the lake."

Ever since their earlier confrontation when Kerian let it slip out that he cared to earn her trust, they had both been a little uneasy around each other.

While Kerian fetched the water, Brieana built the stone ring and gathered wood. While she retrieved the foodstuffs they would need, he started the fire. Together they worked like a well-oiled machine, anticipating each other's wishes and needs oftentimes before the other person became aware they needed something.

Now that their evening meal was over and Zorn had returned, a few feathers hanging off of his mouth and a disgruntled look on his face, she could feel the tension building in the air.

"I think Zorn is still upset about losing his dinner and having you give him drack lessons!" Brieana giggled as she rose to her feet and started for the lake. "You make an impressive drack, Kerian. You caught his dinner with great skill."

155

Stephanie Burke

"Gren taught me everything I know," he almost chuckled and shot the youthling an amused look. "Do not worry, Zorn. I'm sure you will find a woman to do your hunting for you."

Zorn refused to answer the taunt, but instead turned his back on the suddenly playful man and the giggling woman. He was not sure he approved of this sudden sense of humor that had struck the Warlord. He did not like the unpredictable.

"I will walk to the lake with you," Kerian said as he saw Brieana carry the used bowls down for cleaning. "I wish to put cool water on my eye. I believe you have bruised it."

"It was only a small tap, Kerian!" Brieana wailed as she again felt a flush of guilt.

"'Twas merely a jest," he said before he took the lead in their stroll to the lake.

The dim evening light clearly showed the small bruise beneath his eye, but it also highlighted his near perfect profile. Kerian was a handsome man, and now that he was acting interested in Brieana, he was displaying a charm she never thought he possessed.

In truth, Kerian had decided to stop fighting his awareness of Brieana. Too much did he remember of her fiery hot kisses and baby smooth skin. He would be a fool to give that all up! Plus, she caused him to feel something he thought to never experience again. His past history with wary females had taught him to be careful of giving his heart to a woman. And he wasn't thinking about mere lust either.

When he had earlier seen her frightened and nearly hysterical, fighting with feverish intent, he felt the cold ice in his heart shatter into a million pieces. He never wanted to see her that fearful again. He would personally see to it! She had once declared they would be mates, and now he was ready to accept it. She may be the Queen that would unite the Isles, but she was also a woman. A woman who had the same needs as any other woman. After watching her these last few days, Kerian was sure

156

Merlin's Kiss

he was the man to fulfill her every need, but first, they had to complete this quest and fulfill her destiny.

"Shall I help you wash the dishes, Lady?" he asked as he crossed the soft sand and headed for the edge of the lake.

"Let's do it together," Brieana smiled up at him and stepped to his side. "I'm surprised you are willing to help. The men I knew considered this to be woman's work." She knelt and began to heap sand into the small kettle they'd used for cooking.

"I am not like the men you knew." His voice came out a little sternly, causing her to look over at him as he knelt beside her, scrubbing plates.

"I know that, Kerian. You are special."

She wasn't sure, but she thought she saw a small blush begin on his cheeks.

"Kerian, I know that Merlin…"

"*Merlin!*" The voice boomed from everywhere and nowhere.

Kerian and Brieana both jumped to their feet and began to look around.

"Lady, did you…?"

"You dare speak his name, you slut! You trollop! You…you…home-wrecker!"

"Home…wrecker?" Brieana turned a confused look to Kerian then they both continued their fevered search for the voice.

"You dare to come here, reeking of his magic and flaunting your relationship in my face! Are you mad, woman?"

Suddenly, the calm waters of the lake began to churn and bubble as if they were angry with the intruders.

Kerian shoved Brieana behind him as the water began to crash and splash against the shore.

"Bitch!" A large wave slammed against the shore, heading straight for Brieana. And it would have pulled her under too, if

Stephanie Burke

Kerian had not knocked her back to the grass beyond the sandy shore and blocked her with his body.

"Kerian!" Brieana screamed, feeling all the color drain from her face as he was sucked beneath the waves of the now boiling lake.

"And you bring another lover with you! Is not one man enough for you, you little witch?"

"Kerian!" Brieana screamed as she struggled to her feet and began to race to the water's edge.

Again, another massive wave approached, and just when Brieana thought she would be sucked in, something knocked her aside. She looked up to see Zorn being swallowed by the wave meant for her.

"So you can control the beasts of the sky, but that will avail you not, whore! I will deal with you face to face!"

"Zorn! Kerian!" Brieana ignored the voice and the wet gritty sand that covered her body. A cold hard wind lashed her hair around her head and chilled her to the bone, but she felt no discomfort. Her horrified eyes were trained on the once quiet lake, searching for a glimpse of either her courageous Zorn or her beloved Kerian.

So intent on her search was she that she barely noticed the center of the lake parting and the head and naked shoulders of a woman rise as if she was being lifted on a platform.

"Stupid bitch! How dare you come here smelling of him?"

"Kerian!" Brieana cried out again, tears filling her eyes when she saw no sign of him.

"How sweet! You call to one lover, smelling of the other. Where is he? Where is that bastard Merlin?"

"I do not know what you are speaking of!" Brieana sobbed out, screaming to the heavens. "I do not know what you want!"

She turned her anguished eyes to the woman who emerged from the lake. Naked but for the long streams of wet blue hair that twined around her body, the woman's yellow eyes glared at

Merlin's Kiss

her. Raising her arms to the sky, she gave Brieana a nasty smirk that distorted her beautiful elfin face, before lowering her arms slowly.

As her hands reached her waist two large round cages of water emerged from the angry lake. As Brieana peered closer, she saw a flash of platinum hair and knew Kerian was held within one of the watery prisons. Zorn had to be in the other.

"Release them!" she cried, turning her attention back to the naked woman. "We have done you no wrong!"

"You come here smelling of my lover's magic and claim to do no wrong? What are you? Blind or just plain stupid?"

"I have no lovers!" Brieana called out to her, dancing from foot to foot in her helplessness. She knew Kerian had never seen a large body of water before, and it meant he would not know how to swim.

"Don't play me for a fool, woman! I can smell him on you!"

"Who? Who can you smell?" Brieana cried, again turning her tormented gaze to the woman.

"Am I talking to myself or what?" she asked, eyes look up as if beseeching some higher power for patience. "Merlin, that faithless bastard! That's who you are screwing!"

"Screwing? I have no idea what you are speaking of, Lady, and I have not seen Merlin since he cast me into the hand of the Rock of Ages!"

"Liar! I can sense his power on you!" she screamed, her eyes glowing as the wind began to pick up yet again.

"No lie! Truth!" Brieana begged. "I know nothing of Merlin! Please, release them! They have done you no wrong!"

"What kind of fool do you take me for, trollop? I know you have been with him! I can sense his magic, idiot! But I will tell you what! Convince me to let them live and I just might spare their lives, before I send you to your grave."

She crossed her arms over her blue-tinted skin, her hair whipping furiously around her, building with her anger, and exposing her perfectly formed body to Brieana's view. Almost arrogantly, she tossed her hair as she gave Brieana a superior look.

"It would be a shame to kill off such a hunk of man, anyway, but I will if you don't start convincing!"

Falling to her knees in the churning surf, Brieana turned pleading eyes up to the woman. "Please let him go! Let them both go! I am begging you!"

The woman yawned, before flicking her wrist and slowly began filling Kerian's bubble with foaming water.

"You are killing him!" she shrieked as she watched the churning water reach up to his chest. Stoic as always, Kerian watched her with calm eyes, even though she could almost hear him willing her to run away and leave them in this place. "Please!"

"Your begging is annoying me. You'd better try something else, or lover boy will bite it!"

"Bite it? What are you asking for? Your words make no sense to me! But I beseech you, please let him go!"

The woman peered closely at Brieana, as if seeing her for the first time. "Why should I?" She now had the Lady's full attention on her.

"I love him!" Brieana cried out. "I love him so much, it hurts!"

"What's love got to do with anything?" the woman demanded. She gave a flick of her wrist and floated closer to Brieana. Now that she wasn't standing up on her pedestal of water, Brieana noticed that the woman stood no higher than she did. When only a few feet separated them, the woman stopped and eyed Brieana as if she were a particularly disgusting bug she wanted to squash.

"I loved that man, that Merlin, for centuries, and where did it get me? Hmm? I was the occasional booty call for him, but that was it! I loved him and he never even bothered to show up after the first few centuries. And that was fine, he was busy

160

Merlin's Kiss

manipulating people's lives, and I understood that. But then the visits stopped, the messages stopped. He begged me not to give in to the darkness and cease to be, but he never came to keep me company. He begged me to continue this existence and then he abandoned me! And I stayed and suffered because I loved him and believed he would come back to me!" She paused in her tirade against the missing Merlin.

"So where does love get me, you fool? I was better off loving myself! If I had not loved him I could have joined my sisters in oblivion! But here I sit, waiting from some kind of sign from him, and his bitch shows up, smelling of his magic and bringing her own lover with her. And how do you think that makes me feel?"

Her yellow eyes bored into Brieana's green ones, pain and sorrow mixed with anger, causing the yellow eyes to almost glow red.

"I know nothing of Merlin and his intrigues," Brieana began. "And I am sorry he treated you so discourteously, but on the pain of death, I have never lain with him or any man! I was locked away in stone for centuries! I have come here to retrieve Excalibur from you and complete my destiny. But you must understand that man you are murdering is part of my destiny as well. I cannot exist without him! Without him, all of this is meaningless."

"Stone, did you say?" the woman's breath hitched and the wind began to die down.

"Your words are odd to me Lady, but I can understand you. Merlin wronged you, true, but I was no part of it. The only thing I have of Merlin is this torc he gave to me before he tossed me into the hands of the Rock of Ages. If I could remove it from my person, I would gladly give it to you. I would give up a kingdom, my life for him. Please spare him and take me instead!"

The torc around Brieana's neck began to glow and the water around her began to calm. Blindly her hand reached up and gripped the jeweled necklace as she turned pleading eyes towards Kerian, now totally submerged in the water and struggling to hold his breath. "End this! Please!"

"The Woman of Legend!" the Lady breathed and just as suddenly as the squall started, it ended.

With a loud splash Kerian and Zorn's bubbles popped and they both crashed into the waters of the now calm lake. The woman, once again hidden by her long blue hair, stepped back and with a wave of her arm, sent a wall of water rushing up to the beach, depositing a coughing, choking Kerian and a water-logged Zorn at her feet.

"Thank you!" Brieana cried as she dropped to her knees and lifted Kerian's head into her lap. "Thank you."

She dropped her forehead over Kerian's, her hair falling to cover their faces, as she dropped tearful kisses across his forehead and hugged him to her pounding heart.

"You are the Woman of Legend. It is said that you will come to deliver peace to this ravaged land. And I don't talk funny! Everybody spoke like this during the twentieth century!"

While Kerian struggled to regain his breath, Brieana raised a tear-ravaged face to the Lady.

"I am sorry you are here alone, but you need not be. If I can help you in any way, please let me know."

"You, help me? Don't make me laugh! You can do nothing for me human, but you do owe me a boon. For sparing his life, or did you not mean your pretty words?"

"I meant them!" Brieana was quick to assure her. "I will give you almost anything."

"Almost?" the woman said with a sneer.

"I am learning how to deal with people of magic," she choked out.

"You are not as stupid as you look," the Lady allowed.

As Brieana bristled, the Lady ignored her and settled herself tailor style on the calm waters of her lake.

Merlin's Kiss

"I will give you the sword — you are destined to possess it — but it won't work for you until you figure out the secret."

"Secret?" Kerian had pulled himself up to a sitting position, and after checking on Zorn, turned to face the woman who had almost ended his days.

"I see you are with us, tall, platinum and handsome," she quipped, obviously enjoying the way the wet leather became waterlogged and pulled down to expose Kerian's hard muscles to her avid gaze.

"I thought once she possessed the sword, the power would be hers?" Long used to being a pawn in someone's game, Kerian disregarded his near-death experience and in true Kerian form, moved on to the next adventure in this quest.

"So did Arthur-boy. And all it got him was a watery grave."

Brieana blinked a little at this, but otherwise showed no other reaction. Dead was dead, and she had accepted his death the moment she awoke in this time.

"Why did it not work for him?" she finally asked as she turned to assist a dazed Zorn to his feet. The purple drack was a bit woozy but otherwise seemed fine. He snorted water from his nose and eyed the stranger with contempt.

"Because that immature, ignorant, pissant was ruled by his penis and not his heart. It is not a pretty tale. Come back at a later date and I will tell it to you. As for now, I am tired and ready to seek my sleep. We will continue this tomorrow!"

"Tomorrow?" Brieana wailed as she jumped to her feet, Zorn forgotten as she took in the Lady's words.

"Tomorrow!" the Lady stressed. "I have had enough excitement for one night and wish to retire. I will deal with you tomorrow."

With that, the Lady seemed to melt before their eyes, so quickly did she descend under the water.

"Of all the nerve!" Brieana huffed, arms akimbo.

Stephanie Burke

"Yes, of all the nerve," Kerian stated as he struggled to his feet.

He felt a little dizzy but he assumed it was an aftereffect of almost drowning.

"What do you mean?" Brieana asked when she saw he was staring directly at her.

"I have never seen such selfishness in my life! You were supposed to run and save yourself for the Kingdom! But instead you stand and barter with a madwoman. What would have happened to the Isles if you had been killed?"

All semblance of control had been stripped from Kerian as his anger burst forth with every word! Standing there and facing his own death was hard enough, but to watch her barter her life for his, well, that cleared up any confusion and doubt that he had. It also stripped away the protective shell that allowed him to control his emotions.

"I do not give a damn what happens to this world!" Brieana screamed, losing herself in the emotional release of anger. "What good is my kingdom if I don't have my dream?"

"Camelot is your dream!" he yelled back, walking closer to stand toe to toe with her.

"Camelot is my destiny! You are my dream, you idiot!"

"What?" Kerian's face went slack as he absorbed her words. "Me? I am…"

"You are my dream, Kerian!" she declared, quieter this time but with no less emotion. "I have come to realize that I can live anywhere, at any time, and not truly be alive. Camelot is my destiny, by right of honor and birth. You are my dream. Without you, my kingdom will be shallow and my victories tasteless. There is a difference between living and being alive, Kerian. You make me truly alive!"

Merlin's Kiss

Chapter Seventeen

"I make you feel alive?" he asked, a bit dazed and wondering if he had heard her correctly. He shook his head to dislodge any stray droplets of water, then focused his attention upon her once again.

"My very body tingles with your every touch, Kerian. Did you not know? Could you not sense how I felt?"

Kerian stood there, water dripping off of the ends of his hair, utterly amazed. Her green eyes were glowing with some emotion he would rather leave unnamed and that gaze was directed solely at him.

"Lady Brieana, are you sure you know what you are speaking of? I understand if you need my strength to lean upon, or if my body satisfies an urge in yours, but what you are saying..."

"I love you, Kerian!" she finally cried out, unable to contain her excitement any longer. "I love you with every breath in my being!" Brieana blinked as if a weight had been lifted from her heart with her admission. She loved her Warlord! She wanted to shout it to the world! She loved her Kerian, and he set her free!

Kerian's eyes grew wider as understanding shone in his amber eyes. What he was hearing was too good to be true, but the more he watched her excited, sweet face, the more he wanted to believe.

"You love...me?"

"From the moment I laid eyes on you! From the moment you held me on Zorn's back! From the moment you touched me, Kerian. I was destined to find you one day, I just never knew it would take hundreds of thousands of years."

Unable to keep his hands to himself any longer, Kerian leaned closer yet and grabbed Brieana up in his powerful, wet

Stephanie Burke

embrace. Almost delirious with joy, he clasped her small rounded body closer to him as if he wanted to absorb her into his very being.

"Brieana, I am not worthy," he began as he looked down at her happy face. With a trembling hand, he reached out to caress the face that had haunted all of his dreams and tormented his soul.

Reaching up with both hands, Brieana drew his treasured face down to hers. Lips barely touching, she whispered, "Of course you are."

Then there were no more words. As her soft warm breath wafted over his face, Kerian again lost his tenacious grip on his control. With a savage groan, his mouth dropped down to plunder her willing lips.

The taste of her was heaven! Never had he tasted anything sweeter than her lips. He savored her special flavor. It exploded in his mouth and conquered his senses. His tongue plunged in deeper for another taste of once-forbidden delights. His knees began to tremble as her tongue eagerly swept out to taste his.

"Lady," he breathed after tearing his mouth away. "If we continue like this, I will have you on the ground beneath me in a matter of seconds."

"Promise?" she whispered and pulled his head back down to hers, confident he would carry out his threat and eager to feel his hard body closer to hers. The Warlord always meant what he said.

With a groan, Kerian swung Brieana up in his arms and almost stumbled over Zorn, who was eyeing them with curiosity.

Taste good, does she? he smirked.

"Go away!" they both shouted.

With a sniff and a last shake of his purple body, Zorn departed the area, that strange look on his face yet again. "*Await, the chickens do!*" he declared as he regally turned his back and sauntered away.

Merlin's Kiss

Shaking his head at the fates which allowed such a creature to torment him, Kerian turned back to the damp bundle of woman snuggled in his arms.

"I've made you all wet," he spoke softly as he buried his nose in her neck, inhaling her flowery scent.

"How did you know?" she blurted out, then blushed as she realized he was speaking of her clothes. "Ah, pay me no heed, my love."

Kerian smiled at her admission but doubled his speed as he carried her to the blankets that they had earlier spread out.

"Will you now show me how to make love?" she asked as he placed her on her feet and began to struggle with the wet ties of her tunic.

"Will you show me how to love, period?" he countered as he paused in his mad rush to undress her. "Will you show me how to open this heart I once thought dead, Brieana? Will you show me the way?"

"Yes, Kerian, yes," she breathed as she took a step closer to her beloved and wrapped her arms around his waist in a tight embrace, trying to impart her feelings with touch alone.

She gripped the wet material of his vest and moaned as she felt his hard muscles shift beneath her questing hands.

"I have to taste you again," he growled before his mouth latched onto hers.

Stars danced behind her closed eyes as he very slowly stole her breath and returned it to her. Her hand reached up to tangle in his long platinum locks and she moaned her pleasure into his mouth.

"That's it," he breathed against her. "Feel me."

With a glad cry, she tightened her hold on him, forcing the kiss to go on longer, deeper, until all she could feel, smell, taste was him.

Tearing his lips from hers, he began to impatiently tug at her tunic, pulling it over her head.

Stephanie Burke

"I have to touch you," he muttered as he managed to yank the wet leather over her head, then gasped at the perfection of her. He had seen glimpses of her wondrous beauty when he first rescued her from her stony prison. But this...

"You are beautiful indeed!"

Brieana felt a blush steal up her face as Kerian stood there in the warm evening air mesmerized by the sight of her. Her breasts felt full and swollen as he took his time and examined her closely. She had never imagined an intimacy such as this, but she put her embarrassment aside. She wanted to see what would happen next.

His mouth went dry at the thought of taking each berry-colored nipple into his mouth and drinking his fill. Would she taste as sweet as she looked? She stood there, looking up at him as if she were some fertility goddess of old, and he found he could not resist her lure.

Reaching out one single finger, he traced the areola of one plump breast and smiled as she gasped in surprised pleasure.

"Kerian?" she whispered, frightened by these intense feelings that had sprung up between them. Never had she felt so strongly about anything or wanted something so much.

"Be at ease, Brieana," he crooned as he dropped to his knees in front of her. "Let me love you."

His mouth was a moist furnace that burned her with pleasure. Brieana closed her eyes and tightened her grip on his hair as his tongue whipped out and lapped at her nipple. Her eyes widened at the sensation, then closed on a shuddering sigh as he pulled it inside. She moaned as he applied a gentle suction, pulling at her turgid flesh.

Brieana felt as if her knees would give away. His mouth caused surging waves of delight to travel down her body and center in her private woman's place.

Kerian groaned deeply in his throat as he felt her nipple harden further in his mouth. Her taste was divine, her scent addictive, and he had to have more.

Merlin's Kiss

With gentle hands he guided her onto the blankets, then smiled down at the hungry look in her eyes.

Reaching up one hand, she stroked the wet material of his vest. "Take it off." She wanted only to feel his warm skin against her. She had fantasized about the feel of his body and she didn't want to be cheated of that pleasure.

Gaze fastened to hers, Kerian reached down and loosened the cords that held the war vest closed. With one motion, he whipped the constraining garment over his head and tossed his hair behind him.

Brieana shuddered, the nerves tingling down her back, and her nipples hardened even more as she saw his exposed chest. Her skin vibrated with need and the desire to touch what she was now gazing upon. She did not have to wait long.

Kerian rested his arms on either side of her head and lowered his chest, just enough that her erect nipples brushed against the smooth, hairless expanse of chest.

"You burn," she moaned as she tossed her head back, opening herself to his possession.

"For you," he breathed as he skimmed his lips along her exposed neck, inhaling her scent, letting his tongue dart out to taste her.

"I want more," she purred, her hands reaching up to tangle in his damp hair.

Never one to deny her requests, Kerian lowered his head and latched onto her straining nipple again, this time pulling powerfully at her tender flesh.

Brieana parted her leather-clad legs and pulled him tighter to her as she felt his hardness, contained by his wet leggings, pressing against her heated center.

Groaning deeply, Kerian began a slow grinding motion with his hips.

"Oh God!" Brieana cried out as she tossed her head back and rode the waves of pleasure he created within her. His hard hips pressed firmly against her, holding her legs wide apart for

Stephanie Burke

his gentle assault. Instinctively, she clamped her thighs tighter, attempting to protect her secrets, but the firm pressure she applied to his thighs only made everything more intense.

She felt one of his hands reach down between them and slide to the ties of her leggings. A deep aching need settled in her abdomen and she arched helplessly, repeatedly against his touch.

"Help me, Brieana," he gritted out as he pulled his mouth away from her hardened nipple and moved so he could rip her boots from those feet he so enjoyed looking at. Next he tried to make his trembling fingers ease her leggings away from the core of her body he wanted so very much to bury himself in.

Brieana realized her own clothes had absorbed the lake water from Kerian's wet garments. Joyfully, she lifted her hips and felt the cold clammy material being eased past her hips. Glad to be rid of the confining clothing, Brieana sighed and urged Kerian to hurry. These new feelings were wonderful, and drugging. Like a person addicted to sensuality, she waited breathlessly for more.

Tossing her leggings over his shoulder, he again rose above her. With burning eyes, she watched as he slowly loosened the leather tie holding his last covering up. Unconsciously, she licked at lips suddenly gone dry as he slowly undressed for her pleasure. The she sucked in her breath at what was revealed — muscular thighs, lean flanks, and just the hint of an aroused cock.

Standing on his feet, Kerian kicked aside his boots and bending at the waist, eased the last of his clothing off. He hesitated, debating whether or not to expose his fully engorged self to her gaze, but decided it was now or never.

As he stood, proud and aroused before her, Brieana's eyes widened in shock then in apprehension.

"I don't think it will fit!" she breathed as she took in his immense member, all swollen and throbbing and sticking out from his body. "Did it hurt to be squeezed in those leggings?"

Merlin's Kiss

"No, Brieana, and we'll fit," he huffed, trying to keep his laughter within. Most women just stared at him in horrified wonder. His brave Brieana was more concerned about the fit of his clothes.

"Show me?" she asked, not exactly knowing what was going to happen, but knowing her Kerian was something special to behold.

As his large body covered hers, she parted her thighs to make a place for him.

Brieana shivered with delight as she finally came into contact with his hot firm flesh. Her body seemed to know and to welcome her bold warrior, and she could do no less.

With abandon, she threw her arms around his neck and urged him down.

"Will you put it in me now?" she asked as she wiggled closer to his heat. She had missed the feel of him and now savored the hair-roughened texture of his body.

"No, first I will prepare you."

"But I am prepared, Kerian." She wiggled closer to his heat, offering herself up for exploration. "I am wet. I know that I am. I can feel it! And the men always said wet and ready…"

"What?" Kerian's eyebrows rose to almost disappear into his hairline at her admission.

"The soldiers I fought with. They always said the women they liked best were wet and willing. I am willing and wet, Kerian, so will you put it in me now?"

Kerian lowered his forehead to rest against hers as he strove for his legendary control. What fools had she been listening to? But the insistent gyrations of her body were making it hard for him to think! When Brieana wanted something, she went after it with gusto and held nothing back.

"No, I will not, Brieana. Wet is not enough for me. I want you howling and writhing beneath me. I want you mindless with need. I want you to feel what I feel."

Stephanie Burke

Then there was no more time for talk.

Kerian's hands dipped low to discover the wet heat of her, just as his teeth lightly clamped on the vulnerable flesh where shoulder met neck.

Brieana gasped and arched off of the blankets at the powerful duel sensations. She cried out as she felt his fingertips part the soft thatch of hair that covered her secrets.

"Ah!" she shrieked in surprise as one rough finger parted her wet heat then searched for her small kernel of joy.

Kerian moaned as he encountered her creamy softness. Hot and damp, she was already more than prepared to take him. He fought against the urge to ravish her right there as he pictured his rod buried in her slippery heat. Instead, he reached higher and found what he was searching for.

"You are so swollen," he murmured to her as his mouth swooped down to hers again, drinking in her moans and gasps.

He began to rotate his finger in a small, circular motion, causing her hips to jerk and sway. He bit back a curse as he felt her willing response. Never had he had a woman so eager for the joining of their bodies.

Brieana felt as if ecstasy was tearing her body apart. Her head whipped from side to side on the blankets, flinging her hair wildly around her head as her hands fisted in his hair, tugging and pulling. She did not know what she begged and pleaded for, but whatever it was, it was building fast within her.

"Ohhhhh..." she wailed as tears filled her eyes from the awesome power of this act. She could feel her muscles tightening, drawing in, forcing the pleasure deeper, sharper.

"Kerian," she panted, pleading for...she did not know what! "Please!"

"That's it, love, come for me! Let it go!" he urged her on as he took nipping bites of her breasts. "Come on, Brieana, take it!"

Then suddenly her body arched completely off the blanket. "Kerian!" she screamed as the powerful waves of release poured

Merlin's Kiss

through her, making her inner muscles convulse, awakening her to the pleasures of being a woman.

"Yes, love, yes," he purred as he watched her body writhe in rapture.

"Oh," she gasped as the sensations eased off, but stayed just below the surface, simmering. Her trembling arms slid weightlessly from his shoulders and tears filled her eyes, so intense were her emotions.

"Did you enjoy that, Lady?" he rasped as he nursed at her nipple, kneading her breast. "Would you like more?"

"Is there more, Kerian?" she panted, not believing anything could feel as good as that.

"Watch," he commanded as he flipped the long strands of his hair forward to cover her chest.

Brieana moaned as she felt the silken strands of hair sensuously trail over her body. Each cool caress was like a soft kiss, a kiss that trailed lightning in its wake.

Kerian's mouth trailed lower and lower down her body. She felt his hands at her thighs, separating her pliant flesh and making way for his wide shoulders.

"Kerian?" she began, a little uncertain.

"Feel me," he whispered against the tight skin of her stomach as his hands cupped and lifted her bottom for this new invasion.

First she felt his warm breath against the drenched skin of her woman's opening. She felt the startling contrast of the cool air he blew against her burning flesh that made her knees shake uncontrollably. Then she jumped, tense and waiting as he placed a small kiss there.

"I'm going to taste you now," he murmured as his tongue lashed out and quickly sampled her feminine honey.

"Mmm," he groaned, causing her to blush. "Sweet and tangy."

Stephanie Burke

"Kerian," she began, determined to put an end to this delightfully wicked game and get on with the joining. Although she enjoyed this love play, she was curious about the act itself, and wanted to know how he felt inside of her.

But he held her fast as he slowly buried his face in her sex!

"Oh!" she wailed as his rough tongue lapped at her richness and his greedy lips tugged at her throbbing nubbin.

Kerian groaned in response as he thoroughly enjoyed the flavors and textures of his woman. This was a pleasure he never thought to experience, so he relished each wiggling twist of her hips as he immersed himself in her warm, wet offering.

Her hands pounded at his shoulders as he latched onto her vibrating clitoris and gently suckled. This was too much, the heat was too intense, the fire was too hot, the plateau was rising higher and higher.

Kerian reached one hand up and, grasping a handful of his hair, began to rub her nipples, adding extra stimulation to her shuddering body. Then her thighs clamped around his head and his control broke.

With a low shout, Kerian dragged himself up her body, closing his eyes as his hardness dragged against her softness. Pulling one of her hands between them, he molded and shaped himself to her palm. His whole body started as she clasped him in her soft moist hands.

Tentatively, she explored his flesh, marveling at his satiny feel. How could something so hard feel so soft? He felt like the softest of down in her hand. She ran one finger over the raised veins and throbbing skin of his male member and wondered if he would pulse inside her body as well. A drop of wetness pearled up on its tip and she ran a finger through it, delighted to know he became wet for her as well.

"Guide me home, Brieana," he panted, his eyes closed and his mind spinning. Her gentle explorations were sending him over the edge, breaking his control.

"Yes, please!"

174

Merlin's Kiss

But first her hand continued to explore his rigid staff, marveling at its soft texture that concealed an iron core. The heat he gave off was incredible.

At his broken groan, she finally parted her legs wide and led him to the drenched portal of her deepest self.

"Tell me if I hurt you." Again he rested on his elbows above her and tangled his large hands in her soft curls. "Promise me, Brieana," he ordered.

She nodded, breath held waiting for this life-altering experience to begin. She felt as if she was preparing to go into battle, her body flushed with apprehension and excitement. But the battle she now fought was between the blankets and it was sure to be explosive!

"Yes," she gasped, pulling at him, now a bit impatient with how slow he was moving. "I promise, Kerian! I promise!"

Giving in to both of their desires, Kerian pushed forward and sucked in a deep breath at the feel of her scalding heat. Her rich feminine juices bathed the head of his rod and he fought against the urge to pump unrestrainedly into her untried flesh.

Brieana's eyes widened as she felt the large round head of his sex slip inside her. This was a feeling she had never experienced and didn't quite know how to put into words. It was like becoming a part of him, like they were becoming one. The stretching was a bit alarming but was not so uncomfortable as to make her stop him. In fact, it only built up the waves of pleasure coursing through her body, enhancing them tenfold.

"Easy," he murmured, not knowing if he was speaking to her or to himself, and pushed himself in a little deeper.

She was a scalding vise! He closed his eyes and gritted his teeth as her wet sheath slowly accepted his presence.

Impatient with this slow taking, she wrapped her legs around his waist and tightened her muscles, pulling him in faster. She felt he was going too slowly to bring her the pleasure she craved and sought to speed him up a bit.

Stephanie Burke

"Brieana," he groaned as he reached around to try and loosen her grip.

"No, Kerian! Now!" she cried out, her breath coming in pants.

The swirling/falling feeling was returning to her body, but this time, much more powerfully. Much more intensely, just much more!

Kerian groaned his surrender and gripped her waist within his powerful grasp. With one smooth steady motion, he thrust himself into her portal, feeling her small membrane tear. Quickly arching his body lower, he pushed and probed until he reached the very core of her. Shuddering and cursing under his breath, he halted himself to give her time to adjust to his invasion.

"Ouch!" That hurt! But as soon as she vocalized her pain, the sharp sting began to ease. "Ohh!" she sighed, eyes wide as she felt his heart beating from within his male member.

"Kerian, I can feel you!" Her amazed look made him bend down and place a soft kiss on her slack mouth, lapping and moistening her dry lips.

"You feel so good," he purred, giving in and gently rocking his hips against her.

She closed her eyes and moaned as sensation built quickly again, stealing her breath and her reason. Kerian was a large, hard mass inside of her; a throbbing heated gift that touched her senses and promised greater passion to come. Never had she felt this full, this weak, yet powerful, and so complete!

Kerian rose above her, now easing himself almost completely out of her before slowly moving himself back in, soothing her with his gentle movements.

Her hands caressed his back as she began to learn the rhythm of this act. Slowly, but soon moving faster, she matched his rhythm and begged for more.

The hard ribbed feel of him sliding out and pumping back into her heat made her hunger grow! She became a desperate,

Merlin's Kiss

clawing thing, tightening around his length to hold him within, and relaxing her gripping muscles to welcome him back home. It was too much, it was not enough, it was loving Kerian.

Kerian felt his nerves sparkle along his lower back. With each sliding pull of his body, he felt pressure building faster and tighter within his body. Streaks of sharp ecstasy flashed around his body, making his breathing harsh, his skin sheen with sweat, his heart pound in his chest. And his precious Brieana was with him every step of the way.

"It's happening again!" she cried out suddenly as the fire in her body made her legs stiffen and her toes point. A storm broke within her, tossing her body as her inner walls suddenly clamped down on his hardness.

"Kerian!" she screamed as her powerful climax tore through her body, leaving her limp and trembling in his arms.

Kerian felt the rhythmic gripping of her body and lost all threads of his tattered control. With one mighty thrust that shifted their bodies closer together, his seed exploded within her, giving her his life's essence, offering her his soul.

"My love," he cried out as her body drained everything he had to offer, making his arms tremble and his chest heave.

Easing to her side, he pulled her quaking body into the comforting shelter of his. They held on to each other, shaking with the intensity of their release, providing comfort.

"I love you," she murmured against the damp skin of his chest.

"More than my life," he countered as he held her shivering body closer.

Chapter Eighteen

"I have never felt such a thing," Brieana purred as she stroked Kerian's damp hair back from his face.

Unable to put into words his feelings, Kerian grunted and pulled her closer to the warm shelter of his body.

Smiling at his reticence, Brieana ran her fingers over his back, then paused as she felt something other than the smooth firm flesh that covered the rest of his body.

"Kerian? What's this?" She knew she had breached some cut-off place within him, for he stiffened up and pulled away from her.

"It's nothing," he said as he pulled her hands from the raised scars on his back.

"Well, that's a big nothing," she said as she sat up and looked at her lover in the firelight he just moments ago pulled himself away from her to build. His concern for her health and comfort was another way he proved his love for her. But her love for him was making her anxious. Had he been hurt and she knew nothing of it? What was going on?

Rolling to his back, Kerian glared at her for a moment. Then he sighed. Brieana had a right to know.

"You should know the kind of man you have promised yourself to, Brieana. After this, if you want to leave me, I will understand."

"Does this have to do with your claim of having an empty heart, Kerian?" she asked then shivered.

Noting her discomfort, Kerian sat up and draped a blanket over her bare shoulders. Even with the fire burning, there was a chill in the air. Besides, the sight of her breasts, so rosy after their lovemaking, had started a stir of desire in his previously sated body, and he wanted to have a clear head when he spoke to her.

178

Merlin's Kiss

He looked to his wet leggings and turned away with a grimace. He reached for his saddlebags, then he heard her gasp. He had forgotten about his back, and now it was exposed to her in all of its lashed and scarred glory.

Brieana raised her hand to her mouth to hold in her cry of shock. Kerian's back was a mass of raised welts from shoulder to waist. There was barely an inch of skin that was not scarred. What monster would do such a thing?

"I guess there is no point in trying to hide it now, is there?" His voice matter-of-fact, the bags forgotten, he turned to face her again.

"Who?" she gasped out, tears filling her eyes. "Who did this to you?"

"Does it matter?" he sighed, hating the tears that filled her eyes. "Save your pity, Brieana. Don't waste your tears on the past."

"These are not tears of pity, you fool!" she called out, angered he would think that she would pity him. "These are tears of anger! Who did this to you, so that I may cut their hands from their bodies and give them the same treatment?"

Kerian blinked at her bloodthirsty response. Again he had underestimated his beautiful queen. She would never pity him; she would seek to find the person who had hurt him then exact her revenge.

"You can't do that, Brieana."

"And pray tell me why not?" she demanded, pulling the blanket tighter around her as if to keep her hatred inside until it was time to unleash it on the bastard who had harmed her man.

"Because he is dead, Brieana. He died a long time ago."

"And what did your conniving stepmother and father do to you? Did they exact punishment for this?"

"It was my father, Brieana."

"What?" Her horrified cry filled the air, as her eyes grew even wider at the thought. "Your father did this?"

179

Stephanie Burke

Brieana did not have many memories/recollections of her parents, but she did remember that her mother was loving and kind, and that her father was her fierce defender. To have a father so abuse a child was unthinkable to her!

"He held no love for me, Brieana. I was a necessary heir."

"But…but…why?" She still didn't understand. She moved closer to Kerian and took his hand in hers. He smiled down at the sight of her lending him strength and comfort.

"Because he felt I was evil, Brieana. He sought to rid me of the evil by routine floggings."

"But why?" Brieana was horrified! How could a person think his or her own flesh was evil?

"How many others do you see speaking with dracks?"

That gave her a pause.

"No one else spoke with the dracks, Brieana, until you showed up."

"But that is no cause to suspect evil!" she insisted.

"Maybe, but my mother died in childbirth and I believe my father blamed me. For as long as I can remember, he was cold and aloof towards me. The only comfort I had was from the strange whispers in the night, urging me to fly away to freedom."

"Voices, Kerian?" she asked, becoming enthralled by his tale. "What voices?"

"It was Gren. She had heard my lonely ramblings and thinking that I was a fellow drack held captive, urged me to fly away to the mountains. So one day, I did."

"How old were you?" she asked, snuggling closer to his warmth.

"I was maybe six or seven cycles old."

"And no one noticed you were gone?" She was incredulous! For a child to sneak away and no one noticed he was gone smacked of neglect.

180

Merlin's Kiss

"My father never cared, Brieana. And because of that, my nurses were lax in their attentions."

"But you were a child!" she insisted.

"Yes, Brieana. A child who climbed from his bed in the middle of the night and climbed the Dark Mountains."

Remembering the killer rabbits and other dangers they had passed on the way to the drackoon's lair, Brieana shuddered.

"But it was not as bad as you imagine. The drackoons roamed the land freely then. With them out hunting at night, there were few dangers that I faced. Besides, any drackoon coming upon me would have thought I was a youthling lost in the dark. I could hear their thoughts and they could hear mine. But it was Gren I had listened for. It was her voice that comforted me when the days had become especially hard. When I stumbled upon her, I don't know who was more surprised, her or me. I had always entertained the fantasy that she was my mother, not dead, but run away from my father, and that she was calling me to her."

"Gren, startled?" Brieana chuckled. It was hard for her to picture the sage drackoon anything but composed and confident.

"Yes, she was startled," he smiled, "but no more than I. After she called me and I answered, she decided I was her non-son. For nearly a month, I lived with her and Dalis, learning the ways of the drack."

"The ways of the drack," Brieana giggled. She could picture a small, wild-haired Kerian growling and racing around with the large drackoons in their lair.

"I often did more harm than good, but because Gren took me under her wing, so to speak, Dalis decided I would make a fine drack. It was he who first began training me in strategy. I remember him telling me to anticipate what my opponent was thinking, to fight fiercely, but to use my head. In those days, the drackoons lived much closer to Mirage than they do now. So when my father finally discovered I was missing and sent out a search party, Dalis's scouts told him what was happening. I didn't want to return to the cold castle with my father, Brieana, but Gren told me a wise man would learn all he could before he made his way alone in the world. I returned to my father, and even he was surprised to find me well and hearty after almost a month in the wilds. When he asked me what had happened, I told him I was with my True-mother and that she told me to return."

"I can imagine his reaction," Brieana mused.

"I don't think you can," Kerian laughed. "He told every one of his soldiers I was going to be the best Warlord Mirage had ever seen. He was proud I lasted for that long in the wild, and sought to make me his best warrior."

"Typical man," she grinned up at him. "And I bet he took the credit for raising you."

"That he did." Kerian looked to the heavens as if searching for an answer, but shook his head and returned to his story.

"I was put through the most rigorous training he could create. Every morning there were exercises in strength and skill, and every evening that I could, I sneaked off to the mountains to be with Gren and Dalis."

"Poor baby," she soothed, rubbing his chest.

"It wasn't that bad." He grinned down at her, pulling her closer to him and wrapping the blanket closer around her. "At least until my father found out I was still sneaking off."

"Then you were no longer his perfect warrior," she guessed.

"He found me sitting on a boulder looking over Mirage and speaking with one of Gren's sons. Then he went a little mad, because he could see I was speaking to the drack in my mind."

Kerian shuddered a little at the memory of that night, but that was all the emotion he showed.

"I remember him racing towards me, sword drawn and daring this hell beast to harm me. I remember jumping in front of my father and telling Pacal to run. When I stopped my father

Merlin's Kiss

from murdering that drack and told him he was my friend, he went a little mad. He dragged me home and locked me in my room. He forbade me to even mention Gren or any of the drackoons again. He said I was unnatural and unfit to be seen. The only time I was let out was for weapons training and that was with a heavily armed guard. But I still managed to elude him." Kerian laughed at that one.

"I was quite the little sneak, scaling the walls of Mirage at night, hiding in the shadows, blending in. Those were the things Dalis had taught me, and I used his lessons well. But always my father would find me and drag me back. Soon everyone knew I communicated with the drackoon. Hell, if one passed close to the castle, everyone else ran for cover, but I stood outside and had a long conversation and sent word of my health to Gren. My father hated that. Even he was afraid to venture forth when the drackoons were out."

They shared a chuckle over that one, and Brieana reached up to drop a kiss on his chin.

"That's when he found me a new mother, Shala." All laughter stopped.

"What did she do?" Brieana asked, still feeling hatred towards the woman who had drugged her and raped her mind.

"Nothing. But with Shala came the beatings."

"Why would your father beat you, Kerian? What made him think he could beat the evil out of you after all of that?"

"I know not, Brieana, but after my father married the lovely Shala, every evening he would come to my room with his whips and he would hold a cleansing session."

Kerian's eyes went dark as he recalled his father tying him down to the bed, tearing his night robes from his body, and swearing to rid him of the inclination to talk to wicked dracks. He remembered the searing pain of the lash, the cold anger he felt as his father proceeded to tell him he did it for love—that Kerian had to be made normal.

Stephanie Burke

"How old were you?" Brieana asked softly, noticing the anguish on his face even his usual control could not hide.

"The beatings started off and on when I was eight, Brieana, and they lasted until I was sixteen. By then he had his two favored soldiers hold me down for my lessons. But it was Shala, more or less, who made my father cease when he really got lost in his madness and nearly killed me. It was after such a time I finally grew tired of his abuse and ran away."

"Where did you go?" she asked, feeling pain for the young man he had been.

"I ran to Gren. She long knew about the beatings and had launched several attacks in retaliation. Never harming anyone, but freezing my father's stable doors closed or scattering his chum after each beating. I don't recall if he was more frightened at that time or just angered more by what he considered the evils beasts' defense of me. It made him look bad in the eyes of his people for them to know a beast of the fields held me in higher regard than he."

"What happened?" Brieana asked after several moments of quiet.

"I picked a bad time to run away. Pacal had disappeared and Dalis and his scouts were out looking for him. Gren was about to go into lying-in with hatching of eggs and was alone when I arrived bloody from my latest beating and almost out of my mind with pain. I didn't know this, but my father had expected me to run away, planned for it, so there was a soldier always watching my room. He reported to my father where I had gone and the bloody trail I left led them straight to Gren. She was applying some ancient remedy to my back when my father arrived at the lair. I don't remember much, but I do remember him threatening to kill my True-mother and putting an end to all of 'this drackoon nonsense.' I believe he was going to destroy Gren's and Dalis's eggs too! I couldn't let him destroy my brothers and sisters, let alone my True-mother."

"Of course, you could not!" Brieana cried out, shocked a father would murder the innocent and harm his son further.

184

Merlin's Kiss

"I remember racing towards him. I had never been a small child, Brieana, and it was out of parental respect that I never raised my hand to my father. Gren taught me that. But this was too much for me to take. I used the lessons my father had taught me to engage him in combat. I still don't remember all that happened, Brieana, and Gren will never tell me, but that night, I bested my father, unarmed, and he fell from the cliff heights to his death."

Brieana sucked in a deep breath at the thought of the pain Kerian must have experienced, knowing his father died by his hands.

"His soldiers with him said it was a fair fight. I believe they said that more out of fear of the drackoon's retaliation than anything else. Dalis and his scouts had returned at the conclusion of the fight and surrounded my father's men. I remember begging Dalis to let them go, and Gren saying the same. So the men were freed to return to Mirage and I stayed behind with Gren."

"I am so sorry, Kerian," Brieana crooned as she wrapped her arms around him, pulling him closer to her.

"I developed a fever that lasted a long time, then I had to regain my strength. I never wanted to step foot inside Mirage again, but then the hunting began. I don't know who ordered it, and maybe I never will, but there were soon mass huntings for drackoons taking place. I had to do something; I couldn't let the soldiers from Mirage kill off my family. So I returned, smarter and wiser."

"Of course you did!" Brieana declared, knowing the determination that ran within him. "You had to take your place to protect Gren."

Kerian smiled down at Brieana. Any other woman would be calling him odd and a murderer by now, but not his Brieana. She saw things others didn't.

"But the people refused to believe it was me, at first. I had to best my father's old first in command to even be heard. Then,

185

Stephanie Burke

with Shala's help, I took over the reins of leadership and enacted the treaty that protected the drackoons as long as they stayed off Mirage land. That was the hardest thing I had ever done, but I had no choice. Soon Dalis and Gren moved to their lair deep within the Dark Mountains and there they settled. I had to give up my family to keep them safe. Rarely did I get the chance to visit, to plan strategy with Dalis, to get snuffles from Gren, to see the brothers and sisters I protected, but it was worth it."

"You are a special man, Kerian." Brieana sighed as she pulled his mouth down to hers for a deep, wet kiss. "That is why I love you so much," she breathed into his mouth.

"And I...love you, Brieana," he returned, a little uncertain. "With every breath of my being."

"Then show me," she purred as she dropped the blanket. "Show me how much."

"With pleasure," he moaned as he crushed her naked body to his.

Brieana gasped at the contact, still unsure of what to expect even after that first fiery round with her lover. But she anticipated the next move as her body became wet and swollen, ready to take inside whatever her man thrust upon her.

Her eyelids dropped as her hands came up to tangle in his hair. She whimpered at the silky feel of it sliding through her fingers, and tightened her fist in it, pulling his mouth down to hers.

His tongue invaded her mouth, carrying with it his special taste, making her moan and try her best to get closer.

She arched her back, forcing her body against his, and pressing her aroused nipples into the muscled wall of his chest.

Kerian trembled as he felt her legs part to drop him into the seat of her pleasure center.

Her hands slid to his neck, holding on tightly as he felt her knees slowly slide up his sides to clamp tightly around his waist.

Merlin's Kiss

"I need you to be in me," Brieana whispered. "I need that," she bumped her hips against his growing cock, "inside me so badly, Kerian. I need you to be inside of me. I just need you."

"This?" he asked as he did a slow grind against her, the swollen head of his cock running along her moist cleft.

Brieana whimpered and arched herself higher, trying to force him to take her to where her growing need would wipe all thought from her mind.

"This?" Kerian asked again, still not believing this beautiful magical creature was his, belonged to him and him alone.

"Oh yes, Kerian," Brieana whimpered, tugging at his hard body.

The fire from their previous joining was not extinguished, only banked. And now with his words and actions, he was stoking the coals, making her desire for him burn red-hot.

Remembering that she would likely be sore from her first real sexual experience, Kerian placed the mushroom-shaped head of his cock at her entrance, and then gave a slight push.

"Ahh!" Brieana gasped as she felt the thick tip of his cock enter her. "Kerian!"

But just as gently, he eased out before thrusting back in, giving her only an inch of his throbbing cock.

Brieana's legs tightened around him, trying to force his heavy hardness inside her, but using his greater strength, Kerian held back, feeding his cock to her one inch at a time.

"You are killing me," she gasped as slow waves of pleasure began to rock her body.

"I am loving you," he whispered as he slipped his arms under her back, his hands cupping her shoulders, holding her tightly to him as he breathed in her ear.

Helplessly, she let her head fall back to the blankets, his thumbs caressing the sides of her face as his head lowered to nip and kiss at her neck.

Stephanie Burke

Again she whimpered, her body shuddering under his caresses and slow penetration.

As he thrust a bit harder, a bit deeper, he began to lick at the soft skin of her neck, flooding his mouth with her beloved flavor.

But he continued with his slow thrusts and parries, giving her just an inch more with each plunge.

In this position, all control had just about been taken away, and Brieana reveled in it!

Here was someone to take care of her, someone who had her desires at heart, someone who would lead her body into this erotic dance and deliver her into the jaws of sensuous paradise. And she gave in, letting the feeling totally overwhelm her, lost in the sensations her Warlord was giving her.

"More?" Kerian asked, noting the glazed look in her eyes and her ragged breathing.

For the past few moments, she had begun to gasp and whine vocally, telling him of her pleasure in this sex act, no, this act of love.

"I can't...I can't..." she moaned, her head tossing side to side as if denying the pleasure he was bringing.

Her body was going wild, his slow thrusts building to something almost fearsome deep inside of her. She wanted it to stop; she never wanted it to stop. It felt so good!

"Please!"

Her muscles began to tighten and spasm of their own accord, reaching, searching for something she had had a taste of once. Her body knew what it wanted, and it was now relying on her mate to see her through to the end.

Seeing her frazzled state, Kerian smiled as he pulled one hand from behind her and eased it between their heaving, sweating bodies.

"Are you ready?" he softly asked as he nipped at her shoulder and then licked away the small pain.

Merlin's Kiss

"Kerian," she whimpered, lost in a sensual haze.

"Take it," he grunted, then slammed full force into her convulsing body.

"Yes, Kerian! More!" She began to beg, then screamed as wave after wave of pure ecstasy slammed though her body.

"My god," Kerian gasped as he realized he was holding a wildcat in his arms.

Struggling for control, he slipped his fingers through the moist swollen folds of her flesh to gently circle her clit with the pad of one finger.

Her body arched so high it almost bucked him off of her.

She was emitting these little wordless screams and cried as he pressed the swollen lips of her sex against the thrusting hardness of his cock, intensifying the feeling of each thrust.

Suddenly her body froze, stiffening under him while fierce trembling took hold of her.

Her eyes popped open and her mouth opened.

"I'm... Oh, Kerian... Oh... Ahh!"

She began to scream as the tension broke and the force of her orgasm slammed her back into the blankets.

"Brieana!" Kerian managed as he felt her walls rhythmically tighten and release his cock, sending lightning bolts through his cock, up his spine, and back down to his balls.

He felt them tighten and pull up as his cock swelled in the midst of the storm of release.

"Brieana," he groaned as his hips uncontrollably thrust into her, sending his seed deeper, filling her with his white-hot essence.

Shuddering and laboring to breathe, Kerian collapsed on top of her, his head by hers, and he sucked in lungfuls of air.

"Kerian," Brieana said softly, and that alone empowered him enough to roll to his side and bring her body flush to his, pulling her leg over his thigh so they could remain joined.

Stephanie Burke

He loved the slick hot feel of her.

"I love you," he whispered as he reached one arm down to grab the blankets and tug them over their rapidly cooling bodies.

"Oh, how I love you," she responded, snuggling into the moist skin of his chest, drawing in the scent of him, of her, of sex.

She shuddered in the aftermath of her violent release, pulling herself even closer to him.

Closing her eyes, she quickly drifted off to sleep, a smile tugging at her lips.

He'd shown her how to fly without wings.

Merlin's Kiss

Chapter Nineteen

"Gather the men," the dark sensuous voice ordered. "I believe it is time we pay our Warlord a little visit. Don't you?"

Settling back comfortably on a large campstool, Dagon stretched his feet out in front of him and wiggled his bare toes in the plush carpet that lined the floor of his tent. Damn, but it was good to be the leader!

"My Lord." The response was snapped out and the man kneeling at the entrance of this sinfully decadent campaign tent slowly rose.

"And Tybo?" Dagon added as he met his second-in-command's eyes. "What do you think of these...little amusements?" He raised one leathery hand to his chin and smiled.

"I have no opinion, My Lord," Tybo said with a crisp reply as eyes that reflected the ever-changing colors of the rainbow stared steadily into hazy red ones.

"Yes, there seems to be a lot of that going around lately." His droll reply only stiffened the man's resolve as he waited for what his hated and feared ruler would say. Dagon did not disappoint.

"You know, Tybo, I think the reason that no one has an opinion is because no one thinks anymore. Everybody just acts out on his or her impulses, and soon you have a whole lot of stupid reaction without true planning or attention to details. Like mindless chum, one follows the other chasing their tails and baying at the sun. The people need a great ruler. It just so happens I fit that particular bill, to coin an ancient turn of phrase." His red eyes glittered brightly with his amusement as he relished each and every word that escaped his lips.

Stephanie Burke

"And now look at what we have! Chum still, but chum with a purpose! Now what can be a greater purpose than that of seeing my dreams fulfilled?" He raised one dark eyebrow and waited for a reaction. Baiting people was like talking to dracks. When you had the knack, you had the knack. And since only a few could talk to dracks, that made the knack of baiting people all the rarer.

Lazily he extended his wings, his dark leathery wings and compared them to the wings neatly folded on the young man's back. Where his were drab and dull this soldier's wings were light gossamer, looking barely capable of supporting his great weight, let alone flying. Light Magic pulsed through his young body and he possessed an innocent beauty he himself would never have again. Pity. He missed manipulating people with his looks alone. And for really forbidden acts of lust, it just never felt the same when your bed warmer was reluctant to touch certain parts of your body.

Oh, they all loved the man-root, but sometimes he just missed the feel of a woman's tongue lapping across his back or the feel of her wings fluttering against the skin of his thighs as he…But one mustn't digress. Power was greater than a need for feminine caresses. Besides, he had a little power-lusting whore of his own. Some people would just give anything for a taste of true power. Luckily, he was the type who knew how to take advantage of that weakness.

Refolding his wings, Dagon contemplated Tybo, the people's hero. From the time this one was born, Dagon had tried, without much success, to corrupt his young mind and utilize his Light Magic for his own purposes. But Tybo had proven disgustingly resistant to his little suggestions. How utterly boring! But now he was becoming a bit tired with the whole thing. Maybe it was time to stop trying. Maybe it was time to seek other amusements for this light creature.

"The people think, My Lord," finally came the expected reply. "They just don't express what is on their minds."

Merlin's Kiss

"And what is on their minds, young Tybo?" Dagon sneered. For all he cared, the people could, as they said in days long ago, go to hell. But wait, they were already there! Wasting away on the Dark Isles. He chuckled to himself as he settled more comfortably on his seat.

"That you are a vain, egotistical villain who won't stop until what's left of their spirit is crushed beneath your heels."

"The people flatter me!" Dagon's laughter rolled out of the tent, making the waiting warriors shudder with fear as he offered a short mocking bow to her. "Vain and egotistical am I? And I haven't raped or pillaged, as is my right, in hours! What were the people thinking?"

Tybo said nothing, but his face tightened slightly. He must remember to stay calm. If the rumors circulating through the Light Isles were true, then he was needed to make the prophecy a reality.

"I meant only that the people fear you, My Lord."

"As well they should, Tybo." Dagon sat forward, giving his soldier a glimpse of the pure dark magic flowing through his veins. His eyes flashed dangerously red, an evil glowing color that evoked memories of death and destruction. And scarier was the knowledge and wisdom that swirled around in his glittering orbs, proving this was a man who knew exactly what he was and delighted in the acceptance of himself. He was no fool in the guise of power! What he wielded could rule the world, and he wanted to be sure his little underling understood this. "As well they should."

Dagon settled back onto his stool and arched one eyebrow as he looked at the warrior before him, the glowing haze gone from his eyes, and continued as if it never was.

"Maybe some people think too much, would you not say, Tybo?"

In a dark flash, Dagon was across the room, towering over this insubordinate, wings extended, eyes flashing red lightning!

Stephanie Burke

The man was silent. Maybe it was time for a new acolyte? Maybe the child he created would be in his image and have the strength to fight for what he wanted, without compassion, to rule with no mercy!

Lazily, Dagon ran one leathery hand across Tybo's back, enjoying his small uncomfortable tensing, feeling the magic hum through his body. With casual strength, he grasped one of Tybo's brightly colored wings and chuckled to himself as the man forced his muscles to relax, forced himself to accept Dagon's hated touch upon a part of his body he valued almost as much as his life. Dagon raised and extended his wing to its full extension, then just a little bit more, ignoring Tybo's gasp of pain, to prove who was in power. Maybe, it was time for a clip.

"You have your orders, Tybo." He carefully released the wing and smiled as it listed to the side for a moment, before the warrior slowly brought it back into place. "See that they are carried out."

With a short bow, Tybo quit the tent, but not before shooting Dagon a look of disdain from under his lashes.

"Oh, and Tybo," his voice halted the angry man storming for the exit from the tent. "Send me in a woman, someone I have not had before. I fear both my vanity and ego needs to be stroked. I'm sure you understand. I am just trying to give the people what they want!"

"It is so hard to find good help these days," Dagon mused out loud as he settled back in his chair and watched the young man flee from the tent in righteous anger. "But I think, my friend, your usefulness has finally come to an end. And it is such a waste too! But then again, all pawns are expendable."

* * * * *

Something tiny and fluttery would not leave him alone!

Kerian swatted at the thing and sleepily pulled his Brieana closer to his body. The feel of her soft flesh was a joy he thought

Merlin's Kiss

never to experience, so was something to be savored. Besides, he thought as he buried his nose deeper into her soft warm neck, she smelled so good!

But she felt even better, he decided as the tickle thing returned and tried to annoy him out of his slumber.

Again he swatted at it and it disappeared, but now he was quickly drifting towards consciousness. He pulled his love tighter to him, as if holding her would return him to his blissful dream-state. He moved his head further down hoping to return to his twilight land, but something soft yet hard pressed into his face. It had to be her nipple.

Opening one eye a bit, he saw that berry-colored nipple and couldn't resist taking it into his mouth, just for a little taste. It had been a long time, about two hours, and they probably wouldn't get another chance to laze like this for some time. So without guilt, he pulled her into his mouth and moaned at the sweet salty taste of her.

Brieana shivered and wrapped both hands around his head, pulling him closer to her.

Kerian sighed! This was true heaven! Her young and supple body was already arching towards him, her muscles tightening, her whimpers...

The splash of cold water on his heated, naked body jerked him upright!

"*Schlack!*" he bellowed as the freezing water dripped down his face, pulling his sodden hair across his eyes and into his mouth.

"What the hell," he roared as he leapt to his feet and spat his hair free of his mouth. Paying no attention to his unclothed state he instantly scouted the area for the unlucky soul who dared interrupt him in his enjoyment of his mate.

"I'm ready now!" a calm voice cackled from behind.

Kerian turned incredulous eyes on the naked blue woman standing beside their pallet. His mouth opened and closed

Stephanie Burke

several times before any sound emerged from his suddenly closed throat.

"Are you insane?" he roared, the heat of his anger quickly warming him as fast as the water chilled him.

"Get laid on your own time, sport! We have business to attend to!" Her authoritative voice only angered him more.

"And you might want to cover the family jewels, not that I mind the view. But for safety's sake, you understand."

Kerian stood there in the midst of his sopping wet bedroll with a totally incredulous look upon his face.

"What?" he all but screamed, his face screwed up into a mask of confusion as he tried to understand what the blue woman had said.

Brieana's gurgling laughter filled the tense silence and drew all eyes towards her.

"Good morrow, Lady," she giggling as she greeted the woman standing before her.

Brieana had risen to a sitting position and pulled the end of one blanket up to cover her nudity. Although nudity did not bother her overmuch, she still felt she should be at least covered when dealing with an ancient creature such as The Lady of the Lake.

"Quick, get dressed. There is much we need to discuss." The Lady tapped her foot with impatience as she observed a still confused Kerian and a giggling, happy Brieana.

He loves her, she thought, a heavy feeling weighing her heart down. She looked back to Brieana, something akin to envy on her face before she could completely conceal it from the all-seeing eyes of the Woman of Legend.

"But we are all wet, Lady." Brieana smiled in understanding at the woman. "It will take us quite some time to prepare ourselves."

And it was true! The little wake-up splash had soaked Kerian and the bedroll, as well as plastered her black curls to her

Merlin's Kiss

body. They would all need some time to dry out, and the Lady could use the time to compose herself. Brieana had not missed the look of sadness that had, for a moment, overtaken her features.

"We don't have time!" the Lady insisted, again placing her priorities in order. She would not use the time this woman had graciously granted her to pull her feelings under control. They did not have the luxury of spare moments to waste.

With a wave of her hand, the water that soaked them and their possessions bubbled and floated in the air before them. They watched in awe as the clear droplets coalesced into one large clear blob, leaving behind clean dry cloth and flesh. Even the drops that speckled their faces and hair were whisked away, leaving them both bone-dry and strangely tingling. With a negligent wave of her arm, she sent the water mass flowing back into her lake, where in seconds, it dissipated and melded back with its mother waters.

"Now you are clean and dry. You have no excuses. I will give you a moment to gather yourselves, then we must deal with business!"

She turned on her heel and stalked towards her watery home, a look of deep contemplation on her face.

"Laid?" Brieana asked Kerian as he curiously patted his dry hair and body.

"Family jewels?" he returned, a grin pulling at his face.

Brieana was held captive by his smile. Just now she realized she rarely saw him release his emotions in any way, and his smile was a sight to behold. She caught her breath with the joy of discovery and could not help but smile back.

"I think the term is obvious, my love," she giggled. "But hens lay. How do people propose to do that act?"

"I don't think she was speaking of eggs," Kerian muttered. He gazed into her bright green eyes and felt a contentment he had never quite felt before. He could die now a happy man, all because of knowing this incredible woman who smiled and laughed with him.

"We need to get dressed," he said, finally turning away from her. If he watched her for too long in her natural state, he might again be tempted to join her on the bedroll and risk another watery summoning.

"You are correct, Kerian," she sighed. She watched with an avid gaze as he bent over to retrieve fresh clothing from his bags. He really did have a nice ass.

"The Lady's magical waters have left me feeling cleaner than I have since we started this quest."

Brieana chattered as she reached for her own pack and pulled out a fresh tunic, this one the exact green of her eyes. Within moments, they were both dressed and waiting for what the Lady had to say.

Kerian was now dressed in a creamy white vest and a light brown pair of leggings. The color not only made his skin glow and his eyes appear more intense, it also showed to his advantage his incredible strength and musculature. Brieana had a hard time keeping her hands to herself and not exploring the body that fate had bequeathed to her.

"Shall we?" Kerian invited, waving a hand before him, indicating Brieana should precede him. "Let us not keep the good Lady waiting."

Together they hurried down towards the small beach and the Lady's blue waters. She was standing at the edge, anticipating their arrival.

"Took you long enough," she muttered, impatience marking her features. "I thought I would have to come and fetch you two, just to keep you from humping all over the place like a pair of dogs in heat!"

"Dogs?" Kerian asked, one platinum eyebrow going up.

"Humping?" Brieana asked, her whole face reflecting a puzzled look as she tried to figure out what on earth the Lady was speaking of.

Merlin's Kiss

"Never mind!" she exclaimed as she looked towards heaven for answers she was sure she would not receive. "This is wasting time."

"Do you not feel the need to clothe yourself?" Brieana asked. "Not that you are offending me, but I would feel a bit better seeking mystical advice from someone whose breasts were not jiggling with every step."

"What?" the woman shrieked as she turned a frosty look on Brieana. "Oh never mind! I will never understand humans! It's not as if you don't have the same equipment that I do, honey!"

"Huh?" Brieana turned a questioning look on Kerian who merely shrugged as if to say, 'you're on your own with this one.'

"Oh, never mind!" the Lady huffed again and with a wave of her hand, a white frothy foam floated up on the water's surface. With another elaborate movement of her arm, the white froth floated from the waters of the lake to converge upon her body. Within seconds, a large white band encircled her chest, hiding her breasts from view, while a similar skirt appeared around her waist, sinking low to cover the bare essentials but leaving a long length of bare blue leg and thigh.

Brieana thought the new clothing of air and bubbles to be more revealing and suggestive than her nakedness, but she figured she had pressed her luck enough for one day.

"Better?" the Lady growled, turning to Brieana in her barely covered glory, a warning in her eyes.

"Yes, much," she replied and let loose a little grin.

"You are pushing it, sister!" the Lady snorted before her face calmed and she became serious.

"I am entrusting you with a weapon of enormous potential for justice. Make no mistake, Brieana of Belfore, I do not give you this sword. I am just letting you possess it for a time. The magic of this sword chooses its own wielder, chooses for itself who it will bestow its mystical gifts upon. As of yet, you are not ready to utilize its power."

Stephanie Burke

"What?" Brieana cried, shock replacing the wonder on her face.

"Are you deaf, girl?" The Lady cried out. "Or just dense? I said you are not ready! Maybe you will never be ready! That is not for me to say. But I tell you this now, Brieana of Belfore, before you can become this sword's master, you first must be tested by fire and deemed worthy. You have not done that as of yet. This sword will grant you nothing!"

At her pronouncement, a look of utter disbelief crossed Brieana's face! What did this woman mean, not ready? Had she not spent countless years frozen in that stone prison? Had she not used the power of the torc and taken the drack's silent language as her own? Was it not she who read the mysteries of the past with Gren and survived a vicious water attack by none other than the Lady of the Lake herself? What more could she do? How else could she prove herself?

"What?" she breathed in outrage. "What more must I do?"

"I haven't the faintest idea!" The Lady spoke each word as if she were speaking to a lack-wit.

Kerian remained silent for the Lady's pronouncement, but now he could remain silent no longer. Was it not foretold he would be her protector, her equal, and her mate? Then how could he now remain silent while the very foundation of her beliefs was being ripped asunder?

"There must be some mistake, Lady." His voice rang out strong and clear. "Brieana had proven herself worthy several times over. What better person to possess this mysterious sword that is supposed to unite the clans? Surely she has fulfilled her quest and is now suitable to lead."

"You question me, Kerian of Mirage?" The Lady's sharp angry eyes swerved to this man, another man who smelled of power, who was becoming an annoyance to her.

"I question any who would make my mate suffer!"

"I could kill you with one blink of my right eye, fool! How dare you interfere with what is taking place here today!" Her

Merlin's Kiss

anger was livid and for another man, but directed to the handy one who stood before her.

"I will interfere with any who would harm her!" He took a step forward, ignoring Brieana's startled gasp as he eased her a step behind him.

"Proved herself a worthy bed mate?" she questioned slyly, wanting to see what this man would do, looking for any weakness in him, searching for his strengths.

"Proved herself to be the keeper of my heart!" he returned, a cold anger heating in his eyes.

"Going to attack me, little man?" she queried, almost anticipating a battle between the two of them. The waters of the lake boiled and rumbled with her displeasure. "Wanna fight me?"

"No, I pity you!" he stated, an almost cold sympathy ringing in his voice. "How hard it must be for you to wait alone in this lake for a man who played you false. I don't want to fight you, Lady, I feel sorry for you."

He turned towards Brieana, ushering her away from the disappointments found at this beautiful yet lonely lake.

"Ahhhh!" With a loud shriek, the waters of the lake again billowed upwards and shot in angry bursts towards the sky.

Kerian and Brieana both turned towards the lake, horror reflected in their eyes as they each mentally calculated a way to save the other from a watery death.

As they watched, the Lady raised both hands into the air and the wall of roaring surging water rose higher, higher, so high it seemed to block out the very sun! An eerie fog came rolling in, enveloping the Lady in its white wall of mist, obscuring her every feature and making her movements a blur.

The very ground shook beneath their feet as it seemed all the waters of the lake combined to create this giant living wall of liquid, an angry giant that would force the air from their lungs at the same time it filled them with liquid death.

Stephanie Burke

"I love you, Kerian," Brieana muttered, finally figuring there was no way to escape this death the Lady would visit upon them. "I regret nothing."

Kerian took her hand in his, lending her strength to face the inevitable, strength to see her death coming and not shy away.

They both held their breaths as the water wall began to topple. It sounded like a roaring beast as it quivered and shivered in swirling shades of deepest blue to the lightest turquoise. The frothing head on the rippling waves seemed to reach out for them, a white frothy hand of death that extended from the center of the lake and stretched endless feet to the shore where they stood.

Just when they closed their eyes, ready to meet their fate, the hand of water thinned out, became clearer, smaller less intimidating. Their eyes popped open to watch as, out of the center, a glittering object appeared. Twisting in its watery sheath, slowly the form of a sword took shape. Shining, even in the darkness of the water, it funneled its way to the surface and exploded in a sparkling array of droplets that reflected both the light of the hidden sun and the angry colors of the lake. Twirling and dancing, the sword spewed forth, like hot molten silver, to pause in mid air. As if seeking them, finally finding the thing it sought, it changed direction. With a loud whooshing sound, it embedded itself in the earth before a startled Brieana. Excalibur had chosen its future master, and all present were aware of this fact.

"My God!" Brieana shouted with mingled fear and joy. This magical sword was hers, bequeathed by fate, chosen by chance! She would learn its secrets and use it to bring peace throughout this land. She was chosen. And by God, she would rule this land, master and tame it as was foretold. She knew she was the Woman of Legend and she had her destiny to fulfill!

Merlin's Kiss

Chapter Twenty

"Thought that I was gonna do you all in?"

The haughty voice pulled Brieana and Kerian out of their dazed stupor.

Brieana continued to stare at the quivering sword before her. Like a slave returning to its master, the sword dove directly for her, straight and true. The feeling of immense power she felt emanating from it was enough to scramble her mind and steal her breath.

"Why?" Kerian finally managed to get through his tight throat. Fear and anger was replaced by confusion. He might have shown his formidable anger at the Lady, but instead the joy at being alive with his love was too strong of an emotion. It overcame whatever petty arguments he might have had. "Why are we still alive?"

"As if death would trouble you, Warlord," she snorted. "If I wanted to make you suffer, I would take away your pretty little plaything there, but she has work to do."

Her words slammed into him with the ring of truth. He would find life unbearable if anything should happen to his Brieana. His life had been desolate before, devoid of color and future promises, but she had managed to change all of that.

"You make a very wise and strong enemy, Lady," he said, staring her straight in the eyes. "By what name should we remember you by?"

"I am called Nemoae. And I can be a very useful friend, Kerian of Mirage."

As much as she would have loved to blame all men for the failings of one, she knew deep within her heart this man valued this woman more than his life. He would never abandon her with sweet promises and tender lies. He was truly her other half,

203

Stephanie Burke

her soul mate. And the Lady envied the Woman of Legend in that moment. She wished nothing more than to have this type of all-consuming love in her life, but she knew she wished in vain.

"Is it mine?" Brieana finally managed to pull herself out of the void of mindlessness, the call of ultimate power, it had tossed her into. "Is Excalibur mine?"

She looked up at the Lady, knowing in her heart the sword was hers, just needing her to verify it, to validate her dreams.

"I remember holding it before. I remember holding it in my hands before I knew what it was. It called to me then. It calls to me now." She gazed back on the sword that had filled her dreams and thoughts for a very long time.

"It is yours," the Lady said, quite ungraciously. "It has always belonged to you. No one else can master it, and you still can't."

That brought Brieana's eyes snapping back to the Lady.

"What mean you, I can't?"

"Haven't you listened to a single word I have said?" The Lady began to look seriously pissed.

Behind her, the lake had returned to its natural peaceful state and the fog had dissipated, but at her angry words, the lake came to a slow boil.

"You say I am not the one, yet the sword comes to me," she stated, again looking down at Excalibur.

"You are no more ready for it than that fool Arthur."

"Arthur?" her head snapped up at the name. "What about Arthur?"

"The fool couldn't keep his cock in his leggings, that's what! He trusted the wrong man and thought too highly of himself. He never fully understood the ideals that he pilfered from you, I gather. The boy wasn't the sharpest tool in the shed."

"Tool? Shed? What does that have to do with Arthur?"

204

Merlin's Kiss

"Do I have to spell it out for you? The man was a buffoon! He was a fool in king's clothing! He was an idiot, a nincompoop, and an addelpated lack-wit! Understand that, Woman of Legend?"

These words caught Brieana by surprise and cause Kerian to break into one of his uncharacteristic smiles. Glancing at him, she saw a pleased expression cross his face. Why would he smile at the denouncement of Arthur? He really was looking mighty pleased with himself.

"But I thought Merlin was guiding him?" she added, not really wanting to defend Arthur but feeling a little loyalty to him.

"A stupid oaf leading another stupid oaf!" she growled with disgust. "They were two of a kind! Arthur screwed his sister and had a son while Merlin was too busy playing mystic to keep his pet on a short leash!"

"What?" Brieana blanched at the thought. "Arthur did not have a sister, I think."

"He did and boy did he! Can't blame the fool though. She was pretending to be someone else. But if he thought with his head instead of his…other head, a lot of trouble could have been avoided!"

"But what does that have to do with me?" Brieana asked. This Lady spoke in circles and riddles she could not string together into one cohesive thought.

"Learn something, Brieana of Belfore. Take a lesson from Kerian here. Heed his counsel but pay more attention to his actions; then you might be able to control the sword's power."

"But Lady…" Brieana began, but the Lady cut her off.

"Take this ring, Brieana of Belfore. I spared your mate and your winged guardian. You owe me one!"

"But it was you who endangered them in the first place! And I owe you one what?"

"Technicalities!" The Lady brushed off her complaint and waved a hand at Brieana. "Trifles, Woman of Legend. You owe

Stephanie Burke

me a favor for sparing the Warlord and the Flying Rat. I sense you will need me in the future and this is a handy way to keep in touch with you!"

A gold ring, encrusted with sapphires, flew from the waters of the lake. In slow motion, it floated over to Brieana and hovered above her head. The large jewel in the center winked as it caught the morning sun. This was a ring like no other! Its braided gold strands glinted brightly as it waited.

Brieana slowly reached out her hand and the ring floated down to rest against her palm.

"Wear it in good health!" the Lady cried as she turned and began to walk back towards the solitary waters of her enchanted lake.

"But what about the sword?" Brieana called out as she watched the Lady enter the water and began to slowly disappear.

"Do I have to tell you how to do everything? Pick it up! And remember to observe your mate. He is wise beyond his imaginings and you can learn a lot from one such as he for your mentor."

Together, Brieana and Kerian watched as the blue Lady slowly sank from view.

"The Lady has style," Kerian said at last when the lake was free from every bubble of her passing.

"She has something," Brieana muttered as she slipped the ring on her right index finger.

"So pick up your sword and let us be on our way, Woman of Legend. We have a quest to complete."

"But we completed it!" Brieana cried in some delight.

"We have Excalibur! But the quest is not complete until we return to the point of origin. In this instance, until we return to Mirage."

Brieana nodded and reached towards the sword then pulled her hand back.

Merlin's Kiss

"I'm almost afraid to touch it," she laughed as she tried to work up the nerve to grasp her future.

"Courage, My Lady!" Kerian urged, his face showing understanding. "You must retrieve your destiny now."

Nodding, Brieana again reached for the sword. Again she stopped and nervously wiped her hands against the material of her green leggings. Then, again smiling to Kerian, she reached out and her fingers gently caressed the hilt.

Undeniable power dwelled there! With cautious fingers, she reached and carefully explored the bronze handle. It felt warm and strong to the touch.

"It feels like you, Kerian!" she exclaimed before a gentle blush filled her face.

"I thank you for the compliment, Lady. Now take your gift and let us go!"

Smiling at Kerian and still holding his gaze, she grasped the sword hilt in her strong hands and tugged it free of the earth.

It sang to her! Joy filled her being as she held the sword. This mystical magical sword. It felt as light as a feather in her hand, perfectly balanced and weighted. It felt like an extension of her arm, yet she felt it was holding something back.

"It feels odd," she finally said after puzzling over this for a few moments. "Kerian, it feels like something is missing!"

"Well, the Lady said you're not yet quite ready," he said, trying to comfort her. "Perhaps the answer will come to you on the way home. As I have said, a quest is not complete until you journey back to your place of origin."

She nodded her understanding as she brought the sword low to her side.

"Then let us be off, Mighty Warlord, lest I will be tempted to have my way with you on the bedrolls!"

Kerian laughed at her and he took her free hand and guided her to their small camp. "Any more 'way having,' and you'll be walking back to Mirage! You'll be too sore to ride back."

They both snickered over his jest as they packed up their meager possessions in anticipation of the journey home.

The unicorns were unusually docile as Kerian loaded their saddles and belongings. Blaze merely snorted at the man who climbed upon her back and Magic did nothing at all.

"Strange unpredictable beasts," Kerian muttered as he guided Blaze back into the Forbidden Forest.

"Speaking of unpredictable beasts," Brieana said as she followed closely on Magic. "Where is Zorn?"

"I have no idea, but you can be sure the youthling will find us when it is mealtime!"

* * * * *

"Chicken, hunt, must I!" Zorn growled as he stalked the elusive talkative birds. *"Hungry, am I and privacy, the human's must have!"*

He had been tracking a gaggle of the tasty feathered delights since last night and now his stomach was growling loudly, protesting its empty state.

Paying no attention to his surroundings — he could always track Kerian and Brieana by thought later — he continued on his quest. A quest for food.

Laying close to the moist ground, Zorn crawled across the forest floor. With his wings furled tightly across his back, he slithered as quietly as he could along the trail of Y-shaped footprints and the pungent smell of feathers.

The Sage Chickens were smart birds, so catching one required stealth and skill. All of which he possessed in abundance, or so he believed whenever he reflected on his job as protector of the Woman of Legend.

Merlin's Kiss

Spotting a chicken preoccupied with scratching several feet in front of him, Zorn called on the legendary skills of the drackoon and eased his way towards his easy meal. Closer he came to it, his heart pounding faster as he struggled to control his excited breathing. Two yards, one yard, one foot, then...

"Well, what have we got here?"

The voice was loud and unfamiliar! So was the scent!

Zorn jerked his head up and saw several armed men slowly entering the area, clinging to trees and crouching low to the ground.

With a squawk, the chicken disappeared through the underbrush, leaving Zorn to stare in wonder as these fighters approached.

"It's a purple chicken!" one exclaimed, as he emerged from the shadows to Zorn's right. "A big purple chicken!"

"No," cried another voice, as it seemed to float up from the very earth. "It's a bird! A purple bird already plucked and ready for the spit! You can see it is gutless!"

Gutless! That angered Zorn, causing him to rise to his full height, thrusting out his chest and growling low in his throat.

"It's not gutless," another voice to his right laughed. "It's dinner! I wonder what it tastes like?"

Zorn crouched low, ready to attack and defend himself, when a new voice intervened.

"That is enough!" The voice echoed from above, filling the small area with its chilling tones. "We have work to do, and playing the bully is not what we are here for!"

Gently as a cloud moving through the air, a tall figure floated to the ground, iridescent wings fully extended, dark hair wafting in the breeze.

The others backed off as this new arrival gently landed on his feet, knees bent, and turned his piercing, pale green eyes to Zorn.

"This is what holds your attention? This little youthling?"

Stephanie Burke

Slowly he rose to his full height, a gentle wind rustling through the leaves and pressing his dark pants and shirt to his chest, exposing a strong agile frame.

Zorn hissed at the man! Show off! He could fly and land just as gently, yet he did it with style! This creature had a ways to go before he could match the grace of a drack in flight!

"What are your orders?" he rapped out in an authoritative voice.

"Ambush the Warlord," one soldier muttered, casting a chilling glance in the newcomer's direction. "Take his sword and look for the sword from the supposed Woman of Legend."

"You have a problem, Cran?" he purred as he read hatred in the other's eyes.

Ambush the Warlord? What was going on here? No one knew they were journeying into the forests for the sword! No one that is, except for Shala! Zorn thought to himself.

Pivoting on his heel, Zorn made to dash back into the woods towards the enchanted lake, when a shout was heard.

"It's getting away!" Cran shouted, breaking the visual battle with the newcomer to race after the retreating drack.

"Leave it!" Tybo ordered as he started after the soldier.

"He speaks to it!" the man cried out. "He heard us. He'll give away our plans!"

"Get him!" Cran's two cronies urged as the man darted around trees chasing after Zorn.

Must warn and protect! Zorn thought as he dodged around yet another tree. Focusing his energies, he sent out a mental cry to the one man who was sure to hear him.

* * * * *

Kerian jerked Blaze to a halt as blinding pain streaked through his head.

Merlin's Kiss

"*Schlack,*" he muttered as he raised his palms to his temples, as if to block out the noise.

"Kerian, what is it?" Brieana's concerned voice broke through the discomfort in his head and gave him a point to focus on.

"Zorn?" he whispered as he closed his eyes in pain. "It's Zorn, and I've never felt him this excited before!"

Closing her eyes and reaching up to her torc, Brieana concentrated on the younger drack, trying to glean what was being said to Kerian.

"He's in danger!" Brieana cried, eyes going wide and anger filling her heart. "Someone is endangering my Zorn!" Deep concern for her friend caused her to disregard everything she had been taught about going into battle. Her emotions ran too deep for personal concerns.

She turned her unicorn in the direction of the silent scream and instantly kicked him into a gallop.

"Brieana, wait! It's a trap!" Kerian yelled, but was unable to stop her.

Cursing under his breath, Kerian turned his unicorn and gave chase.

Around tall trees they raced, Brieana picking out a path through the dense forest, racing to save her friend.

Seeing no way out of it, Kerian urged Blaze ahead of Magic and took the lead. There would be no stopping his warrior queen! The best he could do was try and guide her through this attack.

Zorn had warned him they were riding into a trap and the attackers knew he was able to communicate with Kerian. His strange description of winged men forced a cold fist to squeeze around his heart! Were these the Dark Isles warriors? How could they defeat an enemy who took to the sky? No matter how well trained his men were, they could not stop warriors who simply flew over his battlements! And if they had sufficient numbers, Mirage would fall.

Chapter Twenty-One

"There he goes!" a loud male voice bellowed as Zorn darted around yet another tree. He was growing weary of this chase but he was desperate to fly away!

But he couldn't fly. He couldn't find an opening large enough for him to fully expand his wings. His heart beat a rapid staccato rhythm in his chest as he lifted his eyes heavenward to once again scan for a break in the branch-shrouded sky. Seeing nothing, he ran on.

He felt his muscles become heavy and then burn as he continued to twist and turn to evade the warriors seeking him. He prayed his message had warned the Warlord and kept him away. If he was to die to protect the Woman of Legend, so be it! He had no need of his life if the whole of the Isle suffered because the one person to make a difference got caught in a trap.

Maybe his mother knew of this. Maybe Gren had seen in her mystical vision that he was the only one capable of discovering this trickery and to warn the Warlord to keep his Lady away. Had his mother weighed the scales between her youngest son and Brieana's life, and decided Brieana was more important? If she had, he faulted her not! He would make the same decision!

He'd always been told there would be a time when he must stand and fight or run away. He was tired of running.

With a snarl of rage, Zorn turned and bared his long razor-sharp teeth and dark purple gums. His eyes narrowed into dark slits and a feral light suffused his whole body. This drack was prepared to fight and die.

"*Schlack!*" Cran cried out as the docile purple lizard tuned into a snarling beast of rage.

In that moment, Zorn attacked.

Merlin's Kiss

Knowing his death was charging him, Cran grabbed one of his two followers and tossed him in the path of the angry drack.

"Help!" the man tried to shout, but only gurgles emerged. In the second it took him to catch his balance, Zorn dove for his neck.

How soft, on humans, the throat is, Zorn thought as he felt his teeth tear through bone and cartilage. He almost gagged on the foul taste of human blood filling his mouth.

He fought against the urge to vomit as he gave one small jerk and the man's head neatly separated from his body, hanging on only by the fragile column of bone that made up his backbone.

Pushing down his revulsion, he quickly turned to the next warrior bearing down on him. With one flick of his long tail, the soldier fell, kneecaps shattered, screaming onto the soft leaf-covered ground.

"Enough!" Tybo roared as he rushed onto the scene.

His thunderous bellow made everyone in the small area halt as all eyes turned towards him.

"Cran!" he bellowed. "Did I not tell you to let this beast go on his way?"

"He killed my men!" Cran yelled back, eyes narrowed because he knew the remaining war party had seen his cowardice.

"He killed my men!" Tybo said in a deadly cool voice.

For a moment, Cran forgot about the crouched and growling drack and remembered whom he had disobeyed.

Tybo was Dagon's apprentice. There was no other man as powerful in the Dark Isles besides Dagon, and he knew it. As he watched the dark-haired man stalk towards him, for a moment all of his fear and hatred coalesced into one serious mixture in his blood.

What did this bastard have that he didn't? Why did the people favor him? Who was he to tell him anything, anyway! He worked for Dagon and Dagon approved of unnecessary bloodshed! It was fun!

"And he won't live to see another day!"

Before anyone could move to stop him, Cran hefted his heavy war blade and hurled it at Zorn.

Before the surprised drack could sidestep, he felt something slam into his back and suddenly his body went numb.

Zorn had been wondering who the dark-haired man was and had let his guard down a little. Now, as he felt a strange lassitude overtake his body, he knew he would pay for his mistake.

"You idiot!" a voice growled and the very earth trembled in fear.

Zorn felt his body list to the side, before ground that seemed so soft before, slammed hard against his head. *Fallen, have I,* he thought in amazement, and felt anguish like he had never experienced before.

He had inadvertently sent his thought to the Warlord. He prayed the Woman of Legend, Lady Brieana was not listening.

"It was my right!" Cran yelled, drawing Zorn's attention back to the cowardly fighter and the dark-haired warrior.

"As this is mine!" Tybo said calmly. Too calmly.

Hell, Cran thought, as the volatile mixture in his blood faded and he realized he had once again gone against Tybo's orders.

Tybo's ever-changing eyes suddenly shone bright red and a hazy sheen colored the gossamer skin on his wings. With a snap, he unfurled those glowing glittering extensions of his power to their full span. A cold smile stretched his full lips and he slowly raised his right arm.

"Please, Tybo!" Cran began to babble as the air around the Dark Isle Warrior began to hum in fiendish delight.

"You severed his wings, Cran," Tybo purred, in that moment sounding like his dark master. "No creature of the sky

Merlin's Kiss

deserves such a fate. That is the punishment of cowards, Cran, more suited to you."

"No! Have mercy!" Cran screamed as he backed away from the glowing harbinger of death. But he had no one else to hide behind. His followers had fallen at the hands of the drack and the rest of the men, seeing his cowardice, refused to even look him in the face.

"No mercy for you, Cran. You haven't earned it." Tybo's pronouncement rang clear and true.

Tybo raised his left hand to clasp the right one gently. With a smile, he slowly began to separate them.

"Nooo!" Cran screamed as he felt his wings being lifted and spread.

"Yes," Tybo said softly and he continued to spread his arms.

First there was a loud ripping sound that could be heard over Cran's screams, then the fighters saw the membranes that attached his wings to his body tear and rip. Then as Tybo spread his arms to their full expansion, Cran's wings were ripped from his body.

Several soldiers turned their heads away in disgust while several others turned and lost their breakfasts into the grass.

As Cran fell to the ground on top of his severed wings, screaming, Tybo's voice rang out clear and true.

"That was for disobeying my orders." But Tybo was not done yet.

"This is for the men whose lives you sacrificed to save your pathetic existence."

Tybo jerked one fist into the air and Cran levitated a foot above the ground. He added the other fist above the first and made a twisting motion. All heard the delicate bones of his legs crack with the force of Tybo's power.

Cran's yells turned into whimpers of agony as he continued to float above the ground, a broken man.

Stephanie Burke

"And this is for taking away the gift from another winged brother," Tybo growled as he clapped his hands.

First there was no reaction to the thunderous clap. Everyone grew silent as they waited for what would come next. They did not have long to wait.

Cran began to whimper, then to yell, finally to scream as his body began to jerk and twist. Suddenly there was silence as his body exploded into a pile of ash.

"Any objections?" he asked as he turned angry red eyes on the observing soldiers. No one answered.

"Then let us be off," he ordered. "We have much to do and that pompous fool has cost us much valuable time."

Silently, his men disappeared into the forests and went to their designated places.

Sadly, Tybo walked over to Zorn, pulling his wings tightly against his back. The red haze faded from his eyes and a deep gray of sadness filled the changing orbs.

Slowly, he knelt beside the fallen drack, knowing the wound was fatal because he made no move to bite or claw at him.

"I am sorry, little bother," he whispered as he laid his palm upon Zorn's back.

At first, he thought Cran's blade had only severed his wings. Now as he took a closer look, he saw that the blade had penetrated the drack's tough hide to crack ribs and pierce his large heart before being dislodged by his fall to the ground.

"*Grrrrr,*" Zorn mournfully growled and more than anything, Tybo wished he could understand the little warrior.

"I don't know if you can understand me, little brother," he said as he brushed one hand over Zorn's head. "But I swear upon my wings that no harm will befall the Woman of Legend. She is the only one who can save us all, and I am sworn to her cause."

Merlin's Kiss

Zorn sighed as he lowered his head to the ground. He was too weak to think, but grateful this powerful warrior wanted to see the Lady safe. No winged person swore on their wings unless they meant what they said.

"I must go, brother. Would you like me to ease your passing?" he asked.

Seeing a negative response in Zorn's weak eyes, he nodded and rose to his feet.

"Until we meet in another life," he said with a small bow, then he too disappeared from sight.

Protected them, have I? Zorn wondered as he closed his eyes and prepared for the great journey. The pain was still absent, yet he knew from his overwhelming sense of lethargy that he was dying.

His eyelids flickered as he remembered all of the things he had learned in his young life. How to hunt with Dalis, how to fly and soar with the clouds, how to appreciate the fine cuisine of the humans, the mighty Warlord, Brieana.

Led a fine life, have I, he decided as his memories flew through his brain. *Fought well, I did!*

As he lay there, he felt his breath start to rattle in his chest, and knew his time was short. He laid his head on the soft ground and a toothy grin spread across his face.

* * * * *

"Zorn!" Brieana screamed as she urged her unicorn faster towards the weakening thoughts of her purple friend, "Hold on, Zorn! I am coming!"

But Kerian feared they were too late.

Leaning close to the neck of his mount, Kerian urged Blaze faster from his position in front of Brieana and Magic.

Stephanie Burke

"Calm, Lady!" Kerian shouted to be heard over the thunder of the equines' hooves. "This is a trap! We must proceed with caution. Getting into their trap won't help Zorn or us."

Some of Kerian's words must have penetrated the thick wall of grief that surrounded her, for she eased up on Magic and slowed his wild gallop to a slow canter.

"He's dying, Kerian!" Brieana said in a rough voice. "He's dying and I can't get to him."

Kerian remained silent. What could he say? He felt the young drack slipping away from him and could do nothing to prevent it from happening.

He slowed their pace and began to cautiously guide Brieana toward their fallen friend.

Merlin's Kiss

Chapter Twenty-Two

Death! It surrounded him, pressed in on him like a blanket, blotted out all sounds and coated his eyes in a dark haze. He had always known death was inevitable, but he never expected to die a sacrifice, no, a martyr. Yes, death would have its way.

A chill breeze blew through the trees, rustling leaves and stirring the silence as Kerian stumbled across the purple lump lying on the ground.

"Zorn," he called as he slid from Blaze's back and ran to the fallen drack's side, his voice sounding miles away.

"Is he...?" Brieana could not bring herself to ask the question that was hovering on her lips.

"Not yet, Lady," he said as he made room for her at their fallen comrade's side.

"Who did this?" she said as she fell to her knees beside her little purple friend and tentatively raised one hand to touch his barely moving side, feeling the cold begin to absorb the heat from his body.

Without a word, Kerian rose to his feet and turned to begin following the prints that crisscrossed over the ground.

Brieana reached one hand for the comfort of the torc as she moved the other hand to Zorn's cool forehead.

"Zorn? Can you hear me?" she asked as she leaned close to him.

A trap, it is, Lady! His voice whispered in her head. *Flee, you must.*

"Wings," Kerian whispered as he came across the pile of ash and severed wings. "These people do have wings! Zorn?"

Disturbed now, Kerian rushed over to the drack's side.

Stephanie Burke

"Zorn?" he whispered urgently. "Zorn! Answer me! How many are there?"

Know not, Warlord, he sighed as he fought for each breath. *Many!*

"Kerian?" Brieana asked as she turned her devastated eyes to him. "Are we in much trouble?"

"You could say that, Lady," Kerian muttered as he began to mentally plan how to thwart an attack against winged warriors.

Trust one, you must, Zorn added on a sigh.

"After they did this thing to you, Zorn?" Brieana asked in amazement. One of his beloved wings was almost severed from his back! The other was damaged beyond repair! The blade that did the deed was still lying beside him, stained black with his blood.

Retribution, that one did take. He sighed as he again closed his eyes. It was getting hard to concentrate. *Rainbow eyes. Drackoon eyes.*

"The pile of ash," Kerian guessed. "He caused this."

Him, you trust! Zorn roused himself enough to say.

"Zorn," Brieana sighed, laying her head against his side. "I don't want to lose you."

Nor I, you, Lady. Flee you must!

"I cannot leave you like this," Brieana said, tears finally choking her up, making her chest pound and her eyes burn.

Leave, you must! Trap! he urged. *Leave me! Join fathers, I do now.* He sighed as if that bit of urgency cost him dearly. *You take,* he ordered Kerian. *You guard!*

"With my life," Kerian assured, dropping to one knee beside the youthling.

Everything I touch dies, he thought as he watched the life seeping from this drack. *Too bad I decided I liked him almost as soon as I lost him,* he thought.

Strong warrior, I am! Tell them! Zorn urged as the light began to leave his already glazed eyes.

Merlin's Kiss

"I will," Brieana whispered, tears running down her pale cheeks. "I will tell them all."

Good day, it is, to die, he sighed. Then Zorn was no more.

Brieana sucked in a deep breath and let it out on a sob. She laid her head against his rapidly cooling body and cried her grief. Zorn did not deserve death! He had not even reached full adulthood! These Dark Isle people were monsters!

"We have to go," Kerian urged her after giving her a moment of time to wallow in her grief.

"We cannot just leave him here!" Brieana argued, suddenly turning fierce. "We have to bury his body!" Her warrior training was overtaken by her emotional feelings for her fallen friend. Her heart was breaking at the loss they just suffered. All rational thoughts were lost in her grief.

"We don't have time!" Kerian argued. He looked suspiciously around the small clearing. The more they tarried here, the greater chance there was of a surprise attack from above.

"I will not move until we have honored his bravery!" Brieana growled, turning heated eyes towards him.

Instead of anger or sadness on her face, there was the cold stoic face of a warrior.

"Listen to me," he grated out as he bent low and got right into her face. "Do you want his death to be in vain?"

"What?" she cried, as she slowly rose to her feet. Kerian knew he was now talking to a royal knight, one of the most feared warriors in the Britons.

"He died," Kerian said as he jabbed a finger in Zorn's direction. "He died so you could live! He sacrificed his life to warn us of the impending attack and of a trap. Think, Lady! What better trap would there be than to lure you here to his dying body and attack while your defenses are down! Worry not about Zorn! The power that spawned him will retrieve the husk of what he used to be. And that is an empty shell, Lady! Zorn is no more!"

Stephanie Burke

Brieana took a deep shuddering breath and fought to get her emotions under control. In her mind she knew Kerian was right, it was her heart that objected.

"It just does not seem right," she sighed finally, her sadness showing on her face.

"Zorn understood the risks, Brieana," Kerian added kindly as he saw her protective mask crack and her true feelings start to show. "Now it is our task to see his memory lives on in you."

Nodding, Brieana gave one last look to Zorn's body before turning away. She was quiet as she mounted Magic and made sure Excalibur was secured to the saddle. Looking over her shoulder, she nodded to Kerian once.

"Then let us be off, Warlord. You are correct. We have business to attend to."

The warrior was back in control. The Queen had spoken.

"My Lady," he nodded as he mounted Blaze and in a flash they were off, neither looking back. Like the warriors they were, they put the past behind them and forged onward.

If they had bothered to look back, they would have noticed a strange glow begin to surround Zorn's body.

* * * * *

"The Woman of Legend," Tybo breathed as he watched the couple on unicorns pass beneath him. "And her pet Warlord," he decided as he observed the tall muscular man that led her protectively through the dense trees of the Forbidden Forest.

She didn't look at all like he expected a great lady to look. In fact, she seemed quite puny.

But upon closer inspection, he decided there was a bit of steel in her backbone, as he watched her calmly scan the surrounding area. They both knew they were being watched, but they just couldn't figure out how. He had to give them credit. Not too many people discovered that much about him before an attack!

Merlin's Kiss

He nodded to one of his five remaining men, and suddenly the leaves shifted, as if by wind as he moved to intercept. He was tired of waiting. It was time for the games to begin.

"Woman of Legend!"

His disembodied voice caused them both to jerk their unicorns to a halt and carefully scan the wooded area around them.

"The time has come."

With a nod, his first man dropped from the high branch he was seated on and landed in front of the woman.

But instead of screaming out in fear, she jerked the reins of her unicorn and forced him to rear. His man never stood a chance as the flashing hooves slammed into him, breaking his wings and nearly punching through his chest.

So much for the surprise attack.

He nodded to two others and, drawing their swords, they converged on the warrior, leaving the woman to fight for control of her high-strung beast.

"Back to back!" Kerian called as two more of the winged men, more cautiously now, dropped from the sky and advanced upon them.

Withdrawing his battle sword and controlling Blaze with the pressure of his thighs, he readied himself to engage the enemy.

But instead of swinging their deadly curved blades, one man closed his eyes and began to shake. In an instant, a circle of the warriors ringed them in.

"What treachery is this?" Brieana cried as she watched, as if by magic, the man began to multiply.

"Dark Isles treachery, Lady," Kerian muttered as he tried to decide which winged man to attack.

"They cannot be real," Brieana said, cold anger in her voice. "They have to have some telling weakness."

Stephanie Burke

Before they could continue with their hurried conversation, the man and his clones attacked and the second followed.

Clutching the reins Kerian knew better than to start swinging at anything that moved, so he waited, sword arm at the ready to defend.

It was Magic that gave him a clue. The aggressive unicorn wanted no others around it other than the two whose scents had become most familiar. So when he smelled the strange person bearing down on him in a fighting stance, his basic instincts kicked in.

Rearing back on his hind legs, he slashed and kicked at the true attacker, ignoring the lesser shadows of the man.

Cursing, the winged man withdrew and darted backwards to avoid the injury-bringing hooves, leaving himself open to attack.

"The unicorns can smell them!" Kerian called out as he brought his sword slashing down, barely missing the Dark Isles warrior as he dodged to the side.

But Brieana was too occupied to answer. While the illusion maker attacked Kerian, the other winged man struck out at her.

But Brieana, used to battle on horseback, dropped her reins and easily blocked the sword thrust directed at her.

With one hand, the man again engaged her sword, trying to get in a quick distracting strike so he could gain control of the reins, but this was a maneuver Brieana expected. Kicking one foot free of the stirrup, she lashed out at the man's face, causing him to retreat and give ground while trying to defend himself from sword strikes that fell like hard rain.

Glancing back to see if Brieana was injured, Kerian kept his attention on the unicorn and which way his head swerved.

Knowing he had lost the element of surprise, the Illusion Warrior decided to end his particular game. It was costing him too much energy.

In a flash, his shadows disappeared and Kerian, never one for wasting time, went for the kill.

Merlin's Kiss

Leaning low over Blaze's neck, he kicked the high-strung animal into a full gallop, straight at the man who thought to use magic as a trap.

"Hell!" the man cried as he saw twelve hundred pounds of angered unicorn flesh with a lowered head and a razor-sharp horn bearing straight down on him.

With a quick leap to the side, he saved himself from being impaled on that spiral horn, but unfortunately for him, his attention was on the animal, and not on the man seated on her back.

Kerian narrowed his eyes into small slits as, with one wide swipe, his sword pierced the man's chest. He grunted as his great, serrated blade cracked bone and sliced through tendon, sliding within him to the hilt. Using the forward momentum of Blaze's lunge, he lifted the screaming, flailing man and tossed him easily aside.

Jerking the reins around, he bore down on Brieana and the man who was skillfully avoiding her swings. The blood lust was now taking over him, melting away his humanity, turning him into the perfect killing machine.

"Mirage!"

His battle cry filled the forest, echoing with his murderous intent as he raced towards the man who would hurt his mate. Driven by the scents of blood and death that now filled the clearing, Blaze was only all too happy to comply.

The warrior, hearing the fierce cry of rage, turned to face a bigger more dangerous opponent! But his lapse of attention cost him dearly.

"For Zorn!" Brieana called out as she swung her blade low.

She felt the jerk, then give of bones and tendons as the man's head neatly flew from his body. Magic, excited by all the action eagerly fought against Brieana's control as he sought yet another victim to maul.

"Lord Tybo!"

Stephanie Burke

Up in the trees, Tybo watched, impressed by the prowess of the two. This situation might not be as boring as he first thought.

"Lord?" the voice intruded in on his musings.

"What is it?" he hissed, his eyes flashing a deep brown, showing annoyance.

"I have sent a message to the Master for reinforcements."

So much for this being easy, he thought as he watched the shaken warrior. It must be his first battle for him to start blubbering for help so soon.

"Did I give you that order, soldier?" he asked in a deceptively calm voice.

"N-No, Lord," the man stuttered as he nervously furled his wings closer to him, a protective maneuver probably because of what happened to Cran.

"Then you will make no more attempts to undermine my authority. I want the Warlord's sword. Go and fetch it for me. That is the proof I need of his destruction."

He settled himself more comfortably on his perch high above and with one finger, scratched at his ear.

"His sword?" the man asked, still remembering what had happened to Cran and weighing that against what the Warlord had done to his fellow soldier.

"His sword," Tybo confirmed. "Lord Dagon knows the fabled sword the Warlord carries. As proof of his death, the sword will assure Lord Dagon the Warlord is no more." At the rate this was going, he would probably wind up sending the whole accursed army out to be slaughtered to prevent any witnesses from popping up at a later, more inconvenient date.

"As you command," the man replied, and launched himself at the excited quartet on the forest floor who now cautiously watched the treetops, waiting for the next wave of attack. And speaking of waves…

"You there," Tybo called out in a low amused tone, pointing to the remaining soldier.

226

Merlin's Kiss

"Me, Lord?" the man asked, fear clearly in his voice.

"Go help him." This was becoming more amusing than he would have imagined.

"Yes sir!" he rapped out, a good little soldier to the last. But then again, they were all pawns in this game.

Tybo watched as the man gracefully dove down to engage the two humans and their unicorn companions in battle. Settling himself more comfortably, he set his strategic mind to figuring out a way to thwart the major portion of Dagon's army, avoid being slaughtered by the two going berserk below, and help them to foil the Dark Master's evil game. His day was looking up!

Chapter Twenty-Three

"Why do they keep coming?" Brieana cried as one, then another winged man dropped, seemingly, from thin air.

"The sword!" the first man cried. "Bring me the sword!"

"Excalibur?" Brieana hissed as she looked to Kerian. "They know of Excalibur?"

There was only one other person who knew about the mythical sword, and she gained that knowledge through trickery.

"The sword," the second man cried. "And we'll let you leave."

The unicorns, enraged by the new scents and the violent activity, pranced and tossed their manes as the men made their demands.

Kerian was applying extra energy to control Blaze, while Magic was intent on making an escape. Both fighters struggled to hold their mounts steady, but it was Kerian who answered to their demands.

"I have the sword for you," he nearly purred as he brought his well-honed blade up in an offensive position. "Are you man enough to come and get it?"

With a cry, the man spread his wings and launched himself at Kerian, making his agitated mount rear and scream.

"*Schlack!*"

With a loud oath, Kerian lost his balance and tumbled from the saddle to land on his back.

Ignoring Brieana's cry of fright, Kerian managed to leap to his feet, a bit dazed, but still a wild and dangerous opponent.

The first swing of his blade nearly took the other Dark Isle warrior's head off as he attempted to rush the downed man.

Merlin's Kiss

Brieana kicked Magic into a position that cut off the remaining man from making an attack on Kerian from behind. But smiling, the man made no move to either attack or assist his friend. He stood there, a smug look on his face, as if he were waiting for something to happen.

Kerian's attacker ducked the controlled swing of the deadly battle sword and clapping his hands, produced a ball of white light that he shot at Kerian.

Now ready for such tricks from these Dark Isles people, Kerian quickly went into a dive that brought him close to the man's exposed stomach. With a wild cry, Kerian jabbed at the warrior's unprotected spot and laughed as he swung his hands down protectively, leaving his face open for a brutal fist that broke his nose and loosened at least three of his teeth.

Falling back, the warrior raised one hand in disbelief as he watched the blood drip from his battered face onto his tunic.

"You son of a…" he got no further than that before Kerian's laughter cut him off.

"You wanted my sword," he sneered, "yet you run from it! Please make up your mind. I grow weary of this game!"

"Then let me not bore you any longer," he growled, his eyes narrowing dangerously as he reached behind his wings and produced a short sword.

"Let us finish this," Kerian agreed as he took up a low battle stance.

With a flap of his wings the other man attacked.

Silver glinted off the narrow beams of the sun that penetrated the dense woods of the forest and shone down upon the combatants. Muscles bulged and sinew stood out in stark relief as the two sword wielders blocked and countered. It was a dizzying ballet of movement as the winged warrior struggled to best Kerian.

All too soon it became apparent that Kerian was toying with the man, slowly draining his power and testing his resolve.

Stephanie Burke

The warrior knew it, too, because he looked over to his partner and his eyes pleaded for help.

With one mighty blow from his sword, Kerian knocked the flying warrior backwards into a tree. The Dark Isles warrior tried holding back a scream as the delicate bones of his wings snapped.

In that second, he let his guard down.

In that second, Kerian moved in for the kill.

Seeing his partner practically bested, the other warrior, ignoring the threat of Brieana and Magic, rushed to aid his comrade. Brieana had been keeping the other attacker at bay. But a moment was all he needed to try and help his falling friend.

"Stop!" Brieana called out as the man raised his hands to toss a magical ball of energy at her mate.

Ignoring her, the man concentrated to produce a ball of flame, but the unexpected blow from Brieana destroyed his concentration. It also defused the ball of energy that he held and drew Kerian's attention to them.

With a growl of anger, the man grasped her foot and gave a hard jerk.

Unprepared for that maneuver, Brieana tumbled from her mount and hit the ground with a rolling movement.

"No!" Kerian's maddened bellows sounded even as Brieana kicked her legs backwards, throwing her body into a flip. She landed on her feet, facing the warrior with her sword, the war sword designed especially for her, held at the ready.

Brieana now had death in her eyes as she glared at the strange winged man. He would pay for unhorsing her, and he would pay dearly.

She absently noted that both unicorns had retreated a safe distance from the battle, but now stood ready, their attention on their riders as if they meant to leap in at a moment's notice to defend.

Merlin's Kiss

She barely paid attention to Kerian, who now stood at her side, his eyes on the man he had not killed because he was rushing to see to her safety.

Now they stood side by side, an impenetrable force against these Dark Isle warriors, watching for a weakness, an opening, as the man with the broken wing rushed to aid his companion, creating a face off between the two sides.

"Enough!" Tybo cried suddenly as he looked up at the sky to judge the time. Soon Dagon's solders would be upon them and he had to end this fast.

Leaping to the ground, he made no move to conceal his entrance as the other two took a defensive step back.

Their surprise was all that Kerian needed. In a flash, he brought up his blade and a whirling dervish attacked.

One well placed kick sent the first warrior flying back into his partner, and crouching low and thrusting up with his knees, Kerian embedded both blades into the man.

He jerked once as Kerian yanked the blades free, then he tumbled face down on the forest floor.

Without giving the second man time to regroup, he twirled, light as air on his feet, and swung the blade into a wide arc. The headless body crumpled on top of his friend, twitching slightly.

"Well done!" Tybo laughed as he stepped forward over the two bodies littering the forest floor, clapping slowly, and faced Kerian.

A stunned Brieana stood behind Kerian, speechless as the man snapped his wings open and shut rapidly. For a second they blazed a cheerful blue before he furled them tightly against his back. Funny, but the color of his wings matched his eyes exactly.

"Now that the exercise is over and you are flushed with victory, maybe we can talk. My name is…"

"Invader," Kerian hissed, amber eyes narrowed to slits.

Stephanie Burke

Never had he been so angry in his life! Because of this man and those like him, his land was in danger, his queen had almost been killed, and he found himself losing to the blood lust he fought so hard to control.

"Well, that is one way of saying what I am," the man concurred with a smile. "But I am an invader you need to pay close attention to."

"You sent them after the sword!" Kerian's voice was low and dangerous as he spoke to this dark-haired man.

For a moment, his eyes flashed purple and his irritation showed, but then they were concealed by a cool wash of green. This man's eyes constantly and rapidly changed colors.

His ever-changing eyes caused a pang of remembrance in Brieana, but she could not remember where she had heard of or seen eyes that were rainbow hued.

"Well, I needed them dead," Tybo reasoned as he faced Kerian, now crouching a bit as if in preparation to defend himself.

"A blade to the back would have been a more honorable death for cowards," Kerian growled, his eyes narrowing further and his vision starting to turn a shocking shade of red.

"Yes, but not nearly as much fun to watch!" Tybo cried, his good humor fleeing in the face of this stubborn man.

"Then watch me, invader," Kerian purred as he tried to draw this man's attention away from Brieana and solely onto him.

"Oh, very well," he sighed as he saw the Warlord was not in the mood to listen. "If we must, let's get this over with quickly. I have information to impart to you two and we don't have much time!"

He quickly slammed the gauntlets on his wrists together, producing a clanging sound a moment before a pair of ornate blades grew down from the leather and metal cuffs on his wrists.

These highly detailed wrist blades caught their attention, with their three-foot blades and their silver sheen. With a flick of

Merlin's Kiss

both of his wrists, matching short swords appeared in his hands, increasing his arsenal and making him a more dangerous opponent.

"If you are going with double swords, I have to match you, Warlord."

"Impressive," Kerian muttered as he positioned himself in a new battle stance, with his right hand held high, the blade held horizontally and the left held low and across his body.

"Shall we dance?" Tybo asked, his eyes turning a violent purple as he snapped his wings, the inside of which changed to match the dangerous color.

In a flash of movement, he sprang at Kerian, blades flashing as he attempted to tire the man. He had already fought three battles and should soon be tired enough to listen to what he had to say. Of course, Tybo was wrong.

Kerian was filled with an unquenchable rage. These people were invading his homeland, the place he had sworn to protect with his life! There were countless beings here that depended on him, including his beautiful mate, and he would be damned before all of that was taken away!

Blades clashed and grunts filled the air as the two fought and battled their way across a clearing, leaping over thick tree branches and keeping their balance among the slippery leaves and needles that lined the floor.

Cautiously, Brieana moved towards her unicorn, meaning to keep the animal calm and guard the sword with her life if need be. She had every confidence her Kerian would win the battle; it was just a matter of when.

"Go back to your own land," Kerian growled as he blocked a swift double blow from the warrior, his forearms bulging with the effort and the swift movements. "You are not needed here."

"But there you are wrong, Warlord," Tybo panted as he sidestepped a vicious blow from the enraged man. "I have something you need to know, or didn't the drack tell you?"

Stephanie Burke

"Zorn?" Kerian called out in surprise, and almost left an opening. With a quick leap to the right, he narrowly avoided a swipe from a wrist blade.

"Yes, damn you," he growled. "My winged brother!"

"Zorn?" That pricked Brieana's attention. She was standing back, but she listened intently to the two warriors, waiting to see if the winged one would let any useful bits of information slip.

Then it hit her! The rainbow eyes! The one who tried to avenge Zorn!

"Wait, Kerian! Do not kill him!" she cried.

Her cry so startled both warriors that they both stumbled, Tybo's foot landing in a deep hole.

"Schlat!" Kerian cried as he saw where his opponent's foot landed. His face blanched as he dropped his blades.

"What?" Tybo called out as he struggled to pull his foot free.

"Why can't I kill him, Brieana?" Kerian asked, as he stood frozen between reaching out towards the man and stepping back to safety.

"Because he is the one who helped Zorn! The rainbow eyes, Kerian," she explained as she stepped forward to offer the man her hand.

But Kerian's hard hand gripping her shoulder stopped her.

"Let me go, Kerian. I want to hear what he has to say."

"What?" Tybo asked again, ignoring Brieana and concentrating his attentions on Kerian, wondering what could make such a man lose color. He never even once shied away from battle and now there he was backing away from him. What would cause him to behave so?

"If you want to save him, Brieana, I suggest you go and retrieve the unicorns, and do it quickly." Then to the warrior, "Stranger, do not move a muscle."

Instantly Tybo stopped all movement and vanished his blades into air again. "What is it?" he asked a resigned look on

Merlin's Kiss

his face. "Nothing else is going right today, so tell me, am I about to be attacked by some deadly poison that will rot the flesh from my bones?"

His eyes were fading into a cautious green and a hint of the same color peeked out from the bottom of his wings, which were now open to give him a bit more balance.

"Nothing that easy," Kerian said quietly as he stored both of his weapons in his war belt.

"Kerian, what is it?" Brieana asked as she struggled to lead both unicorns to his side. She had checked and Excalibur was still in its hidden place, but now the equines were acting peculiar, flattening their ears and pawing at the ground. Even her soft commands could not calm them. "What is going on?"

"Rabbits," he said.

"Rabbits?" the man echoed a funny look on his face, as if he didn't comprehend the danger they were in.

"Oh, shit," breathed Brieana as the color left her face.

Chapter Twenty-Four

"When I give the word, stranger," Kerian said quietly as he inched closer to the winged man. "I want you to jerk your foot out of the hole and make for the trees."

"What is this rabbit?" Tybo asked as he gently maneuvered his foot into position to make a fast break.

"You do not want to know!" Brieana assured him from atop Magic as she held Blaze steady for Kerian.

"That bad?" the man asked, unconcerned as he prepared to move.

"Even worse," Kerian said as he drew his sword in preparation for attack.

"So what did I just step in? And please tell me it's not a hidden pile of rabbit dung."

"Worse," Kerian said, a grim cast to his face. "You just stepped in a rabbit den. You are standing on their young, and the only thing that makes a rabbit angrier than stealing their catch is stepping on their offspring."

"Look at the size of this hole," Tybo argued. "It's small! How bad can they be?" He sniffed in the face of this fearless leader of men. What was he afraid of?

"They hunt in packs and have been known to give a full grown drackoon trouble."

"Schlat," Tybo muttered as he spread his wings and made ready to jump. Maybe there was more to this than he thought. He again reminded himself never to underestimate any danger.

"On the count of three," Kerian said as he motioned Brieana to move away from the area. "One, two…"

"They're coming!" Brieana cried as she saw those familiar beady red eyes glaring at them from behind a nearby tree.

Merlin's Kiss

"Forget the plan!" Kerian bellowed as he threw himself onto Blaze's back. "Run!"

In a flash, Tybo launched himself from the ground and into an overhanging branch, just as a hot ball of fur whizzed by his head.

Kerian wasted no time in seeing to the stranger. With an impressive leap, he mounted Blaze and kicked the unicorn into an all-out gallop through the trees.

"Hurry!" cried Brieana as they dodged trees and jumped the equines over fallen branches and tree roots.

The ground thundered beneath them as they both leaned close to the unicorn's necks and urged them faster.

Observing their flight from the trees, Tybo almost missed the first attack upon his person, so amazed was he, as a gang of rabbits took to leaping from the ground at the branch he perched upon.

At first, Tybo laughed at the small vicious fur-balls that were leaping and snarling at him, but then he noticed several of the little bastards had taken to chewing at the base of the tree, and were clearing a swath rather quickly through it.

"Crafty," he murmured as he observed them, then decided to move.

He quickly leapt to another tree, but then he noticed the sheer numbers of the obstinate little creatures as their growls and grunts of anger filled the clearing.

"Oh, little Dagons," he laughed, his eyes turning bright green with his mirth, until a fuzz ball nearly tore a bite out of his shoulder.

The tiny rabbits were everywhere! They were climbing the trees, leaping into the air, covering the ground in a swarm of writhing fur coats, heralding destruction for any creature in their path.

Suddenly, the Warlord's flight didn't seem that ridiculous and unnecessary!

Stephanie Burke

Deciding that the sheer number of the little beasties was enough to make him move, he leapt into the air, spreading his wings and caught a stiff current of air. Using this wave, he glided through the trees, avoiding the snapping, clawing horde of man-eaters, and followed the clear trail of rabbits giving chase to the Warlord and the Woman of Legend. This day was becoming more interesting by the second.

* * * * *

"Gather the Clans," Shala demanded of the runner she was about to send out. "Gather the Clans and let them know the Dark Isle menace is here. We have no time to lose. I am sure something has happened to my beloved stepson, and we must act!"

Nodding, the runner took off, memorizing her message, horrified at what the Lady had told her. If what she said were true, there would soon be no time to waste!

Shala smiled as she watched the runner quickly exit the room, a fearful look on her face. Fear was a great motivator.

"And I shall use it to motivate you, Dagon, you ruthless bastard!"

"You called, dear one?" a low voice purred in her ear. "I thought I heard you say my name?"

The lights began to dim as Shala whipped around to observe the rather dramatic entrance of the man she'd love...to destroy.

"I just set our plan into action, Dagon." She walked over and closed her bedchamber door, lest anyone happen upon this little conversation. "And I would appreciate it if you would knock before entering my rooms."

"Oh, have we developed a little backbone?" Dagon purred as he glided into view. "So fitting for the mother of my child." He laughed as she winced in reaction to his words. "But a trifle

238

Merlin's Kiss

annoying for one so...gullible. Is that the word that best describes you, dear?"

"What do you want, Dagon?" she retorted, her brow wrinkling in annoyance. "What do you want this time?"

"Why do you always ask the same questions, dear one?" Dagon walked past her and flexed his wings just to see her jump, before continuing on to his favorite chair. "Could I not just want to visit and observe my child as it bloats your body and makes a mockery of that beauty you hold so dear?"

"Bastard!" Shala hissed as she stormed across the room, away from him and his stinging poisonous words.

"Yes, I've been told," he murmured. "My mother always made sure I knew my father never bothered to mate with her after I was presented. You don't have to keep me...'abreast'...of my family history. Besides, we bastards just love to beget bastards. Isn't that right, my dear? Isn't that why you were so ripe for the plucking? And our little bastard child! What will the neighboring Clans think?"

He widened his red eyes in the dim light, feigning concern as he watched the color drain from her face.

"I sent for the Clan leaders," Shala continued as she regained composure of herself. She would refuse to let this monster see how he was affecting her. "They should gather here in the next few days."

"Two," he countered.

"Two what?" Shala demanded, growing angry with his word games and assumptions.

"Two days, my pretty. I want the Clan Leaders gathered in two days."

"That's impossible!" she cried as she stamped her foot in anger.

"Make it possible, my dear," Dagon purred as he stood and crossed to her. "Two days," he spread his dark wings to their full extent, blocking the light of the window, casting Shala in his shadow. "Or I get to have some fun...with your people."

Stephanie Burke

"But Kerian..." Shala stalled as she backed away from the menace Dagon exuded with such ease. "He has to return with the sword and the necklace!"

"Not necessarily, my dear," Dagon purred as he slowly folded his wings, fear reinstalled in Shala. "For you see, I have grown weary of these waiting games. I have decided to eliminate these little...pawns you enjoy playing with."

"I am the only pawn in this game, Dagon!" Shala growled, losing patience with him and his games. "I am the only thing that anyone sees fit to toy with! How dare you order their deaths? You knew I wanted those magical implements!"

"Calm yourself, lover!" Dagon suddenly snapped, his eyes flashing red with his growing annoyance. "I understand women who are with child are extremely emotional, but don't push me too far, female. I can drain off enough of your life-force to leave you near death until my child is born."

"And then what, Dagon?" she snarled, her anger lending her courage. "What will you do with the little winged bastard then? You need me!"

Dagon smiled, then actually chuckled as he stepped forward and ran one taloned hand across her cheek, leaving a stinging line of fire in its wake.

"Need you? A whining, pitiful, pale little bitch?" Shala flinched under his harsh words delivered in such a loving tone. "No, my dear. I certainly do not need you. You are but a vessel for my seed, a container that will protect what is mine. And once your main purpose is fulfilled, you can be discarded, like the insignificant bit of fluff that you are." He smiled down at her before he again turned to take his seat.

"So, in two days' time, Lady, I expect the Clan leaders to gather and bemoan the loss of one of their own. You, being the intelligent and, oh so...ambitious...woman that you are, will immediately bring calm and soothe fears by assuming his role and maintaining peace. And when the time is right, you will

Merlin's Kiss

introduce your ally in this venture—me—and we will rule as one big happy family. Isn't that nice?"

Shala was so angry her eyes took on the red glow that Dagon used so much to his advantage, then a calmer head prevailed.

Yes, I will let Dagon believe he is having his way, she decided as she gently cupped the small bulge in her abdomen. *I will let him feel he is the power behind the woman, but his house of sticks will come tumbling down. I will see to that.*

"Your reply, dearest?" he asked calmly as he easily read her thoughts from her stiff posture. Poor thing still thought she could hold her secrets from him. He would let her play at her game a bit longer. It was so much fun watching the self-righteous crumble.

"As you wish, Dagon," she muttered as she set her features in a pleasant smile and turned to face the man she hated, feared, and most wanted to be.

"Then we are in agreement." He rose again to his feet and faced Shala.

"How is my daughter?" he asked.

"Daughter?" That bit of information gave her pause.

"Yes, my daughter. Can you not feel her thoughts speaking to you? Can you not feel her life's energy? And you call yourself a mother!" he tsked.

"My child, Dagon. My child is doing fine."

"Any unusual cravings?" he asked, struggling hard to bite back a chuckle.

"Cravings for what?" she asked, suddenly weary of whatever he was going to say next. Wasn't it enough her body had to be stretched all out of shape, that she could not keep her favorite sweets down, and that all of her energy was sapped for the little parasite? What more could his child demand?

241

Stephanie Burke

"Oh, nothing to worry your pretty little head about," he assured as he reached out and pressed his palm against her abdomen.

Shala jumped back a bit at his contact, but when he raised a dark eyebrow in her direction, she stood her ground. Dagon chuckled.

"You just begged for my touch not so long ago, Shala. Have I become so repugnant to you?"

She ignored the question, because before she could answer, her stomach gave a little lurch. Startled, she jerked away from Dagon and swiftly used her own hands to investigate.

"It moves, this soon?" she asked.

"She moves, because she recognizes her father," Dagon said as he backed away from Shala's amazed and pleased expression. "Look out for the voices, Shala. Call upon me, my dear, if my offspring becomes too much of a burden to bear."

"Very well, Dagon," she replied, all the while cursing him from underneath her breath.

With one final amused look in her direction, Dagon turned and exited her rooms. Slowly the lights again grew bright with his leave taking.

"You and me, my child," she said as she lovingly rubbed her stomach. "We have a lot to do to teach your proud papa a lesson. And we shall begin by studying that archaic book of magic he tossed at me so many years ago. How would a man-demon sound to put your father in his place?" Her chuckle was every bit as malicious and vindictive as Dagon's.

It wasn't until later that evening, as Shala sat down to meal with the household for the first time since becoming ill, that she first heard the voices.

The slop boy was walking by collecting scraps for his Chigs—the large feathered swine that ate anything—when the voice began to speak in her head.

"Done, My Lady?" he asked as he took the remains of her meal away. She could barely keep anything down, and everyone

242

Merlin's Kiss

assumed it was her worry for the Warlord that stole her appetite.

"Yes," she said in her usual commanding and cold tones. "I find myself not at all hungry this eve, Kelvian, you understand?"

With a nod, the boy lifted the gold trencher and dumped the contents into his bucket.

"What is that smell?" Shala began, but then she heard it.

We are hungry, it purred softly in her mind. *We are so hungry! You are starving us!*

Shala whipped her head around, looking for the person foolish enough to whisper at her, when the boy answered.

"It's the slop bucket, My Lady. I will be away from here in a moment."

No! the voice demanded. *We are hungry! Feed us! It smells so good! You want it.*

"What?" Shala demanded, and the boy repeated his statement.

No! We hunger! the voice crooned, sounding hypnotic and convincing in her head. *We want to see! We want to feed! We are hungry, so hungry!*

"Leave that bucket!" Shala demanded of the startled boy, giving in to the hypnotic suggestion in the voice.

"Lady!" the boy protested, then decided it was best not to argue with the Lady of the keep. He turned and went into the kitchens to report these strange findings to the cook.

"Yes, do it!" the voice urged as Shala looked into the rancid smelling bucket. Inside was a noxious mixture of chum, chig, bread scraps, bits of vegetables, bones and fat from the trenchers of the diners in that hall that evening. It was a disgusting chunky mixture, the main colors being green, brown, and orange, and the smell was enough to turn any stomach.

But suddenly, it looked and smelled very appetizing indeed!

Stephanie Burke

Yes, do it! the voice urged. *Do it! We hunger! We need it! We want it! Yes, eat!*

Shala, almost in a trance, reached for the bucket, reached for its cool slimy contents and was nearly touching them before she was able to break the hold the voice had on her mind.

"What am I doing?" she almost shrieked as she jumped back from the table, the bucket and its contents once again disgusting in her eyes.

She whipped her head around the hall, scanning for the person who dared use magic against her, but all she saw was the disgusted looks from the few servants who remained in the hall. Her face exploded into a deep red blush of humiliation — a first for her since coming to this hall and being educated like a lady.

"I, uh, thought I had lost a ring!" she called out in explanation, and was further chagrined when the staff nodded at her, clearly not believing a word she said.

Knowing that further arguing would make her seem more demented, she turned on her heel and exited the raised platform the table sat upon, almost tripping in her eagerness to leave the hall.

"Dagon, that bastard!" she cursed as she quickly made her way back to her rooms. "He will pay for doing this to me!"

The small voice in her head hissed with laughter.

The servants in the hall nodded their heads in agreement. Lady Shala did not take strain too well. Or maybe what she felt for their Lord and her stepson was more than maternal.

Merlin's Kiss

Chapter Twenty-Five

"Behind us!" Kerian called out to Brieana as they both bent low over the necks of their unicorns. "Keep going! Don't look back!"

"Stranger?" she screamed as the wind whipped her hair around her face, obscuring her view momentarily.

With a curse, she sawed the reins to the right, neatly avoiding a tree that seemed to spring up out of nowhere.

The wind whipped tears from her eyes and caused her lips to dry as they raced headlong into the forest, away from the mass of furry rabbits, the savage, nasty beasts that pursued them.

"He is not eaten!" Kerian shouted as he kept close to Brieana's rear, a human barrier between her and the little harbingers of death that followed.

En mass, the rabbits snarled and growled as they gave chase to the creatures who disturbed their homes, ruined their nest, and now deprived them of a good meal. Devil-red eyes gleamed in the misty darkness of the forest, small red demon's eyes that pierced the fog and created terror in all that observed their passing.

Everywhere, there were rabbits! Leaping from tree branch to tree branch, covering and hopping along the ground, flinging themselves into the air, they came. And along the path they traveled, devastation was left in their wake, grass torn, trees shredded, any live thing crossing their path voraciously consumed. The rabbits were on the march, and nothing could turn their tide of destruction.

From above the carnage, Tybo glided and shook his head at the strange creatures that inhabited this cool green place. There were no such creatures in the Dark Isles, and for that he was grateful. But here, they presented a problem.

Up ahead, he could sense Dagon's troops, the soldiers called by that weak fool who had been destroyed earlier by the Warlord, and the rabbits were driving the ones he sought to save in that very direction.

By the Magic, these people were troublesome.

"Warlord!" He called down to the man who kept a margin of space between his lady and the small stomachs with fangs. "Warlord!"

"Not now!" Kerian cried at the voice that seemed to reach him from a distance. He dared not turn his head and search for the stranger's positioning; he needed all of his attention on the chase, looking for a way to escape the hungry mouths of the rabbits.

"Yes, now!" Tybo exclaimed, surprised and irritated. Just who did this man think he was? "I think now is a good time, Warlord. In just a few minutes, you will run headfirst into your darkest enemy's forces. I hope that is worth a few seconds of your valued time."

"What?" Kerian exclaimed, tearing his sights from Brieana and her mount to glance around, looking for the voice.

"That's right, tall, light, and muscle-headed!" he chortled. "My master's troops are headed right in your direction. If you want to live, I suggest you listen to me!"

"Listen to you?" Kerian sneered. "Why? So you can work your illusions and paint a bright red sign in our direction, stranger? Why should I trust you?"

"Because we both need her to live!" was the reply.

His words bounced around inside of Kerian's head for a moment, and then he came to a swift decision. Even if this man was evil, he would want to take Brieana alive for her sword. No one else knew much about it and she was the Woman of Legend. If he had to kill the man to save his mate, he would do that, but

Merlin's Kiss

it was better to face a single man in combat than to fight an army.

"I am listening," he shouted as he kept the pace, still keeping distance between him and the rabbits. "What would you have me do?"

"Stop!"

How big a fool did he look like?

"Stranger, there may not be rabbits where you come from, but I have seen them swarm! If I stop, we will have seconds to live."

"Trust me!" Tybo argued. "The winged brother trusted me! All I ask for is a second! One second!"

Kerian thought about that too, for a moment, before he whipped Blaze into a faster pace and overtook Brieana. Once he reached the head of her mount, he gripped her reins along with his and led the unicorns off to the side, slowing their headlong race.

"What are you doing?" Brieana screamed as her eyes whipped from her mate to the trail ahead.

Before he could answer, a form dropped out of the sky to land before them.

"Thank you," the stranger cried, before he lifted his hands and a huge ball of clear energy distorted the area around them. He spread his wings, tinted a strange green color that matched his softly glowing eyes, as the ball of energy grew and began to spread. It buckled and moved in waves, making the forest bubble and warp, before it settled around them, a solid shield that made their view of the surrounding area seem hazy and dim.

"What...?" But before Kerian could question him further, the rabbits were upon them.

Brieana stifled a cry, remembering her close brush with the beasts, but they passed by as if the three people and two unicorns were not there.

Stephanie Burke

A few bodies bounced off of the shield, but they recovered their pace and scrambled past, paying the hiding ones no attention at all.

"How?" Brieana asked as her eyes turned towards the stranger Zorn had spoken of.

"Magic," he answered, as he turned his head and gazed at her for moment, before facing front again and concentrated on his shield.

"True magic, not illusions," Kerian breathed, aware now that the stranger could have used magical abilities against him while they dueled, but had not.

"True magic, not the illusions of those lesser than myself." There was no boast in Tybo's words; he only stated true fact.

But all attention again turned forward as the last of the ravenous rabbits scurried by, leaving a dark, torn, scarred path in their wake.

"What now?" Kerian asked as he dismounted from Blaze, absently rubbing and soothing the unicorn who was still agitated from the near miss.

"Now we sit back and have ourselves a few laughs."

"What do you mean?" Brieana asked as she too dismounted from her unicorn. After checking to see that the two swords were sheathed within their places, she approached her mate and the stranger.

"Now we..." But his words were cut off as muffled curses and screams filled the air.

"What was that?" Brieana asked as she moved closer to Kerian instinctively. This man and this forest still made her uneasy.

"I'd say that that was about one hundred of Dagon's best meeting their untimely demise at the hands of those little fur-balls!"

His eyes turned a light blue with his mirth and his spread wings changed colors to match. He was still laughing as he

248

Merlin's Kiss

lowered his hands and the clear bubble that encased them disappeared.

"Dagon?" Kerian asked. Was this Dagon the Dark Isle menace he had been warned about? If so, whom was this man helping them?

"As I was trying to say before I was interrupted by nasty sword thrusts and forced to defend my life from the Warlord here..." Tybo sighed as he furled his wings and faced the couple. "I am Tybo, master swordsman and general of Dagon's conquering army, although now that I think on it, the only thing those hundred are conquering are the insides of a rabbit's stomach!" He chuckled at his own joke while the Warlord and the Woman of Legend looked on in confusion.

"I was sent forth to help you, Lady," he said finally after managing to control his mirth. "I am at your service, Woman of Legend, defender of all peoples. Your coming has been prophesied by my people for ages, and I am honored to be the one chosen to serve."

Brieana stared at the stranger who now executed a perfect bow to her and snorted at Kerian.

"You can start by explaining all of this to me!" she sighed finally. "Why did those men want my sword?"

"Sword?" Tybo began, looking a bit confused. "Oh! The Warlord's sword. It was a handy excuse to get them all killed. That was all."

"Then you don't know about Excalibur?" she asked, stepping forward.

"Ex-what?" Tybo asked as he tried to follow this talk of swords.

"Never mind the sword!" Kerian spoke over Brieana, bringing attention back on himself. "I just want to know what you really want with us."

"To help," he answered without hesitation. "And to warn you about some things that are going on at your home, Warlord."

249

Stephanie Burke

"Shala?" he asked, raising one eyebrow.

"Shala and Dagon." Tybo answered, looking grim.

"I will listen," Kerian decided as he climbed onto the back of Blaze once more. "But I will listen on the move. I have a need to be home as quickly as possible."

"Then you had better listen well, Warlord," Tybo called as he stalked forward to where Kerian halted the unicorn, head raised and eyes open, searching for danger.

"Why is that, Tybo?" Kerian asked, pulling the reins to halt the unicorn still fighting the bit, pausing in his inspection of the immediate area.

"Because your home is infested, Warlord. Infested by the vilest, most ruthless, and most dangerous disease you have ever known. And I ought to know. He raised me."

Brieana paused in her attempt to mount Magic and stared at the two men.

"Raised you?" she called out as she saw pain flash in the young man's eyes.

"By whip and rod!" he answered, noting Kerian's wince.

"Let us push forward and find a place to rest," Kerian decided. "And I will listen."

"Shouldn't we check for survivors?" Brieana asked, as she motioned up ahead. The silence was now deafening.

"What for?" Kerian responded as he motioned her to mount up. "There is nothing left to bury! The rabbits won't leave enough to bury in a basket."

"Charming creatures!" Tybo murmured as he observed the look on Brieana's face. He thought the Woman of Legend would be more ruthless and cutthroat.

"Reminds me of dear old Dagon, at his best."

No one answered.

Merlin's Kiss

Chapter Twenty-six

"Shala is capable of many things, but I don't believe that for one moment!"

Kerian's angry voice sounded firm and direct as he directed his ire at Tybo.

"What reason do I have to lie?" Tybo asked, wondering why this man, this warrior, could not see the obvious. "She has knowledge of magic, and with Dagon's help she has the power."

"She is capable of a great many things, Tybo, but to plot my murder?" he asked as he fought against the very possibility this strange warrior could be right.

"But she loves him!" Brieana added. "She protected him as he grew. Why would she jeopardize her home and her stepson for something as fleeting as power? If I have learned anything during this quest, it's the illusion of power can be shattered quite easily!"

She thought back to the Lady Nemoae and the control she had over the elements, and how she had been kept waiting by a mere sorcerer. Then she thought of the sword that she now had in her possession, the sword forged in the elements that stood for justice and truth alone. Arthur had held it and his kingdom had come crumbling down around his ears. Power was an illusion and control was fleeting.

"One who is power-hungry does not operate with logic, Lady." Tybo stood and faced the two in the dim light of the waning day.

After leaving the scene of destruction, they made their way south, deeper into the Forbidden Forest, yet closer to Mirage than they thought. They were only a day's journey from Kerian's kingdom, and Tybo had one short day to convince these two that Shala and Dagon were working together for the greater bad.

251

Stephanie Burke

"But to plot with our most feared enemies?" Kerian argued. "Even Shala would not dare that!"

"That she has done!" Tybo insisted. "And more! How else do you think I was so easily able to find you?"

That gave them both a pause.

The snorting and pawing of the unicorns tethered nearby was the only sound heard as Kerian and Brieana began to accept what was before them.

"But why?" Kerian finally asked, not expecting an answer. "She protected me from my father's wrath as a child! Many a time I can remember her breaking into a session and throwing herself at my sire's feet begging him to cease. She even…"

He looked over at Brieana and refused to continue that statement.

"She even, what?" Brieana demanded, guessing at what that woman had done.

"She offered to… It doesn't matter, Lady. What was done was done in the past and in a moment of loneliness and weakness."

"She tried to bed you," Brieana said on a growl, picturing that woman with her hands on her mate, running her fingers through his hair, touching his chest, stroking his… "That woman has no shame or sense of decency!"

She narrowed her eyes at Kerian, whose face exploded in an embarrassed flush.

"Nothing happened, Lady," he soothed as he took her hand and began to stroke her palm. "I sent her on her way and she never approached me like that again. Ever! I swear!"

"Then she is scorned and out for revenge!" Brieana decided. "Remember the Lady of the Lake!"

"She is scorned, and out for power!" Tybo interrupted just then. "Do you know what kind of power she would have had as your mate, Warlord? And you would have joined with her," he insisted. "Your sense of honor would have seen to that."

252

Merlin's Kiss

Why was it so hard for this man to accept the truth? It was clear and simple to him! Mate the man, kill the man, and retain the power! It was a simple yet brilliant plan, a plan worthy of him! It was a quick and concise means to an end and could be accomplished with little fuss; a solid plan.

"You are correct on that score, warrior," Kerian sighed. "But Shala has power! She always had! What could she gain by ruling Mirage? She is no mage to protect it with magical spells, no warrior to take up arms in its defense. What is she truly after?"

"Why don't you go and ask her?" Tybo countered. "See what she has to say on the matter. In fact, I'll present myself as witness to her deeds and association with Dagon. Then she can tell no lies. But know this, Warlord. She is planning something with Dagon, and he wants you dead. Probably as much as he wants me to expire."

"Why would he want you dead?" Brieana scoffed as Kerian lapsed into silence. "You claim that he raised you to be his successor. Why would he want you dead?"

"Because, my dear Lady," Tybo purred as he spread his wings out to their full span. "I am the only one fit to truly rival him. And I think for myself. I am too dangerous to have around!"

He rubbed his hands across his chest proudly as his eyes turned a deep shade of gold, his wings following suit.

"And so modest!" Brieana drawled as she observed his actions.

"Merely truthful, Lady," he insisted as he furled his wings and again took a seat on a fallen log.

"And informative," Kerian added, breaking his silence.

"That too!" he insisted, eyeing the Warlord before him. "So what's the plan?"

"We will do as you ask. We will visit Shala in her quarters and demand an explanation. Suddenly, all of her actions begin to add up. She knew about the sword, Brieana, which means she

Stephanie Burke

somehow knew what it was capable of, knew what you are capable of."

"Sword?" Tybo asked, his curiosity piqued. He knew talk of the sword had made them concerned before, but now he knew there was more to it than just a trophy weapon.

"You might as well show him, Brieana," Kerian decided. "If we trust he is telling no lies, we might as well trust him with the knowledge of this too. Even if he turned against us, he could not use the sword."

"Your confidence in my character overwhelms me," Tybo drawled as he rolled his eyes at the Warlord. Then again, it would have been the route he would have taken. Never give anyone you are uncertain of any information that could leave you at a disadvantage.

Now he watched with curious blue eyes as Brieana rose to her feet and went to the saddle her unicorn still wore.

Once there, she unfastened a bundle from the back, a bundle wrapped in a blanket and tied with leather thongs.

"What is it?" he asked, half rising as Brieana brought the package over for them to view.

"Only the fiercest weapon known to mankind," Brieana stated. "And it can only be used by she who holds the key to unlock its power."

That said she ripped the ties away and unveiled the sword, in all its splendor!

"Is it supposed to be rusted?" Tybo asked as he eyed the dubious weapon.

Of course, the sword may at one time have been impressive, but now it was a rusted piece of metal and cut glass.

"What happened to my sword, Kerian?" Brieana growled as she turned her stricken gaze from the tarnished glory in her hands to her mate.

Merlin's Kiss

"Why is everybody looking at me?" he demanded as he sat forward to see what had happened to the mighty sword that had exploded from the waters of the Lake.

Mighty, just now, wasn't the word he would use. It now looked tarnished and old; its jewels lackluster and dull. Even the sharp blade that reflected the light of the sun seemed nicked and blunted. What had happened to it?

"You are the Warlord!" Brieana groused as she glared at him, as if he alone were responsible for the sword's deplorable condition. "You figure it out!"

Kerian looked at his mate's determined features and at Tybo's amused ones and sighed.

"Maybe when you discover the key to its power, it will return to its former glorious appearance," he guessed.

"You don't know how to operate it?" Tybo suddenly asked as his eyes snapped to Brieana.

"Well, I'll figure it out!" she said as she began to rewrap her sword.

"Wait one minute here!" Tybo demanded his eyes turning an angry gray and narrowing in on the Woman of Legend. "You are reputed to have the power to unite the clans and bring lasting peace, is that right?"

"Yes," she answered sharply.

"And you are reputed to have the power to stop Dagon and his pursuit of power both here and in the Dark Isles?"

"Correct!" she replied.

"And this indestructible weapon of mass power you possess is that tarnished twisted hunk of metal you don't know how to use?"

"Yes," she growled, eyeing Tybo coldly.

"Well, this is going to be fun!" he decided as he began to chuckle.

"Just what is your problem, Tybo?" Brieana demanded as she watched his confusing actions.

255

Stephanie Burke

"Dagon!" he replied calmly.

"Then we will deal with him, with or without your help!" she sniffed. She didn't like anyone jesting about her sword.

"Oh, I'll help, Lady!" he stated, mirth dancing in his eyes. "We have had him longer; therefore it will be a privilege to rid the world of him."

"Well, if you had him for such a long time, why haven't your people done something about him?" she questioned as she returned the sword to its place on her saddle.

"What do you know of the Dark Isles?" Tybo questioned them both.

Kerian answered. "I know our ancestors lost contact with the Dark Isles before my ancestors' ancestors were a thought. I know the people, at least some of them, have wings and therefore have sky supremacy in battle. I know that a few of your people have the ability to perform illusions and even fewer possess true magic. I know your people respect the drackoon and have the same prophecies and myths we do, a common past. And I know your people have invaded my home, desirous of power. And most of that I learned today."

"Very good, Warlord," Tybo praised as he nodded in his direction. "Very good at observation, but I would have thought a man of your stature would pick up on those things. But let me tell you things about the Dark Isles you know nothing about, Warlord."

His eyes turned a dark bleak gray and his shoulders seem to strain with the weight of his Isle's problems. He sighed deeply, closed his eyes, and then turned a bitter gaze onto Kerian.

"We are a people enslaved," he said. "Since the coming of Dagon and his plans for peace, we have known no freedom."

Kerian nodded his head in understanding and motioned for him to continue. Brieana settled in closer to Kerian and waited with wide eyes for this dark and twisted tale.

Merlin's Kiss

"Once, we all had our freedom. There were always the poor, and always those who possessed true magic, but most of us worked the land for our living, warred with our enemies, and survived by our own wits. Those of us who possessed true magic often became priests and aided others as we toiled throughout our days."

"The Dark Isles are an arid hot place, Warlord. It is more sand and desert than forest or lake. It is a harsh land, but beautiful in its own way with its bright animals and colorful sunsets. We flew through the skies, unafraid for our children, for we knew we had the ability to protect them. Then came Dagon."

He sighed and shuddered unknowingly as he said the name.

"No one knows where Dagon came from, other than he was a bastard who was raised in the hottest, most arid region of the Isles. They say he came into Baltin, our major township and began to speak. At first, the people dismissed him as a rabble-rouser, a boy that was all talk of peace and unity, for we are a warlike culture, but slowly without anyone noticing, people began to listen."

"Dagon told of how we should work towards one united goal, that we should all be equal, no man higher than the next, and his words had a grain of truth in them. What was wrong with everyone working towards one goal? Same work, same wealth, equality at its highest. Then he said to ensure this peace, we must beat all that opposed us. And that made sense. Wars are fought over opinions, are they not?"

Brieana nodded. She, too, had come from a place of war that fought over rights and privileges almost on a daily basis. She could understand that reasoning.

"So Dagon gathered a righteous army and went to battle with the next largest township. It was there that Dagon exposed his ability to do true magic, something that I understand didn't happen often. The last true mage existed several generations before Dagon made his appearance, so he was a formidable opponent to defeat. As you probably guessed, the next township fell, and all of the cities they controlled fell into Dagon's hands. And still he preached of a united Isle, a place where all did the equal amount of work, equality for all."

Tybo began to chuckle after saying these words; his shoulders quaked with his mirth.

"And the people followed him, this zealot who had the fiery power of truth behind his words. They betrayed their own cities to join his armies, to spread his truth, Dagon's truth. Soon the whole of the Dark Isles were under his thumb, students of Dagon's philosophy, willing to kill to spread his truths."

"And then suddenly, there was peace in the Isles. There was no more war, no fighting, everyone worked the same and for the same cause. For the glory of Dagon."

Tybo lifted sad eyes to his travel companions and sighed.

"He was right, in a way. The only way to have lasting peace was for everybody to be the same. And we were the same. We were suddenly all slaves. There was peace because no one dared oppose Dagon and his legion of followers. Dagon had shown his true purpose, and that purpose was supreme power! Those who objected to sending their hard-earned crops over to Dagon had their lands revoked. Those who didn't send in moneys for his armies had their livestock taken away. Those who thought to object to our leader's glorious ideals lost their lives. Suddenly, everything was for the greatness of Dagon. He told us what to say, how to say it, where to live, what to do with our lives. And if any objected, off with their wings, cut out their tongues, and their families were sent to toil in the desert climates, harvesting desert plants and digging wells. And for over a hundred years, the Dark Isles have existed to serve the glory of Dagon."

"Why didn't your people mount an assault and end this lunacy?" Brieana demanded. "He is just one man, and many are always more powerful than a few!"

In answer, Tybo lifted his right hand and absently gestured to a tree behind him. His eyes flashed white and then a bolt of energy exploded from his palm.

Merlin's Kiss

With no effort on his part, the tree lifted high into the air before it began to split. And not in half, mind you, it began to splinter, each slice precise and even. When the tree was nothing more than a mass of toothpicks, it began to glow red. In an instant, it silently disappeared into a puff of smoke.

"True magic, Lady," he said as he lowered his hand and continued with his story, oblivious to the looks Brieana and Kerian were giving him.

"Well, if you are so powerful, why haven't you stopped him?" Kerian demanded, as he tore his eyes away from the spot where the tree used to exist, to the man who had causally destroyed it.

"Because as powerful as I am," he stated as his eyes returned to their deep gray, "Dagon is one hundred times more powerful."

Both Brieana and Kerian gasped at hearing this.

"Dagon reared me, Warlord, and a tougher taskmaster has yet to be found. I am the only child born of true magic since his conception, and he decided to make me his successor. But you see there are two types of magic, the Dark and the Light. Dagon has sold his soul for the secrets of the Dark magic and it has cost him. He does not cut a, how should I word this, presentable public figure? He has given his heart to the Dark and it shows. That's what the Lady Shala is for. In exchange for some power, she has gone to bed with the devil. He will help her take over Mirage and the Light Isles Clans, and he will rule through her. No fuss, no questions. She will have her power and Dagon will own the land without starting another war. Since the Dark Isles never really recovered from the war he started years ago, he wants to keep this place nice and neat for his takeover. If not for that, he would have destroyed you ages ago."

"Then how can we stop him?" Brieana demanded. "How can we hope to quell this mad demon with unlimited magical powers?"

"Oh, that is what you are for, Lady." Tybo nodded to her.

Stephanie Burke

"I think I am going to be sick!"

Merlin's Kiss

Chapter Twenty-Seven

"Shut up! Shut Up! Shut Up!"

Shala rolled back and forth on the bolsters of her bed, arms wrapped protectively around her skull, sweat beading on her forehead, as the voices in her head whispered, cajoled, and demanded.

Hungry! We are so hungry! they purred. *Hot, we are hot! Air, we need air! Get us air, Mommy! We can't breathe!*

"You parasite, you can breathe just fine! Leave me be!" she shrieked, her voice echoing off of the stone walls. "Give me peace! Shut up!"

Air, Mommy! It's so hot! Give us air! The voices became insistent, and suddenly Shala felt a heat that swept through her whole body, setting her limbs on fire.

She was hot, so very hot! She needed air!

Yes, Mommy! the voiced purred excitedly. *We need air! We are so hot!*

Without any provocation from her, Shala's legs twitched and slid over the side of the bed. As if she were in a trance, her bare feet touched the cold floor and she rose unsteadily to her feet, her arms still wrapped around her head. As if in slow motion, her legs jerked forward, one step at a time, until she found herself standing at the huge stone window that dominated the wall of her bedroom.

The heavy curtains shifted in the breeze, cooling the sweat from her brow, easing the burning of her body.

Yes, Mommy! the voice crooned. *Air, more air!*

"More air," she whispered as she pulled her hands from around her head and her leg lifted for that first step up onto the ledge.

261

Yes, air, Mommy! the voice cried jubilant. *Air Mommy! We can fly!*

"Fly?" she murmured, as the voice took firm control of her body. "Fly like Dagon?"

Fly? She couldn't fly! She had no wings!

Shala shook herself and cried out in fear as she came out of her trance to realize she was standing at the edge of her window ledge, roughly two hundred feet off of the cold hard ground!

"No!" she cried out, but her body refused to obey her, her legs pressing forward towards the cold night and her imminent death. "Dagon!"

Her legs carried her forward, and like an unbalanced vessel, she began to topple forward, her shriek of fear frozen in her throat!

Cool night air rushed past her face, drying her wide open eyes and sending chills down her spine as the earth moved ever closer to her flailing body!

"Dagon!" she managed to croak again, just as fast, strong arms closed about her body, halting her headlong flight, enfolding her in safety.

"You called, dear one?" he asked as she lifted frightened eyes to his face, his red eyes glowing with amusement.

Large leathery wings beat at the night air, lifting them both rapidly as Dagon proceeded to her window, carrying her slight weight as if she were a mere feather.

"Your bastard tried to kill me!" She half sobbed half cried as she tightened her hands around her hated savior and the erstwhile father of her child.

"Hmm," he purred as his feet touched the ledge and he swiftly and easily stepped to the floor. "Must take after you. Murder does run in your blood, my dear. In this instance, this incident is your fault and not mine. I abhor murder. A good execution, on the other hand…"

Merlin's Kiss

"Shut up and put me down!" Shala shrieked, then screamed once more as Dagon tossed her carelessly across the room. She screamed until her bottom hit the thick mattress of her bed and she was swallowed up in her bedcovers.

Struggling to sit upright, she pulled the tangle of hair from her face and glared daggers at that...that...winged man!

"What, my love?" he asked, as he slowly furled his wings. "I did as you asked. You are down."

Shala was so furious she vibrated with her anger. So consequently, her voice shook as she addressed the man standing nonchalantly before her.

"Why did I ever trust you?" she growled.

"You didn't!" he reminded her cheerfully. "And I never trusted you! Hence the bun in your oven, and her abysmal attempt at suicide."

"Suicide?" she shrieked, slamming both fists on the bed and unbalancing herself once more. "That nasty horrid creature you planted within me did this to me! It hates me! It tried to make me eat slop, and then it threw me from the window! Dagon, this thing is insane, just as you are, and I want it out of me!"

"Hmm." He walked over to the bed, and visually examined Shala from the tip of her tangled hair to her bare legs where her gown had ridden up her thighs. "Give it five months, maybe less, and that creature, as you so charmingly call our child, won't be in you anymore! I do so hope the wings won't split you too badly." He shook his head in mock dismay.

"Split? Wings?" her voice rose with each word.

"Yes, my dear, the desire for flight! My child is powerful if she craves the sky at this young stage."

"Wings? Split?"

"Oh don't carry on so, my pretty! It is the way of nature," he soothed. "Women give birth all of the time! And hybrids like my child usually have a fifty-fifty shot."

"Of life?" she asked as her hands went to the small bulge in her abdomen.

"Of killing their mothers during their birth!" he easily explained.

"What?" Shala's face began to match the pale white color of her hair.

"Well, that is neither here nor there, at this juncture, sweet, so the point is moot."

"My life is moot?" she screamed as she looked around for something to hurl at the monster who had put the little monster inside of her.

"No, not moot, exactly. Just expendable." He clarified himself as he crossed the room and sat in his regular seat.

"You will pay for this, Dagon!" Shala muttered as she glared at the man, helpless and not liking it one bit.

We are hungry! the voice interrupted her tirade.

"Shut that brat up!" she screamed as she suddenly looked down at her child. "I have to deal with your father right now, and I can't handle two of you!"

With a negligible wave, Dagon produced a small blue ball of energy and directed it to her.

"And if you think I will absorb more of your energy, you have another 'think' coming, Dagon! Too well do I remember the last time you gifted me with an energy burst!"

Hungry! the voice whined and Shala wanted to scream with frustration.

"Go on and take it, lest you start eating out of garbage piles," Dagon chuckled. "It will not harm you at all, Shala, my sweet. But it will quiet my daughter. She needs things your frail, yet charming body can't provide."

Shala glared at him a moment longer, before reaching out and letting the ball rest within her palm. It was soothing to the touch and almost instantly the insistent voice calmed.

Merlin's Kiss

"You have one day, Shala," Dagon continued as he watched the blue ball flare for a moment before being absorbed into her body. "I trust all of our plans will come to fruition?"

"I ordered an extra runner, Dagon," she murmured as a strange heat began to rush through her body. It wasn't a painful feeling, just warm and strangely exciting. "The Clans will gather one day after tomorrow. A meeting will convene about what to do with the menace that has invaded our Isle." The tingling was starting to feel rather good, actually.

"Good, Lady," he praised, "I knew I could count on you. Tomorrow, my General will bring you your spoils of war, and if this necklace is as powerful as you say, it will feed your need for magic. Of course, it rejected you the first time, Lady. You will have to figure the key to controlling it yourself, as the woman in question will be dead."

"I, uh, anticipate...oh...no problems with that! Dagon!" she muttered as her nerves began to jump and twitch in a most pleasurable way. "Dagon, what have you done to me?"

"Oh, yes. That," he drawled. "There is one side affect to that energy ball, Shala, my dear. Unfortunately, you will experience, um, how can I put this delicately? Uncontrollable, unquenchable passions? No! Frustrated desires! That sums it up nicely!"

"What?" she gasped, gasping because the blood was now flowing hotly through her veins. Her nipples hardened into painful peaks and her clothes suddenly had become an irritant!

"Well, this will keep you busy and away from plotting, lover," he purred as he rose to his feet and approached her figure, now writhing uncontrollably on the bed.

"I would never..." she moaned.

"And now you won't get the chance," he interrupted. "And don't even think about calling a servant or two to service your needs. My daughter wouldn't like that and if you think windows are fun when she is happy, just think what she can do with knives when she is...unhappy."

Stephanie Burke

"Dagon! Stop this!" Shala pleaded as she began to rip the clothes from her body, agitated as she had never been before.

"Not now, lover," he purred as he reached out and laid his cold leathery hand upon her stomach. "I do believe I have a headache. All of this plotting and talk of executions, you understand. Another time, perhaps?"

Shala shrieked and cursed her anger as Dagon smiled sweetly at her, his eyes twinkling merrily.

"Oh yes, our daughter definitely has your desire to see blood shed! And you are right, dear one, my parents were not properly mated. You need not remind me, I never forget."

"Dagon!" she screamed, then panted as the sound of her own voice reverberated through her body, making fires of need burn hotter, making her crave his touch, his kiss, his hard thrusting body.

"Oh! You scream my name and I haven't even touched you! Damn, I'm good!" His laughter filled the room. "But now I must away with myself! Politics of war, you understand."

And as swiftly as he arrived, Dagon exited through the large window, leaving no trace of himself in the darkening sky.

"Tomorrow!" Shala cried, tears running down her face as she fought the cravings of her own body. "Tomorrow we will see who will rule this accursed Isle!"

Her watery gaze sought the hidden place where her book of magic was hidden with its secret, unknown spell.

"Tomorrow, I shall have it all! Mirage, The Light Isles, the world!"

She slowly pulled her quivering limbs beneath her, and made her way to her bathing chamber and some blessedly cool water. It was going to be a long night!

* * * * *

Merlin's Kiss

In a distant clearing, a small cocoon made of light and magic began to shimmer and grow in size. From its depths there was a quiet moan, a low groan from its sole occupant.

The night air wafted gently around, bringing the smell of change, the smell of magic, the scent of power to these creatures that had gathered around in amazement.

The chickens were silent and the rabbits hid in the shadows, their red eyes gleaming, teeth dripping with hungry saliva, but they dared not approach. Something great was happening.

Suddenly a cool draft, a breath of cold surrounded the area, freezing the leaves, frosting the ground, its white vaporous mist floating up slowly towards the night sky.

The forest creatures sat and watched in awe as the cocoon iced over with a sharp snap! A brilliant purple claw tore at the bindings that held it imprisoned, its quiet cry of outrage making the silvery strands shiver. It held power, it held magic, it held a promise of revenge and the desire to keep a solemn vow. A creature of cold was reborn.

Chapter Twenty-Eight

"Do you think she will find the key?"

Tybo's question came quietly from across the campfire as he observed the Warlord.

Brieana settled the unicorns a few feet away from where the men were talking. Kerian had produced a small meal of bread and cheese to break their evening fast and the two men sat waiting for Brieana, who preferred to tend to their unicorns herself.

"I know not what truth is anymore," Kerian began as he gazed at the man, the Dark Isles man, who had appeared to help them. "But I will tell you this. Never have I experienced so many mystical wonders, including all of my years with the drack, and they all center around her. I have seen legends become reality, seen truths I had thought mere childish fables come to life. I now believe anything is possible, Tybo. And I would trust her with my life. She will find the key. The Lady of the Lake promised her she would know what to do when the time was right."

"You believe in her magic that much?" Tybo asked as he turned his curious brown eyes on Brieana, the Woman of Legend.

"I trust in the woman." Kerian's statement left no room for denial.

"She is not what I expected," Tybo stated as he watched her croon to the two unicorns that would have gladly torn any other human's hands from their body and stomped them into the ground, after goring them with that one sharp horn.

"She is…She just is." Kerian said, unable to describe the mixture of Brieana. She was one of the gentlest women he knew, yet she had bested his finest warrior in battle. She treasured life, but would have killed without a thought to protect those whom

Merlin's Kiss

she loved. She was so wise in the ways of the old world, yet blissfully unaware of her own sensuality. She was Brieana, an indefinable mixture that brought so much joy into his bleak life. "And she's mine," he added as he saw Tybo's speculative look.

"She wouldn't have me anyway, Warlord!" Tybo laughed. "So I wouldn't ask you to share."

"Share what?"

While both men stared at each other, Brieana had quietly made her way over to the fire. She cocked her head to the side and observed both men.

"It's not important," Kerian decided after shooting Tybo a warning glare. "And call me Kerian," he said and nodded at the winged man.

"Kerian it is."

For a little while, all was silent, save for a few snuffles from the unicorns and the crackle of the fire as the trio partook of the light fare Kerian had produced.

"Tomorrow...tomorrow will be...amazing," Tybo said finally, breaking the silence.

"How so?" Brieana asked, brushing the crumbs of her meal from her lips with gentle fingers.

"I have a feeling," Tybo said, dusting off his hands and rising to his feet. "I have a feeling we will all be changed."

"Does your magic run to prediction?" Kerian asked as he took Brieana's hand in his.

"Telling the future?" Tybo laughed. "I am afraid, Kerian, that no one is capable of doing that. The future is ever changing!"

"That's a comfort," Brieana drawled sarcastically as she glared at the bright-eyed man.

"Yes, isn't it though?" he drawled as he stretched his wings out to their fullest, their incandescent membranes slowly turning a warm brown that matched his eyes.

Stephanie Burke

"Go away, Tybo!" Brieana laughed, watching as the man tilted his head to the side and observed her.

"You dismiss me?" he growled. "Tybo? Leader of Dagon's first army of the invincible? Master of...*oof!*"

He choked off his statement as a laughing Brieana smacked him in the chest with a piece of kindling. He glared down at her.

"I believe you are a bit of a stuffed shirt, Tybo! If you are to be a member of our court and reside in our kingdom," she laughed at him, "you must simply behave!"

"Our kingdom?" he asked.

"Kerian's and mine!" she answered as she squeezed her mate's hand. "I am a Queen, and to rule properly, I must have a proper King."

Her eyes mellowed as she looked over at Kerian, her mate.

"I can see that I am useless around here this evening," Tybo drawled, his eyes turning an amused green. "You are a lucky man, Warlord. Not every woman would willingly share a kingdom with her chosen. I hope you realize this."

"With every breath, Master of Magic."

Kerian's amber eyes glowed with the wealth of love he had found.

"Then I am off!" Tybo decided as he stretched his wings and prepared to leap into the sky.

"But where will you go without the safety of the fire?" Brieana demanded, standing up in her concern.

"To scout about a bit, to spy, and to make my nest somewhere high and safe, Lady. I am in no danger. Believe me, I am well trained."

"Be safe, Tybo," Kerian called as Tybo leapt into the air. In a flash of brown and black, he was gone.

"Always," the disembodied voice floated back to them. "Always."

After a moment of silence, Brieana turned to her mate.

Merlin's Kiss

"Shall we seek out our pallet, Warlord?" she asked, as she dimpled up at him.

Although there was a smile upon her face, there were deep shadows in her eyes.

Brieana knew what was at stake, even though she tried to hide her fears from Kerian. But Kerian was more observant than she imagined.

"Will you stop pretending you are not frightened?" he countered.

Brieana's eyes widened for a moment. Of all of his possible responses, that was one she did not expect.

"Frightened?" she choked out and she ducked her head low to hide her eyes.

"Yes, frightened, Brieana. Anyone sane person would be. Tomorrow could mean our last day on this land, our last breaths taken. It is normal to be scared."

"Queens are not supposed to be scared, Kerian. What kind of ruler would I be if I were frightened of a little thing like death?" She tried to inject a small laugh in her statement, but it came out sickly and unnerving.

"You would be a human ruler."

He placed on hand on the back of her neck and pulled her head forward. When she was nestled under his chin, he began to softly stroke her back, offering peace and comfort with his touch.

"It hurts so much to be human," she whispered, her voice broken with the sudden onset of tears. "Women of Legend do not feel, Kerian! How can a legend feel?"

"You are more than a legend, Brieana," Kerian soothed as he began to rock her like a child. "You are much more."

"But what if I fail, Kerian? What if I cannot get that blasted sword to work? What if people, good people, die? Should I offer up my life for people I do not even know? Look what happened to Zorn! I do not want to be the one!"

Her disjointed, rambling questions poured out of her like water into a stream.

Through this whole journey, this whole quest, she had managed to keep her fears at bay, deny what she was feeling. But as the time for action drew nearer, she could no longer deny her emotions.

"I might kill us all, Kerian!"

"Brieana, Brieana, My Lady," Kerian crooned as he held her close. "We do not choose our fates, our destinies! They are chosen for us!"

"Why me?" she cried out as she struggled out of his grasp. "Why not someone else?"

"Because," Kerian said as he gripped her upper arms and forced her to meet his eyes. "Because there was no better woman for the job! Believe in yourself, Brieana. Believe, as I believe in you! I would lay my life down for you! And so did Zorn! So does Tybo. So does any being on this Isle that would defend their rights to choose life with free will!"

"But what if I fail?" she asked again as she fought to ease her fears. "What if I, like Arthur, am a token ruler, someone to get others motivated to fight?"

"Then your job is done, Lady! No one asked for a martyr, and no one expects you to be one! We expect a ruler with style and grace, both of which you have already proven! You give us hope, Brieana."

"Is hope enough, I wonder," she sighed as she pulled away from Kerian to wrap her arms around her shaking body. Funny, but she felt a bit better for her outburst. She never before realized that a knot of tension had been building in her chest.

"It is, Lady. And I guess you are feeling quite a bit of resentment, too."

"Resentment?" That brought her eyes up to his beloved face again. Was it resentment that she felt?

"Yes, resentment. No one asked you if you wanted to lead. You pulled the sword out, and accepted all that it entailed

Merlin's Kiss

without a moment's thought. No one asked you if you wanted to be cast into the future, yet I have not heard you complain about your fate. You were told to go on this quest and you did without argument. Are you not tired of people dictating your life to you? You were sorely lacking in choices, Brieana. And I can empathize with that."

"Your gift of talking to and hearing the drackoon," she said as she ran one hand through his loose silvery hair.

"Gift, curse, affliction. It goes by many names, Lady, and it was something I would not choose."

"But you live with it."

"Because it has shaped me into the man I am, because if I want to live I have no choice."

"So if I want to live, I have no choice but to accept my fate."

"No, Lady! You have choices. You can run away, and be sure I will run with you. We can start anew someplace else, someplace untainted by Dagon or his ilk. And we can be happy."

"But Dagon will follow, Tybo will die, the people will suffer, and they will find us eventually."

"True, but for a time, you would have decided your own destiny."

Brieana pulled back and observed the man before her. He was wise, this man of hers. He always knew just what to say.

"How did you get so smart?" she asked as a smile broke out across her lips.

"Experience, Lady. I am very old and wise," he laughed, seeing her answering humor in her eyes.

"Not as old as I, Warlord. So if we must die tomorrow, come and love me now."

With a trembling grin on her lips, she opened her arms to her amber-eyed lover and invited him home.

Stephanie Burke

He knew she would not refute her responsibilities, her destiny. But he also knew making this decision would be easier on her if she had a choice, if she decided for herself.

She would fight tomorrow, possibly die tomorrow, but she would meet her fate with open arms, knowing it was her decision, and not the dictates of some out-dated legend.

She was Queen, damn it, because she wanted to be! Not because of a sword pulled out of the stone! But because she wanted that title, because she knew she could do the job!

Let tomorrow come, she decided as Kerian's lips brushed against hers. She would own tomorrow! But she would live for today.

With that thought in mind, she pulled her lover closer, relishing the feel of his body.

She would live for this, for the passion that lived between the two of them, the love that understood her and knew best how to get a reaction out of her, how to bring the very best from within her. She would live!

Merlin's Kiss

Chapter Twenty-Nine

"Someone's getting laid tonight," Tybo sighed as he carefully scanned the land that surrounded him. "And it ain't me!"

His wings adjusted as he began to glide around the area where Dagon's reinforcements had been set upon by rabbits. *Rabbits!* Who had ever heard of such a thing?

This was a strange land, he decided. Strange, but far more comfortable than the Dark Isles.

Comfortable, that is, unless Dagon had his way with the land. Then you could wave goodbye to all of this beauty.

As he approached the ground, something caused his ears to perk up and the magic coursing through his body began to react.

Something big had just been reborn, and whatever it was, it was headed in his direction.

Before he could complete the thought, a large purple ball of cold hurtled past him, the magic filling him with a screaming silence that seared his inner walls and froze his skin!

Twisting and turning, the purple ball of hot-cold magic zoomed past him, barely missing his wings as he dove out of its path.

The magical backdraft sent him tumbling head over heels and forced him towards the ground.

The only thing that saved him from serious damage was his warrior training. As he hurtled past a thick branch, he latched onto it, determined not to touch the ground that may still be inhabited by the vicious little fur-balls.

"What the...?" he managed as he regained control of his body, his shoulder joints straining as he fought against his freefall.

His body swayed slowly as he quickly turned his head up, searching the night sky for the flying ball of magic, and wondering what had caused such a magical influx!

But all he saw was a pale trail from the end of a flying comet, and felt the magical energy slowly dissipating.

Grunting with the effort, he managed to pull his upper body over the branch, before swinging his legs around to straddle it, his breathing fast but silent.

He shuddered as the last of the energy trail eased, but his ears rang with words that seemed to be heard through all of his magical channels.

That purple ball of furious cold was screaming!

Mother! Gren! it howled, easily translated through his magic — something he had never heard before — but the echoes of that angry, violent, desperate plea left him shaken to the bone!

He decided to give up his hunt for survivors — just on the off-chance that some had survived the rabbit attack — so shaken was he. He collapsed back against the strong tree trunk and tried to get his thoughts together.

Whatever it was that had just passed him was something formidable and nothing to be trifled with. He only hoped it was on their side.

* * * * *

"Kerian!" Brieana gasped as her lover and true mate began to tear the clothing from her body. "Oh my love!"

But Kerian paid no attention to her words. He was too busy filling his hands with the warm full globes of her breasts.

With his Lady's doubts and fears put to rest, Kerian now felt free to affirm their lives, their commitment to each other, and celebrate the here and now!

Merlin's Kiss

Dragging her tunic over her head, he gently placed her on their bedroll, relishing the dim light that cast her body into shadows and pale curves.

To touch her without the full benefit of his eyesight would be amazing! His sensitivity would be magnified a thousand times and he could use his other trained senses to enjoy her.

"You are beautiful," he purred as he bent to lap at one plump breast. "Mmm."

He slowly lowered his upper body over her, gently spreading her leather-clad legs and resting a bit of his upper body against her heated woman's core and her stomach, holding her in place.

"Kerian, I want to touch you!" she gasped as his searching tongue curled around one swelling nipple and sent sparks shooting through her blood.

Her hands latched onto his hair, moaning as the silk of it slid through her fingers. Her body arched underneath his, pressing her feminine junction closer to the hard heat of his body. She shuddered as her heels sought purchase in the spread blankets.

"If you touch me now, I will explode," he growled as he felt his manhood swelling and throbbing with each heartbeat.

The unique scent of her was thick in his nostrils and he inhaled, desperately gasping air, his mouth leaving a wet trail across her chest as he sought her other neglected breast.

"Oh!" she gasped as his mouth homed in on her turgid flesh and his hand closed over the abandoned nipple, tugging and gently rolling it.

Kerian growled low in his chest as he released her nipple with a popping sound and began to place small kisses up to her neck. Dragging his still-clothed body against her naked skin heighten her awareness of her vulnerable position and of his growing passion.

Stephanie Burke

He stopped when his crotch, tented hard with his desire, pressed against her womanhood, making her gasp and shudder in pleasure. And he was still fully clothed!

"You are mine, Brieana," he panted. "As I am yours!"

With that vow, his mouth dropped to take her lips in a searing kiss.

His tongue gently but firmly invaded the wet heat of her mouth, pressing past her teeth to get to the softness within.

Desperately, she began to suck on his tongue, relishing his flavor as his hips began a gentle grind against her.

Her legs came up and around his waist as she tried to bring him closer to her need. But their pants were in the way!

Her hands flew to his waist, to fuss and pull at the ties that held his pants up. But he quickly saw what she was about and slammed her hands above her head.

"This time, I do all of the work," he breathed as he broke off the kiss to lick and nibble a trail down her neck to her breast.

"Please hurry," Brieana purred, as she tugged lightly against his grip.

He would not harm her, but he would hold her. He was determined to have this mating his way. He grunted as he again latched onto her nipple, tugging it into his mouth and sucking hard. His hands moved steadily down, pushing her pants to her ankles and off her feet.

Her body arched against his chest, pushing her breast deeper into his mouth as her head began to roll from side to side and her body began to quiver. Her blood began to boil and she felt a soaking wetness began to flow from between her legs. She wanted her mate, and her body showed it!

"I'll love you enough for all of our tomorrows," he vowed as he pulled away from her tempting heat and tore his tunic over his head.

Heedless of the scars on his back, he came to her, unashamedly in his bare chest and his urgent pulsing desire.

Merlin's Kiss

"Feel me," he urged as he gripped her hands and brought them to his chest, right over his heart. "It beats for you," he whispered, as he closed his eyes in sensual enjoyment of her touch.

Of their own violation, her hands began a slow teasing exploration of her mate.

His nipples, set in two large slabs of pectoral muscles, were erect bronze buttons that hardened at her touch. His chest was firm and hard, the skin felt firm and so tight across the muscles that it felt like it would explode if he but flexed. His powerful heart moved his flesh, tapped out a fast, deep beat against her wandering palm, telling her of his excitement for her.

She sighed in genuine appreciation of his male form and moaned as she realized his affect on her already overheated system.

But at his urgings, her fingers traveled lower, down the rippling abs, down all of that satiny skin, right to the deep impression of his navel.

He gasped a bit as her pinkie trailed there, just pressing in a bit, and his whole body lurched.

She looked up as he opened his eyes, his slumberous amber eyes that dilated in the firelight with the passion her touch invoked.

"Lower," he commanded.

As if in a daze, her fingers trailed downward until the waistband of his pants stopped there movements.

"Loosen it," he purred as he reached out and trailed his fingers down her face, the back of his hand caressing her cheek. "Release me, Brieana."

Mindlessly, her fingers tore at the ties that held up his pants, tearing the thin leather strips in the process, but desperately needing to see him free.

Almost reverently, she lowered the soft leather down his body, slowly pulling the material away from the part of his body that gave her such pleasure.

Stephanie Burke

Kerian said nothing as his mate held her breath and exposed him to the warmth of the fire and her avid gaze.

Her breath caught as she eased the warm leather off of his erection, but he said nothing, just gave her a bit of time to explore.

"Are you always this hot?" she said as her hands neared his throbbing flesh and tested the heat wafting off of his body.

"My nature," he replied as he watched her hand draw closer to the pounding hardness of him. "As it is your nature to be wet and welcoming."

His hand reached out and cupped her streaming wetness, pressing against her pleasure pulse, and eliciting a groan of anguished desire from her parted lips.

His words and his actions sent a thrill throughout her body and a tingling down her spine. Kerian was taking charge, proving that while he was her equal in some things, he was her superior in carnal knowledge.

With a wicked grin, Kerian began to press and rub at her clitoris, remembering how she liked the direct stimulation he had applied before.

Brieana threw her head back, all thoughts of exploration gone from her mind as Kerian's rough fingers pressed where lightning bolts tingled. A low ragged groan escaped her lips as she felt her mouth go dry, her panting breath heating her lips, forcing her to lap at them with her tongue.

Seeing her pink tongue leave a wet shimmering trail across her lips caused Kerian to end the teasing game!

With a low moan of surrender, he parted her legs and dropped between them.

Like a starving animal, he buried his face in her feminine heat, deeply inhaling her musk spreading her essence across his face, luxuriating in her silky warmth.

"Kerian!" Brieana screamed as she felt his swift attack and spread her thighs to give him easier access. "Oh yes! Kerian!"

Merlin's Kiss

Her vocal approval of his action only served to inflame his senses more. Anxious to see her writhing beneath him, he pulled his mouth away from her heat and trailed slow licks up across her trembling belly, tasting the salt on her sweet skin. He paused for a moment at her navel, diving his tongue in that sensitive dimple before traveling upwards to latch onto an upthrust nipple.

One hand replaced his mouth at her inner core, teasing and stroking her points of pleasure, keeping her excitement high, while the other plucked at her other nipple, rolling it between his fingers, pinching it delicately.

Brieana bucked under his body, awash in sensations as her body spread itself for his convenience and her pleasure.

Nothing had ever felt this good, this right before! Maybe it was because of the danger that awaited them on the dawn, maybe it was all of the intense emotions from their conversations, or maybe it was just the fierce lust that accompanied the overwhelming love she felt for this man.

With a sigh, she surrendered everything to him, her pride, her body, her soul. She belonged to him, just as he belonged to her, and this type of brutal, overwhelming, agonizing love needed to be expressed physically as well as emotionally. The two were as one.

"Let me!" Brieana gasped, as her arms wrapped convulsively around her mate. "Kerian, please let me!"

Lifting his head still attached to her nipple, he looked up at her to gauge the meaning of her words.

"I want…need to touch you!" she begged as she arched her body in an attempt to roll him to his back. She wanted the dominant position, and she would have it!

Reading and understanding the desire in her eyes, Kerian slowly released her, allowed her to turn him over and straddle his waist, his leather pants abrading her soft skin, her hands pressing against his chest, balancing her.

Stephanie Burke

"What is it you wish, Lady?" he breathed, his eyes following the glowing planes of her body in the firelight. "Your wish is my command."

"Just you," she answered as she slowly bent over, her breasts swinging to brush her erect nipples against the wall of his chest. "Just to pleasure you as you pleasure me."

That said, she dropped her head and began to bite and suck at the webbing where neck met shoulder, running her tongue along his massive muscles.

"Brieana!" he gasped as his thighs began to tremble and his large hands reached up to torment and tease her breasts.

"Say my name!" she crooned as she began to lick her way down his body.

Kerian closed his eyes, lost in sensation as her hot wet mouth trailed lower and lower. He wanted to open his eyes, God how he wanted to open his eyes, but he knew the sight of her full red lips trailing across his skin would send him over the edge into oblivion.

Instead, he squeezed his eyes shut and concentrated on the feel of her lips trailing down towards his chest, the softness of her thighs as they clutched at his legs as she slid lower, her hot panting breaths that heated the cool trail of wetness her lips left behind. She was intent on proving she was an equal match for him in everything, including desire.

"So hot and hard," she breathed. "And so smooth to the touch. You feel unreal, Kerian!" Brieana breathed as she gently fisted his hardness at the base.

"I'm spinning out of control," he warned her as her hand began a gently gliding motion, squeezing a bit as she pulled up and loosening as she pulled her fist down, imitating the actions of his cock inside her body.

"Then let's spin together," she replied, all shyness burnt away by her intense need.

282

Merlin's Kiss

Even as his body arched and writhed under her touch, her head lowered and she popped the large heart-shaped head into her mouth.

"Brieana!" he all but screamed as she began a hard suction, just as he drew upon her own body, making sweat break out over his skin and his nerves tremble wildly.

"You taste like a man," Brieana pulled off long enough to whisper, before lowering her head again.

But she was not to enjoy this delicacy for long.

In a mighty heave, Kerian pulled Brieana off his hardness and flipped her to her back.

His pants were no longer an issue though, for as soon as she was flat on her back, he reached down and tore them from his body, shredding the leather and freeing his legs for movement.

Brieana blinked up at his sudden action, a bit confused at finding herself in her original position when just seconds before she had Kerian at her mercy. But all confusion cleared up as he gripped her thighs, pulled them around his waist, and slammed home.

"Oh!" was all she could grunt as he began long, slow strokes within her, teasing her body by changing the angle of penetration with each movement, ensuring he hit every pleasure button and forged a few new ones.

Kerian closed his eyes, then forced them open as he felt her hot tight sheath grip and pull at him.

Being in his Lady was like a slow wonderful death, a death because he lost a bit of himself each time he entered her, but it was a welcome death, full of rebirth. Rebirth because even though he gave of himself, she returned his life to him tenfold!

Being lost in his Lady, his Brieana, his Woman of Legend, was more than he could have dreamed of, and more than he had ever hoped or imagined.

The sight and the feel of her were too good for words, as he found himself bathed in her scalding wet heat.

Stephanie Burke

"Mmm," Brieana moaned as she lifted her body to meet each of his thrusts, trembling at the insane pleasure he brought her. Her arms went around the solid arms holding his massive frame off of her body, but holding his chest low enough to brush against her nipples, sending new waves of pleasure to her center where they were so tightly joined.

She would never have believed he would fit inside her if she had not experienced the pleasure first-hand. Luxuriating in the gentle ravishing, she tightened her inner walls around him, loving the feel of the tingling nerves that shot joy throughout her body.

"Stop!" he cried as he felt her work her muscles, exploring this newly discovered way to drive him mad. "Or I won't last!"

Brieana felt it building up inside her, starting at her clenched toes, the spears of pleasure piercing her thighs. Her chest became tight, the sounds of her own panting breaths taking her to a higher plateau. Her eyes began to water and her clitoris to burn; she knew the cataclysmic release she had experienced with him was about to happen all over again.

"Yes!" she whimpered. "Come with me!"

Reading the mounting tension in her face, Kerian realized his love was with him every step of this journey into the dimension of pleasure.

Bending low, he hooked her thighs over his arms, spreading her open for a deeper penetration, even as he gripped her shoulders with his hands, holding her in place for what he was about to do.

"Let's fly!" he growled as he began a series of short, hard jabs, dragging the swollen head of his cock across her inner love spot, making sure his shaft caressed her burning clit with each thrust.

Brieana went wild underneath him, struggling to move against this blinding pleasure.

But his position held her fast, forcing this extreme pleasure upon her body, wracked with trembling.

Merlin's Kiss

"Uh, oh! Kerian!" she gasped, trying to force enough air into her body to gasp the words. "I...love...you!"

"Brieana, you are my life!" Kerian groaned, thrusting harder as he felt the pressure build up in his sac, felt his shaft vibrate with the coming release, then his head tremble as he began to lose himself in a climax greater than any he had ever experienced before.

"Kerian!" Brieana screamed as white lightning tore through her body, shredding her nerves, turning her body into a taut, throbbing thing before she exploded.

"Yes," Kerian groaned again as he felt his seed explode from his body, racing towards her womb, filling her with his life.

"Brieana," he managed to moan as his body collapsed atop her, shuddering and twitching, his hips giving the final sharp thrust to ensure her fulfillment.

"Oh, Kerian," Brieana whispered as her body continued to quake, her eyes to water, and her heart to beat rapidly with its joy.

Slowly he rolled from her, gently easing her legs down, caressing her thighs and back as she rolled into his embrace, seeking comfort and warmth.

"I love you," he said softly into her hair as she burrowed into his neck, trembling and shaken, basking in the afterglow of their love.

"Always," she returned, closing her eyes, feeling his heat next to her, relishing this peaceful, quiet time.

No matter what happened on the morrow, this shining moment would exist in her heart for always, branding her ownership of him onto her soul and hers onto his.

Chapter Thirty

"The time has come," Shala purred as she pulled her book of magic from its hiding place. "The time has come to end this madness."

As she spoke, she gently stroked the small mound that her stomach had become, feeling the cooing of the child within.

Feverishly, she poured over the ancient language, laughing at what Dagon had tossed to her like so many pieces of rubbish.

The spell for the Man-Demon!

She had all the ingredients, and now, thanks to Dagon, the power to call upon. Now, she only had to wait. The bastard would come calling soon, and then she would be rid of him and own this whole isle!

She chuckled softly to herself, running her hands over her stomach. Dagon's reign was coming to an end.

"Something amuses?" the silky voice whispered from behind.

Shala jumped, turning quickly to notice the lights dimming and the curtains ruffling at the windows.

"Dagon," she gasped. "What brings you here at this hour?"

She strove for her usual autocratic voice, but beads of sweat on her forehead gave notice of her nerves.

"What else, my lovely," he whispered as he moved into her view, extending his wings to their full leathery extent, clicking his nails together menacingly as he approached. His red eyes glowed in the dim light of the room, harbingers of danger. "Power."

"Power?" she asked, stepping away from the book as if it didn't matter. "The only power I have is what you deigned to

Merlin's Kiss

give, Dagon. And even that came with a price." She purposely rubbed her stomach, bringing his gaze to the price in question.

"And how is my little daughter?" he purred, stepping close and placing his hand upon her stomach.

Shala jumped as a jolt of pure energy sprang from his fingertips to encircle her stomach, making her clutch his arms in pain as it was absorbed through her skin.

"Good," the small voice in her mind giggled and the baby began a vigorous kicking motion.

"Dagon!" Shala doubled over in pain, her grip on his arms the only thing holding her upright, and panted. Sweat beaded on her brow as her nails tore bloody gouges out of his arms. Eyes widened in shock at the sudden pain, she stared up pleadingly at him. "Stop!"

"If you want to lose a liver, be my guest. But I want my child to live, Shala, my sweet. So until your body expels my heir, I will supplement her growth in this time of need. You do want a healthy baby, do you not?"

He looked at her distress, an amused smile curling at his lips.

"Yes," she managed as her knees began to shake.

"Very good," he purred as he reached out a second hand to stroke her face.

With a sigh, he hefted her up in his arms, folding his wings as he did so, and carried her over to her bed.

"Now, this power, my love. Did you not feel it?" he asked as he lazily ran his fingers through her hair as he settled in beside her, lightly stroking her back, soothing the pain, but replacing it with desire.

"No!" she gasped as suddenly the sharp force zapping through her body became coaxing, drawing warm feelings through her.

She tried to fight it, but his energy was now roaming through her, teasing her senses, exciting her nerve endings, drawing her closer to the unmistakable animal magnetism Dagon exuded with such ease.

"Then you are turning out to be a poor sorceress, my sweet," he whispered as his hand slowly tightened in her hair.

"Dagon!" she gasped in pain as his hand slowly tightened, while the other dispensed the warm pleasure.

"If you are toying with me, Shala, if you are playing a game, best you remember that you gamble with your life!"

Even as her mouth opened in shock, he bent low, lapping at her lips with his rough tongue, touching nerves in her face she never knew existed.

"I would never..." Shala moaned.

"Yes you would, pretty little bitch. That is why we get along so famously!" He breathed against her lips, gently nuzzling her with his nose.

"But..."

"Just remember, lover, as many tricks as you pull, I am still master of the game."

He sharply jerked her head back, forcing her neck into a painful arch, exposing her vulnerable spots.

"You know, I can break your neck without killing you, and your body would still nurture my offspring?" he purred.

"Yes!" Shala gasped, real fear making her voice tremble as she fought to look up at his face to read his intentions.

Had he felt the power from the old grimore? Did he know about the ancient spell?

"That's what I love about you, Shala, my pretty," he sighed as he tightened the pressure holding her head back. "You always know just what to say to make me feel better."

"Please, Dagon!" Shala gasped, fighting to breathe. Her fear and the position of her head were making it hard for her to draw air into her lungs.

"Tell me something, Shala," he answered in his calm midnight voice. "Make me feel good."

Merlin's Kiss

"The men," she gasped. "The clan leaders will arrive tomorrow as planned."

"I feel better," he purred. "But make me feel great."

"I have sent out a message that we were being invaded, that my stepson was murdered trying to stop the menace. The leaders are scared, demanding that justice be served. They are ready for a good fight, Dagon. They all want to be the next Warlord. If for only that, they will all come."

Suddenly the pressure eased off of her hair as Dagon slowly released her.

Gasping for breath, Shala threw her hands around her aching neck, trying to rub the sting of abused muscles away while glaring at the creature she had shared her body with.

"You have made me feel so...good, Shala, my pretty. Murder good...sex good... power-giving good."

"No!" Shala gasped, remembering the pain of the last bit of power he shared with her. "No more of your energy power."

"Not good enough for that?" he leered as he ran one hand down her chest to cup a full breast. "Are you getting fuller, my sweet?" he purred, as he gently kneaded her breast. "Hmm, yes. Pregnancy agrees with you."

Traitor, she hissed to herself, noting that her body still jumped to erotic attention whenever this man was around.

But before she could say anything, try to build her walls up against him, she heard that ominous little voice in her mind.

My Daddy, it hissed and suddenly she felt as if her insides were being torn apart.

"Dagon!" she gasped again as her face lost its color and her teeth clamped into her bottom lip, drawing blood.

"Baby throwing a temper tantrum?" he asked on a chuckle as he dropped her breast and moved his hand to soothe their child. "Baby does not like to share. Is that from your side, or mine, dear Shala?" he asked as he calmed the child.

Stephanie Burke

"What did you put into me?" Shala demanded as the pain subsided and her teeth unclamped from around her lip.

"Why, little mother, it's our baby, yours and mine. The best of both of us, or the worst, depending on how you look at things," he mused. "But she is healthy and strong, and already knows her own mind. Make sure she doesn't know yours too, my love. Our offspring then could be…vicious."

He chuckled as he pulled himself from the bed and glared at the open window.

"I must leave. Evening is breaking and I don't want anyone to see me come from this room. People may begin to question my taste if that ever happens."

"You bastard!" Shala hissed quietly, not wanting to arouse the anger of her child.

"Yes I am, sadly," he returned. "But this child will have a mother and a father — well, at least a father."

"Is that a threat?" she hissed, her temper overcoming her common sense.

"I make no threats, Lady Shala," he said calmly, his eyes now glittering evil rubies, set against the shadows as they swallowed his form again. "I give you probable outcomes for your future."

Then just as quickly as he came, he was gone.

"Future, you winged rabbit! You have no future!"

She pulled herself from the bed, stumbling as her legs began to quake, and made her way to the innocent-looking table that held her grimoire.

"I have something else for you, something that you didn't plan on!"

She hefted the small silken bag, dusty with age and yellowed with time.

"I have held onto this for many a year, Dagon. It is almost time to use it! Then with the help of my slaves, you and your men will rue the day you ever tried to take the Light Isles from

Merlin's Kiss

me! I was using you, you bastard, and now it's my turn to be in control! Tomorrow!"

She smiled grimly in the dim lights, her face looking strangely like the one that had earlier taken his leave.

"Oh, yes, Dagon. I shall have my revenge, a thousand times over!"

* * * * *

"I have a funny feeling," Dagon said to no one in particular as he made his way back to his camp. "That bitch is up to something. I know I would be if I was in her place. This requires careful watching."

He smiled as he neared his hidden encampment, and saw his people, the cattle he had led to this place, shudder in fear.

The women especially, after his earlier interest in a woman for the night, pushed one in front of the other, trying to hide behind each other, leaving the hapless victim in front to face his unpredictable desires.

It gave him an idea.

"I suddenly have need of my scapegoat."

He closed his eyes and concentrated, feeling for his protégé, who was not such a mirror image after all.

"Oh yes, a sacrifice, just in case!" he purred when he felt Tybo's energy. "A shame to lose one so promising, but I needs do what I must."

Dagon trusted no one; it was one of his secrets to longevity.

He motioned a light-haired woman into his tent, chuckling as she fearfully approached, wings dragging in submission.

"I have just the thing, to move my plan along," he chuckled. "And just the right magic."

All was quiet for quite some time, then a loud wail was heard before it was abruptly cut off.

He motioned to a nearby guard and handed him a carefully wrapped package.

"With your life," he told him and then disappeared back into his tent.

The guard would be eliminated later, after he disposed of the contents of the package.

Dagon took no chances and trusted no one.

And he trusted one like Shala even less!

Always, always have a back up, he thought as he returned to his tent and finalized his new plans.

If things didn't work out here, there would always be another day to fight, to conquer, to rule!

Merlin's Kiss

Chapter Thirty-One

"Move quietly," Kerian warned as he crawled through the tunnel that started near the edge of the thick forests surrounding Mirage. "These tunnels lead inside the castle, but I don't want to take the chance of anyone finding us here. There is no room to fight."

"Have you figured out that sword, Woman of Legend, or are we to wait for some grand miracle that will ensure our victory?" Tybo whispered as he folded his wings closer to his body and glared at Brieana's backside as she followed Kerian.

Tybo was bringing up the rear and unhappy about it. More than he hated having his wings touched, he hated being in enclosed areas. Dark Isle men were created to fly free, soaring through the clouds, not to scurry beneath the earth in tight tunnels like parasites!

"That magic must have really unnerved you," Brieana countered, ignoring his growly temper.

When they had broken camp and made their final move towards the castle this morning, Tybo had returned concerned and upset about an energy source that had flown past him, a source of magic like none he had ever felt before.

"It did, Lady, but it was not as unnerving as crawling through this hole in the ground!"

Tybo had seen the necessity of sneaking into the castle, to confront Shala with the information he had, but he didn't have to appreciate their means of getting there.

"We have to know what Shala is doing," Kerian said over the lump of hurt in his chest. He still found it difficult to give up all of the few remaining positive thoughts that he had of his stepmother. He had hoped, had trusted in her for so long…

Stephanie Burke

"She is screwing Dagon and giving your people over to slavery. I fail to understand why that is so difficult to comprehend," Tybo snapped, before reining in his temper.

It was not the Warlord's fault he had faith in the faithless woman. But it was a bit difficult seeing people forget what they were. It took him years with Dagon to see that his intentions were truly evil.

"We don't know that," Kerian insisted as he slid to his stomach to get past a low overhang. "But we are going to find out."

"And what are all these people doing at Mirage?" Brieana asked.

Upon entering the land surrounding the castle, they took cover and hid as several warriors passed, each one looking grave and a bit frightened.

Kerian thought it best to avoid them, not knowing who he could trust, so the unicorns were set free in the forest after they unloaded the swords and proceeded on foot.

"Think, Lady," Tybo said after a moment of silence. "Why would you gather a group of powerful men together?"

"To join them, to make an army," she decided.

"Or to kill them all off and rule independent of any who would oppose you," Kerian said, his words bringing about a ringing silence.

"I never thought of that," Brieana said quietly, appreciating the difference in their approaches to such matters.

"Queen you may be," Tybo said, "you still think like a girl."

"Well, I am a girl, a woman!" Brieana hissed over her shoulder before she too was forced to inch along on her belly.

"Of that, I have no doubt. I could hear the Warlord scream that fact to all of creation!" Tybo hissed, as he lay flat on the ground, giving him the extra inches he needed to get his wings past the barrier. "How long is this tunnel, anyway?"

"Quiet!" Kerian hissed, and his whisper echoed.

Merlin's Kiss

They were entering a higher chamber.

Reaching back, Kerian took Brieana's hand and helped her to her feet, noting that she stretched her back and neck as she regained her balance.

She had insisted on keeping Excalibur strapped to her back, and the sword he designed, her war sword, strapped to her war belt.

Kerian had his great blade strapped to his back also, but his belt and vest were filled with every conceivable weapon at his disposal. He was taking no chances with her safety! And if it came down to it, his life was forfeit for hers.

Tybo entered the chamber with a happy sigh, ignoring the dirt and damp, so long as he could spread his wings.

"Where to now?" he asked, his eyes glowing a curious yellow, his wings shifting in hue to match.

"We go up," Kerian said, pointing to a staircase that lay partially hidden by large spider webs.

"Up is good," Tybo said, feeling them leave the womb of the earth and climb into the air.

"Up, where?" Brieana asked, adjusting the fit of the long sword against her back.

"I can't believe the famed Excalibur looks like that!" Tybo sighed, making Brieana roll her eyes in his direction.

"Up to Shala's chambers," Kerian said, ignoring them both and wiping away the spider webs with his left hand. "If we are going to find any answers, that is where we must be."

Brieana and Tybo agreed and silently followed the dark staircase, each suddenly thinking this was it. The final showdown was approaching and any one of them and possibly all of them, might not make it out alive.

* * * * *

Stephanie Burke

"My friends," Shala called out, ignoring the hissing in her mind as she addressed the council of clan leaders who sat before her in her hall. "The time for action is now!"

She could feel Dagon's presence behind her and knew he was hiding in some hole nearby. His power called to the power within her so she knew he was close. He had delivered something to her earlier and insisted on its use. Time to play the game by his rules, but only for now.

"Why should we believe you?" one burly man called, starting a stream of like comments from the war-hardened men and women in the room.

"Because my beloved stepson is no more! Because the Dark Isles menace is here among us, destroying everything that we have striven so hard to build!"

"I don't believe it!" another called out. "The Warlord is indestructible! He killed his own father and he loved him! He will persevere!"

There were like mumblings as the people demanded proof.

"You want proof?" Shala screamed. "Look at this!"

She pulled a cloth from an object sitting on the table before her with flourish.

There were gasps of surprise and screams of disbelief as they all viewed what lay on the table.

It was the top of a head! Not the whole skull, but just the top, as if someone had removed this small portion just to feast on the brains that lay within.

Shala had to swallow deeply in revulsion, as the child within her chuckled gleefully.

The skin on the bit of bone was covered with cascading platinum hair, the distinctive shade of Kerian's, with its highlighting white streaks that many beatings at his father's hands had added shining brightly in the sunlight.

She had to blink rapidly before she could call the frightened men and women to order.

Merlin's Kiss

"What more proof do you need?" she screamed, wondering where Dagon had gotten such a horrid thing.

If he had killed Kerian and that little bitch, he would have told her. But maybe the deed had been done earlier and this was a trophy to aid in their plans.

She felt a moment's pang of sadness before the rush of power filled her.

Their plans were coming together! They were succeeding, finally! And soon, she would be rid of Dagon, too!

"They must be destroyed! The Dark Isles people must be destroyed!"

She felt Dagon's hiss of indrawn breath, but said nothing as he disappeared towards her chambers.

"They are monstrous, to do this to a man! We must end the threat! We of Mirage, are the most skillfully trained and we hunger for revenge! Let us lead your forces to victory against the hell-spawned demons that are trying to invade our land! We must fight!"

Her little chuckles of pleasure were drowned out by the enraged roars of the battle- maddened people.

But it was still too soon to make a move. She had to deal with Dagon first.

So it was easy for her to feign weakness, and have a few of Kerian's most trusted warriors lead her to her room to recover, leaving the angered mob to think about and to plot their revenge on Dagon and his people.

And with the main tyrant out of the way, she would move on easily as the woman who destroyed the monster, the woman who was fit enough to lead, the Woman of Legend that everyone waited to appear and save them, to unite them.

Even if she was not that woman, what would they know?

After all, they were nothing but stupid men and women!

Stephanie Burke

Chapter Thirty-Two

"That traitorous bitch!" Dagon spat as he made his way to Shala's chamber. "But you have to admire her...determination." He laughed.

"Don't you just," Kerian answered, making Dagon turn and smile at the newcomer.

"Warlord!" he hissed in pleasure, his leathery wings snapping as he raised and lowered them quickly to his back. "I have been expecting you."

"I wonder why?" Kerian asked as he slowly sat up in the chair he had claimed as he waited.

He and his companions had arrived in Shala's chamber moments before, long enough to make out a few of the shouted words of the excited crowd and for them to formulate a quick plan of action.

Brieana and Tybo were to stay out of sight, although Tybo had warned that Dagon could sense his power. It was a given that those who possessed true magic had the ability to find other holders of true magic in close quarters.

"Because you are so regrettably hard to kill," Dagon replied, his eyes suddenly spitting fire in his handsome face as he held his leathery hands behind his back. "By the way, nice trick with the little creatures of the forest—rabbits, I believe? They eliminated a troop I had sent to bring me back your remains."

"Nasty little creatures, aren't they?"

"Oh, yes, indeed, they are, but no nastier than traitorous bastards who bite then turn on their masters," he purred. "Isn't that right, Tybo?"

"Just as I was taught," Tybo said easily as he shimmered into view.

Merlin's Kiss

"Bending light! You were paying attention. But you can't mask the taint of your magic, Tybo. You know, you must needs be punished for this one, oh my, yes."

Relaxed as ever, Dagon strolled over to the chair Kerian occupied and tapped him on the shoulder, his taloned hand a striking contrast to Kerian's golden skin.

"Do you mind? That is my chair."

"By all means," Kerian said as he stood and gave a short bow to the creature that resembled Tybo, but had a nasty, sinister air about him. "Sit."

"And where is this so called 'Woman of Legend?' Is she, too, hidden between bent beams of light?"

"Actually, I am cowering in fear behind you," Brieana said sarcastically as she stepped from the shadows and faced the creature she was to destroy. Excalibur was held tightly in her hand, but was still as dull and lifeless as it appeared after it left the power of the Lady of the Lake.

"Honest bit of goods," Dagon laughed as he examined the small dark woman. Put wings on her and she would easily make a handsome prize for the right man. "And so fresh!"

He inhaled deeply and almost choked as he caught a whiff of her energy signature.

"Oh! I may have been wrong about you."

As a reflex, Brieana's sword came up and Kerian moved closer to her. Tybo spread his wings, now a weary orange as he watched the proceedings with matching eyes.

"Oh, stand down!" Dagon sighed. "Even if this youngling possessed the power of the Old Father, she is not my main concern. The mother of my daughter is."

"Mother?"

Kerian looked puzzled at the dangerous man. Something was not right here.

"Your stepmother, to be accurate," Dagon supplied then chuckled as he watched Kerian's face pale.

Stephanie Burke

"What? Never heard of 'Baby's Mama Drama?' It is an old Light Isles custom, you know, direct from your past. Remind me to explain it to you someday."

"What?"

Brieana moved closer to him, realizing he no longer had a defense for his stepmother, that she had used him all along.

"What?" Dagon rose to his feet, dismissing Tybo with a glance and concentrating his attention on the Warlord. "You thought she cared? That she wanted to help? That she was scared and confused? The little bitch wanted you in her bed, and when the young stuff," he gestured to Brieana, "came along bearing marks of magic, she knew what she wished to obtain would never come to be!"

"She…"

"Used you, abused you, and now wants you dead! I can't fault the dear sweet woman. I want you dead, too."

He crooned a little tune as he clicked his talons together under his chin, his eyes intent on his prey.

Brieana made to step in front of Kerian, to protect her mate, but Dagon began to speak again.

"But I wanted you dead for more than abused vanity, my dear boy. I want you dead for your power."

"It would do you no good," Kerian replied, easing Brieana back behind him, accepting the truth—Shala was not being misguided by this creature. "My men would never follow you."

"But they would follow the Woman of Legend."

"What do I…?" Brieana began, but was interrupted.

"Not you, my dear. If Shala could get rid of you, she could step into your place."

"Excalibur?" she asked softly, clenching the sword tighter in her grasp.

"What? I have no idea who or what that is, my dear. But I do know with you gone, it will be easy for Shala to take command, and then pass off power to me."

300

Merlin's Kiss

"Why don't you just take it?" Tybo demanded. "Like you have taken over the Dark Isles!"

"Well, because this place is not a hellhole, Tybo! Please stay with this conversation! And I thought I trained you better than to ignore the obvious!"

He turned away from his apprentice and focused on Kerian again.

"War has a way of making a place...less than habitable."

"You want an easy conquest," Kerian snarled, the heat of battle filling his veins. "You want to rule without proving yourself capable of controlling what you acquire!"

"Give the boy a prize!" Dagon crowed in delight, his laughter circling around the room. "He is not all brawn and good looks after all."

"You will never get away with it!" Brieana growled, catching the battle fever.

"I already have," Dagon smiled. "After I take care of a certain walking womb, my plans will come to fruition."

"Not necessarily," a female voice said from behind. "You see, I have created a few obstacles for you to overcome."

"Shala, my love!" Dagon smiled, his red eyes glowing in delight. "It is about time you joined this gathering. Now the circle is complete."

Even with her swollen belly, Shala moved with grace. A wicked smile played at her lips and her golden eyes glared at all in the room.

"Now," she purred, her hands resting on her belly, "the killings can begin."

Chapter Thirty-Three

"Planning on committing suicide, dear?" Dagon asked, his lips turning up into a sly grin. "It really is no way out, dear. Besides, what would our daughter think?"

"Daughter?"

Kerian's sharp gasp filled the room as Shala strode casually inside, smile in place.

"My daughter. The future ruler of this land. Now that you are dead, Kerian."

"Yet I stand here," he pointed out, still amazed the woman he had grown to trust, that he defended, would not only betray him but his people as well.

"Well, they don't know that."

She walked over to the window and pulled back the thick drapery, letting in the sounds of war-hungry warriors crying out for justice.

"What have you done?" This from Brieana who took a step forward, eyes blazing her fury.

"The question should be, you silly child, 'what am I about to do?'"

Reaching into her pocket, she pulled out a small velvet bag.

"Another incantation, Shala?" Dagon drawled as he rose to his feet. "I thought you had grown bored with getting backlash from your own spells?"

"But this, dear Dagon, is an incantation from the high mages. Something I believe you overlooked."

"Do tell?"

"The legendary Man-Damon, Dagon. Part drack, part mage, all power. He comes from a spell I cast that in no way uses my magic. Can you imagine such a thing? Or has your ego gotten so

Merlin's Kiss

large you no longer believe there are forces out there, other than yours?"

"Well, I won't stand here and let you cast unknown magic," Tybo shouted as he took a step forward, his eyes flaring red with his anger.

But before he could make another move, Shala threw a pinch of powder from her bag into his face.

"What," he coughed. "What have you done?"

Almost immediately, a silvery sheen covered the winged man. His breathing increased until he was fighting for each breath, as if his lungs were seizing up. His wings turned a sickly shade of gray, the same shade repeated in his eyes and skin.

"Tybo!" Kerian shouted as he moved forward, his hands gripping the man's chest.

His eyes widened in amazement and fear as he felt the man's skin grow hard beneath his very fingers.

Tybo tried to open his mouth, to shout a warning, but he was now powerless to move, a living statue of what once had been a powerful magician and soldier.

"What did you do?" Kerian growled, turning to face the woman he was growing to hate more and more each second.

"I'm sure you remember that slimy lizard you tried so hard to find, Kerian."

"Gren's lost offspring?" he breathed, trying hard not to even think about what his logical mind was now concluding.

"Yes, that unnatural beast's offspring. Behold what is left of him." Shala laughed as she shook the bag in delight.

As Kerian gasped out in maddened anger and disbelief, Shala threw back her head and exploded in maniacal laughter.

"Oh, Kerian! You should see your face!" she snickered. "Your father took great delight in beheading the beast, and I took far more pleasure in ripping his still beating heart from his chest."

Stephanie Burke

"Your bloodthirsty ways remind me of why I chose you in the first place, Shala," Dagon chortled as he made a few motions behind his back. "Your...ambition...has always been arousing to see."

"How could you?" Kerian asked, horror spreading through his mind at the thought of the gentle drack he often played with as a child. "How could you dare kill him? That's murder!"

"To hunt a poor stupid beast? Please, Kerian. You act as if they are human."

"You are the only inhuman thing I see around here," Brieana hissed as she reached out and touched Kerian's arm in a comforting manner. "But what does that have to do with what you have wrought here?"

"Well you see, the heart of a drack contains powerful magic, Brieana. And Kerian, I almost had your father's approval to hunt the wretched beasts down and take what I needed. Their hearts. You see, it has a nice paralyzing effect on humans, and those not quite human."

She gestured to Tybo's wings, and then turned her gaze to Dagon.

"And I know you have cast a spell of protection, Dagon. So wasting this powder on you would be foolish. But there is another use for drack hearts. It is a great tool for summoning."

"Enough of this!" Dagon reared suddenly. He turned to Shala and made to move in her direction.

But before he could reach her, Shala ran to her bedside table, putting distance between them and ripped her eating knife from her belt.

"Like that will work," Dagon snorted as he prepared to rush her. But his actions, even as fast as he could be, were not quick enough to stop her from performing the ritual.

But Shala quickly sliced across her palm and clenched her fist, squeezing out her precious life's blood to the floor.

"I summon thee, Man-Beast, Creature of Legend. Awake from your eternal slumber and release the cosmic energy in your

Merlin's Kiss

soul. Come to me, my minion of darkness, creature of element, thing of power. Creator of kings and destroyer of fools. I summon thee! Come to me and do my bidding! From the fires of the pit of earth, to the frigid heart of the sea! Come to me, creature. Three times I summon thee."

She tossed a pinch of drack powder into the puddle of blood and the whole room seemed to freeze.

"No!" Kerian yelled as he moved in slow motion towards his treacherous stepmother.

Brieana moved just as slowly as she tried to maneuver her sword and face the evil woman.

Dagon skidded to a halt, his eyes on the spot on the floor that had begun to shimmer and smoke.

And then, like a bubble popping, the force holding them back exploded.

They rushed in their motions at an exaggerated speed, moving faster than the eyes could follow for just a second.

Then the spot exploded, sending shimmering powder and dark smoke across the room.

Kerian threw his arm up, protecting his eyes as Brieana ducked low into a warrior's crouch, balanced and ready, yet protecting herself from most of the blast.

Dagon's spell of protection instantly erected an invisible shield that the smoke flowed around like river water around a stone.

Shala threw back her head in laughter, ignoring the hissing of her child from within her mind.

"Who dares summon me?" a deep voice bellowed, a voice that shook the very rafters with its resonance.

Instantly, Brieana's head popped up.

It couldn't be!

But it was!

"Merlin!" she screamed as she rose to her full height.

Stephanie Burke

"Lady Brieana?"

Merlin's Kiss

Chapter Thirty-Four

"Kill them! Kill them all!" Shala screamed, one hand on her slightly swollen stomach, the other pointing to Dagon and her stepson.

"Merlin!" Brieana breathed, her hand going to her mouth, eyes wide and glistening with unshed tears. "It is you."

"Lady Brieana. You seemed to have landed in the middle again."

"Are my words not heard?" Shala screamed, growing impatient and fearful. How did the Man-Demon know that stupid little girl?

"Quiet, you!" Merlin snapped and instantly Shala's hands went to her throat.

Try as she might, not a word would pass her frozen throat. Her eyes widened in sheer fright even as a hissing laughter filled her mind.

Stupid, the voice of her child hissed. *You are so stupid.*

"My Lord Merlin," Brieana said as she stepped around the frozen Tybo and her stiff warrior. "Please, you must help me!"

"I cannot."

"But you have to! Excalibur is dead in my grasp," she explained as she walked over to the man who looked amazingly the same.

His long dark hair wafted in a breeze of his own power, his eyes were intense as they observed her. He even smelled the same, of musk, magic, and man.

"This continent that I am supposed to rule, this place, is being overrun by dark forces. How can I help? What do I do?"

"You know what to do, Lady," Merlin sighed. "But I have sworn an oath never to interfere again."

307

Stephanie Burke

"But you said it was for the good of the Britons. I understand that now, but I need your guidance. That was the Britons, Merlin. That was another time and another place. This is here. This is now!"

"I cannot, little Brieana," Merlin sighed, his eyes looking sad as he stared at what he considered his one true miscarriage of justice. People were not meant to be pawns, and yet he had turned this delicate creature into one.

"But why?"

"I created a puppet king, Brieana. One the people could follow. And while I pulled the strings, the Britons prospered. Despite the guilt I felt for your fate, dear Brieana, I pulled the strings of my puppet until he decided to cut those strings free. Lust and desire are within us all, child. But lust and desire, running unchecked, started the downfall of the kingdom, your perfect kingdom, Brieana. And lust, desire and greed not only corrupted it, they brought it to its knees. The age of magic was lost, child. And with it the ideals of truth and justice, very lofty and proper goals, were ground into the dust."

"And Arthur…?"

"He died because of his unchecked lusts, Brieana. All that was right and good seemed to fade with him."

"And the kingdom fell." Brieana sounded tired.

"Camelot fell," Merlin repeated.

"But this is not Camelot, Merlin. This is the Light Isles. You can make a difference here. Please! Advise me, My Lord. Help guide me on the right path. I am no puppet Queen to blindly follow your word, but I will gladly accept your advice. How can I make Excalibur live? How can I end the scourge that is threatening the land?"

"And the skies," Dagon felt a need to add. This sickening sweet, touching, and oh, so moving moment, was making him ill.

All turned to look at the demonically beautiful man.

Merlin's Kiss

"What? Did you think I would not attempt to have every advantage? Air supremacy is the key, Woman of Legend," Dagon sneered.

"We will stop you," Kerian snarled, drawing his big sword and stepping forward to meet Dagon.

"You will try, you muscle-bound oaf. You will try and you will fail. Who do you think controls the people now? Shala with her fertile belly filled with my essence? This Woman of Legend with some unknown sword that is supposed to bring me low? This mysterious Man-Demon who can't stop making chum eyes at your woman? This is ridiculous," Dagon sighed as he turned to leave the room. "I will see you all dead." He turned to Shala. "You, after my offspring is born from your wasted body, but all of you will be dead soon."

He chuckled as he calmly walked towards the door.

A fierce roar made him turn on his heel, leathery wings drawn tight to his back, as Kerian rushed him.

There was a clank and sparks bounded off of the magical shielding Dagon held around his person, as Kerian's sword slammed into it.

"Fool," Dagon hissed as he raised his hand to summon his dark inner power.

"Enough of this!" Merlin bellowed, and everyone froze.

"Is this what has become of the world?"

He turned to Shala, then to Tybo frozen with the drack heart powder, then to Dagon, a creature with some great inner strength but a dark core. To Kerian who was poised to lose everything in the defense of his woman and her kingdom. And finally to Brieana, who was once again confused, lost, and stuck in the middle.

"It appears I have wronged you again, Brieana. Mayhap I was thinking like a Briton when I sent you to this place. But you need more than what I have given you in order for you to succeed. So I give you this. The key to controlling Excalibur has always been within you, in the decision you make."

Stephanie Burke

He turned to observe the room again.

"In our time, my dear, perverted magic such as this didn't exist. There was no place for it to grow this strong, because the elementals kept things in balance. And I feel so very little of them left in this place. So I give you this."

With a wave of his arm, Tybo began to lose the gray tint that held him imprisoned. He blinked rapidly and inhaled a deep breath while stretching like he was awakening from a long nap.

"I cannot interfere with your destiny, my dear, I gave my word. But I can aid you in stopping those who would defile the natural order of things."

Merlin stepped back and just as suddenly, the players began to move once again.

"No!" Shala screamed and darted between Kerian and Dagon, out of the room.

Her plans were in ruins! The Man-Demon would not aid her. That little bitch was the Woman of Legend. She had lost her chance to grasp real power. Now it was time to rely on brute force.

Tybo started to dart after her, but instead turned towards his former mentor.

Dagon shook with shock. Despite his strongest shield, the mysterious creature managed to freeze him in place. Curious.

He turned towards Tybo, and smiled.

"It appears there are forces greater than me, my protégé."

Before anyone else could move, there came a great hue and cry from the courtyard.

"They are here!" Shala screamed as she ran. "They have invaded the castle! The Dark Isles monsters are here!"

"Schlack!" Dagon hissed as he turned to the people in the room. "I guess it is time for me to take my leave."

Merlin's Kiss

"You are going nowhere!" Kerian growled, but before he could move, a blinding light emanated from Dagon...and he was gone, all but his voice.

"I left something to keep you occupied, Lord Kerian," the voice whispered as it faded. "Look to the skies."

They all rushed to the windows, but Brieana and Merlin held back.

"Thank you," she whispered.

"Small enough thing to do, My Lady," he replied.

"That kiss...?"

"Is better left between the two of us. Otherwise, who knows what may happen?"

He began to fade. Just like that! No flashes of light, no blast of energy, just began to grow more transparent until there was hardly a shadow of him, like he was never there.

"Where are you going?" Brieana asked urgently. "Where...."

"To explore this new world of yours, my Queen. It feels of magic and it calls to me."

"Schlack!"

The curse made Brieana turn towards Tybo and Kerian at the windows, trying to see what had upset them. She glanced back at Merlin, but he was gone, not even the smell of him remained.

"Thank you," she whispered, before turning back to the window to see what plague had descended upon them now.

And plague was the perfect word, for the sky was filled with leather-clad winged men.

"What Dagon does not keep, he destroys," Tybo hissed as he watched his fellow Dark Isles warriors fill the sky and begin to rain destruction down upon Mirage.

Chapter Thirty-Five

"We've got to stop them!" Tybo shouted as he bolted for the door.

"Wait!" Kerian screamed as he and Brieana turned to follow.

"No!" Tybo yelled back. "I am second-in-command! They will listen to me!"

Kerian, sword drawn, raced after his new friend, while Brieana gazed at Excalibur, said a brief prayer and tossed her bag, with the sword Kerian had given her, into the corner of the room.

"Please, let me find the answer," she prayed, before turning to follow them.

She managed to make it to the outer chamber when some instinct born of years on the battlefield told her to duck.

As she did, a sword went soaring over her head.

She dove into a roll, came up on her feet, and turned to face her attacker.

Shala stood there, eyes blazing fury as she watched the child who stolen her dreams.

"Whore!" she hissed. "It's time you die!"

The sound of metal clashing against metal filled the room as the two powerful women met in open combat.

* * * * *

"Wait!" Kerian shouted as he followed behind Tybo. "My people will…"

His voice trailed off as he saw a glittering jewel in the distance.

Merlin's Kiss

Even Tybo halted his mad rush, as a rainbow seemed to appear in the afternoon sky.

"What is it?" Tybo breathed as the feel of magic and power tickled his skin and made his hair stand on end.

"True-mother," Kerian breathed as felt the warmth and love she projected to him fill his being with comfort.

The drackoons had arrived, Gren and Dalis in the lead followed by a large pearlized purple being.

"Zorn!" Kerian screamed, eyes wide in wonder as the drackoons filled the sky.

But a fearful murmur from the courtyard drew his attention again to his people.

"Trapped!" someone shouted. "The Dark Isles and the drackoons! We must fight!"

And as the first icy blasts struck the Dark Isles menace, the first spears cast with fear and hatred struck the mighty drackoons.

"No!" Kerian screamed as he fought his way towards the courtyards. "No! Not this! They are here to help!"

All the while, Tybo was scrambling to get into a position to be heard by his people.

"Halt this madness!" he roared as his fellow winged warriors began hurling sulfur bombs at the people of Mirage and the drackoons alike.

Seeing Kerian wade amongst his people gave Tybo the idea to reach higher ground, to be seen by his people, to make them understand this attack was not wanted.

Spying a lookout tower, he spread his wings, pale gold with frustration, and launched himself upwards into the air.

As he landed and opened his mouth to shout instructions to his people, he heard a voice scream, "The Dark Isle menace has breached the castle!"

The voice carried and several stout warriors turned in his direction.

Stephanie Burke

Just as he felt hands grasp the muscles below and above his wings and twist them painfully and a knife sliced through tendons, immobilizing him, a voice hissed in his ear.

"What is mine, I keep or destroy as I see fit. You were mine, Tybo. And your destruction begins at my hands."

"Dagon," he breathed before he was shoved off of the tower.

The sky, the one thing that sustained him for all these years, his one source of freedom and his true love, for once in his life, rejected him.

He tried to scream as the wind rushed past his face, blinding him as he plummeted down, through the fingers of wind that for once refused to catch him.

He managed to throw his hands in front of his face, but his wings were paralyzed, refusing to spread wide and capture the current that usually caressed them.

Down he fell, the wind tearing at his clothes, his useless wings, his pride, and all that he was, down into the arms of the enraged Mirage warriors.

* * * * *

"Stupid girl!" Shala hissed as she drew back her sword and thrust again at Brieana, attacking her with the flying steel, keeping her on the defensive. Her warrior skills coming back to her after so may years as Lady of Mirage.

"Old hag!" Brieana hissed back as she blocked thrust after thrust from the pregnant woman.

"Old enough to know better, little girl, than to mess with another woman's castle!" Shala screamed as she continued her frenzied attack, driving Brieana back towards the halls that led to the outer courtyard.

"And see what your wisdom has brought you?" Brieana asked as she blocked a blow, knocked Shala's sword to the side, and curved her blow inward, trying to strike the woman's wrist.

Merlin's Kiss

But she missed by a hairsbreadth and had to leap backwards to avoid getting a slice to the side or the neck.

"It brought me a child of power, little girl. It brought me knowledge that I will use to rule this Isle."

Brieana retreated, moving further and further back, until her she heard the roar of the crowd fighting in the courtyard.

She closed her mind to what was going on around her, failing to see the drackoons knocking the winged warriors out of the sky, or the spears cast by the fighters gathered on the ground, wounding the Dark Isles men and drackoon alike.

"It brought you destruction!" Brieana screamed as she pushed a running servant out of the way of Shala's frantic sword blows.

This caused Shala to step to the right against the castle wall, and for once gave her a glimpse of all that she had wrought.

"No!" Shala screamed as she saw her people, her castle, her land being destroyed.

Chunks of stone were falling, turned into solid ice by the blast of the drackoon's breath while those she would have ruled fell dead and injured to the cobbled stones of Mirage's courtyard.

"This is all your fault!" the woman screamed, returning to her attack, determined to make Brieana, the Woman of Legend, pay for making her dreams fall.

* * * * *

"Stop this!" Kerian bellowed as he waded through the piles of people, kicking weapons out of their hands. "Cease this at once!"

A few warriors, recognizing who was speaking, stopped in confusion. The Warlord was dead, wasn't he?

More and more of his people lowered their weapons and stared in awe at the man, seemingly back from the dead.

315

"Cease!" he bellowed, shoving one archer aside as he took aim at a drackoon and knocking him off of his feet.

A murmur began to fill the vast courtyard, and gradual silence as more and more of the warriors stopped and looked around to see what was happening.

"True-mother!" Kerian bellowed.

Even the Dark Isles forces seemed to freeze for a moment, then a large scream rent the air.

The large platinum-white drackoon swooped through the sky, knocking winged men aside as she raced towards her human son.

Kerian cried out in gladness to see at her side, Zorn, fully transformed and large as the female who had spawned him, racing along.

The warriors of Mirage gasped and ducked as the angry avian lizards swooped over their heads, yet no one thought to lift a weapon as the magical lizards swept through the skies.

"Zorn!" Kerian shouted, a smile growing on his face as the drackoon swooped down and hovered over Kerian.

Returned to you, I have! his voice thundered in his mind. *Woman of Legend, I protect!*

"More purple hide for my leggings," Kerian responded, though all could see how happy he was to see the no-longer-small purple drack.

Because you needed me, I come, my son! Gren's majestic voice filled his head, making his eyes water with the love he felt for his True-mother.

"True-mother…" he began, "I have news."

But before he could continue, the winged warriors got over their shock at seeing this puny magic-less man speak to a fellow winged creature.

Silently and deadly, they began their attack again, raining sulfur and illusion down on the crowd as well as at the lizards in the sky.

Merlin's Kiss

Kerian's people instantly retaliated, striking at the Dark Isles soldiers, leaving the drackoons alone.

"Stop!" Kerian bellowed, as pandemonium began to take over the courtyard once more.

"We can make them stop!" a voice screamed from behind him. "We have their leader!"

Kerian turned and horror filled his face as he watched the beaten and bruised body of Tybo being carried towards him.

"Tybo! No!" he bellowed as he watched his friend, body being propped up, blood running from his various injuries, nose and mouth. But what horrified Kerian the most, what made his blood turn cold, what made him bellow to the heavens in anguish, was that Tybo's wings were gone.

Chapter Thirty-six

Silence filled the courtyard at Kerian's bellow.

The joyous people carting around Tybo froze as Kerian drew his sword and raced towards the fallen man.

Even the Dark Isles soldiers paused, eyes horrified as they looked upon what was left of their second-in-command.

And in that silence, a new sound began to ring.

Curious, several people looked up towards the courtyard entrance.

What they saw made even the most battle-hardy warriors pause.

Shala and Brieana were oblivious to the attention they were gathering as they each fought for what they believed in.

"You killed my people!" Shala was shouting, as she seemed to fight the strange dark-haired woman back. "You caused all of this!"

"You fucked that thing with wings who started all of this!" Brieana countered. "You tried to kill Kerian and you invited the invaders into the castle! This is your doing, Shala!"

Screaming out her rage, Shala brought her sword up and rushed Brieana again.

"Your pitiful sword is no match for me!" she hissed as Brieana wielded the rusted Excalibur. "You will fall and this land will be mine!"

"This land already has a Master!" Brieana hissed in response as she ducked a blow and leapt over a knee strike. Where did the pregnant woman get her energy, her strength?

"You dare to take what is mine?"

"It's Kerian's!" Brieana shouted...and Excalibur began to grow warm in her hand.

318

Merlin's Kiss

"It's mine! You are stealing it away from me!"

"It's his, by right and might!" Brieana screamed again. "It is his, and as rightful Queen, as the Woman of Legend, I rule it by his side!"

Excalibur grew almost hot to the touch, but Brieana was too busy parrying Shala to make much of it.

"You mean you will rule it! You took him to your bed and now you rule through him!"

Shala took another mighty swing, drawing on the energy that Dagon gifted her with, but that would soon be used up.

"I mean to rule it with him! Do not paint me with your brushstrokes, Shala! This land was meant to be ruled by someone who understands right and justice as well as might with a sword! That person is not you!"

"It is mine!" Shala screamed. "Justice decrees it to be!"

"What do you know of justice?"

Both women were panting now, sweating heavily with their exertions.

Shala's gown was torn and dirtied from her movements. Even the baby within her was silent, seemingly listening to the words that Brieana spoke.

"This place is mine! I fought for it! I protected it from those accursed lizards! I brought the people together to subjugate themselves to me!"

"You lied! You schemed! You brought destruction!" Brieana declared, her voice growing more majestic and her sword arm strengthening as she suddenly went on the attack.

"You brought death and misery! You destroyed the land you tried to rule! You murdered innocents! You are not fit to rule! You are not fit to live!"

As she took a mighty swing, Shala brought her own sword up in a defensive position, only to have it snapped in two.

Shala looked up and screamed as Excalibur seemed to take on a life of its own.

The sword gleamed and hummed as it sang through the air. Brieana herself glowed with an internal power that Shala knew her stolen magic could never match.

She watched, wide-eyed, as the now razor-sharp tip of the transformed sword arched towards her neck. They watched as it stopped a mere hair's breadth from slicing her throat.

All those in the courtyard held their breaths, waiting to see what would happen.

All had heard Brieana's accusations and noted that Shala did not deny them. They all heard how she schemed and lied to get to a position of power. Now all waited to see what Brieana, who could only be the legendary Woman of Power, would do.

"You don't deserve to live!" Brieana hissed again, her voice carrying across the courtyard. "You tried to seduce then murder your own stepson. You tried to kill me because you perceived me as a threat. You murdered the drack in order to obtain its heart for you dark rites."

Gren seemed to freeze, to drop several inches before recovering herself. But only Kerian heard her anguished wail as she lost the final dream of her beloved lost child returning home.

"You invited invaders inside your people's castle gate, Lady Shala," Brieana continued. "You destroyed everything that was right, perverted the good, murdered the innocent...all for want of power. You do not deserve to live." Her voice rose to a righteous shout as she stared at the cowering woman. "But I cannot kill you."

There was a collective gasp as Brieana's words were heard and repeated.

"It is not my place to cast judgment over you, Shala of Mirage. No one person should have control over life and death. This is what you forgot. A ruler is supposed to love her people, not the power that lets her lead them. The land is nothing without the people, Shala. And that what makes a real ruler. The love she has for her people. The willingness to die for her people!"

320

Merlin's Kiss

As these words passed her lips, Brieana felt as if a great weight was lifted off of her chest.

"All this time, I fought for a rulership, for a place to call my own. to rule as I was destined to rule. I never once considered whom I would be ruling. I am not fit to rule either. No one should rule Mirage but Kerian."

As these words left her lips, the sword seemed to jerk out of her hand.

All watched in awe as the sword rose above her head and began to spin wildly.

Bright flashes of color filled the courtyard, filled the sky, as the sword shook off its ill-used and rusted appearance.

As they all watched, the powerful symbol of justice and kingship began to glow.

"Behold. The true and righteous ruler." The voice boomed from nowhere and yet was everywhere. The sword seemed to spin out of control, spinning, flying around the courtyard, sending light and majesty in all directions.

Faster and faster it spun, its light falling on everyone who exuded even the slightest of leadership abilities. It even swung over the assembled drackoon who hovered, waiting, anticipation in their eyes as the true ruler of this land was picked.

Then just as fast, it was over.

The sword shot towards Brieana, headed straight for her heart.

But instead of piercing her chest and taking her life, it granted her a new one.

The sword flipped over, hilt first, screaming to a halt inches in front of her chest.

Almost of their own violation, her hands reached up and wrapped around the hilt of the glowing sword.

"Behold! The Queen!" the voice bellowed as all fell to their knees stunned as a bright glow suffused Brieana, making her leadership known.

Stephanie Burke

"Behold, My King, consort, and co-ruler!" Brieana shouted as she pointed.

As if by magic, the crowd parted to expose their new king.

But Kerian was on his knees, not in supplication to a new ruler. He held the battered body of his friend in his arms.

He lifted tear-streaked eyes to his mate, his body hunched protectively over Tybo.

Before he could speak, the sword flew straight at him, spinning and twirling, looking as if it would strike him dead, but instead, came to a sudden stop and hovered above him.

Again, as if his limbs were being controlled by another, his right hand lifted and the sword stilled within his grasp.

"Behold!" the voice bellowed. "The King."

Chapter Thirty-Seven

"Tybo!" Brieana whispered in horror as she raced from the walkway towards Kerian and their fallen friend.

Kerian lowered his fist, Excalibur warm and glowing in his grasp, and dropped the sword to the ground.

Even Shala gasped at his audacity. That was a thing of magic he was mistreating.

But Kerian had eyes only for his mate and his friend.

"His wings," Kerian whispered as he pressed his hands to the terrible wounds that bled freely.

"Tybo," Brieana whispered as she ran her hands over his face, brushing bloodied hair out of his eyes. "Tybo?"

"My Queen," his split lips parted as a weak voice whispered out.

"Tybo!" Brieana cried, tears making tracks in the dirt and sweat that covered her face. "Hang on. We can save you, my friend. Please fight."

"My wings," Tybo whispered, his eyes blank and pale as death opened to watch the two people who seemed to care for him. "They are gone."

"That doesn't matter," Brieana began. "The healers…"

"Cannot give me back my wings," he countered, groaning as shudders wracked his body. "Let me die," he whispered as he lay back in Kerian's arms. "Without my wings, my magic, I am nothing. Let me die in peace."

"No, Tybo, no!" Brieana murmured. "You have so much to live for."

"Brieana, My Queen," he whispered. "What made me, me, is gone. My soul is gone, Brieana. Better to die now, a warrior's death, instead of suffering for the rest of my days, half a man, half a soul. Let me die."

He struggled as he spoke, his breathing becoming more labored until he closed his eyes and his body shuddered.

"No, Tybo! No! Not like this! This is not your fate!"

Brieana began to cry in earnest, her hands wiping the tears from her eyes but leaving her face covered in her friend's deep red blood.

"No!" she cried. "Not like this! Not for my war!"

As she ran her hands frantically over her face, a sharp pain made her look down at the ring on her hand.

True power, she thought. Elemental power.

Throwing her head back, she bellowed at the top of her voice, "Nemoae!"

Her voice carried to the skies, echoing and bouncing off the stone, the walls magnifying it, and sending it hurtling through time and space.

As the last echoes of it faded from the sky, a great rumbling filled the air.

Dark clouds filled the sky as the air suddenly dropped in temperature.

"You rang?" a deep feminine voice rippled out, amusement filling its tones, as a large silver cloud dropped from the darkened skies.

People began to scream and even the drackoons parted company to allow the cloud passage.

Nemoae, the Great Elemental, the Lady of the Lake, stepped out of her cloud to stand before the assembled peoples, cloaked in nothing but sea-foam, billowing blue hair, and a smile.

"Nemoae," Brieana, whispered. "Lady, please help me! It's Tybo! He's…"

Merlin's Kiss

"Almost dead as a doornail." she cut Brieana off as she stared down at the man. "I am getting a taste of power from this one, but it is fading fast."

"They tore off his wings!"

The men responsible inhaled deeply as Nemoae's eyes seemed to search out each person in the courtyard, and read deep into their souls.

"Want me to kill them?" she asked, and the guilty parties fell to their knees, heads turning to the ground in supplication.

"No. They didn't know what they were doing. But please, you are the only person powerful enough to help him!"

Nemoae sighed as she looked down at the fallen man in Kerian's arms. He was barely breathing.

"I wish I could help you, I really do," Nemoae sighed. "But I am an Elemental. I can fuse magical energy into his body, but the body is too torn for me to be sure it would hold fast. Key magical elements, components," she tried again at Brieana's confused look. "Body parts are missing."

"His wings?"

"His wings."

"How can we…?"

"I only know of one wretch who can recreate wings, and that is because the bastard has a set of them that he hides internally."

The Lady of the Lake's eyes began to glimmer and glow like they did when she was referring to…

"Merlin!"

Nemoae jumped as Brieana placed her fingers upon the torc around her neck and cried out that bastard's name.

"Yeah, that's him," Nemoae said before the air around them began to shimmer.

The Lady jerked her head up, scenting the air a moment before the bastard himself winked into view.

Stephanie Burke

"You called?" he asked, his robes flying around him in a wind created of his power.

"You bastard!" Nemoae shouted as she launched herself at the wizard.

"Nemoae?" he asked, a moment before her fist connected with his face.

He went down in a flurry of robes and hair, the Lady of the Lake riding his body to the ground.

Once he hit the ground with a rather loud boom, Nemoae planted her lips on his and gave him a kiss that had been stored up for eons.

Merlin's hands flew out across her back, pulling at her hair, then slowly tugging her closer.

Soft moans and whimpers filled the air as Brieana felt a blush creep up her face.

Indeed, most of the people in the courtyard found a reason to look somewhere, anywhere, else. Suddenly toes, fingers, drackoons, the hovering winged men, all looked very interesting.

"Okay!" Kerian finally bellowed, breaking the two of them apart. "Lust later! Tybo now!"

The two stared, sightlessly at each other for a moment, before slowly rising to their feet.

"Ty- uh, Tybo?" Merlin asked with a dazed look in his eyes.

"Help him!" Brieana demanded. "Please!"

"You know I can't interfere in your life, Brieana," Merlin sighed sadly as he felt the life force leaving the brave young man. "I want to help but…."

"Stuff it, Merlin!" Nemoae snorted as she rolled her eyes at the wizard.

"Stuff…it?"

"Stop the bullshit. You can help that boy if you want to."

"But my word! I gave my word, baby!"

Merlin's Kiss

At this endearment, Brieana turned to stare at the Lady, whose blush was kind of purple under the blue-tinted skin.

"What?" she snarled, snapping her fingers and sending a shower of icy cold rain on Brieana, and every one who stared at her in amusement.

Merlin rolled his eyes at her antics.

"As I was saying," she growled as everyone found something else to stare at and the rains stopped. "You gave your word not to interfere in Brieana's life. But what about the daughter?"

Merlin blinked, then closed his eyes and muttered something under his breath.

"Hell," he hissed as his eyes landed on Brieana's face.

"Daughter?" Kerian asked blinking at his mate.

"Too many damned daughters!" Merlin growled, his eyes cutting to Shala, who still remained in the courtyard walkway, on her knees in shock.

"What?" Brieana asked, her eyes going from Shala, to Merlin, to Kerian.

"Daughter?" Kerian whispered again, eyes widening in joy and no small amount of fear.

"Daughter!" Nemoae laughed. Then, pointing to Tybo, she whispered, "He is for the daughter."

"Brieana?" Kerian whispered, his eyes filling with love and longing as he stared at his mate.

"She didn't say which daughter," Shala's voice cut through the silence.

All eyes went to Merlin.

"Oh, no! I'll fix him because he belongs to the daughter, but telling which daughter would interfere with their lives!"

He crossed his arms and glared at Nemoae, daring her to contradict him.

Stephanie Burke

"You are right," she conceded. "But that one," she pointed to Shala, "is too dangerous to have running around loose."

"First things first," Merlin nodded as he threw his arms in Tybo's direction.

Immediately, the man floated free of Kerian's lap and a glowing cocoon of white light began to enclose his body.

Within seconds, he was covered from head to foot in strands of pure magic. Into this Nemoae thrust her power, and the cocoon began to glow blue.

"This will heal and protect him," Nemoae reassured Brieana as the new Queen stared in awe.

"Until...?" she commented, but was cut off by Merlin.

"Until someone with a righteous heart, a determined mind, and a rare power frees him." He added softly, "With a kiss."

With that the cocoon flashed bright blue then cleared. The spell was cast and set. Tybo resided within a clear case of pure magic, his face healed and cleaned while a translucent set of magnificent wings wrapped around his body.

"Not again!" Nemoae groaned as she stared at Merlin.

"What?"

"You did it again! You know, I am not so sure that I'm happy to see you? You pull this magical shit all the time, Merlin! This has got to stop!"

"What?"

"This kiss bullshit! It always causes more harm than good, you bastard!"

"Bastard! I'll have you know that my mother..."

"Was a fucking witch and your daddy was a lizard boy!"

Old Father! The drackoons chorused as one as they hovered above.

"Old Father, my ass!" Nemoae was...pissed.

"That is the way I do things!" Merlin defended, his anger starting to show.

Merlin's Kiss

"That is the way you screw up people's lives! I thought you had learned your lesson by now! But I guess not! So that leaves me only one choice!"

"What?" he growled as he stared at his lover of old. Actually, that sea-foam was slipping and he was catching an enticing view of her blue-tinted flesh. Was that a ring of silver through her left nipple?

"Until I grant you a kiss not clouded with anger, you remain in my water bubble, with me!"

"Wha...?"

Before he could complete the word, Merlin was encased in a large clear bubble. It floated over the crowd, around the people of Mirage, and into the Lady's cloud.

"I told you I was more powerful," she whispered to Brieana as she stepped back onto her cloud, beside the pouting Merlin.

"Wow," Brieana breathed. She had never truly believed Nemoae's boast, but now seeing what she just saw...

"It's not in what you know, toots," Nemoae called back in her strange way of speaking. "It's all in who you know."

Just as quickly, the cloud was gone, the skies lightened up, and all hints of magic faded from their view.

Kerian, looking down at his friend, was content he was healing until... He was unsure who would wake him up. But he knew he would protect his friend until then.

Turning towards those who had ripped the wings from his body, Kerian commanded, "You will take him to my chambers in the castle. And you all will guard him with your lives."

The men scurried to obey, grateful for their lives.

Brieana raced down and picked up Excalibur. Again, it appeared to be a normal sword. No longer rusted and nicked, a beautiful example workmanship, but still just a sword.

"What now?" Brieana asked Kerian.

"You are Queen," he replied.

"You are King," she returned.

Stephanie Burke

And away, they get, the winged warriors, Zorn added as he spoke into both of their heads.

They looked, and sure enough, the Dark Isles winged men, leaving illusion in their wake, disappeared from view.

"After them!" One Mirage warrior shouted as he looked up and noticed the winged men disappearing from sight.

A loud rumble, and a surge towards weapons greeted his announcement.

"Enough!" Kerian shouted, raising his hands as he stared at his people. "Have you not seen enough violence? Do you want to die?"

Murmurs met this pronouncement.

"If you want to die, I will kill you myself!"

Silence.

"This should be a time of learning, a time of peace! The threat is gone! The danger is passed, and still you thirst for war, for blood! To survive, we need peace!"

Taking Brieana by the arm, he led her over to the courtyard entrance.

Shala rose to her feet and sneered at them both.

"These people don't want peace, Kerian. They want to be led to glorious victory. What can you and your little girl do for them?"

"That is it!" Brieana snarled as she walked over to face Shala.

At her approach, Shala threw up a hand, striking Brieana across her face.

Her face turned with the force of the blow, but as she straightened, she looked at Shala and smiled.

Before Shala could blink, Brieana's fist shot up, striking her dead in the nose and knocking her to the ground.

Merlin's Kiss

"I've never hit a pregnant woman before, but I make an exception in your case. And stop calling me girl! I was born over two thousand years ago. I'm older than you!"

"Behold, your Queen," Kerian called out, amusement in his voice.

A loud cheer greeted his shouted comment, making Brieana blush.

"And as my first act as co-ruler, I want that bitch locked away. Because she is pregnant, make her prison a comfortable one. And no magic."

"No!" Shala wailed, but the people, filled with awe at the magic their ruler possessed and glad to have the one man who always gave more of himself than he asked of others, drowned her cries out.

Gentle but firm hands dragged Shala off, the laughter of her unborn child resonating in her mind.

"We are a people united!" Kerian shouted, and taking Excalibur from Brieana he thrust it high in the air. "United in justice and peace!"

The roars of approval filled the air and he wrapped his arm tighter around Brieana.

Looking up, Brieana saw something she thought to never see again. Her dear friend flew through the air, directly towards her.

"Zorn!" she exclaimed, and the little drack, now a fully-grown drackoon, swooped done before her.

Back to you, I've come, he murmured softly in her mind as she pulled free of Kerian and threw her arms around the purple drackoon's neck as he bent down to her.

"Oh, Zorn," she whispered as happy tears fell from her eyes.

Kerian laughed as Zorn shot him a superior look over her shoulder.

The people stared in awe.

Stephanie Burke

"Peace between us all!" Kerian stated and his True-mother nodded her head, before she and Dalis led their family back to the caves high on the Dark Mountain.

Be back, I will! Zorn stated, before he eased away from Brieana, threw his head back, and with one leap soared high into the sky, a shimmering, glistening beacon of hope.

"To our future!" Kerian roared, and Brieana's hand went to her stomach.

"To all of our futures," she whispered moved back a few steps to take her place beside her man, and rule her kingdom.

She was prepared to live happily ever after... but...

Merlin's Kiss

Epilogue

Shala sat and fumed in her new set of rooms. Sure, every comfort was offered to her, every wish fulfilled. Every one but the thing she wanted most—her freedom. Her freedom and her revenge.

She narrowed her eyes and rubbed her stomach as hissing laughter filled her head.

Her daughter could not contain her amusement at her mother's incarceration.

"I will be free," she snarled back, her hand rubbing her stomach, willing her child to love her.

When you are dead, her child answered back, hissing laughter filling her head again.

* * * * *

Dagon sat in his chambers in the Dark Isles and fumed.

His plans had not gone accordingly. There were some things he had not foreseen.

He drummed his fingers on the table as his mind whirled in contemplation.

He still wanted the Light Isles for his own. He wanted to claim his daughter when she was born. He wanted to make sure Tybo was dead or at least suffering. And he wanted revenge on those who thwarted him—the Man-Demon she called Merlin, the Woman of Legend, the Warlord. They all must pay.

But instead of giving vent to his temper in some explosive display of power, he closed his eyes and contemplated the future.

He smiled, his red eyes glowing wildly, as his mind raced with his newest plan.

His plotting was interrupted, however, by a tap at his door.

"Master," the young woman whispered, head bowed as she entered the room, her wings tightly coiled around her body.

"Just what I needed," he purred as he pointed to his crotch. "On your knees, my dear. And do remember not to use teeth."

It was good to be the Master.

* * * * *

Brieana screamed as she arched her back, her head dropping to her folded arms, forcing her bottom back towards her pleasure-giving man.

Sweat poured from her body and she moaned as the silken sheets abraded her swollen nipples.

The bed swung in countermotion for each thrust, emphasizing the pleasure streaming through her body not only from the direct stimulation to her clit, but also from the head of his cock striking that hidden spot within her.

"More!" she wailed as he slowly pulled out, feeling each bump and vein of him stimulating her swollen walls. "Kerian, more!"

One hand around her waist holding her firmly, Kerian bent over her body, making her push up into him at the feel of him covering her, dominating her, protecting her, loving her.

His other hand reached up to gently cup her swollen breasts.

He marveled at their increased girth, the only sign of pregnancy she showed. That, and their sudden extreme sensitivity. And so soon, too.

Gently tugging, he bent low and whispered into her ear, "You are so wet for me Brieana, so hot, so tight. I want you to explode for me, love. I'm going to make you scream."

Merlin's Kiss

His erotic words sent a tremor through her body and pushed her senses that much closer to climax as she tightened her muscles around him.

He groaned and thrust a bit harder, grinding his hips at the end of the thrust, stimulating her swollen woman's flesh as he gained maximum pleasure from the move.

"Mmm." Brieana moaned, her whole body tingling and tightening around him.

"I can feel you, Kerian," she whispered, her voice high and breathy. "You feel so deep in me."

She closed her eyes and began to rhythmically tighten her muscles around him, bringing a gasp to his lips as he rose up and grasped her hips in both hands.

"This ends," he growled as he pulled back and thrust deep inside sharply.

"Yes!" Brieana screamed, losing control and pushing herself up on her arms desperate to get closer to the pleasure he was giving. "Harder!"

But Kerian kept at a slow deliberate pace, slowly pulling out and thrusting deeply back in, striking spots that made her gasp and scream as she tried to meld their bodies closer.

"Let go for me," he demanded as he held her in this position, drawing on her loss of control and turning it back to her as pure erotic pleasures. "Let go."

Brieana moaned as she felt the tingling numbness in her clit that signaled release was at hand.

Her muscles began to tighten slowly, almost against her will, and pleasure zinged through all her nerves and raced like fire through her veins. Her eyes closed as colors and stars began to cloud her vision. Her toes began to curl and her legs to stiffen as her stomach shuddered in ecstasy at each of his plunges.

Her mouth opened to scream aloud her pleasure to the world, but her voice was stolen as sensation built on top of painfully hot, wonderful, beautiful sensation.

Her breath caught, her body stiffened, and then her climax was upon her.

"Kerian!" She screamed his name through the waves of fire that washed over her body, even as her inner muscles began to dance around his hard cock. "Oh God, yes!"

"Brieana," Kerian gasped as her sudden release took him by surprise.

The feel of her inner walls massaging his cock was too much!

The tingling he felt at the base of his spine intensified as he felt his sac rise up to the base of his cock. He felt his hot seed churning inside, ready to explode free, and suddenly, all his muscles bunched.

"Brieana," he managed to gasp as he felt his cock swell even larger inside her. Then the need to thrust took over his mind.

Almost mindlessly he pounded into her, feeling his engorged cock ready to fire deep inside her.

Suddenly, a great wave of passion flooded his senses!

All he could see was Brieana, all he could smell was Brieana, all he could taste was Brieana!

His cock began to pulse, shooting his hot essence deep into her willing body, as his hips automatically kept up the thrusting motions, sending waves of delight through his body.

"Brieana!"

Then just as suddenly, his body turned boneless, all of his strength expended in pleasing his mate and slaking his own lusts on her beloved body.

Kerian retained enough of himself to move to the side, pulling her slack body with him as he tried to remain deeply inside of her for as long as he could.

"Love you," he whispered into her hair as he pulled her back to spoon against his body, enveloping her with his touch, making sure she felt protected, safe and loved.

Merlin's Kiss

"More than my life," she whispered back, still trembling from her massive release. "More than my life."

And her words were her vow.

She was the Woman of Legend, and she had the man who would help shape her dreams into reality.

About the author:

Stephanie Burke welcomes mail from readers. You can write to her c/o Ellora's Cave Publishing at P.O. Box 787, Hudson, Ohio 44236-0787.

Also by STEPHANIE BURKE:

- Keeper of the Flame
- Dangerous Heat
- The Slayer
- Seascape
- Lucavarious
- Hidden Passions Volume 1
- Hidden Passions Volume 2
- Wicked Wishes anthology with Marly Chance and Joanna Wylde
- Threshold anthology with Shelby Morgen

Why an electronic book?

We live in the Information Age—an exciting time in the history of human civilization in which technology rules supreme and continues to progress in leaps and bounds every minute of every hour of every day. For a multitude of reasons, more and more avid literary fans are opting to purchase e-books instead of paperbacks. The question to those not yet initiated to the world of electronic reading is simply: *why?*

1. *Price.* An electronic title at Ellora's Cave Publishing runs anywhere from 40-75% less than the cover price of the <u>exact same title</u> in paperback format. Why? Cold mathematics. It is less expensive to publish an e-book than it is to publish a paperback, so the savings are passed along to the consumer.

2. *Space.* Running out of room to house your paperback books? That is one worry you will never have with electronic novels. For a low one-time cost, you can purchase a handheld computer designed specifically for e-reading purposes. Many e-readers are larger than the average handheld, giving you plenty of screen room. Better yet, hundreds of titles can be stored within your new library—a single microchip. (Please note that Ellora's Cave does not endorse any specific brands. You can check our website at www.ellorascave.com for customer recommendations we make available to new consumers.)

3. *Mobility.* Because your new library now consists of only a microchip, your entire cache of books can be taken with you wherever you go.

4. *Personal preferences are accounted for.* Are the words you are currently reading too small? Too large? Too...**ANNOYING**? Paperback books cannot be modified according to personal preferences, but e-books can.

5. *Innovation.* The way you read a book is not the only advancement the Information Age has gifted the literary community with. There is also the factor of what you can read. Ellora's Cave Publishing will be introducing a new line of interactive titles that are available in e-book format only.

6. *Instant gratification.* Is it the middle of the night and all the bookstores are closed? Are you tired of waiting days—sometimes weeks—for online and offline bookstores to ship the novels you bought? Ellora's Cave Publishing sells instantaneous downloads 24 hours a day, 7 days a week, 365 days a year. Our e-book delivery system is 100% automated, meaning your order is filled as soon as you pay for it.

Those are a few of the top reasons why electronic novels are displacing paperbacks for many an avid reader. As always, Ellora's Cave Publishing welcomes your questions and comments. We invite you to email us at service@ellorascave.com or write to us directly at: P.O. Box 787, Hudson, Ohio 44236-0787.

Printed in the United States
38613LVS00001B/34